For Arve, my old
Friends friend.

Dlapper

76. Gin on the rocks
is **NOT** a martini!

SHOT
BY
HARP

SHOT
BY
HARP
D.E. HOPPER

Deeds Publishing | Atlanta

Published by Deeds Publishing in Athens, GA
www.deedspublishing.com

Printed in The United States of America

Cover design and text layout by Mark Babcock

Library of Congress Cataloging-in-Publications data is available upon request.

ISBN 978-1-947309-73-9

Books are available in quantity for promotional or premium use. For information, email info@deedspublishing.com.

First Edition, 2019

10 9 8 7 6 5 4 3 2 1

ACKNOWLEDGEMENT

BRINGING A BOOK TO FRUITION IS MUCH MORE DIFFI-
cult than I expected. If I had ever felt I was by myself in this
often lonely endeavor, I doubt it would have been finished. Most
importantly among those I must thank, with major contributions
in encouragement and editing, is my loving and talented wife
Mary. Whether or not I was a good writer, or my writing was
good, she said that I should keep going. My brother-in-law Dr.
Robert G. Stephens, III, went so far as to say parts of this book
were very good. The public will decide that, but I greatly appreciate him saying it. Reader Richard Peckham has been a long-time
supporter of all my creative endeavors who even read this book in
rough form twice! And, finally, I want to thank my sons Joseph
and Jefferson who give me the greatest support a man can ask for
by simply loving and believing in me.

FOREWORD

THIS BOOK IS MOSTLY ABOUT VETERANS. I COME FROM A family of veterans whose service stretches from WW2 through Desert Storm. In my family, we are veterans of the Army, Air Force, Marines, Navy, and Coast Guard and we are men and women. We have served and we are lucky. We all came home. We weren't all unharmed, but we all came home. To say thank you for the service given to this amazing country by veterans is not enough but then, nothing is. The debt the country owes them is never adequately paid and exists forever. I sincerely hope my words add a little bit to the understanding of how great that debt is. So, a salute to my father, my uncles, my cousins, my niece, my nephews, and my brothers-in law – we all proudly served. This book is dedicated to them.

1

HE HAD FOUGHT MANY BATTLES. HE HAD BEEN WOUND-
ed many times. He had killed many men. But that was over. He
was discharged and home. He had gotten to where he sometimes
felt moments of peace in a mind too familiar with violence. Then
she had marched into this delicately constructed civilian world
with her damned briefcase full of trouble and put him back in
the killing business.

In the end, he did what had to be done to protect her and,
finally, to protect himself. In between, he had inherited a cursed
farm, taken her to bed, put together a crew of damaged souls, sold
the damned farm for a lot of money…and killed again. But he
was a civilian now, so this was murder. It didn't matter that the
first guy was an unprincipled bastard who had threatened the
lives of her and her family. The death of that one guy, done just for
her, was supposed to be the only one. But it opened gates to the
deadly necessity for even more killing. They all deserved it, but
the whole damned thing became ridiculous. They all died because
a man who just wanted to be left alone inherited a goddamned

farm. How this piece of land could hold such monstrous secrets with such deadly results was almost beyond imagination.

The problem was, for that first one, he made a big mistake. He used a bullet with a history. Civilian cops didn't know about that cartridge. They tried their best but couldn't make a case against him. All they had was motive. Nothing else. He was home free. Almost. Then came a couple of deadly spooks from some Fed agency buried so deep they made their own laws. They knew him when he was active military. They knew what he had done and what he was capable of. They used him a long time ago on a special mission. It was just bad luck that they saw the report, and they put it all together. They knew about the damned bullet. They knew its story. So, just when he was back to his comfortable routine, learning again to forget the past, they came for him again. This time the target was stateside.

Shit.

2

IT WAS AROUND FIVE IN THE AFTERNOON IN EARLY
spring on an ordinary day in a worn-out saloon in a working-class
neighborhood of Trenton, New Jersey. He didn't know anybody
who came into this haven for lost souls and worked hard to keep
it that way. Then came the I'm-here-on-business heels hitting
hard on the old wood floor. He refused to look up, even when
they stopped behind his left shoulder. She waited, then sighed,
hitched a long perfect leg up on the next stool, slid her shapely
butt the rest of the way, and slapped an expensive leather briefcase on the bar. It landed way too close to his first drink of the
day. Neat. Small chaser.

It had been worked out the hard way, but he had a rhythm in
this new freedom to drink any time he damned well felt like it.
He knew how much, how fast, and how long to make it last. His
first drink had been happily quivering under his nose waiting for
that delicious beginning sip. Bourbon. Second shelf. He deeply
resented the interruption in the day's rhythm. Pointedly raising

his left shoulder and turning away, he stared with marked intent at his drink.

He was sitting at the bar in the Battle, a long dark narrow drinkers' cave where everything was rubbed to a greasy polish by decades serving people like him who just wanted a place to buy a drink and drink it alone. Everything about it was brown, even the light coming from ancient fixtures hanging from a fifteen-foot high pressed tin ceiling. It was just called the "Battle" and was a neighborhood tradition, supposed to be the same, year after year. That's what its customers wanted. No surprises. Probably the bartender, a little guy—broken nose, bullet head, scarred eyebrows—had been here for years. He might even be the owner. To find out, Harp would have to ask. He wasn't interested enough to break the silence he coveted. He had heard enough noise to last two lifetimes. Sharp, painful noises from exploding shells and torn bodies.

Harp saw the place on one of his despised rehabilitative jogs through the neighborhood. It had a dull brown storefront with old iron columns set back from the sidewalk with a worn marble shallow trapezoid stoop. Sad curtains covering the bottom half of its grimy windows. No neon, no nothing. Defying time and economics, it said nothing about itself other than a mostly flaked and peeled gold leaf word on the front window. It said "--ttle" having neither inclination or need to replace the long missing letters. He had assumed it was another failed business until one day he saw a patron stagger out as he was slogging by. He went back later and found that it was exactly what he was looking for. A man could enter and march straight forward to the far end of a long bar and sit by himself in the dim stillness and no one would say a word in greeting. No jukebox. No hellos. Any talkers sat at the few tables near the grimy windows at the front. An old television stuck on the side of the wall stayed permanently tuned to the hopelessly banal chattering of a local sports channel. Desperate souls in trouble sometimes sat together there whispering so intensely they made more noise than if they had been screaming.

He liked leaning on the old mahogany and oak heart of the place. No Formica, no marble, no copper, no cute, just wood. The smell was as expected in any low budget blue collar neighborhood bar. It was a combination of smoke, spilled liquor, stale beer, bar rags, with subtle notes of urinal cake. Even with a clean bar top, even with clear glasses and white aprons, the smell is still there—an invitation to drink your drink and mind your own damned business.

Harp didn't even have to order now. He had asked for it weeks ago and now, without a word, the bourbon was there with a small beer chaser. When it was empty, it was refilled. Though he would never admit it, he was grudgingly pleased that the bartender could serve him without either ever saying a word. They said nothing when he arrived and nothing when he left. It was an almost military efficiency to which he responded with instinctive approval. When he was finished, he upended the glass, put the money on the bar, and walked out the door. If asked, the bartender would say that he could never remember him saying anything. Maybe the first time—just to get the order straight. Jack neat, beer back. Harp didn't know the bartender's name and didn't want to. That kind of familiarity led to bar conversations. He hated bar conversations. They were always about either hope or revenge. Or how unfair the world was. Or shitty jokes. Or fucking politics. Or fucking baseball. Harp felt that loud voices in bars belonged to assholes. Worse, there were too many people whining about their failures. Those failures were never their fault.

He knew his failures were his fault.

Arms on the rounded edge, looking down, face only inches from the glass, he could see the reflection of one amber eye at a time floating on the surface of his neat bourbon — breaking into nervous lines when someone bumped the bar. Sometimes, after a few, he silently asked the eye questions. The questions usually started with a regretful, disbelieving, "What the fuck were you thinking?" It was a time in his life when peacetime, whiskey, and distance from a life at war were opening some hard-shut doors to places in his mind where he knew he had to go. He felt strong enough to go there now and he knew it was time. But, he would not let anything or anyone challenge the foundation of a belief that he had done his duty. He was a soldier who had fought bravely and often. Of course he had painful memories. He remembered very well the faces of his buddies, his troops; some alive and some dead. Sometimes he felt the dead were his fault. He walked around with this extra weight. He was their sergeant and was not supposed to let that happen. He could also remember faces of some of the ones he had killed. They didn't bother him at all. He would kill those fuckers again if he got the chance.

Harp knew about PTSD. But, he also knew that you can learn to handle bad memories. Some guys walked away from the shoot or die world and got on with civilian life. He was determined to be one of them. He didn't want a fucking stateside shrink telling him how to cope with the horrific visions from past missions. They were his identity at the same time they were his punishment.

6

To let them be taken away would be, to him, a form of cowardice. So, he coped with these memories even when they tore apart his sleep. This was, to Sergeant H.B. Harper, a continuation of his duty.

It was his debt to pay. He paid every day.

That's why he usually had six drinks. He was a big guy and could hold it fine. Six were enough to help ease the bodily aches and pains from a lifetime of physical conflict. But, mostly, he could relax a little. Eight shots were enough to replace with moments of forgiveness some of the most persistent fragments of doubt that still crept in against his will.

Ten shots were too good. He could even laugh. But, it also released the rage — and he didn't dare to lose control. There was a hot core of anger that surprised even him when it erupted. He was careful to keep it buried. Plus, he never wanted to sleep on the sticky goddamn pool table in the back of the bar where he had seen others crawl when they were too drunk to walk. He wanted to be able to walk two blocks to his little third floor apartment without falling into the gutter. He wanted to stay in bed in the morning when he felt like it. He wanted to spend all day reading new books and old books on military fuckups down through history. He looked forward to the point in the afternoon when this new routine began. He could now casually stroll to this perfect oasis and quietly drink the number of drinks the day required. Returning home, he would massage his leg, curse the news, hit the rack, and read himself to sleep.

He was a guy whose appearance made it easy for him to sit alone. A look was enough to drive away any patron foolish enough to sit anywhere near him with a phone or, god forbid, a laptop. A broken nose and scarred chin marked a sun-creased face. A dime-sized notch at the top of his left ear was a gift of a 7.62 round from an AK fired by a now deceased idiot in the sand-pit. He was not at all unhappy with this little memento because the bullet could have been two inches to the right. It was mostly covered with a tangle of graying hair that grew too fast and stayed uncombed for most of its existence—just as his face remained unshaven most of the time. Any concern about the way he looked in the mirror was usually solved with a shrug and a "fuck it." He wore khakis and an untucked shirt every day. Sometimes he wore socks with his old boat shoes or running shoes, sometimes not. In his pockets he carried only a small folded wallet with his VA ID card, credit card, driver's license, and some cash. He always carried a camo folding knife he had liberated from military control.

Army pal Tillis, now deceased, said his nose made him look like a fucking Indian. Eyes an ordinary gray stared out from under bushy eyebrows with the look of total disinterest in what they were seeing. Yet, if those ordinary eyes flashed in anger, there was that cold readiness that comes from a lifetime of fighting back. Overall, with a flat mouth hidden under a unkempt mustache, slouching, looking straight ahead, he always looked like he was in a shitty mood. Usually he *was* in a shitty mood and did his best to maintain it.

When he strode out, looking nowhere but straight ahead, a slight limp became evident. Shrapnel, a couple of large pieces, had shattered his femur and brought about long hospital stays involving grafts, plates, screws, and intensive therapy. The leg was about a half inch shorter and was operating at about 80 percent, which was enough for Harp. No one ever saw this as a chink in his armor. He moved too smoothly and with too much power, even with that limp. That shrapnel made him a civilian. Little pieces of metal would still emerge from the skin on his leg and hip from time to time. They were pulled loose and flicked into the trash. Much as he hated it, he would don his sweats and jog a couple times a week to keep it from stiffening up. The leg could do it, but it ached like hell afterward. On those days, he rewarded himself with extra bourbon — seven, maybe eight.

One could never tell from the hardness of his visage that Harp was in the midst of this personal revelation. He was finally finding a quiet rhythm to a civilian life after years of dangerous tours. He was shedding the tension of a constant wariness and had accomplished what, for him, was a monumental achievement: he had almost relaxed. He was still learning to sleep more than five hours and now sometimes felt rested. He saw, to his wonder, that he might actually be whole again.

3

BUT, AS LUCK WOULD HAVE IT, HARP COULD NOT FLOAT along with this sense of contentment he was quietly marveling at. Of course it must be interrupted. It was too perfect. What's worse, this interruption was delivered by a fucking lawyer. What was even worse was that the lawyer was a woman. He compared female lawyers to vampires. Harp and lawyers were not meant to get along. They always declared that he must bow to the vagaries and subjectivity of the laws and their interpretation of it. Harp hated to bow to anything he thought was stupid and unreasonable. He hated people who explained what he *had* to do. The law, they said, was the law. Then, when he glared in anger, said they didn't make the law. Also, it did not help that, where he had been in conflict with the legal system, almost always it was Harp who had been wrong. This lawyer brought with her a scent that smelled expensive — thus totally foreign to this place. After the briefcase had been deposited, she put her purse next to it and shrugged out of a light jacket and fashionable scarf. She piled them on top of her purse. Everything looked expensive.

"You're a hard man to find," she said while busily opening the briefcase. "We knew only that you were military and the DOD would have you in its system. Our researcher told them you were a relative. A couple more lies and some tears convinced some E-3 in records to give her your last known address which, by the way, needs to be updated. She found you anyway and followed you to this, ah, colorful oasis." She scanned the room again and shook her head. "This place stinks. Smells like dog pee." She looked around again. "I probably should have waited and gone to your place of residence, but I wanted to get it done today. Now that I see the quality of your hangout, I probably should have waited." She looked at the old back bar, stained walls, and tin ceiling. "It would have to be better."

She continued as if Harp wanted to hear her explanation. "Okay, we lied a little to the United States Army, but sometimes a lie is okay if it's for the greater good. Usually the only time I lie is when I must defend some dirt-bag in court. I don't represent dirt-bags anymore so don't think this is something I do all the time." She apparently did not feel the need to introduce herself just yet. "Well, maybe if it is a very rich dirt-bag."

Just when everything was getting right, Harp thought sadly, slowly shaking his head. She had a distinct, powerful voice, developed over years in courtrooms, and, try as he might not to listen, he had no choice but to hear her. A vocal coach would say she was a perfect alto.

"Hey there, Rufus," she gracefully turned and wiggled her long fingers, summoning the bartender in that courtroom voice, "how about scrubbing a glass extra clean and bringing me a gin and tonic? Something high up?" The bartender, whose name was definitely not Rufus, brought her the drink and a scowl. He looked at Harp for a sign. Harp shrugged.

She was watching with a smile. "It's okay, Rufe, I am a great big girl and you don't need his permission to serve me a drink." She put a twenty on the bar. "And get my uncommunicative friend here another one while you're at it."

With that she began pulling a sheaf of papers from the briefcase with those very attractive hands. "Here's the story, Mr. Harper, my firm was contacted about a month ago by another firm in a little town called Bardberg, Pennsylvania. I never heard of it either. It seems you are the only surviving relative of a Mrs. Pauline Harper Kuykendahl. Great name, by the way."

Harp was moved to speak at the enormity of this claim. He turned his head to glare at this interruption and said, "Listen, sweet cheeks, I happen to know for a fact that my only living relative died years ago in Topeka. So, take your scam back to 'the firm' and leave me alone. Thanks for the drink." He turned back to his Bourbon and shifted his shoulders away from her steady gaze.

She smiled. She had lots of time in the courtroom. This amateurish brushoff was laughable. "As I was saying, our firm was contacted to find a Mr. Horace Baldwin Harper which is you and which is why we are here." She continued as if he hadn't spoken. She focused on a single page in the file she had taken from the briefcase and commenced reading. "My name is not Sweet Cheeks. It is Sandra Kowalski, with an "I" not a "y" and your last *known* relative was your Uncle Titus Harper who died five years ago in Topeka. Apparently you are unaware that, before he moved to Topeka, he was married to and divorced from Ermaline Harper, nee Penson, from Callensburg, PA. She kept the Harper name. Callensburg is right down the road from Turkey City and Turnip Hole and right up the road from Sligo and Huey. She flashed a wicked grin as Harp turned in disbelief. He noticed that her eyes smiled honestly. He winced at the thought of her knowing his full name.

"Jesus Christ," Harp muttered and took an extra-large sip of whiskey. This was now going to be an eight-drink night. "Turnip Hole?"

Paying no attention to his muttering, she continued. "Before he broke camp for Kansas, he managed to get his former wife heavy with child. Whether or not he knew she was pregnant is unknown and of no importance. He never acknowledged the existence of the child and contributed nothing to its support. In other words, your last genuine relative was a real shitheel. Sorry, that's personal." She removed another page from the stack and sipped from her glass. As she was reading, she was curling a lock above her left ear around her forefinger.

"That child was your cousin Pauline Harper. Pauline was raised by her single mother who, by all reports, did a good job. Your "unknown" aunt Ermaline worked hard and died young. Must be that she told Pauline about you. Pauline grew up and married Lars Kuykendahl and they were together until he was killed in an oil rig fire. She thus became sole owner of a good-sized farm near Vowinckel. Last month she died in an auto accident. They had no children. It's too bad you did not know about her because you might have been some help." Harp shrugged. Kowalski had turned toward Harp and absently planted her foot on the rung of his bar stool.

"As requested in her will, and after your existence was confirmed, her lawyer back there hired us to find you." She put the pages back on the pile. She had paid no attention to his comments as she was reading. She looked up and studied the side of his head and spoke with much greater intensity.

"To cut to the chase, Mr. Harper, you have inherited 487 acres of land near Vowinckel. It is described as mostly hilly with some flatlands, mostly cropland and pasture, and a little creek frontage on the south side. Some of that land reaches all the way up to Gilfoyle." She added with a barely suppressed grin.

"Christ on a crutch," Harp muttered again. "Vowinckel. Gilfoyle."

"Bring us another drink, Rufus. You are not pretty but you make a pretty good drink." Another scowl came with another round. Harp had still not finished the first one. Kowalski was really sucking them down. "There are several buildings on the property, including a 4-bedroom, two and one-half-bath house with attached two-car garage, a large barn, equipment shed, a silo, a small pond, a farrowing house, hog shed, and a large chicken house. There is also a small abattoir that until recently was used for livestock slaughter. They killed hogs, chickens, and beef themselves. One assumes they ate a whole lot of meat. They even had some bee hives which are now vacant. You might learn to make your own honey." She suppressed a giggle.

"Unbelievable," he muttered in disbelief. "I grew up in Trenton. What the fu ... hell is a farrowing house?"

"You will have to figure that one out yourself. You get a John Deere tractor, several pieces of farm equipment, an old Ford stake body truck, a 2011 John Deere ATV, a 2011 Ford pickup, and a snowmobile. There are also, by the way, two old oil wells that were capped long ago. Unlike many properties in this area, the mineral rights have been retained and pass to you along with the property. Even if you sell the property, you have the option of retaining the mineral rights—which I strongly recommend."

Leaning heavily on the bar, Harp had put his head in his hands and was quietly whispering "shit" over and over.

Kowalski was inexplicably and suddenly tempted to reach out and smack him on the back of his furry head. Where the hell did that come from, she wondered? Why would I want to touch this sullen animal? She quickly shook off the thought and continued reading. "The livestock has all been sold as per instructions in the will. The property is free of encumbrances and will pass cleanly to your possession. There is a small checking account with several thousand but a larger savings account holding, as of last month, about 320,000 dollars, most of which came from a settlement arising from Lars' death. She actually got a cool half million but the goddamn lawyers took their cut off the top."

Harp could not help it. His head rose quickly and turned toward the now smirking lawyer. He was squinting in disbelief. She was grinning triumphantly. The highly regarded city lawyer was trying to figure out why she wanted to make an impression on this scruffy Jersey drunk. It came as a shock as she realized that this was the first man in a long time whose presence she found intimidating. Yet she knew instinctively that he posed no physical threat. She hid these strange thoughts behind her lawyer face and continued.

"Got your attention, didn't I?"

"And all of that is mine?" He was still dubious, but now interested. He had a good military retirement with disability but this was real money. He wouldn't even know how to spend that much but he'd like to try. The trouble was, he didn't really *want* anything that he couldn't easily buy himself. Except maybe top shelf whiskey. Okay, one of the new LED TV's — maybe even a fifty-incher. Maybe some new shoes. Really good ones.

"Sign on the dotted line when you get there, and it's all yours," she stated, somewhat smugly, having got his full attention. "As another goddamn lawyer, I will also get a small piece of your inheritance.

"Oh, I forgot one thing. You also inherited a mongrel dog named Fart." She snorted loudly at this. In disbelief, Harp grimaced and roughly scratched his head with both hands.

"If that's a joke, it is not funny." Harp said.

"No, it's not a joke." She giggled. "Your cousin, her husband, and previous owners from over the years are all buried in a small cemetery which, by the way, you also now own. Their dog was totally dedicated to Pauline and still stays by her grave. So, they have decided to leave him there for the heirs to handle. So you are now the owner of a dog named Fart, whose name, I would guess, is not happenstance." She sipped her drink and chuckled. "I gotta tell you, I have done lots of these inheritances before, but this one really has some dillies. Rufus, give us another round."

Harp just sat shaking his head. "Are you sure that I'm the right guy? Just say I am, how soon can I sell this place?"

"Just as soon as all the title work is done. As a matter of fact, people will be lined up to take this property off your hands. You can unload it in a day, easy." Kowalski polished off her drink just as "Rufus" slipped another one in front of her. She absently began drinking her third drink as she went down the list of items to cover.

Harp followed national news only so far as one hearing it in the background. But, he had heard enough to know that the current economy was making it hard to unload real estate. He wondered aloud what was so valuable about this piece of land that would make it sell so easily.

"Let me give you a clue." She laid the papers on the bar. She held up her left hand and was somewhat unsteadily pointing at her fingers with the right and she made her points. "Towns in this part of the state have names like Oil City, Derrick City, Coal City, and Burning Well. What do those cute names reveal to your alcohollicky, alcoholly — boy these are good drinks — alcohol damaged brain? Even better, they are fracking gas wells all over that part of the state. You know what fracking is? Does? Do they explain things like fracking in these dimly lit, smelly caverns wherein you choose to spend your life? An' get that dirty look off your face. The word is *fracking*, not the one you're thinking of." Why, she wondered, am I *yelling* at this guy?

Her sarcasm did annoy the hell out of Harp but he was damned if he would let her know it. He also noted that Miss Kowalski was getting plastered. He leaned forward and, with raised eyebrows, looked past Kowalski at the bartender who grinned and held up a bottle of gin with his fingers showing how much was gone. According to the rough measure of Rufus's hand, she had just finished about a fifth of a bottle of gin in the short time she had been here. She should have learned by now to never piss off the person making your drinks. The pay-back options are endless.

Harp turned to look at her straight on. He bumped her knees as he swung around. Her blue eyes were wandering slightly. He jabbed his finger on the bar as he made his points. "It tells me that Bardberg is a smelly place with pig shit, bad air, and bad water. It tells me that I never want to live there. It tells me that it's a backwater hole in the woods without good bars and probably under the control of religious nut-jobs. It tells me that I am going to take the money and run. And I am going to run right back here and sit right here in this goddamn seat in the middle of the dog pee smell and try to spend every bit of that money on the most expensive bourbon they got! How about that, Mrs. Lawyer Kawinsky?"

Kowalski had stared back with eyes which were having difficulty focusing as he made his declaration. She said, "I told you it is *Miss*, and it is *Kowalski*. And whatever you want to do with your loot is up to you, you unappreciative shitheel." An observer might have wondered how they could have developed such animosity in such a short time. She had carelessly jammed the papers back in the briefcase and turned toward Harp with right hand pointing a finger and with the intent of putting her left elbow on the bar. She was going to fire a final parting shot before leaving. But, her elbow missed the bar and she toppled forward. Her face landed square in Harp's lap.

For just a moment Harp left her there, looking down at the back of her head as she struggled to sit up. It was just too satisfying to see this overconfident, aggressive lawyer-type with her carefully done hair face-down in his crotch. But, then, as she struggled to sit up, he took pity and, holding her by the shoulders, easily lifted her back into a somewhat upright position. Then she started tipping sideways instead and was grinning. Some of those expensive curls had fallen over her forehead. He straightened her up again.

"Do you know how many assholes have tried to get my face in their junk? You are a lucky man, Harper." Her head was now nodding and turning on its own. "We've known each other for about an hour and already I have done a face plant in your probably doman…dominit …di-min-u-tive lower parts." Drunk or not, she was still taking shots. Harp thought he knew what that word meant but wasn't sure. He *was* pretty sure it was an insult.

It hit him now that Kowalski was in no condition to drive. Hell, she was in no condition to walk. Reluctantly, he paid his tab and the rest of her tab not covered by the twenty and stood up. Wouldn't you know, Harp thought, not only was he stuck with a drunken lawyer but he had to pay for her goddamn drinks. And he didn't get to enjoy his hugely anticipated daily course of bourbons. He scowled at the barkeep who quickly turned away to hide his grin.

"Where's your car?" he asked gruffly. She was not his damned responsibility but he was stuck with her now.

"Took a cab," came the slurred answer.

"Shit." Harp muttered. Talking like people do when they are trying to get a kid, or a dog, or a drunk, to do something, he said, "Come on, sweetie, stand up and let's get you out of here."

"Nah Sweetie, either, ash hole, I am Shandra." She corrected again.

Other patrons were watching and grinning as he tried to hold her upright while at the same time carrying her jacket, scarf, briefcase, and purse. When Harp turned and glared, they all took sudden interest in their drinks. He made it out of the bar holding her arm around his neck with one hand and his other arm with all her possessions around her waist.

Cabs were safe but not safe enough to dump this lady and her belongings into the back of one and hope that everything would arrive safely. He didn't even know where she was going. Her office was downtown, but she was in no condition to go there.

"Shit," he said loudly now. "Shit, shit, shit."

"Shi, shi shi," she responded, having lost some consonants shortly after the last drink. "Shi." Her head flopped backward as she looked up at Harp and smiled in a happy drunken way. "You ol' shi'heel.

Considering all the options, Harp decided he had no choice but to take her back to his place. The thought was more irritating than she would ever understand. It was his hard-won domain. It was his turf, his place, his personally crafted environment. It was, in terms of the sniper, his hide. He could go in there and disappear. He had no land line and no computer. He bought bubble pack phones when he needed one.

But, his apartment was close and it was the only solution. So, in the fashion of drunken couples everywhere, they weaved and staggered to his building, where he had to almost carry her up the stairs and through his door. He needn't have worried about her reaction to the casual mess which required sweeping pillows and magazines aside. As soon as she landed on the sofa, she was out.

Harp enjoyed the company of anonymous women from time to time, but never here. It implied a sharing and he wasn't ready to share anything with an emotion attached. He went to their place or a hotel. She was the first. He looked at her as she lay there, already snoring. The features of her face were a little too strong for Harp. Her nose was too big, her mouth was too wide, and her eyes were too far apart. On the other hand, she had dark curly hair, nice teeth, big tits, and long legs. All of those legs were now showing as her already short business skirt was hiked up way too far. Very nice legs, indeed, topped with lacy pink undies.

Harp entertained some dirty thoughts for just a second but angrily concluded that, even though he had been screwed by lawyers, he could not bring himself to screw an unconscious one, even in what he considered would be justifiable revenge. Disgusted with his own conscience, he threw a blanket over the lucky long-legged attorney and went to bed. His last thoughts were of piles of money and a dog named Fart. He went to sleep shaking his head.

***

"Do you have a gun?" Harp woke up with a start. His first thought was anger at his failure to realize that someone had come into his bedroom without his sensing their presence. His second thought was the curious message.

"Do you have a gun?" came the voice again. It had a definite note of pleading.

Harp finally was awake enough to listen. Kowalski was leaning over his bed and holding her head tightly between her hands.

"Please, I beg you. Shoot me! Oh, God, do something. My forehead is going to explode if you don't do something."

Harp didn't have to do anything. Suddenly, she clutched her stomach, covered her mouth, and looked around in panic. Harp pointed toward the bathroom and she ran. She failed to close the door and the sounds coming out were disgusting—even to an old drinker.

21

With clothes over her arms, dressed only in bra and panties, wet face, wet hair, she came out of the bathroom about a half hour later. She started walking toward the living room and said, "To hell with it." Instead she threw her clothes on a chair, jerked the covers aside and flopped in beside Harp, who was watching with a sort of wonder.

"Touch me and you die" was all she said before she was soon snoring again. Harp had still not said a word. He figured that, because it was going to be a Saturday, she could probably sleep in so he wouldn't wake her when he got up. He was tired. His leg ached from carrying her up the stairs. It was still dark. He went back to sleep.

A bright morning brought the smell of perfume. Not exactly perfume, but a nice smell, like freshly shampooed hair. It was a different thing for him to wake to. Harp opened his eyes and found that he was looking into another pair of eyes. She was lying on her side, propped on an elbow, wet hair, watching him. She had spent some time studying the various white scars scattered around his head and torso. She quietly snickered at the erection with which he began every morning.

"I have never seen anyone as beaten up and scarred as you are." She was matter of fact, speaking in a quiet voice. "That leg is a total mess. Half your damned ear is shot off. I have seen better looking autopsy photos. You have apparently been otherwise shot and stabbed. The funny thing is that, as battered as you are, and as tough as you probably are, I am not afraid of you. Why is that?"

Harp shrugged.

She flopped on her back and continued. "Look at me. Here I am, a 32-year-old successful lawyer, well-respected in my field, and

I get drunk and crawl into bed with a bum I met in a Westside dive. Worse even yet is that he is a client. What the hell is the matter with me? I am such an idiot. I used to wonder if I could be a genuine slut. Now I know. Now I am one." She covered her eyes with her arms.

Harp was just smart enough to recognize a purely rhetorical question. He wasn't sure he liked being called a bum. He wisely said nothing.

"I am naked under these covers. See?" She lifted the covers so he could see. He looked with great appreciation. His regular morning erection suddenly became very serious. "You don't realize what your kind of beat-up, scarred, ragged, male does to women, do you?"

"I decided I want to make love when I looked at all those scars. What the hell does that mean? Do women atavistically gravitate toward men showing marks of battle? Like, if you have scars you're more virile. I somehow think we could have great sex, which unfortunately is not a big challenge considering my recent history." She stared at the ceiling. "I started to masturbate in the shower, which I just have to do sometimes. I stopped, though. Can you understand where that left me?"

Still, Harp said nothing. She was sharing more than he could assimilate on short notice. She turned to her side facing Harp. She was stunned by the level calmness of his gaze. She realized she had seriously underestimated this man. There was wisdom in that look, as if he had seen too many things and absorbed the deeper meanings from each. Harp slowly pushed his covers down and kicked them aside.

Kowalski lay back again, spread her legs, and raised her arms. "Okay," was all she said with a slightly cracking voice, eyes closed, afraid of what she was doing, afraid of him, but strangely ecstatic. For the first time in her life, even considering her horniest college years, Kowalski had an orgasm the moment she was entered and a second a minute later and a third five minutes later. She was in heaven.

Harp too was in heaven. He found himself making love to a woman who was nothing but orgasms. The sensations were overwhelming. It was impossible to resist and, try as he might to continue this earthshaking ride, he exploded. Even then, they did not stop. She was grunting and pounding on his back with her fists and he was doing his best to reach her heart with his penis. He came again and bragged to himself. Forty-two and twice in twenty minutes!

The bed was not big enough to contain their thrashing. They found themselves on the floor, done, panting, and wet. Kowalski was on her back, body still quivering, with tears falling from the corners of her eyes. Harp still had not said a word. He was speechless. He was trying to understand what had happened and why he had gotten so old before it happened.

"Harper, you cannot know how much I love your silence. If you said one damn word, I know it would be the wrong word. So, don't say one damned word!" She shifted around and sat up with her back against the bed, knees against her chest. He was lying on his side watching her face. She looked back with sad intensity. "This has been one of the most incredible moments in my entire life. Now, I have to carry it around like a diamond I'm afraid of losing. Even worse, you bastard, is that now I am afraid that it will never happen again. When I fall in love with some ordinary person and want to marry him, I do not want to be thinking about a freaking Trenton bar fly covered with bullet holes."

He was having some difficulty following her thought process and felt only slightly miffed at the ways she had described him. If he had any idea what to say, he might have tried something but, so far, silence appeared to be the wisest course. He maintained course. She stood and looked at Harp who was still lying on the floor.

"I am going to get dressed and leave. I have a normal life I need to live it and so do you. I will leave the papers for you to sign showing you have been contacted. Keep your copy; send the rest back to my office. The address is on the letterhead. That's not responsible on my part but right now I do not give a shit. I just need to get away from you." She stood, gathered up her clothes and went to the bathroom. Harp put on some shorts and a t-shirt and waited.

Kowalski came out of the bathroom looking again like a lawyer—or at least a lawyer with a flushed face and wrinkled clothes. She gathered all her gear and walked to the door. She paused and turned back toward him. Her eyes were shining. "And I promise you one thing. If ever I see you again, no matter where or when, I am going to try not to jump on you. I will try not to let you hump me against a wall or on the bar or on the floor. It doesn't matter, you shot-up son-of-bitch." She slammed the door.

Harp had still never said one word. He had just realized that Sandra Kowalski was actually a beautiful woman. He straightened the room and showered. He signed the papers, kept his copy, and would mail the rest later. He knew that he and Kowalski were not finished. There was just too much there to ever forget. But for now, the memory would have to be enough. He had a lot to do. He was sure that selling a farm would not be as simple as she made it. Nothing was ever as simple as planned. One thing for sure, he had to at least get out there and see what he owned before selling it.

4

HARP BOUGHT A PICKUP TRUCK, THE FIRST ONE HE HAD ever owned. He assumed there would be things on his farm that he would want—he shook his head at those words—*his farm.* "Harp's Farm," he said aloud, and laughed. He still could not imagine living in a place where you could not simply walk to a bar for a drink or a restaurant for food. He assumed there would be food. Farms had food, right? Anyway, he figured there might be things he would want to keep and bring back to Trenton. They might have had guns, knives, etc. Maybe some little tables, things like that. His apartment could use some stuff. He could more easily haul things back with a truck, he reasoned. But, having a natural affinity for camouflage, Harp didn't want to drive a brand new shiny truck into this strange place. He would rather sneak in, sell, and sneak out. That way he wouldn't have to meet anyone and play nicey nicey.

Harp bought a brown 2010 Dodge four-door quad cab with four-wheel drive, extra fuel tanks, and a huge diesel engine. It reminded him of vehicles they drove in the sandpit. It was noisy with the distinct diesel clatter, and smelly, had some scrapes and dents, but would run forever and had the power to pull a tree out by its roots. The engine, drive train, and tires were totally checked out and were in perfect condition. For Harp's needs, it was ideal, because it had been a contractor's vehicle and there was a large interior space where the rear seats had been removed and he could stow the tan foot-locker he just happened to have left over from a strange assignment while in the pit.

***

In Afghanistan during the later years of U.S. involvement, Harp had been recruited for a small incursion into Pakistan. This was before the States had admitted ever crossing the border between the two countries. He had "volunteered" to go with a team of two civilians, obviously spooks from some agency, on a special mission. These guys were operating in the area and had said they needed someone ASAP who was qualified to carry out a "long-range removal project." They explained somewhat cryptically that their current contractor had been neutralized. It was quickly ascertained that Harp was the only G.I. available nearby on short notice with the skills they needed. His MOS was certainly not sniper but he was known to be very good at it.

It was amazing how easily Harp was taken from his Company and assigned to work with this crew—which meant they had some serious pull way up the ladder. They asked and it was done, just like that. His Company Commander didn't like it but he agreed to just one mission. Harp was given a fake ID—just in case, they said. In case of what they never explained. They took a dusty gray Nissan SUV for the night drive into Pakistan. Harp knew he was way out of his league when he heard the team leader speak in easy Pakistani at the border crossing and hand over a fistful of American money. They never actually introduced themselves. They said he could just call them Pat and Tim and laughed. Harp didn't get the joke. They explained that they couldn't remember which one was supposed to be Pat and which one Tim. They were just mission names. Their real names were many miles and many missions behind them. It didn't matter, they said, because he would never see them again after this job.

The only mission info they would or could share was that they had a location on a target they had been after for months and they had to move fast. He was known to change locations week to week and, as Tim put it, "They had a spot and they had a shot." They arrived at an empty three-story shit, straw, and mud dwelling where they quickly set up housekeeping; the first thing they did was cover all the windows. It was very clear that they had done all this many times. They brought in with them a desert tan metal military foot locker full of the latest mil-tech goodies, including a Barrett 50-caliber rifle with a giant scope. The locker was smaller than most, lower and shorter. The location of this place was no accident. Once settled, Pat laid out the plan. It was simple. They would take out the target and clear out. Harp assembled the rifle. The object was to eliminate a ranking terrorist leader. Though a long way away, this was the closest they found where they could even get a shot. They had a picture of the target and a drawing showing his location. It was a little less than a half mile away. A clear shot was possible and a miss would have the serious consequence of driving the target out of a known location and back into deep hiding. That would be simply unacceptable. They had two options: Kill, or forget it.

Now that they were on site, they explained with real regret that neither of them had the ability to take the shot. They asked again if he was certain that he could do it. Through a small gap in the rags over the window, Harp studied the target area through a spotting scope and responded that it was within the range of the rifle and scope but not an easy shot. Factors such as wind, heat, light, and the rifle itself, which he had never fired, could affect the outcome. They knew this already and were ready for that risk level. The target was aware of the danger from snipers, but felt he could sit safely on this carefully chosen tiny patio sipping a tea. He couldn't have known there was one place from which he was visible because he couldn't see it. Who can see an opening of about two square feet a half mile away? Yet, far away, down a sight lane threading past and through hundreds of buildings, there was a tiny black dot hardly recognizable as an opening. But it was a window, and inside that window Harp waited far back in the room. He was wearing heavy duty ear protectors and sat on the trunk which had carried the rifle. In front of him was a folding table with a sandbag rest for the Barrett. While waiting, Pat was surprised by a call on his cell phone. He and Tim imme-diately huddled in a corner away from Harp. Pat told Harp that it was a go but they had another issue of some urgency to deal with immediately after this mission.

The target appeared as had been predicted and sat on a small stool with his tea, right on schedule. Harp considered all that had to be considered, guessed that the heat from a series of tall building on the right would push the bullet a little to the left. He aimed slightly high and to the right, held his breath, and gently squeezed the trigger. In a few seconds the wall behind the man was splashed a bright red as arms and feet flew upward. Harp had opted for a body shot to make it ninety-nine-point nine percent odds. He wasn't sure of the heat effect going past all those buildings but had guessed right. There was no doubt about the kill. A fifty-caliber round will explode the human body. The watching spooks slapped him on the back with thanks for the good work.

They quickly began packing everything back into the locker. When the room was clean, they told Harp to wait while they took care of this other matter. When they came back, they would all run back across the border and Harp would go back to his unit. They also said, if they were not back in two hours, Harp was to take the truck and equipment and get back the same way they had come in. The border crossing was bought and paid for. They gave Harp a fistful of cash in case he needed it. He didn't even count it. Tim stopped at the door. He turned to Harp. "I know you know this is black ops. We are not supposed to be here and there is no record that we *were* here. Go back to your unit and forget everything. Okay?" He waited. Harp nodded. They left.

They never came back. He hoped they hadn't been killed because they seemed like competent guys doing a tough job. After two hours, Harp humped the locker down the stairs and into the back of the SUV. He was apprehensive about driving through this country but obviously arrived at the crossing before any word had gotten out about the kill. The guys at the border, taking the wad of American dollars, were happy to wave him through. On his way back to his assigned billet well after dark, Harp couldn't help but think about the foot locker. They hadn't told him what to do with it. He had caught a brief glimpse and was pretty sure that none of these things were listed on any regular inventory. That meant, at least at this moment, all this stuff belonged to Harp. On a whim, he drove directly to the supply depot of a neighboring command and, using his temporary spook ID, directed that it be shipped to a military storage depot back in Jersey. If it was there when he got home, fine. If it was not, fine. It was tightly locked and had the strange fed seal, so he was fairly certain that it would not be inspected.

Later, after he had gotten back to the States and semi-recovered from his wounds, he got curious. He went to the New Jersey Military Depot and there it was, waiting for him after years of storage. Recovered from a bored supply sergeant using that same fake ID they had given him long ago, he loaded it into a cab and took it right to a storage unit. Now, he didn't know why he was taking it to Bardberg. Just instinct, he guessed. Now it was in a truck heading into who knows what. A farm of all things. His farm.

***

And on this farm there were some small, shiny, iridescent bubbles peeking out from a rusty cast iron seal. This bubble and its mate would change his life and end other lives. Such was this inheritance.

5

HE PAID IN ADVANCE TO KEEP HIS TRENTON APARTMENT. Hell, he could afford things like that now. He paid for three months but felt sure he would be gone only a couple weeks. When he was packed, he hit the road heading west. He planned to wrap everything up and return ASAP. He didn't see how it could take any longer. See the farm, sell the farm, come home. Plus, even in the totally impossible event he didn't come back, there was nothing here that he couldn't walk away from. He might even take a little trip to Hawaii. He remembered with fond recollection some sweet nights on the beach during an R&R to the Islands.

Harp learned from maps and his new GPS that a person can cross the Appalachian Mountains in central Pennsylvania going from east to west only a couple of ways. The mountains ran from northeast to southwest and that's the way the roads went. The best way would be to hop on the Interstate and let those federal dollars do the work. All he had to do was get up to I-80, head west and put it on cruise control for three hundred miles or so at seventy miles per hour. About a five-hour drive. Nothing to it.

Along the way, Harp was noticing pockets of activity in strange places along the route. Trucks carrying long pipes were common. Large tankers with strange markings were also common. The exit that would take him to Bardberg came up sooner than he expected. He had enjoyed the drive. It was beautiful country. The town was small, so the address of the law firm was easy to find and he pulled into the drive at about 2:30 in the afternoon. The firm was Billups, Parsnip, and Port. Harp was supposed to talk to Mr. Parsnip.

The firm was in a beautiful old house which was no doubt the residence of one of the community fathers long ago. It was a tall two-story, light blue with darker blue gingerbread trim all over. Steep roofs covered little porches and dormers and looked out over perfect landscaping. It was the kind of house that some of his classmates lived in back in his hometown. He hated them and he hated their houses, so he just naturally hated this house. Harp drove up the perfect concrete drive and parked in a small lot that had once been a lawn between the house and a huge, architecturally decorated barn built as a carriage house. The sign directed clients to enter at the front, so he plodded down the drive and up several steps to an ornate walnut door with frosted glass panels. Entering a large, all mahogany front hall, he stopped at a desk behind which sat a sharp-faced woman whose age was somewhere between fifty and eighty. Her name plate said Phoebe Loftus. She did not look up immediately but let him wait for just a hair longer than he liked. "Yes?" she asked.

"I'm Harper, to see Parsnip. We're supposed to meet at three."

"And which Harper would that be?" she asked.

Irritated in the first place at even being in a lawyer's office, he was further irritated at the silliness of the question. He could not resist. "How many Harpers are there in this entire world who have a three o'clock appointment with a Lawyer Parsnip?" he growled.

"We have a busy practice, Mr. Harper, with many Harpers. In the legal world, it is important to be precise in all things."

"My name is Horace B. Harper, Mrs. Loftus, but most people know me as Harp." Harp was feeling definitely irritated at this exchange, but he understood her need to assert control over her domain. "Is that precise enough?"

"I find it interesting, Mr. Harper, that you eschew a fine old name like Horace and would prefer to be called Harp Harper. People do make interesting choices, don't they, Mr. Harper? If you will wait here, I'll tell Mr. Parsnip that you have arrived." She rose from her chair and walked stiffly through a large set of pocket doors on the right side of the hall. Her shape reminded him of one of those primitive African carvings. Big round head on top, pointed breasts, stomach sticking out in front, butt sticking out in the back, all supported by pencil legs without one bit of tone. She soon came back out and stood by the door. He assumed that was his signal to enter. "And it is Miss Loftus, thank you." She said as he passed by.

Harp could not resist. "I think it's interesting, *Miss* Loftus, that a woman of your obvious charm is still unmarried." The door closed behind him with a bang.

At that sound, the man at the desk in the middle of a large room looked up. Harp figured this was the library in the old house because of the bookshelves along one wall. On other walls were works of art which Harp guessed were originals. He stood for a moment looking around the room, assessing its qualities. He had learned long ago to study his surroundings before moving. He was standing on a very nice Persian rug artfully located on a Walnut plank floor. Several steps away was a large, ornate desk. To the left was a fireplace, which appeared to be functional, and to the right was an expensive library table with six chairs around it. It was a very rich room which seemed a little too rich for the size of the town and what he assumed was the size of the practice. Parsnip finished signing something and rose from his chair and walked around the desk. He was dressed casually with pressed khakis, button down shirt and cashmere V-neck. He approached Harp with a smile and proffered hand. His grip was firm and cool and his look steady as he returned Harp's usual direct gaze. "Mr. Harper. My name is Andrew Parsnip. My friends call me Andy." He exuded charm.

"Nice office." Harp said, glancing past Parsnip.

"Yes," the lawyer said. "We were lucky to acquire this property for our practice. It fits our needs perfectly though these old houses require unending maintenance." He turned toward the table where a packet of documents was waiting. After chatting about the trip from Trenton and the weather, he put his hand on Harp's shoulder and steered him toward the table. "Let's sit over here and we'll go through the transfer of ownership. It's all pretty much pro forma. The title is clear and the instructions are very simple. Let me say that I am so sorry for your loss and, on behalf of the entire firm, extend our most sincere condolences." They sat side by side at the table. Parsnip opened the folder and arranged the documents.

"Just out of curiosity, do you have any plans for this property?

Just guessing, but you just don't appear to be a farmer, heh heh."
His gaze was very intent, even during this weak attempt to be
jovial.

Harp responded as they took their seats. "My plan is to go
to your little bank, take out all of my money, spend a couple of
weeks at this farm of mine, sell the whole thing to the highest
bidder, and then return to Trenton."

Parsnip could not contain his pleasure. "How I admire a man
who knows his own mind. It sounds like the perfect plan for you.
And, you will be happy to know that I have already had prospec-
tive buyers contact me and, as soon as you are ready, we can begin
negotiations. I can guarantee a quick sale at a very fair price."
At the table, Parsnip finished making small stacks of documents
according to purpose. He was fast and practiced and obviously
knew what he was doing. Harp appreciated the lack of small talk.
He still just wanted to get the whole thing over with and get back
to Trenton.

"For the record, I need to see some picture identification and
other documents proving you are the heir of record." He smiled.
"Of course I do not doubt for a minute that you are Horace B.
Harper, but the law requires this confirmation." Harp produced
his driver's license and handed it over.

"This is good but the law requires us to have two forms of
identification. Do you have something else?" Parsnip asked

"I have my Veterans Administration ID card. Will that do?"
He was mildly impatient with the procedure. But, he knew from
experience that you could do nothing these days without some
proof of ID.

Suddenly assuming an attitude of deep respect and what

was no doubt his courtroom voice, the lawyer said. "That will do just fine. I have the utmost respect for men who have served our country. How many years, if I might ask, did you serve?"

It was a strange way to feel, but Harp could not help but be mildly nauseated by the way some of the people who never served treated veterans. It was okay if an old soldier slapped him on the back and said thanks, but it was different when an unctuous, well-fed young frat boy who had never served pretended to deeply appreciate and understand what Harp had been through. If he appreciated it so much, why didn't he enlist? "I did twenty-four plus years. Got out about a year ago."

"What was your specialty?" The earnestness was palpable now.

Harp thought *my specialty was killing people* but certainly did not want to answer that question. "Is this still part of the identification process?"

"No, no." Parsnip hastily retreated. "Just my own curiosity. Sorry." He paused and turned back to the documents. "Okay, we know you are who you say you are." He chuckled and started handing documents to Harp to sign. Forms for deeds, taxes, equipment titles, law firm disclosure forms, and more. Parsnip would pass a form over with an explanation and Harp would sign—mostly without looking. He just wanted to sell and be done with it. After he had signed most of the forms, Parsnip casually passed another form saying, in the same bored voice as with the other forms, "Mineral rights transfer form," and moved on to the next form. Harp signed them all.

With everything signed, a statement Kowalski made came back to Harp. She had recommended that he keep the mineral rights. He wasn't sure he wanted to bother with a complication to the process, but the thought occurred that he could sell the property and maybe get some money from the mineral rights on down the road. Parsnip had stood up with his copy of the forms under his arm. With an expansive smile, he thanked Harp and started toward the door.

Harp stopped suddenly and asked, "Mr. Parsnip, I have another question."

Parsnip did not completely stifle an irritated look but smiled and said certainly. "Of course, what do you need to know?"

"I want to look at both sets of documents together, yours and mine, and just kind of review what each one says. Could we do that?"

"Well sure we can," Parsnip said, acting jovial once again.

***

Back in their chairs at the table, the lawyer started from the beginning and briefly outlined what each form accomplished. Harp turned his over as Parsnip finished with each form. When he got to the mineral rights forms, Harp casually reached over and picked up the lawyer's copy of the mineral rights transfer form and placed it next to his copy as if to compare.

"Tell me again what this form does."

Parsnip was suddenly and obviously tense. But he forced a smile and explained. "This is simply a way to appoint an agent to be responsible for the transfer of the mineral rights to the property. When you sell the property, this says where and to whom those rights should go." His hand moved almost of its own volition toward his copy. Harp placed his arm in the way.

Harp held up his hand and motioned Parsnip to wait while he read the document more carefully. "It says here that you would be that agent. But it looks to me like I am transferring those rights to you. And it looks like you get to sell the mineral rights regardless of what I do with the property. Am I reading it right? In other words, it kind of makes you the owner of those mineral rights. Am I reading this correctly?"

With a sickly smile, Parsnip agreed saying, "It is just a way to simplify the process. It's done all the time. I would probably be doing it anyway on your behalf. You would of course enjoy the profits from such a transfer." He twisted toward Harp and made ready to snatch the forms.

"At your discretion, of course." Harp said. The lawyer weakly agreed. "Well, I guess it's okay." Parsnip heaved a deep sigh of relief. "But, I think I'll just keep both copies for now and give this some more thought."

"I'm sorry but you just can't do that!" He blustered. You could tell he was used to blustering and getting his way. "You have already signed and tendered a legal form to an officer of the court and do not have the option of arbitrarily taking it back. I'm afraid you absolutely must return that form to me!" Parsnip was now sweating. He reached again for the form. Harp casually turned away, folded both forms together and put them in his inside jacket pocket.

"Like I said, I just want to think about this some more. Besides, I always thought nothing was legally binding until it's filed at the courthouse." Harp stood up, took his packet of forms. "Thanks, Mr. Parsnip, for all your help in this. I am sure I'll get a bill in the mail and you can count on quick payment. Just send it out to the bank." Parsnip was slumped in his seat, staring at the forms. He was desperately trying to come up with a way to salvage a situation which had suddenly veered out of control. But, looking at this rough scarred man called Harp, he realized that he suddenly did not dare to make idle threats. He would have to find another way. Harp coldly smiled and waved and left him there.

On his way out, he asked Phoebe Loftus for directions to the bank. Her bony hands were clenched on the desktop and her mouth was a thin angry line. "Well, Horace Baldwin Harper, if you turn right out of the driveway, you will see it on the right about three blocks up the street." She then wheeled her chair all the way around so she was facing away from him. He grinned and saluted her rigid back. He concluded that for future legal representation, he would have to get another lawyer. He was disappointed in Phoebe. He thought she would have a more inventive way to vent her anger. After Harp had passed through the front door, Parsnip hurried to the back of the house to see what he was driving. He noted the big Dodge and wrote the license number on a sticky note. As he was returning to his office, the phone rang and he knew Phoebe would be transferring the call to his office. He thought he knew who it would be and he was right.

It was a simple question, asked with no preamble, hello, or how are you. "Did you get it?"

"Well, yes and no." Parsnip equivocated. He really did not want to answer this question.

"Explain." The voice was suddenly flat and wary.

"Just as we predicted, he intends to take his money out of the bank, sell the property, and go back to Trenton. He signed all the papers, asked a couple questions, and started to leave."

"So what's the problem?"

"He gets to the door, and then he says he's got a couple questions and wants to go back over the forms. I couldn't say no to that. We sat down and went over all the forms, one by one, and when we get to the mineral rights, he reaches over and takes my copy—like he's going to compare them. Then takes both copies, folds them and puts them in his jacket pocket." The lawyer's voice had risen in disbelief as he finished his explanation.

"Why didn't you just take it back? That seems fairly simple. He was not within his rights to do this." The voice had become quite hard.

"Listen, if you saw this guy, you would know why I couldn't do it. He is a big, hard guy, retired military, and the way he looks at you would stop a bear in its tracks. There's no way I could physically make him give me the forms. No way!"

"So he's got the forms with him right now?"

"Yes, and he's on the way to the bank. He should be there by now."

There was a long pause, as the caller was thinking. "Okay. He's probably going to take out some of that money she left him and go on out to the property."

"Well, I have done as much as I can do. I don't want to be involved any further."

"Let me remind you, young Mr. Parsnip, that I have sent enough work on these leases and deeds to your firm, including you and your partners, to make you all rich men." The caller paused. "I want you to call Button and tell him that Harper has arrived. Tell him what Harper is driving." The line went dead. Parsnip was sweating. He was wondering how this had happened.

How had he gotten involved in things which his instincts told him could be serious trouble? He was legally clear, he thought, but knew that the caller could bring him in any time.

***

Harp found the bank was right where she said it would be, with easy parking right out in front. It was small as banks go, just two stories and a small footprint. But it had the look you want to see on banks. It was solid, clean, and cool. You could trust this bank. It looked slightly newer than the buildings around it and he guessed it had outgrown its original location.

The bank was definitely small town with a short row of tellers on the left and small open cubicles straight ahead. This was one of those banks where the officers still sat out where the customers could see them. Harp went to the first desk and introduced himself. It was a young lady whose nameplate said she was assistant cashier. With a genuine smile, she asked how she might help him. When he explained why he was there, she gasped slightly and said, "My goodness. We have been waiting for you. You must talk to our President, Mr. Harrison Johnson. If you will wait just a minute, I'll let him know you're here." Rather than use the phone, she jumped from her chair and hurried to a door behind the desks. She was in the office for a just brief period then hurried to the gate in the low barrier and motioned him through.

"Mr. Johnson will see you now, Mr. Harper." She then hurried back to her desk to continue whatever she had been working on. Harp was impressed.

Standing in the doorway, Mr. Johnson smiled and motioned for Harp to enter his office. Johnson was tall, a couple of inches more than Harp, and had a full head of white hair which was neatly parted and combed. His gray eyes were level and knowing. His grip when shaking hands was strong and Harp could feel calluses that did not come from pens and pencils. After Harp had entered, he checked the interior of the bank for a long moment, and then closed the door. His office was simply decorated with wildlife pictures on the walls, a desk, credenza, and a couple of walnut filing cabinets. There was an American Legion Plaque and a Rotary award. Johnson motioned Harp to a very comfortable chair close to the front of his desk and returned to his large leather office chair which looked well worn.

Johnson asked Harp for identification and looked at the same documents that Harp had provided Parsnip. "I see you are retired military. That would place you in service around the time of Kuwait, Iraq, Afghanistan, and all that mess."

Harp nodded. Johnson continued, "I also see that you probably did not come home the same way you left."

Harp nodded again. He was aware that Johnson was studying him but was surprised at the accuracy of his observations. "I didn't either. Two days ago, another little piece of shrapnel worked its way out of my left leg. It took about 40 years for that little piece of a mortar round to work its way out. I don't know if there's any more. I'm getting old and sentimental and every little piece that comes out reminds me again of what we lost over there." He didn't say where but Harp figured it had to be Vietnam. "In a funny way, I think I deserve the pain of it. Do you know what I mean?" Harp knew exactly what he meant; the guilt of surviving when so many buddies had not. He just nodded. This was why he could not resent his ongoing pain. It was his penance.

Harp and Johnson sat for a moment comfortably regarding one another. Soon, Johnson nodded as if a decision had been made. And it had. He pointed at the thick file of documents Harp had carried from Parsnip's office. "Okay, Mr. Harper, I am going to trust you. Let me start by saying that you are the heir to much more than you realize—a much bigger heritage in many ways. You may be just the man to handle it. We will just have to see."

Johnson pushed away from his desk and opened the large middle drawer. He removed a file and dropped it onto his desk. "Do you agree that you have signed all the proper papers and are now the owner of the farm and all attached items passed down to you by Pauline and Lars Kuykendahl?" Harp nodded again. "You have also inherited a checking account with $4,563.21 in it and a money market account with $321,987.56. Either of which is immediately available to you in any form you wish. If you want cash, it will take a day to get that many $100 bills delivered to the bank, but it is all yours. There are some bills, electricity, gas, heating oil, and such which have been paid by Mr. Parsnip's office out of the checking account but each of those accounts is up to date and will be transferred to your name today. Most importantly, all the taxes are paid up and current. We have the receipts for everything. All you have to do is go out to this farm—which is quite nice by the way—and move in." Johnson smiled somewhat grimly at that.

"Wow," was all that Harp could think to say. "Is it really that simple?"

"Nothing, as you well know, Mr. Harper, is ever that simple."

Johnson turned his chair to the side, rocked back and stared at the ceiling. "Let me ask you something. Did you give up the mineral rights to this farm?"

Harp grinned. "I did, but I recalled something the Trenton lawyer said about keeping the mineral rights, even if I sell the property. But I had already signed the papers naming Parsnip as my agent in selling those rights.

"Oh, hell." Johnson said.

"But I took them back, both copies." Harp pulled the copies out of his jacket pocket and handed them to Johnson.

"How in hell did you do that?" Johnson was staring with wonder at the documents.

Harp explained what had happened and the lawyer's response. "Parsnip got hot and demanded them back. I told him I wanted to think about it. Now I don't know what to do with them."

"Mr. Harper, documents like this have a pretty important potential. I would strongly recommend that you either destroy them or put them in a very safe place. To do the former would mean that it never happened. The latter might eventually provide an opportunity to nail that little prick for this kind of unethical behavior. Which would you prefer?"

Harp gave it some thought. "I think for now anyway I would like to hold on to them. Do you have a safe deposit box available? I'll stick them in there for now."

"Mr. Harper, you already have a safe deposit box in this bank." Harp's eyebrows lifted in surprise.

Johnson continued, "Before Pauline died, she paid in advance for a safe deposit box. I have a document signed by her and notarized, allowing me to hold the other key. It is to be tendered to the heir upon my best judgment that the heir is of sufficient integrity and intelligence to receive the contents of the box."

"Boy, the surprises just keep coming," Harp muttered.

Johnson continued. "This was done because Pauline was very specific about keeping the contents of this box separate from the rest of the probate. At this moment, you and I are the only people who are aware of this agreement. I have the key in a sealed envelope which, as you will see, remains unopened. I do not know what is in the box. I believe this is legal because the will, which I have seen, clearly states that you are to receive everything. That would include the items in this box. I have decided that you are of sufficient integrity and intelligence to receive this key. I would, however, advise you never to reveal the existence of the box. It is apparently nobody's business but your own." He handed Harp an envelope with very stiff paper and a large wax seal over the flap.

Johnson stood up with a slight groan and limped around the desk. "If you will follow me, I'll take you to the vault. You may remain in there as long as you wish but we close in two hours." He produced another key from his desk and led the way down a short hall. They went into the small vault together. Johnson went to a shoe box sized safe deposit box and inserted his key and held out his hand. Harp tore open the envelope and removed his key. Johnson inserted both keys and turned. The locks opened simultaneously and Johnson pulled the long box from the wall of similar boxes. He handed it to Harp and stepped toward the door. "Let me know when you are finished."

Harp took it to a table. Inside was another small box, like a jewelry box for a necklace, a sealed letter and a map. The map appeared to be a detailed map of the farm, including the topography—which he could see right away showed some relatively flat fields and lots of hills. There were some pencil markings on the map—which he would have to figure out later—and small squares indicating buildings at the end of a long driveway off the main road, maybe a couple hundred yards. He laid this aside and looked into the small box. There was another key.

Harp opened the letter. It was several pages, obviously printed on a cheap home printer.

Dear Horace:

It seems like I have seen this done a hundred times on TV but if you are reading this I am dead. I know we don't know each other but I remember talking to your mother's sister a long time ago and she said you were in the service and doing something really dangerous. I am really sorry we never got to meet. You would've liked Lars. He was a real man too. I hope you learned how to take good care of yourself cause you are going to need it. Don't pay any attention to my poor writing. I did okay in school but I was never much good at writing. Mom hated that I could only get C's in English.

Don't thank me too soon for all you inherited because I hate to tell you but you have landed in a shitstorm. Sorry about that. I spent my whole life on a farm and been up to my knees in some kind of poop the whole time. The one good thing I can say about our place is that it is all free and clear. We don't owe anybody anything and that sure bothers the hell out of some people around here. They even tried to get us on taxes but we was able to prove they were all paid in full ahead of time.

I am leaving you this stuff separate from all the legal stuff that that law firm with Parsnip will handle. I somehow don't trust that little fellow. He does not know about what I am telling you here. I needed a lawyer and they are local and they offered to do the will and stuff so I let them have it.

We have got a beautiful place out here with about 490 acres of hills and fields and me and Lars just plain loved it. We could sit on our front porch and see all the way down the valley. It was too bad we couldn't have kids cause it woulda been nice to have them carry on with it. But, it looks like you are going to have to do that. Lars would work a couple of weeks on rig maintenance in oil fields up north of here and then come home for a week or so and we would get caught up on the chores and just spend good time together. He made real good money so we never wanted for anything. We grew our own meat and veggies and lived a good, quiet life. It got so I could pretty much run the farm while he brought home the bacon. Ha, ha.

Everything was fine until that damn fracking started. We didn't pay much attention at first because we weren't in any way interested in it. Trouble was, everybody around us got right interested and sold out real quick. That made those frack-ing people just hot to trot to buy our land. Seems like we are in a prime spot, which is a kind of a geo-something center of their field. They said they could start right here and go in every whichaway from our farm. Even worse is that they can't le-gally go UNDER our land cause we own all the way down to China and we got those mineral rights free and clear. We told those bastards no, and no, and hell no. Then the neighbors got mad cause we was the only ones who held out. Lately a lot of strange stuff has been happening around here. We even talked one time about maybe some of these people might get really serious. You know what I mean?

By now you seen what all was in this deposit box. This letter you are reading, a map of the farm and the little box with a key and a patch of cloth. That cloth came from Lars's coveralls. They say he burned to death which is a thing I don't want to think about. They said a line broke and the gas lit some kind of solvent on his clothes and he fell back on a bolt of some kind. I hope that's what killed him. And somehow nobody saw it. That is weird. He works on these far apart pumps but still how could nobody see that? They gave his personal effects and clothes and all to me and there wasn't much left of them. He ended up on his back so this part of his clothes didn't get all burnt by the fire. When I got them, I noticed this neat little hole right in the middle of the back part of his coveralls. Anyway, the coroner, who is the undertaker, said he died from falling on that bolt and then got burned up by the fire and that was that. I still wonder about it being an "accident" and all. How come after all those years poor old Lars falls on a stuck up bolt? Anyway, it all got me to thinking, suppose something happened to me? What would happen to this place? I sure don't want it to go to some fracker. That's when I did all the will work and wrote this letter. Maybe I'm crazy. But one thing is really different around here. Now everybody has got lots of money and from what they say there is lots and lots more to be made. As you know, money changes people. There have been two different agents out here trying to buy this place and they offer unreal amounts. But I ask them what can I do with all that money.

Do they think I can just pick up and leave Lars out there in our little cemetery? I tell them not only no but hell no. I want to stay here til I die.

Do you know what a root cellar is? Anyway, me and Lars dug one in the back wall of the basement to keep our canned stuff and some potatoes and such and to be a place to sit out bad storms. Just for the heck of it, we decided to keep it hidden. So it's got a set of shelves in front of it but they slide out of the way real easy and show a metal door. The key is for that door. We dug a little tunnel in there while we were at it. Lars knew about mining and stuff. It was hard work but we had the tools so we had some fun with that. You will see where it comes out. After Lars died, I could go down there and just sit in the dark in that root cellar and could kind of smell him and see him the best of any place on the farm. Maybe because we made it together. I hope you like canned stuff because there is a bunch of it down there. Try the canned beef. Most folks don't know how to do that. It will fill you up with good solid proteen. The veggies are really good too.

Well, I have gone on long enough. It is funny to talk this way but I do not know what happened to me. I am in pretty good health and all. If I get sick and have the time, I will add a page to explain that. On the back of this page is one of those sticky things with some numbers and our computer password on it. I expect cause you are military and all that you will know what those numbers are. We never wanted nobody else to know about it. Lars saw it and told me about it but he was so shook up he said that it was enough to make anybody pray. If you decide to see it, and I know I'm kind of talking in riddles, you will realize what I meant about a shitstorm. It would probably be a good thing if you could memorize those numbers then get rid of that piece of paper. Nobody knows about them except you now. Maybe when you know, you will just forget about it. God, I would hate for anyone else to get a hold of this letter. Please take care of everything.

Best wishes from your Cousin Pauline.

P.S. I hope you decide to keep the farm. The alfalfa on the westerly field grows real fast and will need regular cutting. You might need some help doing farm stuff. Ask Harry Johnson to find someone. Also, take good care of our old dog Fart. Ha ha.

In planning missions, Harp had learned the hard way not to let the actions get ahead of the thinking. After reading the letter twice, he slumped back in his chair and let the many thoughts tumble around in his mind. He hoped that, in this process, these jumbled images would arrange themselves in some order of priority.

Rising to the top of the mixture was the fact that he kind of admired Cousin Pauline and she was, after all, the last of his family. Second was the fact that he was a little angry. He was angry that so much had happened to this brave woman and he might have helped if he had known about this situation sooner. The next thought to occur was that Harp might be able to stay a little longer just to see what happens next. With that final thought in mind, Harp took the key and the map. He placed the small box, the letter, the two copies of the mineral rights transfer form and all the deed documents in the safe deposit box. He looked at the piece of denim very closely and from experience could see where the fabric edges were pushed in from the outside. Harp could tell from experience that metal of some sort had been pushed through the cloth. He wasn't sure what the significance was but he put it back in the box along with the other items. He studied the sticky note long enough to memorize the numbers then tore it into smaller and smaller pieces which he put in his shirt pocket. They would be scattered along the road on his way to the farm. He relocked the box and left the vault.

Johnson looked up from his computer as Harp walked into his office. "Everything okay, Mr. Harper?"

Harp dropped into a chair in front of Johnson's desk. He asked without preamble, "How did Pauline die?"

Johnson's eyes widened briefly at the abrupt question. He pushed the keyboard aside and laced his fingers on the desk and looked at Harp in a calm manner. "Interesting question. She died in an auto accident. Her car was found upside down in a creek where the water was just deep enough for the top of the car to be totally submerged. The autopsy showed that she died a slow death from drowning while hanging upside down from the seat belt. There was no indication of mechanical failure. The assumption was that she lost control of her car on a perfectly dry road with no traffic that she had driven daily for many years and landed upside down in the creek. That's how Pauline died." The distinguished bank president finished his statement in a dry noncommittal voice. "And, as with Lars' death, no one questioned the coroner's ruling."

Harp was silent for a long moment. "When I got here, I was certain that I was going to sell this place to the first person who made a decent offer. Now, I don't know. What I do know is that I am going to spend a little time on this land just to see what happens next. According to what Pauline said in her letter, I have to cut the alfalfa and feed a dog named Fart." He smiled grimly. The letter, its meaning, and even the presence of a solid man like Johnson somehow made the notion of ownership real. Maybe he owed Cousin Pauline at least a little attention to her beloved farm.

Mr. Harrison Johnson suddenly felt that this man would be all right no matter what happened. He felt a great sense of relief.

Harp placed the easily identified deposit box key on Johnson's desk. "I think I would like for you to continue holding this key. If something happens to me, I don't want anyone else to know about the stuff in there." Johnson took the key and put it back into another envelope and sealed it. Each initialed across the seal. "I put those copies of that mineral rights form in the box along with all the deed stuff." Johnson nodded and agreed that it was the wise thing to do. "For right now," Harp continued, "I would like you to move about $20,000 into checking and give me a couple thousand cash. Is it alright to do this?" It was still hard to believe this was all his money.

"Of course," Johnson replies. He called his assistant to come in with a counter check and transfer form which Harp filled out and signed and Johnson approved. "In a couple of days, you can come by and pick up your new supply of checks."

As he stood in preparation to leave, it occurred to Harp that it would not be very smart to be stopped by a local police force. His truck would not withstand a determined search and the hidden weaponry would be very hard to explain. He asked Johnson if there was some way to the farm that allowed staying off main roads and getting on the place unobserved. Johnson was puzzled but nodded and produced an area map. He marked a series of small country roads that would take Harp to his farm. It would, however, start with him leaving Bardberg the way he came in and bring him to the farm from the direction of another town. A long drive. Johnson's knowledge of the area was impressive. He explained that he had driven these roads and hunted in the area for decades.

Map in hand, cash in his pocket, Harp hurried to his truck and hit the road. He noticed some locals lounging around the street but none seemed to be overly interested in his departure. One of those locals, however, was very interested and dialed his cell phone as soon as Harp's truck pulled out. "He just left the bank. What do you want me to do?"

"Call Cecil and tell him to wait out on 53. We know where he's going. You stay there and keep an eye on Johnson." A click ended the conversation.

Cecil waited two hours before calling back. "I thought you said he was just leaving. He ain't come by here yet."

"Hell, he would have to be by there by now. Maybe he didn't go straight on out. I'll call the boss."

"Boss, he never went by Cecil. We don't know where he went. Oh, and Johnson went home."

The voice on the phone was unperturbed. "Don't worry. There's somebody out there who will know when he pulls in. You go on home too."

According to his map, Harp drove north out of town instead of the obvious west. After a series of back roads, he only had to

turn off on what would be one of his own farm roads a quarter mile before he got to the front driveway. He would cross his
pasture and go down the other side of a rise in the pasture and
approach the back of his new home on a well-used track in the
field. He drove the truck right to the rear of the large barn. After
a quick look-see, he easily pushed open the large sliding doors
and quietly drove the truck inside. He pulled the doors closed
and studied the barn's interior in the available fading light. He
didn't know much about barns, but he supposed this one was typical. It had a huge central bay for equipment with various rooms
and stalls along the sides. There were large hay storage areas atop
both sides and they appeared to be full of bales. First things first.
The locker went into one of the small tackle rooms and was buried under blankets and leather straps whose uses were a mystery.

Harp figured that he had arrived undetected but decided
to wait until it was completely dark before reconnoitering. This
would also give him an opportunity to use the night vision goggles that were in the tan locker. Maybe they would work, maybe
not. The batteries were old but they were lithium. It was almost
dark and he figured if he knew his way in the dark, he would
surely know it in the daytime. It was a hell of a way to come into
a new home, he thought to himself. To the right of the large
equipment door at the front of the barn was a smaller normal
door through which he exited when it was dark. A nicely planned
graveled drive with fences on either side led toward the back of
the house.

The goggles worked. Infrared mode showed nothing alarm-
ing outside or inside the farm structures along the way. He was
startled just for a second when a large bright green rat wandered

along the edge of the equipment shed and disappeared under ground. He figured that the house had been empty for several weeks and had to be cooled down. Therefore, any heat generated had to come from warm bodies. He very slowly circled the house while aiming the latest iteration of the Ultra infrared TAC10 developed by the military to show heat signatures even inside thick clay walls. All he saw was a couple more rats around the base of the house. Harp felt it was safe to go in. The rats would have to go, but in good time. He hoped the only rats were these non-human kind.

He entered through a back-door mudroom with an unlocked outer door. He was struck by the racks and hooks holding boots and work coats used by Pauline and Lars. Even to the hard-nosed Harp, it was sad to see this evidence of their active lives on this land. The smell of the farm was a little too obvious to Harp's city nose. Animal shit on shoes was something he hoped he would never personally experience.

Coming through the door from the mud room, even with the night goggles, he could tell it was a comfortable, homey kitchen. It was cool and smelled clean. He was thirsty and hungry but had some work to do before he rested. His personal luggage was still in his truck and had to be brought in before he did anything else. He went back for the essentials and brought them into what appeared to be Pauline and Lars' bedroom. He was tired and his leg ached like hell. He went to sleep in seconds.

Harp got up at first light and used the adjoining bathroom. Like everything else, it seemed like it had been prepared for the arrival of company. He guessed that's what he was. He was going to visit for a while and then leave. After looking at the pictures of Pauline and Lars that were hanging around the bedroom, he found his way back to the kitchen. He was starting toward the fridge when he heard something outside the kitchen door. Pulling the curtains aside slightly, he looked down at what was the most mournful, sad looking animal he had ever seen. It had red-rimmed eyes, wet jowls, drooping tail, and appeared to be having trouble holding its head up. This had to be Fart, Harp concluded. He looked like a cross between a hound and a boxer—which created the homeliest dog face ever created. It had a short nose but long drooping ears, long legs, and fur of varying lengths around a heavily shouldered body.

Because Fart looked as though he didn't have enough energy to attack, Harp opened the door. They stood there looking at one another for a long moment. With a big sigh, Fart walked to the corner of the mud room and collapsed with a thump next to a large bowl. Harp assumed this was his dinner bowl. Looking around the room, Harp found a bin with a large bag of dog food inside. Not knowing how much the dog needed, he filled the bowl. With zero enthusiasm, Fart ate about half the food while Harp watched, marveling that this animal had enough energy to swallow food. He took this opportunity to see what he was feeding the dog and found it was nothing but vegetable matter with some fake protein. He was pretty sure that dogs were meat eaters and decided that he should get some real food for this sad creature. When he finished eating, Fart slouched over to look up at his new owner.

"What?" Harp asked. He didn't know what was next. The dog started to turn away when Harp asked, "You want to come inside?" Fart paused for a second then gave a dog shrug and followed Harp into the kitchen. He had only reached the middle of the room when he made the slightest of fart sounds. A small squeak was all it was. For some reason, dog farts are among the most volatile gases in the universe. It took no more than two seconds for the kitchen to be totally given over to an overwhelming odor that instantly surrounded Harp in a sickening cloud.

"Holy shit!" Harp shouted. "What the fuck was that? Son of a bitch!" Harp threw open the door and pointed outside with a shaking arm. "Get your ass out of here. Now!" Fart sighed and turned back toward the door as if he knew this was inevitable. He slunk outside, stopped, looked back at Harp, sighed again, and ambled off. Harp was desperately trying to fan the air with the door. He had been thinking about finding something for breakfast but no longer cared for food.

Instead, in wonder still at the twist of fate that brought him to this moment, he began a study of his house. The whole thing was decorated with a nice touch with a lot of country items. It was plain that Pauline did the decorating and it was plain she liked cute things. Ceramic cherubs seemed to be her favorite. They were everywhere. Probably Lars didn't give a rat's ass as long she was happy and he had a large recliner. The house was basically a huge country kitchen on the back, a big living room on the front, an office/den on one side in the middle and a large bedroom on the other side. A long porch reached across the front and a smaller porch came off the side of the kitchen. There was a half bath off the kitchen and full bath off the downstairs bedroom. Harp supposed there were three bedrooms and a bath upstairs. The stairs were in the hall, and he started going up.

6

HE HAD JUST PUT A FOOT ON THE FIRST STEP WHEN HE
heard heavy footsteps on the porch outside the front door. Whoever was out there was not trying to be secretive. The heavy footsteps clumped across the wide porch and stopped at the front
door. There was the soft clink of keys being searched then the
clicking as the right one was inserted and turned. Harp had quietly slipped down the hall and across the living room and was
pressed against the wall behind the door. As it opened, admitting
a large man, Harp stepped forward, grabbed the man's collar and
put a finger in his back.

"Do not move another step or I pull the trigger. Get those
hands up where I can see them."

"Jesus Christ, mister, don't worry! I'm not going to do anything. Just tell me what you want!"

"Go over and sit in that recliner. Keep your hands in your lap."
The man carefully walked over, turned and sat. Harp kept his
hand behind his back, not yet ready to reveal that he was armed
with just a forefinger.

The man was still shaken but worked up enough courage to bluster. "You better have a damned good reason to be in this house!" He was pointing a shaking finger at Harp. "I am responsible for this house and you are trespassing."

Harp did not answer for a moment. He studied the intruder, who looked like a hard-working farmer gone soft, maybe fifty-seven or fifty-eight, farmer tan, sun-wrinkled face. He was thinking that this man, because he had the keys and entered with confidence, probably had legal reason to be here. "First thing is that you are no longer responsible for anything here. I am. This is my house and, while I understand you might be keeping an eye on the place, your services are no longer needed. Thank you very much for your help. What is your name?"

Calming down somewhat, he replied, "I'm Marvin Benson. I own the place next to yours about a mile up the road. A lawyer named Parsnip asked me to come by once in a while and make sure everything was okay. He didn't tell me about anybody moving in. Just who are you, mister?"

"I am H. B. Harper, Pauline's cousin. She left the farm to me. I got in last night."

"Hell," Benson sputtered, "Nobody saw you arrive."

"Why would they?" Harp asked. "Is somebody supposed to see who comes and goes?"

Benson's eyes suddenly shifted away as he appeared to consider his answer. Harp could see that Benson was thinking about his answer, which meant he was probably about to lie. "Why no, it's just that folks along this road usually see who is coming and going. We might be a little nosy that way." He chuckled unconvincingly.

Harp stood silently. He brought his hand around from behind his back. Benson watched the empty hand come around with tightened lips. He was a big man who was not usually bluffed so easily. "You probably won't be able to do that to me again, Harper," he said in a tight voice." He stood up, chin out, tight fists.

"Wouldn't think of it." Harp said.

"I'll be leaving now. I guess we'll be seeing each other around." He started toward the door.

"One thing, Benson, I'll need those keys."

"Can't do it, Mr. Harper. Mr. Parsnip gave me those keys and I reckon I should give them back to him." He took another step toward the door.

With sudden grace, Harp glided to a spot between Benson and the door. He smiled, "I'll have the keys *now*, Benson." This time there was no mistaking the hardness. There was also no mistaking to Benson that his options had narrowed down to just two. He could hand over the keys or he could try to get by Harp. Big as he was, he realized that he was not ready to go up against a man who looked like Harper. There was no question that Harp was a warrior and Benson was not. He pulled the keys from his pants pocket and dropped them in Harp's hand. Harp stepped aside and held the door for Benson.

"Another thing, Mr. Benson. You are no longer invited to come and go on this place until we get to know each other a little better. Understood?"

Benson was standing on the porch. He nodded. "Let me make a prediction, Mr. Harper. You don't know how things are happening around here. Pauline and Lars were good people but they just didn't want to get along with their neighbors. You seem the same way. Things are moving real fast. If I had to guess, I would guess that you are not a farmer. I would also guess that you are soon going to be offered a great deal of money for this place. I would also guess that you will take it and leave. To me, that will be a good thing. I recommend it. Goodbye."

Benson crossed the porch and went down the steps to enter a giant new Cadillac SUV. It started silently and silently glided away from the house. Somehow it did not seem like the kind of car that Benson would drive.

Benson's visit reminded Harp that he had certain things to take care of. No telling who might come by next. Most importantly, he had to move the damned locker to a more secure place, like maybe that root cellar Pauline mentioned. He quickly loaded it back on the truck, drove to the back door, and carried it inside. It wasn't too heavy but, like all foot lockers, awkward to carry.

A quick search found the stairs to the basement off the hallway.

After locking front and back doors and making sure no one was approaching from any direction, he laboriously carried the thing through the house to the top of the stairs. The top part of the stairs was lit from the hall lights but the basement was in darkness. There was a wall to the right so, after putting the locker on the floor at the bottom, he felt around until he found a light switch. Suddenly the room was brightly lit and Harp was struck dumb with amazement at the vision to his left. It was a beautifully made, fully stocked, private bar. Mouth hanging open, he ambled over to gaze upon one of the prettiest sights he had ever seen. Harp walked to the end of the bar, marveling at the completeness of it.

It was a fateful discovery. To the eventual consternation of many people and even in wonder at his own vulnerability when certain treasures were offered, this was the moment when Horace B. "Harp" Harper decided that maybe he would not sell the place as quickly as he might have. The back bar was stocked with some of the finest whiskeys and liquors he had ever laid eyes on—along with some very fine crystal glasses to pour them in. Under the back bar was a small fridge, an ice maker, and shelves with more bottles. Under the bar was a double sink and shelf with drink mixing paraphernalia. More light switches revealed tasteful lights and overhead variable lighting. The bar itself was glowing mahogany with four magnificent wood stools ready to be occupied.

Up until now, the magnitude of his inheritance was something that had lacked definition. Harp could only define it within the context of his existence. What the fuck was a farm anyway? To him, it was just money. He wasn't going to stay, so why work to understand a new reality? Now, however, this was different. Now he understood that this was *his*. All of this was his—and nobody else was going to get one goddamned drop. He decided in a flash in the basement of this farmhouse that there was no real hurry to get back to Trenton. He would at least stay long enough to drink it all. Right here was a sofa, huge coffee table, television, and bathroom. Except for some food, he didn't see why he would have to leave this room for anything. For the first time in his life, he felt lucky. Life, he thought, could be something other than a shit sandwich.

Harp was trying to decide which of the bottles he would sample first when he remembered what he was supposed to be doing.

With some resentment and now in a hurry, he turned away to search for the entrance to the secret room. He knew it had to be on the back wall of the basement and that it was behind a set of shelves, so it must be in the room to the right. He entered and found a combination workroom/storeroom with a large freezer, a steel work table, and three sets of wood shelves lining the back wall. The shelves were pretty much full of odds and ends. At first inspection, they all looked exactly the same. About four-foot-wide and six-foot-tall, they had solid wood backs and appeared to be attached to the cinder block wall behind them. Harp knew the door had to be on the back wall of the basement and that a handle of some sort was hidden among the contents of these shelves. He soon found that handle behind a set of books. It wasn't too tricky, he thought, but, if you didn't know about it beforehand, you wouldn't easily find it. He flipped the handle up, turned and pulled and the whole set of shelves easily swung away from the wall. Now revealed was a steel door about two and a half by five and a half feet with a good quality lock. The key from the safe deposit box easily turned in the lock and the door smoothly opened inward.

The contents of the room were another revelation. It had been carefully planned. The walls had been cut from the native clay and then covered with a coating of some kind of cement. It was very cool and dry and had the slightly musty but pleasant odor of damp earth. As Pauline had said, there were countless jars of canned food. But there were also many gallon bottles of water, tightly sealed containers of kerosene, glass jars labeled with sugar, salt, rice, flour, and more. Harp was impressed at the determination of Lars and Pauline to survive no matter what happened in the world. He would be willing to bet there were candles, matches, knives, lanterns, batteries, flashlights, and more in the cases stacked here and there. Most importantly, it was cool and dry and a perfect place to secure his gear. He placed the locker in a corner on the concrete floor. It was as safe here as anywhere he could think of and, who knows, he might need one of those "tools." This kind of prep had saved his life on many occasions.

Harp saw the small door at the back wall of the room, which had to be the tunnel Pauline mentioned. Roughly three by four, it was secured with just a sliding bolt. With some apprehension, he opened the door and looked into complete blackness. He noted that the door could be secured from the other side so, once you were in there, it would not be easy to be followed. Harp wondered again at the thinking of Pauline and Lars and assumed that they must just have been very cautious people. It was a simple dirt tunnel with a plank ceiling, plywood flooring, and supports every three or four feet. Harp concluded that it must lead away from the house to hell only knows where. He decided he would find out later. He was feeling a certain tension that he could not quite put his finger on. If someone told Harp that maybe he was feeling a small sense of proprietorship with this inherited property, maybe even a family connection, he would have laughed. But, deep in a heart scarred by brutal losses was the need to believe that he could truly trust a gift like this—that he could *own* something with value.

After a final look around, Harp concluded it was time to hit the bar. He was going to pick out the oldest bourbon and start with a double neat. After he swung the shelves back in place, he did something that was definitely not Harp-like. He rubbed his hands in glee and did a little awkward shuffle which could in no way be interpreted as a dance step—but it was the best he could do. It was a pitiful limp-shuffle. While the other kids were learning to dance, he was learning to start cars without keys. His lack of success at this endeavor was one of the reasons he left town for the military. The judge said it was an either/or situation. Harp took the "either" and enlisted because the "or" involved confinement.

***

Harp woke up on the basement sofa with no idea what time it was or how long he had been sleeping. The first thing he noticed was that he had no hangover—which he attributed to drinking thirty-year-old bourbon. He contentedly sighed at the memory. He was already looking forward to the next session. The second thing he noticed was that he was ready for a shower and shave. After another loving look at *his* bar, he opened the basement chest freezer to gawk at pile after pile of perfectly wrapped frozen beef, pork, and chicken. He grabbed several packs of frozen meat and went back upstairs.

It was early morning with gray light showing through the curtains. His duffel was still on the floor in the downstairs bedroom, so he decided to use that shower. Having grown to like and admire Lars and Pauline, Harp was saddened just a bit to be using items as intimate as their soaps, brushes, and shampoos. This heightened the sense that he owed them something. He wasn't quite sure where this notion came from, it was so foreign. He could only conclude that he liked these guys. If they had been

67

victims, as what little he knew showed, maybe he kind of owed it to them to find out. Still, Harp shuddered slightly at the thought of owing anybody anything. He had spent a lifetime getting to a place where he owed nothing. But, he was also a man of honor and a debt was a debt, no matter how distasteful.

So, as owner of a farm, this made him a farmer, he joked to himself. If he was a goddamned farmer, he ought to have a hearty breakfast and get out there and plow the pasture and slop the chickens, or hoe the corn, or something. Then, after all the chores were done, he could come back in and reap the harvest of whiskey. The fridge had been cleaned out before he got there, but there was unopened coffee to perk and frozen steaks. That was breakfast. He nuked the steaks and fried one, then gave the other to Fart, who happened to be the total of his livestock and who happened to not be around at present. Satisfied with a stomach full of nearly raw steak and several cups of coffee, Harp realized he had not even been upstairs in his house. Carrying a last cup, he went up the stairs. There were large rooms to the right and left, each with a queen bed, and one larger bedroom across the front. A large, modern bathroom was in the hall. Each room was decorated very nicely with a country look and uncomfortably neat—like company was coming. In addition to being nice rooms, Harp's logistical mind noted that each commanded a great view—one out the front of the house and one out each side and the back. There were several closets. They were full of clothes. Harp tried on a checkered red flannel shirt to find a perfect fit. He shrugged at the thought of wearing a dead man's clothes. It wouldn't be the first time. He and Lars were both extra-large. So now he had farmer clothes too.

Still wearing the shirt, Harp went back downstairs. He started a list in his mind of things he needed to do. High on the list was food. He needed to find some groceries somewhere. Probably there would be a store in Bardberg.

First, though, was a walk around the farmstead. Walking slowly from place to place, he examined all the buildings, trying to guess what each was for. An open equipment shed held all the farm vehicles plus a very dirty, very old, late forties Chevy four-door sedan squatting on tires that had obviously been flat for years. He studied with great interest the huge tractor and decided he would have to have lessons before he even thought of starting the monster. Several other machines seemed to have something to do with handling crops because they were a clutter of shafts, chutes, and cutting blades. He had seen them on TV but had no desire to operate the damned things. Off by itself was a perfect little model house. He soon found that it was a prettified well-house that housed a small tank and a box for electrical power. The chicken house was easy and so was the hog shed.

Going back to the house, he realized he hadn't looked in the attached garage. He went in through the kitchen and hit the garage door opener. In one bay was the big Ford pickup the papers had mentioned and in the other was a new looking four-wheel drive John Deere ATV. It was almost as big as a small pickup. Now this, he thought, is what I need. It was a highly-polished green with a good-sized truck bed behind a wide comfortable seat. It had a roof and a windshield but was open on the sides. Fortunately, the keys were in it and it started easily. Finding the gear selection understandable even to him, he backed it out of the garage and drove it around the farm yard just to get the feel of

69

it. What the hell, he thought; this might be a good time to have a look at the far reaches of his property. He had no idea how big 487 acres were. He went back and got the map that Pauline had provided via the safe deposit box. He spent a few minutes studying it before he mounted his ATV and drove it out of the garage. He still didn't know why she felt this map had to be secured like that. The pencil marks were the only things making it different from any map available at the county office. Right now, he had no idea what the marks meant.

Harp operated the vehicle with a sense of anticipation and pleasure at driving such a fine piece of equipment. The thought of taking it back to Trenton flitted across his mind and was quickly forgotten. Leaving the yard behind the house, he first followed a path between fences toward a small knoll where the headstones of a cemetery were visible. As he drove up, Fart rose from the ground next to the newest grave and stood looking at Harp. Harp cut the motor and sat staring back at the dog, which hadn't changed in appearance or manner. For some reason, as big and mean as the dog looked, Harp did not sense any threat. The dog just looked like he was lost.

After they had looked eye to eye for a couple of minutes, Harp spoke. "Listen pal, you and I don't have to be buddies or anything like that. But it looks like I got you along with this place so you gotta let me know what you want to do. You want to stay out here and whine, okay. You want to get over it and come with me, okay." Harp slapped the seat beside him which startled the dog. "Now come on." Harp said in a commanding voice. He slapped the seat again. "Get up here!" Fart turned and looked at the grave one more time then, surprisingly, loped over and jumped on the seat beside Harp. As if he had been waiting for the moment, Fart put his head on Harp's thigh and heaved a huge dog sigh. Hell, Harp thought, he didn't mean he wanted the damned dog to start liking him. There just wasn't room in his life for a fucking dog. He had to admit to a certain thrill over this display of trust, though, and tentatively patted Fart on his big ugly head. Fart sighed again. "And another thing, I don't why they have been feeding you that vegetarian stuff. I'm switching you back to a mostly meat diet. Maybe that will cure your case of atomic asshole. Broccoli makes *me* fart."

7

PARSNIP WAS WORKING ON ONE OF HIS BREAD AND BUT-
ter cases involving an auto accident when Phoebe buzzed to tell
him that HE was on the line.

Parsnip picked up and said, "Hello, Adam."

"Is he out there?" Adam asked with no preamble.

"Yes, as far as we know. Benson went out as usual and was
shocked to find Harper had moved in. I was going to call you."
Parsnip said.

"What happened?"

"They had a little run-in and Harper took all the keys back.
He told Benson he was no longer welcome."

"What did Benson do? He's a pretty big guy."

"The way Benson explained it, Harper kind of got between
him and the door and more or less threatened him with bodily
harm. He said that Harper was really mean looking and he did
not want to get into a scrap in somebody else's house or he would
have kicked Harper's ass." The last was said with a sardonic tone.

"So this guy backs Benson down and Benson does nothing?"

"Yup, that's about it." Parsnip wanted to get back to work.

"Do we know how Harper got out to the farm without anyone seeing him? How could a stranger to this area do this?"

The lawyer replied, "I thought about that. About the only way he would be able to do that would be to get directions from somebody local and come in on the north side of the farm. I don't think even the GPS would show all those little roads out there. As far as I know, he talked to just two people before he headed out there. He talked to me and he talked to Harry Johnson at the bank. I think it must have been Johnson. You know that he has never been convinced that the whole area should be fracked. Plus, he was pretty close to Pauline and Lars."

"Harrison Johnson may find that, bank president or not, he has some vulnerabilities."

Parsnip cautioned, "We need to be very careful there. Johnson is real popular around here. Even with his doubts, he has many friends in high places. Not to mention that he really is a great guy."

"He has no concept of high places," Adam said sarcastically.

Parsnip waited. He knew what was coming. He had heard it enough times.

"Not including that land is like owning a billion-dollar ship with a big hole in the bottom. We have to have it."

"I know, Adam. But we certainly have some time to observe and see how things develop. He could decide to sell it tomorrow. One thing I can tell you for sure is that he is not a farmer."

"This is true and that is why I am being patient with you. No one likes it when I get impatient. Do you understand?" The imperiousness could be irritating, but the lawyer kept his tongue. He was in too deep to be impertinent.

"Yes, Adam. I will keep you apprised of events."
"See that you do." Adam was gone.

***

Now there was a new beautiful, black, iridescent bubble forming, just barely visible, but there.

8

FINDING A PROPERTY LINE IN THIS KIND OF COUNTRY
without specific markers was next to impossible, Harp found, especially when he didn't know what he was looking for. Yet, driving slowly while looking at the map allowed him to see generally
where a property line probably was. But this land was shaped by
ancient geological forces then reshaped by glaciers that reached
almost all the way to Pittsburgh. When they retreated, their tor-
rents of melt water created a new roughness in the underlying
land. Today it is part of the Allegheny Plateau and is dissected
by so many valleys that it makes a very rugged terrain. Under it
lie strata full of natural gas and petroleum. Harp did not yet understand the blessings and nightmares that stemmed from those
geological factors. All he knew was that his 487 acres had an
amazing number of mounds, escarpments, ravines, and gullies.
Beyond the fields behind the house you could hardly go in any
direction without having to either back-track or drive around
cliffs, sudden drop-offs, deep ravines, wooded slopes, and rock
piles. He found that this had challenged owners of the land for

eons and, as a result, there were narrow trails everywhere providing access you could use to see pretty much everything. Those trails explained the need for a smaller four-wheel drive ATV like the one he was driving. This land was beautiful in its wildness, however, and he could see how the Kuykendahls grew attached to the place. They had the best the topography could offer. Adjacent to the farmstead, they had plenty of land for crops, but they also had plenty for hunting and wildlife, and, what Harp appreciated, lots of privacy.

After a couple hours of driving around, Harp and Fart were ready to head back home for some food, which he thought would again consist of only meat. He had to get some groceries, he reminded himself again. Then he remembered all the canned stuff he could try. He would open the green beans. He promised Fart he wouldn't have to eat any of it. "Green beans and ribeye and bourbon," he shouted in a sudden fit of uncharacteristic joy. "Goddamn, Fart, let's slap some vittles on the table back at the ranch and stuff our guts with some real rib stickers!" Sensing his upbeat mood but still a semi-sad dog, Fart responded with a baritone "Wuff."

On the way, Harp checked the map and found he was around one of the penciled X's. It was on the side of a small hillock in an open area that was easy to spot. He saw as he got closer that there was obviously a small fenced spring flowing from the steep side of the hillock. The fence was three-sided and C-shaped, extending no more than eight feet from the bank which was the fourth side. It was quite new and obviously intended to block access to the spring, which seemed odd, even to Harp, for an area that appeared to be pasture. Even while still in the small truck, he began to smell a slightly sulfuric odor. The water did not appear to be flowing beyond the fence but was easily reachable when he dropped to a knee and reached through for a sample. From a cupped hand, he cautiously sipped some of the water. He was immediately repelled by a strong chemical taste in the water and quickly spit it out. He stood up and looked around, trying to imagine what could possibly be contaminating water clear out here. There was nothing but green as far as he could see. He would check later but guessed that the other X's indicated similar conditions. But he knew the water in the house was fine, for which he was very grateful. Because the location of these springs was something that Pauline did not want to reveal, Harp decided to do the same. He needed to find out a lot more before he said anything about it.

It was getting late, so they went back to the house. As soon as the ATV was parked in the garage, Fart jumped down and ambled around the house to the mud room where he went directly to an old blanket in the corner where he flopped and waited. That was his customary spot apart from his graveside vigil. It looked like the vigil might be over. Harp entered through the kitchen and began meal preparation, which involved dumping the canned green beans in a sauce pan, throwing a huge rib eye in a frying pan, followed by a quick trip to the basement for the bottle of the evening. He took another thawed rib eye to the back door and soon noticed Fart in the corner waiting. "My friend, until we get you some proper animal food, you are just going to have to eat steak." Harp dropped a pound and a half steak into his food bowl and went to get water for the water bowl. When he returned a minute or so later, the steak was gone and Fart was asleep. Harp found himself smiling and was disgusted when he realized what he was doing. But, because he didn't want to wake the snoring creature, he put off the trip for groceries until morning. Harp decided to do more homework this evening.

In rural areas like this, most farm houses are heated with fuel oil or propane. Harp realized this after a quick look at the bills neatly categorized in the farm office off the hall. He also realized he didn't know where the tank was. He hoped it wasn't near the house. Harp had a lot of unpleasant experience with exploding fuel and its proximity made him nervous. He searched the entire desk and found the usual junk in many drawers. He saw that one of the Kuykendahls was a good bookkeeper. Everything was filed in such a way that even Harp could understand the order of it. He would need to get the management business under control first thing, he thought. Even for a short stay, he would still need to be sure everything was paid up.

There were many thick files relating to animal sales and purchases. Looking at the details made him cringe. No matter what, he swore, he would never, ever buy a goddamned cow. A computer was tucked away under one side of the desk and fired up when he hit the start button. He pulled the keyboard from under the desktop and waited. As expected, it asked for a password and, now that the mouse was awake, he fed the computer MyDahl-y4Me and it bloomed to life. This brought about another slight twinge of guilt at the knowledge that he was poking through other peoples' belongings. He consoled himself with the excuse that he was doing this because she wanted him to.

But then, there wasn't much of interest to Harp anyway. Huge files on raising hogs and cattle took up much of the memory.

There were some Excel files, but apparently they liked to keep books the old-fashioned way, with ledger entries and checks. Because he had lots of time, he kept going, however, and eventually stumbled across a folder innocently titled *Springtime*. If he hadn't just come from that strange little spring with the foul water, he wouldn't have picked up on this title. But, because of that experience, he paused to look at this file. It dealt with the bad water in the springs.

Lars wrote:

Just for the record, Pauly and I decided we ought to have a record of what is happening to our water. Don't have a plan on what to do about it yet. Don't want to sue or anything. Anyway, the water in the north spring went bad around the end of July. It isn't much of a spring and it is in an area where we don't keep any livestock. No doubt in my mind what happened. What they do not realize is that there are men all over this part of the state who know what is down there and have felt with their hands a drill bit working. That new gas well on the Benson place is the problem. When they put that one in, they did not do a good job on the concrete well liner. Reason I know is that I talked to Bobby Place, a driller I have known for years. He was kind of nervous and not happy I was asking these questions but he talked to me because we are old friends. He said that they only went 120 or so feet with the liner when it set up because the mix was bad and they knew it was supposed to go 200 feet. They would have had to start all over if they tried to correct that by digging it all out and they did not have the time or money. So when they did the injection, they knew it could leak but didn't know for sure or how deep so they rigged the

79

numbers to show 200 and hoped for the best. I asked what did they do with the used injection fluid and he said they were putting it in some old capped oil wells which I know are all over the place up there, which is legal. We even have a couple here. I guess the thinking is that if those old wells did not leak oil then they would not leak this chemical stuff. I did not say anything about our problem and Billy said for God's sake do not tell anybody that he talked to me. I told him do not worry because it is just one old driller talking to another. Tell them I was looking for a job closer to home. Being gone for half a month at a time is getting pretty old to tell the truth. I hate leaving Pauly alone so much but she is a good old girl who can take care of herself. She just smacked me on the back of the head. Anyway, Bobby has left that job and is working on new gas wells in West Virginia as far as I know. It looks to me like what we might have is maybe leakage from two places. It might of come out of the original well because the liner was too short and then maybe came from them injecting the drilling fluid back into old dry oil wells. Do not know which. We already know about those old wells, how they sometimes would cross through the layer holding our water. Me and Pauly know about that in person when you talk about oil. They did not have the same strict rules back when they were drilled. The thing is that I know about ground water all to hell but what I do not understand is that I always thought springs ran down from water in a higher place. So how does this shit get into surface water? Maybe we got something else. Whatever it is, we know that the bad stuff is coming up from under the ground and it might be getting forced up. Anyway, now the second one of these springs has gone bad. I may be wrong in blaming the boys who are drilling the Benson well cause for all I know our water is coming from a different direction. We don't dare to do anything right now because of this other thing we don't want anybody to know about. Then the shit would really hit the fan. If anybody went there, they would see what I mean. Pauly just said it already has, ha ha. So anyway, we are kind of holding fire to see what else happens. Sometimes I think they know what is going on over here and they are really scared of what we will do. If we said something, it might shut everything down then everybody would be pissed. We want to be good neighbors but they all kind of sold out for money and said to hell with the land. I put some samples of the water in those two springs in the gun safe. Do not know what to do with them yet. That other thing we just ain't ready to deal with right now. We figure that pretty soon we'll know what to do. Life is funny. You go looking for a lost calf and you see something you can't unsee. The world will have to know about this someday, but not now. We are going to

Lars's narrative just quit there, presumably to be picked up later. Harp sat looking at the computer screen, trying to figure what he should do next. One of the first things he needed to do was get out his GPS unit and go to that spot indicated by those numbers. Harp knew as soon as he looked at them that they were coordinates. He turned the computer off. The gun safe was in a small closet opposite the computer desk. Pauline had said nothing about a gun safe key or combination. He needn't have worried because it was unlocked. The first thing he noticed was that there were no water samples. There were three rifles: two twenty-twos and one old thirty-thirty, and two twelve gauge shotguns, one pump and one double barrel. None were expensive, just working farm and hunting weapons and several boxes of ammunition. Harp checked and none were loaded. They all looked as if they had been used regularly but were cleaned and oiled. He wondered aloud why the water samples would not be where Lars said they would be and, for a moment, suspected Benson, who had the run of the place. That didn't make any sense, though, because anybody could go out and get more samples—which is what Harp added to his list of to-do's. Only now it was from three springs.

Ready to turn in, Harp had a decision to make: Upstairs front or back bedroom? He felt there was too much of Lars and Pauline in that downstairs bedroom and he wasn't quite ready to push them out. Their pictures were everywhere. He would have to pack them up sometime. The wedding pictures were especially sad. They looked so young. He noted that he and Lars were similar in build and general appearance. He chose upstairs front for the time being. It had that great view and a great bed along with a nice little bathroom with no personal effects. He wondered for a second about making it from the bar in the basement all the way to the second floor. Not a problem, he concluded. If the booze was of sufficient quality, he was not averse to sleeping where he fell. When Harp turned off the light next to the bed, the house went dark. The last thought that crossed Harp's mind before he drifted off was the realization that he had not talked to a person all day. That made it a perfect day. He smiled as he went to sleep. He dreamed of barren landscapes and explosions with dogs running toward him. They were trying to bark around the human arms in their mouths. This made a strange strangled sound that Harp imitated in his sleep.

***

The black coffee on the front porch while sitting in a very comfortable old rocker at sunrise was the best cup of coffee he had had in a long time. He was barefoot, in khakis and flannel shirt and, for a city boy, was enjoying looking out over the countryside. He had too little experience with pastoral scenes to easily process natural, nonthreatening beauty. The nature of his upbringing had not provided opportunities for trips to the countryside. He went straight from the streets to the Army. So, this sudden rush of the look, sounds, and smells of a perfect country morning had to wedge past decades of mostly military and practical landscape perceptions to a place in his mind where this rich scented land could be seen with the simple pleasure of watching nature happen.

Making it somewhat perplexing to Harp was the notion that he could own this country morning. There was not one single human noise to be heard as he studied the blue sky, the many greens from trees and shrubs, the sounds of songbirds, the fragrance from flowers, and wondered how this could actually belong to him. In the end, he sighed and shook his head. He sipped his coffee, ruffled the fur on Fart's head, rocked just a little, and let his eyes relax. He enjoyed a moment of peace. All he knew was that it was all green and it was all his. It was maybe a little too green for Harp, who thought the brown and red of brick was the real color of home. Worse, it sometimes seemed that Harp's life was spent in sand. Kuwait, Iraq, Afghanistan, and even a short time in Libya, were the main stations in his career. He did not even think of the sojourn into Pakistan which was a journey settled into nonexistence by the need for secrecy.

Sand. It defined his life. He had been in love once, only to find that it too was sand. Love, trust, faith, and belief shifted and changed shape so many times, blown around by passion and anger, that in the end, there was no compass good enough to show them the way back home. He tried. She didn't. He had no idea where she was and liked it that way. Fortunately, they hadn't married and there were no kids. As breaks go, it was clean.

Fart sat beside him, having already devoured another pound plus steak. He was looking much better and hadn't farted lately—as far as Harp knew. He appeared to be contented also. He would look at Harp periodically and inch closer as Harp rocked. Finally, Harp rubbed the dog's head and the response was a pitiful whimper and tail thumping which, to Harp, was sad for a beast that could easily kill a man. Harp warned him again that this was not a permanent arrangement and resisted the temptation to rub his head again. He didn't want to spoil the ugly mutt. All Fart heard was the loving voice of his new master offering praise just for being there. To a dog, this is the sweetness of life.

Harp realized that he was hungry for something from his former diet. He hadn't had any of those tangy, salty, sour calories in days. He loved pickled eggs and pickled pig's feet. He loved kielbasa and beer nuts. If it sat on a bar or back bar, it was something that food evolution had determined was of special need to drinkers. He needed to get some of this stuff and laughed when he realized he could not remember ever making a grocery list. He had made weapon lists, ammo lists, manpower lists, supply lists, liquor lists, communications lists, and even dead body lists. He had never made a grocery list. He had no idea how much he should get and how much things cost. He was sure that he had never written the word "flour" in his entire life. But then, he wasn't going to buy flour because he had no idea what to do with it. Proud of his final effort, which even included eggs, he decided at the last minute to leave the Dodge in the barn and take the Ford pickup.

Carefully backing the truck from the garage, he was about to turn down the driveway when he saw Fart standing and waiting. What the hell, he thought, let the beast come along. He got out to find Fart waiting behind the truck. Harp walked around and opened the passenger door and still Fart waited by the tailgate. Finally guessing what he was supposed to do, Harp lowered the tailgate and Fart easily leaped into the truck bed. If a previously sad looking dog could suddenly look happy, the dog did it. He was almost prancing from side to side and back and forth. Probably at some point in the past the dog had been inside the truck and released one of his sinus clearing bombs. If a little squeaker could destroy the air in a large kitchen, one could only imagine what it would have been like in the small confines of a truck cab. Harp shuddered at the thought and slammed the tailgate shut. Fart knew where he belonged. When they were on the road and moving faster, Harp almost laughed when, looking in the large rear-view mirror, he saw Fart's lips and ridiculous tongue loosely flopping in the wind with dog saliva stringing away in the wind. If a dog could grin, this dog was grinning.

The truck drove very well and he enjoyed its silence and power. He drove slowly while finding where all the controls were. The truck came with everything. It had cruise, four-wheel drive, compass, remote control everything on the steering wheel, and about a half dozen speakers. He was pleasantly surprised to find a Pink

Floyd CD in the radio. Either Lars or Pauline was cooler than he thought. It reminded him of their fire-base in Afghanistan where Perkins, who didn't make it, always seemed to be listening to Floyd in his ear buds. Perkins was afraid of dying and was trying to block out the everyday horror and fear by overwhelming them with the beauty of their music. Even in that shithole, the piercing guitar solos would rip their way past the misery and, just for a moment, erase the visions of blood and gore piled up behind the eyes of kids too young to cope with that unimaginable horror. Now, whenever he heard their music, Harp listened as his own homage to Perkins, who had been a good soldier.

The road was blacktop, probably called macadam in this part of the country, and wound its way between crumbling rocky clay cliffs and wooded slopes on either side. And, next to these hill country roads, there was always a creek with an Indian name. The shallow, fast-moving water would guide you to a village or town where folks drank it, cooked with it, and bathed in it. Occasionally there were wide, flatter spots in the small valleys where there would inevitably be a house or small farm. Buildable sites in this kind of topography had been found long ago and none were empty.

On the outskirts of Bardberg, he noticed a gas station coming up on the right and decided this would be as good a time as any for a fill-up. He could also ask about groceries. An attendant had just waved at a car that was leaving as Harp pulled up. The man looked at Harp and the dog and his face paled until the man looked again and then relaxed. Harp was wary as he opened the truck door.

"Good God, almighty, mister, I thought for minute there I

was seeing a ghost. You looked just like Lars there for a minute and you driving his truck and with his dog. Whew!" He made the wipe the brow gesture. Harp remembered that he was still wearing Lars' shirt.

Harp smiled and got out of the truck. He was pleased to see that Fart stood and watched.

"You must be that feller who got their farm. Word gets around a small place like this." He stuck out his hand and introduced himself. "My name is Pete Shultz. I been running this place for thirty-some years and I guess I've met everyone in the whole damned county, excuse my French." He was in his mid to late fifties, small-framed with drooping pants and blue work shirt. He had the lined and wrinkled face of a man who smoked and worked out in the weather. His hands were hard and calloused with permanent black arcs under his fingernails.

Harp was about to introduce himself but Shultz continued. "It's a damned shame, excuse my French, what happened to Lars and Pauline. They were a couple of the nicest people. We were all shocked when first one then the other bought the farm, so to speak. What was your name?"

"My name is Harp Harper. Pauline was my cousin." He shook hands with the gas station owner.

"When Lars got killed in that crazy accident, that was bad enough. We all hated for that to happen to Pauline. She was such a great person. She was a friend to all of us. Then when she goes off the road for no reason and gets drowned upside down, it's really a damned shame, excuse my French. Can't imagine anything worse." He shuddered dramatically. "You need some gas?" Harp let him do it because he didn't know where the filler door was.

He was glad that he didn't have to search for it while someone was watching.

"Yeah, go ahead and fill it." He watched as Shultz went to the driver's side of the Ford. Harp was relieved that he had pulled up with the correct side toward the pumps. Pure luck.

"She's got dual tanks. You want both filled?" Harp nodded. "Sorry about the price of gas these days. Nothing to do with me. Damn Aye-rabs, excuse my French. I gotta charge enough to keep the place open. Tell you one thing; I ain't making much anymore what with taxes and insurance. I got enough work for three people and can't afford to pay more than one other than me who ain't much 'cause I'm too damn old, excuse my French. Where you from?"

Harp told him Trenton, over in Jersey. Shultz was silent for a couple of minutes as he pumped gas. Fart came to the edge and watched Shultz.

"He your dog now?" Shultz asked. He apparently knew the dog because he was comfortable with his nearby presence. He reached up and rubbed the mutt's head. Fart seemed to enjoy it.

"Well, I guess so. He seems to like my company. Never had a dog before. I guess they make up their own minds about things."

"Lars got him as a puppy. Just a mongrel. They was close."

Pausing because he was getting more personal, he finally blurted out what was on his mind. "You done any farming?" Harp shook his head. Shultz was so harmlessly candid with his questions that Harp was not offended as he would have been with someone else.

"Didn't think so. Well, there are lots of folks around who can give you a hand. All the land that went into that damn fracking, excuse my French, put a lot of farm labor out of work. You don't want to let a nice piece of land like you got go bad, you know."

Harp had found that head nodding and shaking was all that was necessary. It was quite pleasant standing here in the shade of the gas island roof listening to a person who had no agenda and who posed no threat. Harp leaned with arms crossed on the tailgate and mostly listened. The dog would come over for a touch and then go back to watching Shultz.

"Still hard to find the ones who ain't lazy, though." Harp nodded in agreement.

"That will be $93.68 for the gas. Sorry. One tank was empty. One half empty." Harp paid with two fifties and got his change.

"I need to stock up on groceries, Mr. Shultz. Where's the best place?"

"Call me Pete. Everyone does. You probably need to stock up on basics so I would drive a little bit and go the Piggly Wiggly outside of Clarion. They got everything and then some." He turned to go back into his station, then stopped. "This mean you gonna stick around for a while?" He waited for Harp's answer with surprising intensity.

Harp shrugged. "Yeah, maybe for a little while." He didn't want to explain about staying just long enough to drink all the liquor. Shultz looked hard at Harp, then nodded.

Harp thanked Shultz and drove off. He decided that he would be damned if would ever get caught buying anything in a store called Piggly Wiggly. He drove instead into Bardberg and took his chances. The Bard Mart was easy to find with a tall sign announcing Blatz Beer for eight bucks a case and eggs, only ninety-nine cents a dozen. He soon found that one cart was not enough. He bought cases of real meat dog food in cans, cases of bottled water, toilet paper, and paper towels. He loaded up on pickled eggs, sausage, candied peanuts, and other such bar fare. He could live on kielbasa, potato chips, pickled pig's feet, and bourbon if he had to. He was enjoying this. He liked buying things by the case. Then he remembered he would need things like salt, pepper, coffee, ketchup, and bread; sandwich stuff. He bought extra amounts of everything. He was especially happy to see the shelf with Spam. God, he loved fried Spam. He bought ten cans and vowed that his next meal was going to be fried Spam sandwiches loaded with mustard and onions. He actually salivated a little just thinking about it. As he was paying up, he noticed a rack of no-contract cell phones with one hundred free minutes. He bought two, not knowing when he might need one.

Harp had loaded the contents of the first cart inside the truck while Fart watched with great curiosity. When he got to the grocery door with the second cart load, he saw through the glass three men standing next to his truck. One of them was making stabbing, poking motions into the back of the truck. The other two were laughing and drinking beer from cans. Harp moved his cart to the side and pushed through the doors. He calmly walked to a point behind the three to find that the biggest one was jabbing at Fart with a length of iron pipe. Harp quickly pushed the others aside and roughly muscled between the man with the pipe and the truck. He was tremendously relieved to see that Fart was alive and mobile. But he was overcome with a sense of fury when he saw that Fart's mouth was bloody where he had been biting at the pipe. When the dog saw Harp, his sense of relief was palpable. Just as Harp was about to turn and face the attackers, he felt a tremendous blow across his back. The pain was stunning and would have driven a lesser warrior to his knees. But Harp had been hit before. He had been shot before. He had been blown into the air and lacerated by shrapnel. He knew that when you are hit hard, the first thing you do is respond; only after that do you focus on recovery. He knew also that if he acknowledged the pain, he would give in to it.

Within a split second, Harp ducked and spun and had a pointed fist sunk many inches into the man's gut before the guy knew what was happening. His mouth dropped open, his eyes bulged, and he was frantically trying to catch his breath. It was easy to take the piece of pipe from his hand. Without pausing, Harp broke both of the man's forearms with hard fast swings deliberately aimed at the thinness of the arm just above the wrist. Then, wheeling to the left, he crushed the kneecap of one of the laughing pair. He wheeled toward the third man to find that he had taken off running. Harp threw the weapon into the truck and went back to get the rest of his groceries. People were lined up at the door and front windows. They regarded Harp with open-mouthed awe. Few had ever seen that kind of violence in person. The two injured men were on the pavement. The big one just kept looking at his arms saying, "Jesus Christ!" over and over. The one with the shattered knee was clutching it and screaming.

"Any of you know who those guys are?" he asked a small group watching from inside. Finally, an elderly woman said. "I think they must be with one of them traveling drilling crews hired over east of here. Don't know any names. They ain't like folks here." Harp thanked her for the information. Old enough to be free of inhibitions in her observations she added, "When I came in just now I saw what they was doing to your dog. You just don't treat animals thataway! I saw him smack you with that pipe and I'll tell the Sheriff if you want me to. I'm glad you kicked their butts."

Stepping over and ignoring the man still on the ground moaning and holding his knee, Harp loaded the remaining bags of groceries into the back seat of the Ford. He checked Fart again to be sure he was okay. On closer look, he saw where the skin had been slightly torn on one of the dog's cheeks and his right shoulder from being jabbed with the rough pipe edge. It appeared that there was nothing serious. Fart stood calmly while Harp looked him over. Harp couldn't help it. He grabbed the dog's head between his hands and gave him a gentle shake. Fart licked his face. No question they had bonded. For the first time in his life Harp said the words "good boy!" to an animal and his heart gave a strange lurch. He heard sirens coming and decided he would rather meet with the law on his own ground. He knew there were witnesses and his actions were obviously in self-defense. Harp quickly left town and drove back to the farm and began unpacking the provisions.

It didn't take long. As he was putting the first of the groceries away, he heard the sirens approaching. The beer and dog food were still in the truck. There were two cars and they blasted their sirens even in his driveway. Harp smiled at the show. Wincing at the pain in his back and the possible broken rib, Harp took his shirt off and went out to the front porch and stood waiting. He didn't know what his back looked like, but the pain indicated that he had some serious bruising. Fart came around the house and came to stand beside Harp.

In one car was the Sheriff and in the other two deputies. They all piled from their cars with guns drawn. "Get those hands up, now!" the Sheriff shouted. Harp tried to comply but the pain made it difficult. "I said, get them up!" Harp finally managed. "Now turn around and put your hands against the wall!" When Harp turned, they gasped. He slowly placed his hands against the wall of his porch. Fart growled at the posse. Harp told him to sit, and was surprised when he did it.

One of the deputies spoke in shock, "Holy shit, boss, they said they didn't touch him."

"Shut up, Manley." The Sheriff walked closer. "Keep him covered."

"Turn around, Harper." Harp found it curious that the Sheriff knew his name.

The Sheriff stood at the bottom of the steps studying Harp. "I know what you are going to claim. I know you are going to claim self-defense. I also know, looking at your back, you would probably get away with it."

He started up the steps. "Put your hands down, Harper. Sit down in that chair and keep your hands in your lap." After regarding Harp for a long moment, he turned to the deputies, "You boys go on back to town." They holstered their Glocks and reluctantly got back in their cruiser and left. They had to be satisfied with baleful glares at Harp when they were hoping instead for the opportunity to manhandle a reluctant prisoner. One had still never used his Taser, and he put it away with disappointment.

The Sheriff took the other rocker, crossed his legs, and put his hat on his knee. Harp sat and watched. "I have been out here and sat on this porch many times just for friendly visits. Lars and Pauline were good people. We all hated to see them pass. They got a great place here. They bought it when the prices were reasonable.

So did I. I have my own land a few miles south of here. My name is William Senter. Until I ran for office, I raised corn and hogs and everybody called me Billy. Now it's just Sheriff Senter."

After a long pause, he spoke almost reflectively, looking out at the view. "You went up against three young guys. You broke both arms of a big healthy boy. You trashed the knee of another one and made the last one turn total pussy and run off. And, by all accounts, the whole thing took about five seconds; one-twelfth of a minute. Can't imagine how you could do that. There's nobody else around here could do that or I would know about it. I've had a lot of training and I couldn't do that." He looked down at his boots. "Heard they hit you with a piece of pipe. That right?" Harp nodded. He was studying Senter. Senter was a big fit-looking man with curly blond hair and perfect white teeth. He had a tan line over his eyebrows and probably weighed over two hundred pounds. Senter calmly returned the regard, looking with no embarrassment at all he could see of Harp's body, as if noting for the record all identifying marks.

"Probably they left fingerprints all over it." He looked at Harp with raised eyebrows. Harp nodded. He sat, hands in lap, curious to know where Senter was going with this soliloquy. He was not afraid of Senter, but was very curious.

"Can't help but notice the other scars. You military?" Harp nodded. "Iraq? Afghanistan?"

Harp nodded. "Both, plus some others. Little things."

Senter raised his eyebrows at this. He rocked some more. "Would I know about those others?"

"Nope."

"Could I ask about those others?"

"Nope."

The Sheriff nodded and rocked some more. He seemed relaxed. He laughed, "What I am about to say reminded me of some of those old westerns. The tired gunslinger would come to town saying he just wanted to see his wife, or his momma, or son, one last time. Some fool kid would challenge him and of course the gunslinger would kill the dumb kid. Not even his fault that the gunfight happened. Self-defense all the way. But the sheriff would always say something like, 'We got a peaceful little town here and we don't want your kind coming around starting trouble. I reckon you best be gone by sunup,' they always said."

"Is that what you are telling me, Sheriff?" Harp didn't see how anyone could tell him to leave his "home" and get out of the territory. "You want me out of here by sunup?"

Senter smiled. "Nah. Even I can't do that. What I am telling you is that we have seen huge changes in this little part of the state and finally reached a balance in my jurisdiction. Everything is going smoothly. We have what is basically a whole new economy. Everybody is getting rich off natural gas. We got all these gas field workers taking up every room and trailer in the county. Pretty much everybody has agreed that we are going to accept this use of our land. Crime is down. Nobody needs to steal anything because the ones who didn't have any money have been displaced. They give me credit for all this peace and crime-free living and I am happy to take it. I like my job. I can get re-elected for as long as I want. I'm looking at another twenty years at least." Harp waited. He rolled his shoulders to loosen muscles tightened up against the pain.

"Now you come along and pose a threat to this balance. You

come out of nowhere with no connections to this place at all and you move in on the land that belonged to a well-known and liked couple. You all of a sudden own a piece of land that has some importance to the overall picture. Now, certain people are worried. What it all boils down to, Mr. Harper, just between you and me, is that you have the potential to pee on my flowers." Senter stood up and leaned against the post at the top of the stairs. "You are wondering how that is. Let me tell you. You come to my town, my county, you seriously hurt two citizens, and there is a whole gaggle of my constituents who watched you do it. Now they're wondering what I am going to do about it."

The Sheriff descended the stairs. He stopped and looked back at Harp, who was still sitting in the rocker. He understood that Harp was not meekly following his order to sit. He was more like an animal quietly watching for the moment to attack. "And I am not going to do anything about it because, as an officer of the law, I recognize that it would be a waste of time to try to prosecute you. A lot of people saw those boys hit you. However, my voters are going to wonder how somebody could do all that damage and me not do anything. There are other people and institutions vital to this area that are also going to wonder about it. This will be the first time I've had to explain my actions. The first time in twelve years. In another words, you might have cost me some votes and some campaign money." The Sheriff turned and looked down the driveway. He scratched the back of his neck. Harp was thinking, so what?

"You know and I know that you don't belong here. You are a soldier and city boy, through and through. But, I admire you. I want you to have some time sitting on this porch and looking out at my world. Then I would like for you to sell this land and get the hell out of here. Go back to Trenton." The Sheriff was still turned away as he talked.

This was getting serious, Harp thought. "Why?" he asked.

Now he turned to face Harp. "I don't know if you understand county politics, Harper, but the Sheriff is all powerful and can do certain things, completely within the law, to make anybody's life miserable. I have to think of what's best for *all* my voters. Even the ones who might be a little corporate. Think about it."

"What is the overall picture?" Harp asked.

Senter just raised his eyebrows.

"You said this land has some importance to the overall picture."

Sheriff Senter didn't answer or give any indication he had heard the question but Harp knew he had.

He walked to his car and stopped next to his car door. He paused as if he were going to answer but instead opened the door and tossed his hat into the rider's seat. "Enjoyed our visit, Mr. Harper." He drove off. Near the end of the driveway, he whooped his siren a couple of times as if to punctuate his warning.

Harp sat for a long time calculating his next move. He agreed with Senter that he didn't belong here. But that didn't mean he was packing up anytime soon. He would just have to be careful not to attract the attention again of the Sheriff and his deputies, at least for a while. As if to punctuate that thought, one of the county cars slowly drove by on the road below. A uniformed arm waved lazily out the window. It had been only twenty minutes since the Sheriff left. Fast work, Harp thought. He wanted to get up and get inside where he could stretch out and rest, but his back hurt so bad he could hardly move from the rocker. Fart sat and watched his every move. Finally, Harp got to his feet and shuffled toward the basement. He needed some medicine. Maybe ten-year old sour mash will do it. But this time he did something totally out of character as he headed for a highly anticipated meeting with a bottle; he stopped and reconsidered. It was still early, he thought, he should get out and do something physical instead. If he lay down now, no telling when he could get up.

Reminding himself that he needed to get new jars of the bad water and put them in a safe place and he needed to see where those coordinates would take him, he got busy. Maybe some vigorous hiking would loosen up his aching back. He knew where two of the bad springs were and the third should be easy to find with the map. He found three empty canning jars in the kitchen pantry. He wrapped them in towels and put them in a rucksack. He couldn't stand a backpack over his back yet. He found to his disgust the GPS unit needed charging so he wouldn't be able to find that spot just yet. His small digital camera was ready to go, however, so it went into the pack. Two bottles of water, one for him and one for Fart, completed the preparation. He was navigating by a small hand-drawn map that merely replicated the X's on the larger map but just in general relation to the lay of the land on the farm. The place was not so big that any spot could not be found, he thought.

Vigorously swinging his arms as he walked, he decided that it might be a good day after all. There was a slight breeze, bluebird skies overhead, and temperature in the low seventies. He even noticed a pleasant smell in the air, though he could not identify it. One thing he knew: that smell was a long way from the smell of death and poor waste management with which he was so familiar.

Dressed in desert sand pants and khaki tee, with feet in tan combat boots, baseball cap on his head, he felt more alive than he had in months. He considered carrying the beautiful little nine-millimeter from the locker but was not sure about PA laws on carrying. That was another thing on his growing list. He really didn't know if he was allowed to even *own* a handgun, much less carry one. He did carry a favorite knife, however, and welcomed it as an old friend when it was strapped to his belt. It felt good to be moving, even if his back was still very painful. Rolling his shoulders and moving his arms felt good and he knew this would help loosen the bruised and stiff muscles across his back. He already dreaded getting up in the morning because he knew from experience that this was when the worst of the stiffness would hit.

With no knowledge of paths and trails, he took off on a direct heading. There were no farm roads or paths where he was walking. This was probably more difficult but it made it more natural to study the landscape around him. He noted fence lines and different kinds of grasses. He supposed some of the stuff was planted and some was natural but had no idea which was which. The cropland part was easy because of furrows that were still very evident. The fencing looked good and the gates opened and closed easily. Harp identified pasture because of the old cattle droppings he saw everywhere. Even Harp knew what cowshit was. And he had worked under enough asshole superior officers to know what bullshit was.

***

He had decided to go to the spring furthest to the north first.

He calculated that his land was roughly one mile deep and three-quarters of a mile wide, with the house and outbuildings sitting in the front middle. So where he was going was on a diagonal about one-half mile away from the house. He would go to the north spring, back across to the middle spring, and then try to find the third one at the southern edge of the property, or at least where it was indicated with another X on the map, then back home. He believed it should not take more than a couple of hours.

As far as the dog was concerned, it could take all day. He had run these fields many times, so this was a joyful reunion with nature for him. He would gallop off in the distance to track and sniff, stop and stare, pee, then run back to Harp with tongue flopping and saliva dripping just to bump Harp's legs then take off again. He acted like an animal that had been turned loose after a long time in a cage. He could have done this anytime he wanted, Harp thought, but he could not leave Pauline and Lars until someone said it was okay. Dogs lived in a strange world, Harp concluded, where everything they did was based on what they thought another creature wanted. That seemed to a very independent man to be pretty damned pitiful.

With minimal meandering, Harp found the first spring. This one was not in an open area but was inside a rock outcrop on the edge of the woods. Here the water flowed more freely and generated enough flow to make a pleasant sound. Before he took up a sample, Harp scouted the area within forty or fifty meters around the spring. He found an old fence line north of the spring, which he calculated would be the edge of his property. He was surprised to see signs of fairly regular narrow wheelbase, probably

ATV, traffic along the other side of the line. It was easy to see a
footpath where someone had crossed the fence and had often
come to Harp's spring. Harp thought about it and concluded that
this spring had been here for eons and had probably been a common source of water for man and animals over the years. But, the
map showed a mark indicating that this was bad water. He hoped
it hadn't poisoned anyone. Harp filled one of the jars, carefully
wrapped it, and put it back in the rucksack. He thought it would
probably be safe enough to taste it and spit it right back out if it
was bad. And, he had the bottle of water he could use to rinse his
mouth. He sipped cautiously but the water wasn't bad. In fact, it
was cold and, he thought, excellent water. It would go beautifully
with bourbon, which he believed was the highest and best use
of this liquid. He still spit it out without swallowing just in case.

"No, no, no, Fart!" He had forgotten about the dog and turned
to find him noisily lapping up the water behind Harp. He
rushed over and grabbed Fart by the ruff and pulled him away
from the little stream. Fart yipped in surprise and jumped away
from Harp to stand a few feet off, looking very confused. He
obeyed, however, when Harp sat down on a rock and called him
over. Harp told him to sit and held the dog's head and watched
his eyes and listened to his breathing. Fart returned the gaze
and waited to see what was going on. They sat like this for five
minutes. Finally, Harp decided that, if the dog was poisoned, it
wasn't going to show right away and, even better, he wasn't going to have to carry the poisoned hundred twenty-pound animal
back to the house. Also, if the water had tasted as bad as that in
the middle spring, he didn't think that even a dog could drink it.
He let the dog go to resume his loping survey of the area. Harp

remained by the spring and watched for any sign of distress as the animal cruised the edge of the woods. There was none. So he began walking due south toward the middle spring, which he *knew* was bad.

It took only twenty or so minutes to get there. Oddly, there was no smell this time. The area around the spring still looked bad, with yellowed grass and slime around the edges of the small pool. The water looked fine, but he knew it was seriously polluted. After getting the sample, they walked toward the southernmost spring. They found themselves on a long uphill grade which led Harp to check his small hand-drawn map again. He had somehow not noticed that this spring was at a higher elevation. He found it at the head of a small ravine. Again, he surveyed the area before taking the sample. Again, the water seemed fine. Now he was really puzzled about the notation on the map. As he was standing, rucksack in hand, sample secured, he heard Fart give a brief woof. He looked around but couldn't see him. The dog woofed again and this time he looked up and found the dog looking down at him from the point atop one side of the ravine. Retracing his path back to the entrance and looking to the right, he found a vague but easily traversed trail that climbed up to a spot about twenty feet above the base of the ravine and several meters behind it. He found Fart waiting at the top of the trail. The dog woofed and walked a few paces then stopped. He would look back and trot a few more paces. Harp finally got the idea that he was supposed to follow the mutt. Fart led him to a small area a couple of meters wide where the trees opened up and revealed a beautiful view of his property. Harp was at first taken at the beauty of the vista and the fact that his house, barn, outbuildings, farm roads, *everything*, was visible from this vantage point.

He was then appalled to find that it had been used quite recently. There were well-worn vehicle tracks leading up to the area with signs of use over a long period. Cigarette butts, wrappers, and cans were scattered around. Harp saw that the detritus had never been rained upon, which meant they had only been there for a matter of days. It was apparent that someone had been coming here regularly to view or keep watch over his property. They could have been up here watching *him*. This made Harp nervous and when Harp got nervous, he became resentful of the person or thing that made him nervous. He followed the track leading to this spot and saw that it would be a long hike through the forest. He was not prepared to take that hike now. He did not know how far it would take him and he did not want the dog along. Fart would be too unreliable in a strange and perhaps demanding situation.

But, it was a hike that Harp was soon going to make. He wanted to find out where these people were coming from and why they had been spying on his property. There was not a doubt in his mind that the person or persons using this spot were watching his farmstead. He wanted to know who and why. Harp and Fart began the pleasant hike back to the house, now with a lot more to consider. Harp was still warily watching Fart for any effects of drinking that supposedly bad water but could detect no change so far. He would have to figure out how a person got water tested. He supposed he would have to carry it somewhere.

As they walked toward the house, Harp saw a car pull off the road and enter his driveway. He hurried to the back of the house and entered through the kitchen. From the front room, he watched as a woman, about fifty, went to a rear door of her car. She pulled a briefcase and another folder from the back seat and walked toward the porch. Harp stepped through the front door and waited. She was startled when she looked up and saw him standing there. "Well, hello!" she blurted. Harp just smiled.

"My name is Edie Martin. I'm a Realtor with PennDepp Realty. Mind if I come up and talk to you?" She placed the folder on the step and drew a card from her jacket pocket. She was a full-figured woman who wore her clothes very well. She had rimless glasses and her graying hair was nicely shaped on the sides and drawn into a loose bun in the back. With her warm smile and pale blue eyes, she looked more like your third-grade teacher than a real estate salesperson. Harp took the card and motioned toward one of the rockers. He sat in the other. Fart flopped next to his chair and promptly went to sleep. He had had a great day. Harp hoped the dog could contain himself.

She sat down and fanned her face with her hand. "Whew! It's been a long day. Sorry to drop in like this, but I've left several messages trying to set up a meeting and didn't even know if anyone was here." She gave him a warm smile of apology. "So I thought I would drive out and see for myself." She opened her arms and smiled. "And here I am and here you are!" Harp was wondering where the answering machine was. He smiled. Of course, they would have a phone, he thought. He was surprised that he had not seen it.

"According to the papers filed with the county, you are Horace B. Harper and you are the heir to the property formerly owned by my dear friends Lars and Pauline Kuykendahl." She held her hand over her heart as she said the last. "I am so sorry for your loss."

"I didn't even know them," Harp said with a certain satisfaction just to see her reaction.

"Well, I am sorry you never got to know them. They were wonderful people." She gave the gentle smile again and withdrew a packet of materials from her briefcase. "I understand that you do not have a farming background and have indicated an intent to sell the property."

"Where did you hear that?" Harp asked. He thought he knew the answer.

Her smile faded slightly. "My good friend Andy Parsnip. I've known him since he was a boy. I assure you that he would not reveal anything confidential." She raised a hand as if taking an oath. Harp thought that good friend Andy had already revealed too much.

"In any case, you are now the owner of this property and, as such, are in a position to sell it. To be perfectly frank with you, because you also inherited the mineral rights, this is an extremely valuable piece of land. I have been authorized to make a very generous offer." She removed a piece of paper from the folder. "You have 487 acres on this property. I represent a buyer who will pay you $5,000 per acre for a total of $2.435 million." She grinned widely in triumph. "That's a lump sum cash, by the way."

Harp was stunned. My God, he was thinking, with the other money, he could walk away from this deal with close to three million dollars. He was careful to let his face show nothing, however, and her disappointment at his lack of reaction was obvious.

"That is a whole lot of money," Harp said. "And I am definitely going to sell the place." She smiled in triumph, already counting her seven percent commission. "But I don't see the hurry. I am kind of enjoying the fresh air and countryside. I think I'll just stay a while before I decide what to do." The change in her face was remarkable. Even though she caught herself quickly, Harp saw the kindly visage grow cold and hard for a split second then quickly revert to the kindly teacher. "Well that is certainly within your rights, Mr. Harper, but sometimes when we put off major decisions like this, especially in this economy, it can be a costly mistake. I cannot promise that this offer will be on the table for very long." Harp just smiled at the implied threat. She did not smile back.

"This is all about the gas thing, right?" Harp asked.

"Of course it is. That's what's been driving all of us to distraction in recent years." She paused as if thinking about what to say. "The industry and all its components are very complex. I'm not sure anyone understands all of it. I would advise you not to bother yourself with the politics of it. When everybody is making lots of money, it changes just about every equation. You won't be here long enough to get into the details."

She silently began putting her materials back into folders as Harp watched. With everything assembled, she stood and spoke with a much cooler voice. "I hope, Mr. Harper, that when you do decide to move the property, you will let me know. I promise that I can get you the best deal around." She held out her hand for a handshake. While still holding his hand, her gaze was direct and cool. "Another thing; be advised that there aren't many buyers who can afford a piece of land like this. I may be your best chance to move it."

By the time she left, it was getting dark. Harp and Fart were hungry so Harp fried another meal for both. Now that he had some different food, he fixed some vegetables to go along with the meat. He found that the dog liked steak cooked just as much as raw. Good dog. He had to admit, this inheritance was getting very interesting. It might be kind of fun just to hang around for a while and see what happens. The phone ringing reminded him that he was going to look for it. He walked around the kitchen trying to zero in on the sound. It was coming from a small cabinet by the hall door. He opened the cabinet to find a modern telephone answering machine with a cordless handset resting in the charger base. After some thought, he decided to answer but he was too late so the call had gone to the message machine. Harp listened to the most recent messages to see what Martin had said.

It's Edie Martin again. I guess I'll drive out there on the chance I might find you in. Thanks.

Mr. Harper, this is Edie Martin again and I don't want to be a pest. I'm just not sure you are getting my message. Hope you're having a good day.

"Mr. Harper, my name is Edie Martin. I am a Realtor with the PennDepp Real Estate Company. I represent a client who is quite interested in buying the property you recently inherited from Pauline Kuykendahl, bless her heart. I was hoping that we could set up a time when we might get together and discuss an offer. Thanks, and have a good day."

Harp decided to listen to all the messages while he was at it. He went all the way back to the beginning.

"Hey Pauly, this is Margy. Us girls are getting together for a canasta night at my place tomorrow night. Come on over. You need to get out girl! Call me.

"Pauline, this is Harry Johnson. Just wanted you to know that we have some one percent CD's you might be interested in. That's not much but they are safer than the money market right now. Let me know if there is anything I can do. You know I am always there for you.

Pauline, this is Andy. This is a follow-up to our talk the other day. I know you are reluctant to discuss future plans right now but we both know it makes sense to sell. Why not take the best deal? I'll be in my office every day. You can call any time.

"Good morning, Pauline. This is Reverend Thomas. Just wanted to remind you that I am here if you need me. Come see me and let's talk about God's plan. Bless you."

Congratulations! You have been selected to receive a free home security system! Just respond within twenty-four hours and a representative will be at your door with a totally free system!

He felt like he was eavesdropping. None of this was his business. He also felt like an impostor who had no right to be listening to these words. It was interesting to note, however, that Parsnip had been pressuring Pauline to sell. This only confirmed Harp's dislike and suspicion of the lawyer.

It was getting late and Harp considered hitting the sack. He did not feel like turning in and his mind kept going back to that spot where someone sat watching his house. To a private person like Harp, the thought of someone watching him was very irritating. Along with this memory came the idea that he had not been on a night mission in years. Suddenly the idea of getting out there in the dark seemed very enticing. The plan was to sleep for a few hours and head out at about 3 a.m. He had all the necessary equipment and was confident that he could follow those ATV tracks in the dark with the now charged night vision goggles.

He left at 2:45 a.m. This was just about the darkest hour with only a half moon. Fart was safely locked in the mud room. With the goggles on, it was almost like walking in daylight. He was dressed in black jeans and shirt with black stocking cap to pull down over his face. He carried only a knife as a weapon but on his belt was a can of disabling spray, camera, and infrared detector. He stuck a small bottle of water in his pocket just in case. It took only twenty minutes to traverse the half mile to the small ravine where the spring was located. Beginning at the watcher's location, Harp followed the track through the forest. It took only another few minutes and he came to a fence line which he assumed was the edge of his property. It had a wire loop gate which was used by the intruder. He carefully crossed the barbed wire fence and stayed on the trail. It wound its way along easily walked paths that were open enough to allow wheeled vehicle access. Harp didn't know whose property he was crossing but assumed he could find out later. What he did know was that he was being watched from this property, which meant that the owner was to some degree responsible.

After about twenty minutes at a good pace, Harp soon came

to a small dwelling in a clearing that he could immediately see had been used for human habitation for a long time. Though he was unfamiliar with the tradition, he was looking at a typical hunting camp built around a small prefab cabin. It was well-built with a steel roof, windows on the sides, and a small window next to the front door. A short galvanized chimney pipe indicated the presence of heat. The presence of electric lights hung on tree limbs indicated there was a generator somewhere. A camouflaged patterned ATV with a large game basket on the rear was parked near the front door. Lines hung with clothes ran from tree to tree. A crude wooden table with benches and two folding chairs provided outdoor seating and dining space. Atop the table was a propane stove and a box of pots and pans. It looked as if someone lived here.

On the opposite side of the clearing, the track continued. Harp watched and listened carefully for many minutes to get a sense of life in this camp. There were no signs of dogs present, and his infrared detector spotted no cameras. He concluded he could enter the camp. Carefully avoiding stepping on or kicking trash scattered around the camp, Harp drifted silently to the wall of the cabin. As he approached, he passed a mass which, when the cover was removed, revealed a fifty-gallon drum set on a rough cradle. There were no markings on the container but, when he sniffed the tap, it smelled very familiar. He would take a sample when he left. Continuing to the cabin, he put an ear to the wall and heard snoring. Slowly rising to the level of the window, Harp studied the interior. There were two bunks but only one was occupied and that was the source of the snoring. The other bunk was heaped with clothing. Harp very quietly tried the door and found, as he expected, that it was unlocked. The occupant apparently felt there was little to fear in this isolated place.

Now that he had succeeded in finding this place and the person who had been spying on him—he thought of it that way now—Harp realized he hadn't planned the next step. He did not have enough reason to take extreme measures with this person. After some thought, he developed a plan, such as it was. Because it was a modern well-made little building, Harp could silently enter the cabin with no creaks or squeaks giving him away. Approaching the sleeping man, Harp waited for the inhale and sprayed the open mouth with the disabling spray. It was a special DOD concoction that combined Rohypnol with a concentrated nitrous oxide. It was packaged in a can that looked like a common medicinal spray for athlete's foot. One short sniff rendered a person, or animal, unconscious and unhurt but with absolutely no memory of what occurred during the hours they were out. The spray was highly illegal outside the military or certain government agencies.

It worked as promised. Harp gently slapped the man's face, then slapped harder and watched the man's eyes. There was no reaction at all. Nobody is cool enough to hide a reaction to having your face slapped while sleeping in the middle of the night. It was safe now to do a search of the premises. He removed the goggles for a minute and rubbed his eyes. Extended wear of these things did cause a kind of eye strain. While they were off, he saw that he was standing in pitch darkness, which was good. Again wearing the goggles, he searched the room carefully. He first looked for the guns and found them in the corner to the left of the door. Hanging on a peg was a .357 Magnum in its holster with a belt full of cartridges. That's interesting, Harp thought. Does it mean that this guy is a licensed carrier? The only other thing of importance was a laptop computer. He considered taking it but, at least for now, thought it would be best if there was no sign of his visit. Thinking that it would have been so easy to bring one along, he looked for a jump drive. He knew there would likely be one somewhere in the room, and if it turned up missing from rough quarters like this, the owner would assume he lost it.

He found two. One was on a shelf with shaving gear and one was mixed in with odds and ends scattered on a small table. He took the one on the table. Harp knew that he must slowly adapt to the light from the computer screen, so he removed the goggles again, draped a towel over the screen and turned it on. By looking through slitted eyes with short glances, it still took a long two minutes before he could look at the screen. He was finally able to see well enough to insert the drive and copy the documents and picture files. It appeared to be mostly a dated list of simple activities. It was just the numbers one, two, and three with dates going back over the past several weeks. He would look at everything in detail later. He closed the files and turned the computer off. He put it back exactly where he had found it. Looking around, he made sure that he had left no sign of his visit.

As for the sleeping interloper, that was another matter. In a sort of revenge for his spying, Harp thought he would mess with this guy's mind. He pulled the man from the bunk and carried him, wearing only boxer shorts, to the large game carrier on the back of the ATV. Fortunately, the guy was a smallish slender man. Harp carefully curled him into position and secured his body with the stretch cords that were already there. In some pain from his injured back, he went back into the cabin for a final recon. There was a new bottle of vodka on a shelf. Harp cracked the seal and dumped all but an inch in the bottom on the ground away from the camp, poured a little in a glass, then put the bottle and glass on the table near the bunk, spilling just a little on the table.

With no idea where he was going, Harp drove the vehicle away from his property along an obvious track, with no lights. He drove slowly and as quietly as possible for another quarter mile. He stopped when he saw lights moving along a road still some distance away. It appeared that the trail he was on went to that road. Driving as close as he dared, Harp stopped and rearranged the man's inert body. He placed him on the seat slumped forward with his head resting on the steering wheel. Just for the hell of it, he removed the man's shorts. He would wake up probably at early daylight next to the road, sitting naked on the ATV with absolutely no memory of how he had gotten there. If nothing else, it might cause him to re-examine his current occupation. Now hurrying, Harp wanted to get back to his house and get some sleep. On the way, almost as an afterthought, he emptied his water bottle and stopped at the cabin to gather a sample of whatever was in the drum. He was again struck by the familiar odor.

Harp's leg was aggravated by the time he returned to the house. It had been a long hike in the dark. He apologized to a frantic Fart, then let him out for the night to run and whatever. Dawn was just breaking in the east when he went to bed at 5 a.m. He fell asleep with a greater sense of satisfaction than he had felt in a long time. There was nothing like a night mission to get the old adrenaline up, he thought, before falling into a deep sleep. He dreamed of running across a hayfield as a boy. He had run across factory ruins, city streets, and building roofs. He had run across desert sand and down bullet riddled streets. But, he had never run across a field of grass. He felt a different kind of freedom. Then, his running was interrupted by the raucous sound of bells at PS 231 where he had attended school. He was unsuccessful at that school. He left with no diploma and no one behind who remembered him.

The ringing finally evolved from the school into the sound of a telephone. It was just 7:30 a.m. so he had gotten only a couple hours of sleep. He waited for the ringing to end, but he had somehow managed to turn off the answering machine. The ringing continued. He arose with great pain, cursing at the feel of it, then went downstairs and answered with a mumbled hello.

"Mr. Harper!" There was an urgency in the voice which caught his attention immediately. He was accustomed to being awakened and called to action within minutes. Tired as he was, he was suddenly very attentive.

"Yeah, who's this?" The voice was familiar.

"Mr. Harper, this is Harry Johnson at the bank!" Harp remembered the man as being very calm and self-contained. This was a surprise.

"Sure, Mr. Johnson. What's going on?"

"I'm really not too sure of that any more. But I called to tell you that someone has talked those guys you hurt into pressing charges against you. We all know what the real facts are so we don't know why they would be doing this. Anyway, my nephew is a deputy sheriff trainee. He often comes by the house to drop stuff off from his mother on the way to work. This morning he was excited about the big arrest they have planned out on the

Kuykendahl place. He said they were going to take a whole crew out there to bring in a real bad ass."

"And I am the bad ass?" Harp was thinking fast.

"It looks like it. Apparently, they want to either get on the place to do something or get you off the place to do something to you. I don't know which. I just wanted to alert you that something is about to happen. I really don't know what's going on around here, but I know I don't like it."

Harp was thinking of what might occur. He suspected the idea was to get him off the property for some reason. Why else would they come with a warrant for his arrest? He didn't know if the root cellar could withstand a determined search but doubted it. The average burglar would never find it but a group of experienced lawmen would. This meant he had to move all his gear and move it fast.

"Tommy, my nephew, said they are getting the warrant from Judge Lawson and I know he will not do one damned thing before 9 a.m. You've got a couple hours to do whatever you can."

"Mr. Johnson, I have a couple of things I have to do really fast." He dug Kowalski's card out of his wallet and gave Johnson the information. "I would really appreciate it if you would call this person and tell her what's happening here. Ask her if she would hire a good lawyer over in this part of the state to come and represent me. I am going to let them put me in jail but I want to do it on my schedule."

"Consider it done, Mr. Harper. I know some lawyers but none like what you need. I assume money is not an issue."

"Yeah, right now, that's the least of my worries. If this lawyer starts talking money, you have my permission to advise him or her of my recent assets."

"Will do. Good luck." Johnson hung up.

Harp swung into action. The top priority was getting all his gear out of the root cellar and into a safe place. He was probably crazy for holding on to this stuff anyway. A small rented storage unit would do just fine. Quickly repacking the gear, he loaded the tan trunk on the back of the ATV. He drove it to the barn and transferred everything back into the Dodge which had been sitting there since the first night. As an afterthought, Harp carefully packed the water samples along with the one from that cabin in the woods. He also threw the pipe that had bruised his back on top of the pile.

By 8 a.m. he was ready to roll. Fart was standing by the tailgate. Harp felt it necessary to explain to Fart that he might be gone for a while. "Listen Pal, you can stay in the mud room or wherever. I dumped out a bunch of food so you will be okay for a while. I would advise you to get lost when these people get here. Sorry." What the hell, he thought; he was apologizing to a damned dog. Fart stayed by the barn and watched him drive out of sight. He could not believe a damned dog was making him feel guilty.

He drove back out the same way he came in that first night. Probably the area close to the interstate would be most likely to have what he needed so he aimed the Dodge Ram truck south. What he found was a rental storage site of massive proportions. It covered many acres with row upon row of yellow cinder block buildings with retracting red doors. He rented a five by ten for six months prepaid, bought a ridiculously protective combination lock, and drove to the unit. After assuring that there were no observers, he pulled as close as possible and removed the container from the passenger side of the truck. He doubted anyone could see what he was moving, even if they were watching. They had given him a card with the unit number which was part of the code needed to get through the gate. To a mind often required to memorize lists of coordinates, this was too easy. He tore the card in tiny pieces and dropped them into a storm water grate. Thinking of this reminded him of the coordinates that Pauline had asked him to remember. He remembered the GPS unit and left it with the other stuff. He now had no weapon other than a small pocket knife.

He knew the truck was going to be searched because of his next step. It was 9 a.m. and he was about an hour from the jail at Bardberg. Harp guessed that he could be at the jail before the "posse" was done driving out to the farm, searching, then driving back. He hoped to be in a jail cell when they got back. He surely did not want to be alone on his farm or in the back of a police car. Too many things could happen where there were no witnesses. Planning as he drove, he found the Sheriff's office and jail with little trouble. It was behind the courthouse. He picked a good spot for the truck where it would be out of the way for a while. Harp walked in with a great show of confidence and approached the front desk. An elderly black deputy was manning the desk and laboriously filling out some kind of form. He was probably too old to be going out on raids and was working the office until retirement. Harp stopped in front of his desk and asked, "Is this where you get a Pennsylvania hunting license?" The deputy looked up with great annoyance. He had answered this question a hundred times. "No sir, they do that at the courthouse right out in front of this building." He went back to his forms.

Harp continued. "I recently moved onto the Kuykendahl farm and figured I'd better get a PA hunting license. I might need to shoot some deer or coyotes or something."

For a moment, the old deputy ignored Harp, but then, as Harp watched, the realization came to the old man. It started at the fingers that dropped the pen, progressed to the arms, and finally got into a brain dulled by the sameness of his work. "You're that fella they went out there to get!" he squeaked. He slowly rose from a creaking chair and straightened his back and pulled up his sagging pants. He was not armed. His sidearm was nowhere in sight. He was pointing a finger while trying to figure out what to say.

"What, you mean they were going to get me?" Harp spoke with wide-eyed amazement. "I know there must be some mistake. Can I just wait here until the Sheriff gets back? We will get it all straightened out."

The deputy was now running on most cylinders. Looking almost comically crafty, he motioned for Harp to follow him. "Sure you can. You can wait right here with me." Then came the next level of craftiness. "You can wait right back here." Harp followed, trying to look innocently interested. "If you will just take a seat in there, we can wait for Sheriff Senter to get back," he intoned in a most ingratiating way. He motioned toward an open cell. Harp casually strode in to the cell and sat on the bunk. "Okay, I'll wait right here, deputy."

The old man slammed the door and yelled, "I gotcha!" He stomped out of the room, practically rubbing his hands with pride at his cleverness.

Harp knew the whole series was on camera. He played his role a little further. "Wait, there must be some mistake. I just came in for a hunting license. Why are you doing this?" But the deputy was gone. Harp smiled to himself and made himself comfortable. It really was a fairly nice bunk. Apparently they did not get many smelly prisoners. As a matter of fact, he was the only prisoner. After last night and the activity of the day, he was very tired. His back still hurt. He was soon asleep and it was just after 10 a.m.

Harp heard the clatter of the returning group of deputies, dropping equipment, falling into chairs, chattering about the morning's activities. Then there was silence. They now knew he was here. Harp listened and smiled and remained on his side facing away from the door, as if still asleep. He heard footsteps approaching and stopping right outside his cell. He was certain it was the Sheriff. Harp even snored a bit. He knew he was safe as long as that door remained closed.

Senter knew. "You know, Harper, you are just too much a smart ass. I kind of admire that but as I told you before, I just can't abide a smart ass like you in my house."

Harp rolled over on his back, put his hands behind his head, and coolly regarded the Sheriff. "All I know is that I got out early this morning to drive around getting to know the territory when it came to me that I might need a hunting license. I came in to your office to ask about it. Next thing I know, your ace deputy tricked me. He led me to this cell and locked me in. I knew that you would get it all straightened out when you got here." Senter just stood, leaning on the cell bars looking at the floor.

Harp continued, "So now that you're here I can go home. Right? I haven't broken any laws that I know of."

"Where do you do all this driving around? I'm just curious to know." Senter was watching Harp now. His gaze was steady but very serious.

"Heck, I don't know these roads yet, Sheriff. I just drove all over the place. Can't remember any road names." Harp shrugged. "Can I go home now?"

Senter shook his head. "Well, you see, Mr. Harper, you have been accused of breaking the law and we cannot let you go. You are facing some serious charges.

"That's bullshit, what are these charges?" Harp acted indignant because he felt indignant, even though he knew what was going on.

Senter smiled. "Those boys you cruelly assaulted have decided to press charges. We have a long list of reasons to keep you in jail."

"Sheriff, that is pure stupidity. You know what happened and you know there were witnesses to the fact that they attacked me first. You even know that it was a piece of pipe that they hit me with. Hell, just having their prints on that pipe makes them guilty of lying. You know those prints weren't put on there *after* I got through with them. Those prints mean I was telling the truth."

"Which brings up an interesting question, Mr. Harper. Just where is that piece of pipe? Of course, you didn't know we went to your house to arrest you this morning. You just happened to be gone." The sheriff pulled up a folding chair, sat and crossed his legs. A deputy stepped into the room but the Sheriff waved him away before he'd taken three steps. Senter continued. "Because we were there to arrest an accused felon, we felt it our duty to search the premises for the weapon in question and any other weapons said accused felon might be hiding. In the process, I am afraid that we might have caused some justifiable damage.

Things can be hidden under floorboards, behind sheetrock, and who knows where. It was our duty to investigate all potential hiding places."

Senter took out a pocket knife and began cleaning his nails. "It was just a shame that we had to look inside mattresses and on top of cabinets 'cause Lars and Pauline had such a nice house before you got there. And, in those other buildings on the property, weapons could have been anywhere. Of course, you may bill the county for any damage we might have caused; provided of course that you are innocent of all charges."

The Sheriff was pleased to see that he was getting under Harp's skin, in spite of Harp's determination to show no reaction. "Doesn't matter. You'll be my guest for a while until the prosecutor says you can go. You might even get the chance to make bail." With a satisfied smile, Senter stood up and turned to leave. This was his house and he was the boss. The door to the cell block burst open and a deputy rushed in. He ignored the Sheriff's motion to leave and rushed up next to the Sheriff and whispered a few words.

Senter turned back to Harp. "Well, well, Mr. Harper, you continue to amaze me." He turned to the deputy and said, "Give me a couple of minutes, then let him in." He turned to Harp. "Take some free advice, Harper. Those boys that you hurt were pure amateurs. For reasons I do not yet understand, you pose a real threat to someone important. The next ones you meet will not be so careless. As of now, I only hope I am done with you and all that's going on out there." He turned and yelled, "Let him in, Luke."

A fit, immaculately dressed man with a hundred-dollar haircut and five-thousand-dollar suit brushed by the Sheriff and approached Harper. He placed a tape recorder on the chair. "Are you Horace B. Harper?"

Harper nodded. "My name is Anthony M. Everston, III. I have been retained as your attorney through the offices of Sandra L. Kowalski Esq. Do you accept?" Harp smiled and nodded. Said yes. Goddamn, he liked Kowalski. Everston handed his card to the Sheriff and Harp.

"Good. Mr. Harper, were you attacked by the complainants?" Harp said, yes he was.

"Did they harm you in any way?" Harp said they hit him in the back and maybe cracked some ribs.

"Please remove your shirt." Harp removed his shirt and turned his back toward Everston. His back had had time to develop the bright yellow and purple that bad bruises show after a day or so. Senter sighed and shook his head. Everston clucked his tongue and said, "Sheriff Senter, I am doing you a big favor by *not* taking you to court." Everston removed a camera from his briefcase and took several pictures. He motioned Harp to come closer to the bars, then, before Senter knew what he was doing, he moved away and took a picture of Harp's back with Senter standing next to him outside the bars.

"Now hold on there, Mr. Everston. I did not approve any pictures of me." But the lawyer had quickly placed the camera in his briefcase and placed it under his arm. He ignored the Sheriff. Strangely, Senter did not pursue his objection.

"Mr. Harper, do you have the weapon with which you were beaten?" Harp said he did not have it but might be able to find it. Senter nodded with a wry expression, which said of course Harp could find it.

"Okay, Sheriff Senter. Here's what I'm going to do. I am going to leave here and go talk to the prosecutor who's behind this. I am going to talk to the judge who approved the warrants to search this man's house. I do not feel they were adequately informed. I am going to show each of them these pictures. This will do several things. It will establish that you knew of these injuries. It will establish the extent of the injuries and show that any further injuries which might happen to occur would have been while in your jail. It will further establish the fact that my client was brutally beaten by the complainants before taking action to protect himself."

Harp was not watching the lawyer. He was watching Senter. He wanted to see if this would be the end of it. Senter turned to look at Harp with a thoughtful look which said only maybe. But he wasn't used to being manhandled like this. The Sheriff exhaled noisily. "Go ahead and get the charges dropped. I'll release Harper as soon as the papers come over."

Everston responded with firmness. "No, Sheriff. *I* will bring the papers personally and I will see my client walk out those doors. I will be back."

And he was. In less than an hour, Everston briskly walked back into the Sheriff's office and placed the documents on his desk. Senter looked at the papers briefly and shrugged. He called a deputy to release the prisoner. "I would like to know who contacted you."

Everston smiled. "Sorry, that is attorney/client privileged information. Oh, FYI, the DA and the judge are both now curious about your activities. They said they will be in touch." Harp was brought into the room with a deputy still holding his arm. "Let him go, Charlie." The deputy reluctantly obeyed and was motioned out by Senter. Another deputy came in with a bag containing Harp's personal effects. Harp checked and it was all there.

"Are you ready to go, Mr. Harper?" Harp nodded but remained standing erect in front of the Sheriff's desk. He wanted Senter to look at something he had been hiding until now. He wanted Senter to see a killer's eyes. He put his hands on Senter's desk and leaned forward until he was into Senter's personal space, staring with the intense focus of a battle-hardened man into the eyes of this country Sheriff. He wanted Senter to see what it was like to stare into the eyes of a man who had killed many men and would kill again if pushed too far. He wanted Senter to see a man totally in control; not the slightest bit afraid. Senter looked back, confidently at first, but then his eyes widened at what he saw there. For the first time, Senter truly considered this man called Harp. A new feeling for him, a kind of chill, shook him. He instinctively understood that he would never defeat this man. Harp nodded once. The message had been received. Senter looked down, strangely confused at his own reaction. This had never happened before.

Harp and Everston paused on the sidewalk outside the jail. It was a beautiful day. Harp looked at the sky and put his hands in his pockets and said, "I'm not very good at thank-you's because I don't say it much, but I really appreciate what you did in there. I will pay whatever you bill me for it."

Everston gazed at Harp and smiled. "I shouldn't even charge you. I'm really a corporate lawyer and don't get much chance to jerk the tail of these small-town bullies." He polished his glasses with his tie. "I was one of the senior partners with Sandra's firm when we hired her. We knew she was special because she showed right away that she had balls—in a feminine way of course."

They walked toward the lawyer's car. It was a four-door BMW sedan, the large version. "I'm from Pittsburgh. I left her firm with another partner to start our own firm over here." Harp remained silent. "But, to tell the truth, I wish we had had the foresight to invite her in. She is really topnotch."

Everston unlocked the doors with his key fob and threw the briefcase in the back seat. "I'll send you a copy of those pictures when I get back to the office." Harp nodded and said thanks. "Of course I have wondered why my former colleague, who specializes in estate law, called me with some anxiety in her voice to get over here and represent you." Harp smiled and looked off down the street. Everston waited and Harp volunteered nothing. The fact was, Harp didn't know either. "And, I assume that now I will just keep wondering." He stood next to the open door and looked with some amusement at Harp. "I don't know what's going on in this little burg but if you need me again, give me a call. If I can't help you, I will find someone who can." He grinned, "And tell Sandy I said hello." The door closed with a quiet thump and the car whispered out into traffic.

Harp turned to look at the jail. Two deputies were standing at the top of the step grinning. As he walked toward his truck, he was wondering what those grins meant. But the truck was okay. Everything remained in the glove box and it started easily. He pointed it toward the farm, his farm.

"So, Billy, you just opened the door and let him go." Senter was aggravated by the call coming so close on the heels of this minor humiliation. How in hell did he know damned near everything that happened?

"Adam, there are some things I can do and some I can't. One

125

thing I can't do is make a photograph lie. I already have some explaining to do to the judge and DA. I told you that this was a bad strategy and I was right." Senter loosened his tie and threw a foot up on his desk. "Those three idiots are not even smart enough to perjure themselves in a way that the dumbest jury would believe. You're lucky we didn't have to take it to court."

The voice remained measured but the intensity was inescapable. "Billy, you have no idea what's at stake here. I am protecting you by not telling you what it is. One way or another, I have to have that pissant little farm and I don't have a lot of time to get it."

"Well, why keep farting around? Why don't you make him an offer he can't refuse?" Senter was honestly puzzled.

"We have offered him two and half million and he turned it down. He said he was going to sell it but he was going to sell it later. We can't accept 'later.'"

"Holy Mother of God, he turned down two and half mil?" Senter knew that land in this area was going for ridiculous sums, but he rarely heard a number *this* size for a small area farm.

"Yes, and we are going to double our offer. So, you see how serious we are. Do what you can to help him make a decision—within the law, of course." The last was spoken sardonically. It was followed by a loud clatter as Adam's phone bounced in its cradle. Senter was stunned. What the hell was going on? Another thought intruded before he could push it away: If there's that much money at stake on this one piece of land, maybe he could somehow get some of the action. Then he reminded himself that he was Sheriff and that was enough. He also recalled the look Harper had given him. He knew that, even though he was

Sheriff, Harper was not a man he should mess with. If he pushed Harper, he had better be ready for a push back.

***

Adam hung up after talking to Senter. He still used a land line for certain calls. He did not trust such vital information to the randomness of cell phone transmission intercepts conducted by various agencies. It would not be a good thing if anybody else knew what he was doing or had done. But, he explained to himself, the stakes are high enough to justify the most drastic actions. Anyone would agree if they only knew. For the tenth time, he read the report from the geological consulting firm that he had engaged over the years. Because they were privately hired, their reports and conclusions were his alone. Adam made sure that their firm understood the necessity for absolute secrecy. He also made sure that they were paid enough to be more than happy to do anything he asked. But, the latest report was very troubling. Based on field test anomalies, the firm had added seismology models to the mix. The results had the potential for standing this whole part of the state on its ear. Adam wanted to be the first to profit. And the report was clear; pressure was building. They also made it clear that, money or not, it was their duty to report dangerous situations. He did not have much time left.

The first thing Adam needed to do was terminate the polluted spring strategy. It was an ill-conceived idea from the outset, but it was simple enough to give it a try. Just to get the Kuykendahls thinking about selling, the plan was to have them believe that work on neighboring properties was polluting their waters. It was hoped that this would cause them to *want* to sell their land, believing that all their water would soon become undrinkable. But, it would be too easy to show that those springs couldn't have been affected by area drilling. Adam's people were then going to go in and apologize then make a great offer to buy. It was a bad idea which hadn't worked. A stubborn Lars had questioned how a surface water supply could be polluted by an underground activity and still refused all offers. He was right. Their springs were actually as good as they ever were. Further, the idiot who was supposed to be periodically dumping the fracking fluid near each of the springs was found passed out drunk and naked on his ATV next to the Hannyville Road. He claimed that something funny was going on. He didn't even remember opening the bottle. How many drunks have used *that* explanation? He was fired as soon as he brought the drum full of extremely complicated fracking chemicals back in to the firm's warehouse. The fluid's chemical makeup was a closely guarded trade secret, and Adam did not want that to get out. The cabin would be cleaned up and reverted to its original use as a seasonal hunting camp. Adam had even hunted from there in the past. Got a nice 12-pointer a few years back.

9

HAPPY TO BE FREE FROM THE JAIL AND FEELING A SENSE
of satisfaction, Harp drove toward the farm, slouching with windows down, left arm on the sill, right hand drooping over the top of the steering wheel. He was careful to obey all rules of the road. He did not want to go back to that cell. He now understood that he was fair game and would be hauled in on the slightest pretext. He just wanted to get to the house, settle in with bourbon and Fart, and simply vegetate for a while. He needed time to think things out. It all seemed much more complicated than it needed to be. He was damned well ready to sell the place and get the hell out of this mess. He laughed to himself at Pauline's prediction. She knew what she was saying when she said he had inherited a shitstorm.

As he drove up the driveway, the picture of his house was all wrong. Everything was open: The front door, the garage doors, and on past, all the outbuilding's doors also. Harp now knew what the deputy's grinning was all about. He drove on to the parking area behind the house. The back doors were open too, mud room and kitchen. Fart had been waiting. He had been hiding in the cemetery. As soon as Harp stepped down from the truck, Fart started baying with the sound that only hounds can make. He was running and baying with what could only be a joyous sound, like his ancestors made when the quarry was sighted. Only Harp was not the quarry; he was the beloved master. Fart made that perfectly clear as he first skidded to a stop then quickly rose and placed his dirty paws on Harps chest. The surprising thing about this encounter was not that this formerly reserved animal was sloppily licking Harp's face. The surprising thing was that Harp let him do it and was grinning widely as he roughly shook Fart's head and laughingly told him to stop. Finally, both were satisfied that the reunion had run its course and turned toward the house. "Okay, let's go see how bad it is." Fart stopped at the door but Harp motioned him to come in. What the hell, the dog was part of this. Harp needn't have worried; nothing Fart could do would be worse than the scene greeting them inside the door.

Bad would not cover it. It was an unbelievable mess. It was a destructive rampage with the sole intent of making his house unlivable. Under the guise of searching for something, everything had been pulled from shelves and left on the floor. Cans, dishes, pots, pans, sugar; all had crashed to the floor and then been trod upon as the search continued. All the furniture was upended. Pictures were pulled from the walls and holes had been punched into the sheetrock where they had been. The central light fixture, a nice hanging leaded glass shade, was pulled down and broken. Water was running in the sinks but had drained past rough plugs stuck in the drains. In the downstairs bedroom, the pillows had been cut open, the mattress was sliced to pieces, and every liquid item in the bathroom had been dumped on the floor. The sheet rock in the walls was holed too many times to count.

The rest of the house was the same. Nothing was spared. Furniture cut, pictures smashed, rugs stained with all kinds of fluids. The office was especially bad because of all the paper records that had been pulled from file drawers and scattered about. The computer was thrown on the floor. Harp guessed that they had not gotten into the hard drive without the password. The rifles and shotguns were gone. Harp guessed he was supposed to ask for them. Harp stood in the office trying to wrap his mind around the situation. Then it hit him! The bar! If those sonsabitches had touched his bar, there would be hell to pay. Harp ran down the stairs to confront one of the saddest sights he had ever seen.

"Oh, those miserable son of a bitch bastards!" Harp shouted. The bar had been wrecked. Not every bottle was broken but most were. The stools had been kicked away and the beautiful wood had been pried away—as if a hiding spot would ever be made there. Behind the bar was a mess of broken glass and spilled whiskey. Along one wall, water was dripping where it had leaked through from the kitchen above. It was almost too much. They would never know how close, with this skirmish, they came to winning the battle. Harp had to ask himself if it was worth it now. He had lost one of his main reasons for staying; he could no longer devote himself to enjoying all the liquor in the bar before selling. He had known all along that, while this goal was superficial, it still had been an enjoyable challenge that he would have been happy to meet.

He assumed that they had found the root cellar and trashed that also. But, he was relieved to see that, while all the things that had been on the shelves had been pushed onto the floor, the book shelf was still in place. Kicking the mess aside, he pulled the shelf aside and opened the steel door. Though he had maybe wasted a lot of time moving his gear, he happily noted that the room was intact. It was good to know that this space was now almost officially off the books. He could now bring all his equipment back—and it looked like he might need it. That minor victory buoyed his spirits just enough to get him thinking of the next step. It was supposed to be pack up and leave. Harp could not leave this way. Who knew what would happen to the house if they thought it was abandoned? But he had to make it even just a little livable before he could stay in it. Most of the cleanup he could do himself, but he realized he needed help if he was going to spend any time here—which he was now going to do just to spite all the fuckers. He was still going to eventually sell and leave this goddamned place, but he was damned if he was going to be driven off. It was *his,* dammit all. It was the only thing of substance he had ever owned. The big question was, who could he trust to bring into a situation which could conceivably be danger-ous? Harp knew the answer almost as soon as he asked himself the question.

You trusted the ones who had had your back before. You trusted the guys you had fought with. They had formed a bond that was deeper than most people would ever begin to compre-hend. Harp knew that if he called, they would come. The problem was that he needed skilled tradesmen, not trained warriors. These guys could handle a long list of weapons, but they couldn't patch a hole in drywall or plumb a sink if their lives depended on it.

Wait, he thought. Maybe I can have both. These guys had

shown in the past that they could do anything with the proper training. They had been forced to learn an incredible array of skills just to stay alive. There was no reason they could not learn a little painting, carpentry, and plumbing. They would be especially motivated when they learned how much Harp would be able to pay. All Harp needed was a teacher. In addition to these new skills, Harp was beginning to get an idea of uses for their less obvious capabilities. Then, of course, there was the other problem with this plan. These guys were the walking wounded. Marion Bondurant had lost his right foot a little above the ankle. They cut off a little more to make a better prosthesis. Phil Weeks lost his left arm above the elbow. All this happened in the same IED explosion that blew Harp's femur into pieces and peppered the rest of his body with shrapnel.

After their lives had been saved at the field hospital, they had all ended up at Bethesda at the same time. Harp had been discharged after they were and, like military men everywhere, lost track of his buddies. They were younger guys and had little in common with the "old man" Sgt. Harper. Marion, or "Bonny," was doing really well the last time Harp saw him, but he heard Weeks was still having flashbacks and needed more time. But that was a long time ago. The team of Harp, Bonny, and Weeks; maybe it was ready for a reunion, Harp thought. Plus, if he was going to ask people he could trust to help him, he would like it to be them. Who knows, he thought, it might be good for all of them.

It wasn't easy to find them. He used up all the minutes on one of his throwaway cell phones. He found Bonny first. He was divorced but okay with it. He didn't blame her. He had his disability pension. He was working for a hospital in D.C. as drug and organ conveyance specialist. He was delivering kidneys, hearts, lungs, and rare drugs that needed to get from one institution to another in a hurry. He said it was interesting but he was ready for a change. He knew where Weeks was but could not recommend contacting him. Weeks, he said, was still in and out of rehab and couldn't seem to get his shit together. Bonny said that Weeks was having serious flashbacks and overreacting to some pretty ordinary daily stuff. Bonny and Harp discussed pros and cons but concluded that, whatever happened, Weeks needed their help. The question was, would he come to Bardberg?

They needn't have worried. Phil Weeks was in serious need of some get-far-away time. Living off disability checks, he had gone home to North Carolina to find that there was no place for him there. Family and old friends tried to relate. Almost without fail, they could not. How could they know what he had gone through? How could they know that the primitive people he fought did not view death the same way as a stateside Baptist? How could they know that he had become as primitive as those people were just to stay alive? You just had to pull the damned trigger and shoot anyone who shot at you. You killed and killed to not be killed. The best his old friends and family could come up with was a lot of hearty thank-you's while trying hard not to stare at his prosthetic arm. One brother even said he envied Weeks because he didn't have to go to work every day. No matter what they said, or how they said it, Weeks always thought he heard a cloying pity that dripped off the edge of their words.

To a proud man, a man who had distinguished himself in battle among other soldiers, pity was an acid that ate away at his ability to accept and move on. Yet his anger was not at them. His anger was not at the enemy. It was not at the men who sent him into battle. It was not at the loss of an arm. It was not at the twists of fate that placed him in that fucking sandbox. He was angry because there was a thing inside him that was very important and he was having a hard time holding on to it. He desperately wanted to remain who he had always been. He wanted to scream "It's still me, godammit! I'm still me!" He had finally admitted that he needed some serious help. More rehab was ahead, but he wasn't sure he was going to try again. He wasn't sure he had the strength to say he would keep trying. Then Harp called.

When Weeks answered his cell, he heard a voice he hadn't heard in way too long. "Hello, asshole, this is Sergeant Harper. You learned how to jerk off with your other hand yet?" Weeks nearly collapsed in relief. Here was normalcy. Here was something he understood. "Sarge, you old piece of shit, I know you must be calling me from a lockup somewhere 'cause there is no way you could be out walking around. And, no I don't have any money so I can't bail you out."

Harp laughed. He was just as happy to hear Weeks' voice. "I'm walkin' and I'm talkin' and right now I want to do some talkin' to you. You got a minute?"

Minute? Weeks thought. Do I have a fuckin' minute for the Sarge? "Yeah, man, I got a minute, or an hour, or a whole damned year if you want it. I'm suckin' air, man. I am about two steps away from the edge of happy valley."

"Pretty rough, huh?" Harp knew how it was and he knew not to be too solicitous. "Well, shake it off. I need your help." Better words could not have been spoken. "Is that piece of hardware you are wearing working now?"

"Sarge, you would not believe the things I can do with this arm. I can thread a needle with the sumbitch. The trouble is, nobody wants the rest of me. I got kind of a record now and the mealy-mouth bastards who do the hiring look at me like I'm some kind of animal. In other words, I am totally screwed."

"Well, I need you and I can pay you some real change for helping me out. And, don't say you won't take any money. I got a ton of it and I want to share with my buddies."

"Ah, shit, you went into robbin' banks?" Weeks was worried for his old Sarge.

"Hell no. I just inherited a bundle. I'll give you and Bonny each twenty grand for a couple of weeks' work. What do you say?"

"Fuckin' A is what I say. Where and when do I report? I can drive but I don't have a car."

"Don't worry about that. Bonny's got a car and he will pick you up."

"Don't shit me, Sarge. You found Bonny!? Hoo boy! Harp, Bonny, and Weeks together again."

"You got it, my friend. Bonny is up in D.C. He'll be calling to set up a time to pick up your sorry ass. I'll give you the whole story when you get here."

"Get where?"

"Believe me, Corporal Weeks, it will be easier to show you than tell you. You won't believe it even when you see it."

"Okay, Sarge. Thanks for calling." Weeks paused. "You caught me at just the right time, if you know what I mean."

Harp was struck with a heavy sadness that such a good man who had given so much had been brought to this point. "Yeah, Weeks, I know what you mean. Put it away and come on out. I'll see you in a couple of days. Bring your basics. We'll be kind of camping for a while."

Harp was so used to this story, he no longer wondered why it had to be this way. Like people everywhere who see unending cruelty and violence as part of their jobs, he now simply shrugged and did not ask the rhetorical "why" posed by tortured people who are desperate to understand the new convolutions in their battered brains. He was happy that those two guys were coming but he still had a problem. They would do anything he asked, but who was going to show them how to do what he needed doing?

Taking a break from picking up pieces of his house, turning off water, and making a place to sleep, Harp thought that this would be a good time to see where those coordinates took him. He was not a clean-up guy and he didn't even know where everything was supposed to go, so he couldn't put it back. Fuck it, he thought. I'll wait 'till I get some help. Just to be doing something and to get away from the depressing mess of the house, he focused on the coordinates that Pauline had given him. He also needed time to think of the next step.

He knew the miracle of today's Global Positioning System could put him within a meter of any point on the map. As he and Fart sat on the seat of the ATV, he plugged in the numbers. It was so simple. The unit first located him and then showed the spot under the numbers. They set out slowly heading toward the northwestern quarter of the farm. In a matter of minutes, they were there. They had motored up a gradual slope and arrived at a limestone outcrop about fifteen feet high. They were within feet of the location on the GPS but there wasn't anything there. The outcrop leaned out over a shallow circular area which cut back under it by just three or four feet.

A small natural bench sat under the overhang. Aside from being an attractive spot, Harp could see nothing special. Certainly nothing that would cause such obvious concern to Lars and Pauline. Then Fart barked and there was an echo. At first, Harp assumed it was a trick of the overhang's shape. The dog barked again and this time there was no doubt in Harp's mind that the strange semi-echo indicated something hollow, like talking near the end of a very large pipe. But, except for the overhang, there was nothing like that in sight. He walked up very close to the bench and whistled. It was in front of him. He leaned over the bench and found it. There was a jagged slot, invisible to any angle but the one Harp used, perfectly hidden behind the bench. It was about six feet long and two-foot-wide at the widest point. Harp picked up a small stone and dropped it. The sound of it landing came very quickly so it wasn't very deep.

Puzzled, but satisfied that he had found the mysterious spot, the next step was to go down into this hole and see what was there. Though daring in many circumstances, Harp was not foolish enough to descend into an unknown pit without the guarantee of a way out. He would wait until the guys got here and they could do it the right way. Harp studied the back edge of the bench and easily saw where a rope had left rounded indentations as if a heavy weight had been raised and lowered into the hole. Harp guessed that Pauline had used some kind of machinery to get Lars in and out. What had he seen that was so shattering?

Before returning to the house, Harp motored south to the lookout point above the third spring. There was no evidence of any recent visits. At the last minute, he turned to the track he followed before to the cabin in the woods. He and Fart stealthily approached the place on foot to find a completely different appearance. The area around the cabin was totally devoid of any signs of inhabitance. A look in the window showed a neat room, empty except for the bunks, a couple of chairs, and the table. Harp looked behind the cabin and saw that the drum of strange fluid was gone. This reminded him that he needed to find out how to get all those samples checked. Fart inspected everything carefully before selecting a corner of the cabin to piss on. Harp thought this was perfectly appropriate. He pissed on another corner. They returned to the house. Fart worried around outside. He did not like what was going on around his home. Harp went to work again inside.

While waiting for the men to arrive, Harp busied himself with the most basic cleanup of the mess left by the Sheriff's men. He had turned off all the running water but that was about it. In an old telephone directory, he found a dumpster company which agreed to bring a medium sized container and drop it outside the back door. They came from a long way off so it was expensive but, in Harp's newfound financial freedom, he did not even quibble. It seemed like most of the house's contents would end up in that giant green container, including most of the furniture.

While the deputies had cut up all the mattresses and cushions in their "search," they had not bothered with the foundations under the mattresses. They would be their beds until new sets could be bought. Hell, they had slept for months on canvas cots. Bonny and Weeks could each take one of the upstairs bedrooms if they wanted to. The kitchen was such a mess that it was beyond his capacity to even start cleaning. Everything had been dumped and scattered and broken. Probably there was not a bit of food left for Harp and his arriving crew. Harp did not even want to think about cleaning the kitchen. A quick visit to all the other structures on the farm showed various degrees of disarray. Give legal freedom to a crew of five or six determined assholes for a couple of hours and they could wreak havoc on any property.

Of course, the most painful was the cleanup behind the bar. There was some good news, however. Harp found a few unbroken bottles on the back bar and more stored underneath. He did the basic cleanup, getting all the broken glass and spilled booze off the floor. It would take a lot more work to get rid of the stains and smell. It was painful. Harp would pick up a label of a twenty-year-old bourbon, and shake his head sadly while smelling the glass with reverence. If only the Sheriff knew: this was the *least* effective way to get him to leave.

10

"THEY DELIVERED A DUMPSTER. IT'S OUT THERE NOW. He's started hauling trash from the house. What the hell happened out there anyway?" Pierce was reporting to Adam. He did not know who he was calling. Just the name "Adam." Pierce was the rural mail carrier. He had gotten behind in mortgage payments to a finance company Adam owned. Adam had agreed to refinance and not foreclose if Pierce would keep him updated on activity around the Kuykendahl place. Pierce stretched the rules just a little bit but drew the line at opening mail. He had principles. Plus, he did not want to screw up his federal pension or go to federal prison.

Adam did not answer the question. He was still not sure that harassing Harper was the wisest strategy. "Has anybody else been out there?" he asked. He remained very calm and casual with Pierce. He did not want him to have even the slightest idea that something immense was at stake. He knew that Pierce was a gossip. All Adam asked was to be the first to know.

"Nah. It's just him and that dog. That dog has changed by the way. He don't hide out by that little cemetery any more. I take the mail up to the house—just to be neighborly, you know—and now that dog he just watches me all the time I'm there. He never did that before, even with Lars." Pierce was in his own home. It was late afternoon. His route was done in the morning, so he watched the grandkids in the afternoon while his wife worked at the old folk's home. Everything was working out real good now that the house payment schedule was worked out. Putting money in his nephew's sure-thing used car business was the dumbest thing he had ever done.

"Has he gotten any mail yet addressed to him?"

"Nah. It's that same crap we carry to every house. Mostly ads for pizza, chicken, car loans, and life insurance. The usual stuff."

"Well, keep up the good work, Mr. Pierce." The phone clicked and Adam was gone. Pierce finished eating his cold fried chicken and hollered at one of his grandchildren to stop pestering the cat.

11

HARP WAS SITTING ON THE PORCH WITH FART LYING
comfortably beside his rocker. For some reason, they had not
trashed the rockers. Probably because they were in plain sight.
Who knows? Around three in the afternoon, a late model 4-door
Chevy sedan tentatively pulled into the bottom of the driveway,
then slowly drove to stop near the porch. The front doors opened
and Staff Sergeant Bondurant and Corporal Weeks got out. To
Harp, they hadn't changed much. Bonny looked a little older but
was still in his late twenties. He was a big bearded guy with heavy
torso and long legs. His hair was still military length. Like many
former GI's, once he had all his hair cut off, he found he liked
it that way. Now his hair and beard were the same length and
kept that way with electric clippers. Bonny had a gentle face with
friendly eyes and regular features, but there was an air about him
of contained strength. Harp had seen him turn those gentle eyes
on a group of Taliban attackers and kill them all. No one would
ever know how many men he had killed. And no one ever made
the mistake of saying that Bonny was a sissy name. He was a little

taller than Harp. He stood clear of the car, grinned, came to attention and saluted. He was wearing khaki shorts, short-sleeved shirt, and appeared to be navigating with no trouble on his metal foot.

Weeks was average height and slender. Yet Harp knew he could carry the same weight as any man and hump it all day without undue complaint. He had black tightly curled hair, bright gray eyes, and very bright teeth against his brown skin. The team was not kidding when they told Weeks not to smile while on a mission. His teeth were like a little light going on, even at a distance. He was wearing a long-sleeved shirt and a glove on his left hand. He too stepped away from the car, gave a flashbulb grin and saluted. Despite the smile, Harp could see the pain in Weeks' eyes. He knew his men.

But they hesitated before approaching. Bonny turned back toward the car and motioned for someone to get out of the back door. Weeks looked at Harp and shrugged in an apologetic way. The door opened and another man got out. Harp's first reaction was anger. He had always trusted his troops, though, so he said nothing. The door opened and a third man stepped out. As he exited the car, only the right side of his head was visible to Harp. Harp's first impression was that this was an incredibly good-looking guy. He was shorter than the other two, maybe five nine. His hair was blond and wavy. He had a movie-star profile with perfect nose and wide mouth. When he turned, Harp saw a crude, insufficient patch which failed to cover the damage to the left side of his face.

"What's your name, soldier?" Harp asked.

"I am not a soldier." He declared bitterly. "I did not want to be in your fucking army! I was never a fucking soldier!" Bonny looked at Harp and shrugged again. Weeks just waited. Nobody moved.

"Okay, what's your name, *mister!*"

He was still standing next to the door of the car as if ready to get back in. "My name is Wellington Kipling Finch-Smithers, the Fourth. Okay?" He said it as if it was supposed to mean something. It meant nothing to Harp.

"Sure it's okay," Harp responded. This kid's attitude had gotten to Harp. He knew lots of guys who were hurt a lot worse than this one. "I just want to know your name before I send your ass right back where you came from, Mr. Wellington Pinch Fisher whatever the number." The kid jumped back in the car and slammed the door. He slumped down in the seat with resignation.

Bonny looked at the car for a moment then approached the porch. Harp came down the steps and they hugged with lots of manly back-slaps. Then he and Weeks did the same. They all looked at each other with misty eyes. They had been through hell together and the emotions they felt did not need words. They could look at each other and not feel the usual embarrassment men do when caught teary-eyed. They had watched each other cry.

"Sarge, he needs us." Bonny said, motioning with his thumb over his shoulder.

With a sigh, Harp asked, "Okay, what's his story?

Military reports are necessarily brief. Bonny reported: "Rich kid from upstate New York. Got busted at Yale on possession. Enlisted to spite an asshole father. Caught one while on patrol. Always carried his share. Lost an eye and part of his cheekbone.

145

He won't do what the doctors tell him to. Won't go home. Won't talk to his parents. Sarge, he can't be more than nineteen."

Bonny paused, then gave the rest of the story. "I met him while making one of my deliveries. It was a kidney in the cooler. I took it in and got the receipt. When I left, he was at the back door of the clinic, smoking. I saw his face, he saw my foot, and we talked a little. His face was real bad fucked up then, a lot worse than it looks now. Then I kind of got the feeling he was waiting for me on my deliveries. He started talking and he talked and talked over the last few weeks. It was kind of like I was his shrink."

Shifting his weight to his good foot, he continued. "Then you called and I told him I was leaving. I was just letting him know to be nice, you know? Anyway, he just says, 'I'm going with you.' I told him that I actually didn't know where I was going. Then he says that that would be perfect because he didn't know where he was going either. He said that I was the only one he could talk to and then begged me to take him with me. I just couldn't say no. So here we are." Harp stood with hands on hips thinking about the ramifications of keeping the kid here. He then strode to the car, opened the door, and motioned for the kid to get out. Sullenly, Finch-Smithers climbed from the car. Harp walked back to Bonny and Weeks and stopped. He motioned the kid to come join them.

Most of what Harp said was for the kid. "Okay, there is going to be four of us. Kid, you are in because Bonny has stuck his neck out for you. We are going to be working together for a while so let's have some ground rules. The big one is, no bullshit. If you lie, cheat, or steal, you are down the road. If you don't carry your load, you are down the road. If I hear any whining, I will kick your ass before you go down the road. My men don't whine. We have got a lot of work to do here and each of you will have an equal share. Agreed?" Weeks and Bonny nodded with smiles, they knew this was not for them. The kid slowly nodded. "We are all fucked up a little or a lot," Harp continued. "And none of us are going to think that what happened to us is any better or worse than the others. Bonny, we can see your foot. Weeks, do you have to wear that glove and that shirt?" Surprised, Weeks shook his head.

"Okay, take 'em off." Weeks hesitated. He had been covering his arm for so long, he found it strange to display it to other people. Then he removed his shirt and glove. They stood looking at the whole apparatus with appreciation for the genius it displayed. He stood there in sleeveless tee shirt waiting for any wisecracks. There were none. From his experience, Bonny asked about some technical details in the construction of the arm. Soon they were talking about the good and bad features of their respective mechanisms while the kid and Harp listened.

They looked at the kid's eye patch and waited. It hit Harp that the kid was not accustomed to taking the patch off around other people. Then, almost in defiance, he ripped it off. Harp had seen human suffering in the most gruesome and obscene ways man could invent, so his face showed nothing in response to the kid's glare. The bullet had come from high to the right, entered the forehead above the nose, caught the front of the eyeball and blown out the left cheekbone. Without the patch and, with a bright blue good eye, he glared at Harp, daring him to comment. From his eyebrow to a spot about two inches from his ear, the left side of his face was pretty much torn up where bone frag-

147

ments had exited. Where the bullet had entered, there was only a small indentation. The first of many surgeries had closed the gap in his cheek but it was still a pink and purple tangle. This guy has a bunch of operations ahead of him, Harp thought. He should still be in the hospital. "Bonny, do you see anything special here?" Bonny made a point of examining the kid's face. He replied, "Nah, I think he's lucky. That bullet could have taken his whole face off."

Weeks, sensitive to what was happening, said, "I would swap with him in a minute. I would rather have my arm back." The kid stood, mouth open in wonder at the casual acceptance of his wounds. It was an important first step toward accepting them himself. "What about you?" the kid said, in a challenge to Harp. Without a word, Harp removed his shirt and dropped his trousers to show the mangled leg and other scars. The kid nodded, somewhat chastened. "Okay," was all he said. Harp put pants and shirt back on.

To the kid, Harp said, "What do we call you?"

Somewhat shyly, he answered, "My parents called me Wellington, which I always hated. I had an aunt with a cottage on the ocean where I would visit a couple of weeks during the summer. She would call me Kip. That's the only name I ever liked." The serenity of those summers was reflected in his face, the good side, for a fleeting moment.

"Kip it is. Guys, say hello to Kip." They all laughed and said Kip in as many ways as they could think of. Loudly, softly, falsetto, deeply, until the name was adopted permanently. Even Kip laughed. Harp would have bet that this was the first time Kip had laughed in months

Fart had come up to stand beside Harp. He was carefully watching each of the men as they spoke. It was clear that his master accepted these people but he was waiting to be sure. "This is my adopted dog. He is like us. He has been through a lot. He is the first dog I have ever had. He took up with me and I took up with him. He is to be treated with respect. Right now, his name is Fart." Harp waited until the laughter stopped. "He deserved that name at one time. Be aware that, in a closed space, his farts can kill. With a better diet, I think he might have quit farting." Harp continued. "Probably we can get this place back to normal in a couple of weeks. As agreed, I will pay each of you twenty thousand for two weeks' work."

They all made sounds of dismissal saying it was too much and they would help for nothing. Harp went on. "I inherited a bundle and will make a ton when I sell this place. So take the money and enjoy it. I *want* you to have it. Understood?" Bonny and Weeks shrugged and nodded. Kip did not.

Harp looked at Kip. "What?"

"I've already got a lot of money." Kip said quietly. "I don't even want to say how much I will inherit when I turn twenty-one. Give my share to Bonny and Weeks." The three of them grinned in appreciation and did knuckle bumps all around.

"All right then. Come on in and assess our situation. We are going to be roughing it for a while. You'll understand better once you see the mess." He led the way through the door. "Go ahead and scout the whole house. Upstairs, downstairs, nothing is off limits. Take your time. While you're at it, pick a place to crash. I'll take the downstairs bedroom. There are three bedrooms upstairs. Each of you get a room. Take your pick. Go out and look at all the other buildings. We'll meet on the porch in about an hour. I'll tell you the whole story then."

While Harp sat on the porch with Fart, the three of them wandered the entire farmstead. They studied each room, went through the barn and poked through every other building. When they returned to the porch, they were all visibly angry.

Bonny started. "You say this was done by Sheriffs' deputies?" Harp nodded. The others shook their heads. "Sarge," Weeks said, "I wouldn't even know how to start fixing everything. We can clean it up sure, but we got to *fix* everything. We don't know how!"

Kip was silent but you could tell he was thinking. "Is it the usual thing in situations like this to not think about getting even?" Harp grinned. It was not a pleasant grin. More like a wolf's snarl.

He answered, "First things first. Top priority is to make this place livable. We need the basics: water, food, and a place to sleep. Then we work out a strategy. But, in answer to your question, we are definitely going to get even somehow. Let's work on that later. Right now, I get the feeling that just being here is driving somebody nuts."

"You all sit down and get a load off, I want to tell you the whole story. I wish we had a beer or something but…"

Bonny grinned. "Way ahead of you Sarge. I got a case of Rolling Rock in the trunk." He laughed. "I sent Kip in to buy it and they wouldn't sell it to him. He's just a baby." Kip flipped him the bird. Bonny went to the car and came back with a cooler full of bottles.

Kip spoke up, "It's not funny. I'm not old enough to drink and lost my fake ID." Once again, they were reminded of the incongruity of drinking laws and military service minimum age. *Old enough to get shot but not old enough to buy a shot.* Weeks slapped Kip on the back. "Goddamn, Kip, someday you're going to be old enough to have a legal beer. Just don't die or get crippled first." There was a round of bitter laughter. Kip was surprised to find himself grinning. The grin felt strange on his face, especially where it pushed against the new mass of scars.

When each of them had a bottle of beer in hand, Harp told the whole crazy tale, beginning with Kowalski coming into the bar. For some reason, he left out the part about Kowalski spending the night at his apartment. When he was done, several bottles were gone and it was dark. Everyone was silent as they digested all this startling information.

First to speak was Bonny. "So you *are* going to sell the place, right?"

"Yeah, Bonny, I don't see myself spending the rest of my life, or even a few years of my life here."

Weeks was next. "So what are we doing here? Why not just take the money and walk away now?"

Harp thought about it. "I'm not sure I can explain it. First thing, of course, is the fact that I don't like being threatened like this. I, we, have seen too much shit and survived to take this crap from rear echelon mother-fuckers who don't know doodely-shit from Shinola. I just naturally want to push back. Another thing is that I kind of got to admire my Cousin Pauline and her husband Lars. There was something wrong about the way they died. They were good people in a bad situation. Then, they left everything to me so I guess I feel I owe them." He could not bring himself to confess that the original reason for staying was to drink all the liquor.

151

"And that's it?" Kip asked.

"Well, not exactly. I get a chance to spend some time with three genuine Army issue assholes and might not get that chance again." Harp feigned ducking as they laughed and threw air grenades. "Anyway, I want to return the place to the way I found it. We are going to be here for maybe a couple weeks and we need to be able to eat and sleep here. First thing will be to clean out all the busted and broken stuff. Next thing will be to refurnish the place and get everything operating the way it should." Harp looked at the three attentive faces. "I need someone to go on a big time buying trip. I want him to go buy a house full of furniture and whatever else we need. Basically, we need replacements for anything with a cushion. Sofas, chairs, mattresses, pillows, stuff like that. One of you will go into the city with cash to buy from a list we will all put together. Who volunteers?"

"Not me, I'm not ready for something like that." Kip said. Harp and all understood.

"There's too much I can be doing here while Bonny goes." Weeks said. His need to stay close was understood.

"I'll do it, then," Bonny said, "if that's you want me to do, Sarge." He was sensitive to the fact that he was entrusted with a sizable bundle of cash and the judgment to fill a house with essentials.

"Good. It's decided then. Take the Ford truck. It will hold more. Everybody can give Bonny a list. We'll have the furnishings delivered. The rest he can load up. Bonny, do you think ten grand is enough for now?"

Bonny thought for a minute. "We got four bedrooms, a living room, an office, the downstairs den, and a kitchen. We need mattresses, chairs, sofas, tables, rugs, kitchen stuff, blankets, and a hell of a lot more. No, I don't think that's enough."

"Okay. I'll get fifteen thousand."

"Plus we need a good computer," Kip added to everyone's surprise. "We need to find out what the hell is going on around here and I can do some research through the internet. Get me a top of the line laptop. A good one with a seventeen-inch screen and lots of memory." Bonny was visibly worried about this purchase. He had never bought a good laptop and said so. Kip suggested that he just buy a name brand that cost a thousand dollars.

"Do we even have internet?" Harp asked.

Kip pointed toward the north side of the house. "You've got a dish up there and you said the bills had all been paid so you probably got it." They were impressed. None of them had seen the dish which was between two dormers. "I had a bunch of computer classes so I think I can find the information we need," he added, smiling. He was still not quite ready to leave his patch off. But they did not say a word about it.

Harp told Kip to give Bonny a better idea in writing of the kind of computer he wanted along with the software, some flash drives, and a good camera. Then they started listing important items like Pepsi, Coca-Cola, bourbon, vodka, beer, potato chips, corn chips, pickled eggs, Spam, etc.

***

After a night of camping in their trashed surroundings, Harp called Harry Johnson. Johnson answered "Hello, Mr. Harper. How's it going out there?" Apparently, he had not heard. Harp quickly described their situation. "Those bastards! What the hell is going on out there? I don't get it! It's just not like us!"

"Mr. Johnson, all I know is someone wants this place and they are desperate. For the time being, I am staying. I have some friends out here and we are going to repair all the damage those guys did. I need some cash to do it."

"No problem. You have an incredible balance with us. What do you need?"

"We need money. We also need someone who can show us how to do all the repairs. None of us has any experience or training in the basic stuff, but we need to learn how. It would be nice if you could recommend someone who could come work with us on this stuff."

Johnson listened intently. He was rubbing his chin and considering possibilities. "Okay. First, the money. How much do you need?"

"I need fifteen thousand in cash and I do not want to come in there and get it. What can we do?"

There was a moment of silence as Johnson thought about it. "Tell you what. I will bring you fifteen thousand of my own money and you can repay me when you do come in. How's that?"

Harp was speechless. "Mr. Johnson, I don't know what to say. That is way beyond what anyone has done for me."

"When I decide to trust a man, I trust them all the way. I have never been wrong. I will be out there with the money after closing. Probably about five thirty or so. Will that be okay?'

"Hell yes, anytime you can make it is fine with me." Harp hung up with a look of wonder on his face. He had never in his life met a man who put that much faith in him while knowing him so briefly

"Sarge, I got a problem." Bonny was standing there looking worried. Harp waited. "I have never bought furniture in my life. Every place I lived was furnished. I don't know what to buy for you guys."

"All you got to do is walk around the house and look at the rooms and write down what would look good in it." Harp had no idea what he was talking about but didn't want Bonny to know that. "Look around the place tonight and make a list. Just don't buy anything with pink, green, orange, or purple in it. Buy man stuff, you know, black, brown, red, like that. Make sure they deliver." He walked away before Bonny could ask him any details. He had no idea what he was talking about. Mostly, he didn't care, none of them cared, as long as the stuff was big and soft.

"Before we all get started, there's something I want to show you." He led the way to the basement, walked to the bookcase and pulled the hidden handle. Several appreciative expletives were uttered as the hidden door was revealed. Harp opened the door, flipped the light on, and led the way into the root cellar. "I was really worried that those assholes would find this—but they didn't. This is our secret. We do not mention this outside our group in any way shape or form." Harp gave each of them a hard look. Each nodded. "There is plenty of good food here, I guess. I never had canned food but, if Pauline and Lars made it, it has got to be good." Harp waited as the crew inspected the space. As if in agreement, they all ended up at the small door in the wall and looked at Harp. Harp shrugged. "I don't know where it goes but we need to find out. I would guess that it's safe and well-built but don't know how long it is or where it comes out." He grinned, "Do we have a volunteer?"

155

Kip stepped forward and said, "Hell Sarge, I'm the one who should check it out. You and Bonny are too big and Weeks' robo arm might get dirty," he said without thinking. Then he realized that what he had said could be taken as a jab at Weeks and was immediately contrite. Weeks, however, grinned and said, "Just don't get anything in your eye." Harp found a flashlight on a shelf and handed it to Kip who climbed into the tunnel without hesitating and disappeared in the dark. They looked at each other and silently agreed; the kid has balls. He belongs here. They yelled at Kip several times to ask if he was all right and he answered, "I'm cool" each time but they could tell the distance was growing. Then there was no answer at all. As they were deciding what to do, now very worried, Kip walked in behind them. He was only moderately dusty and wore a huge grin. They all jumped in surprise. Harp swore to himself at this serious lapse in security. He had allowed someone to come in the house from the outside and walk into this concealed room with the door wide open. This would never happen again. In the joy of the moment, he decided to let it go this time.

"You will never guess where it comes out." The kid said laughing. "You know that old car in that shed back there, the shed with all the machinery? This thing comes out in the trunk of that car!" Expressions of disbelief followed. "There's no trick or anything. You get to the end, go up about six steps, push up the trunk lid and you're out. You just open the door and step out! The tunnel is easy. Any of us could get out that way!" To these soldiers, knowing they had an escape route had special meaning. After more banter with Kip, they went to their duties.

While they were working on the mess in the kitchen, a car

156

horn gave notice at the front of the house. Harp went to the porch and saw Harry Johnson getting out of his car. Another man, a black man who looked to be in his late fifties, stepped from the passenger side. Harp stepped back to the front door and yelled inside, "Guys, come on out here. I want you to meet someone who has been a big help to us." Bonny came out first and stood there in his shorts with metal foot in full view. Weeks came out next wearing a sleeveless shirt, followed by Kip, who was wearing his inadequate eye patch. They stood in a row waiting for the introductions. "Mr. Johnson, this is my crew. This is Bonny, this is Weeks, and this is Kip. We all served in the same theater." He addressed his group, "Guys, you should know Mr. Johnson got the Heart in Vietnam."

Harry Johnson was speechless. He was deeply, deeply impressed with the extent of giving represented in this small group. He was a soldier and understood what he was seeing. He understood the devastating impact of such injuries. He understood the pain and rehab they had gone through. He had to fight back tears because he knew damned well that tears were the last thing these guys would want. When he found his voice, all he could think to say was, "Jesus Christ, Harper. What the hell." He stopped and took a deep breath and determined to get down to business. "I brought you the money. It's in hundreds. You can have whatever the hell else you want, too!" He walked to the porch and handed Harp a fat envelope. He looked each of them in the eye as he vigorously shook their hands and, knowing that Johnson had also been shot at and shit on, they were as earnest in the greeting as he was. He was smart enough not to thank them for their service. They knew what he was thinking.

Johnson then turned toward the black man who was still standing near the car and motioned for him to join them. "Come on up here, Calvin. I want you to meet this bunch. Men, this is Calvin Jones." Instead of walking toward the group on the porch, however, Calvin turned away and walked a few paces away from the porch and appeared to be taking deep breaths. He stopped and looked down at the ground for half a minute before turning and walking toward the porch. "Sorry Harry, sorry gentlemen, I needed a minute to get my head together."

Then it hit Harry Johnson, "Oh God, Cal, if I had known about these guys, I never would have called you. I am so sorry. Let's get back to town." He quickly started down the steps. On top of being confused at the interplay, Harp and his men were beginning to feel a little insulted by the implications. Calvin held up a hand. "Hold up, Harry. I only needed a minute. I'm okay now." Everyone waited as he gathered his thoughts. "I have not talked about this because, up until now, I have not been able to." He took a deep trembling breath and continued, "My son was killed in Afghanistan one year ago. I thought I had buried the knowing of it deep enough just to allow me to go on living. Seeing you four brought it all back. Now I realize I have got to get it out before it eats me alive."

He paused and swallowed. "He was a college graduate, the first one of our family. He did ROTC all the way through. He made First Lieutenant. One of those ignorant piss-ants over there put a bullet through the brain of my only son. My heart just can't seem to accept that." He closed his eyes. "Right now, I don't think I can say much more than that." One could imagine what he was seeing, perhaps a happy young boy playing in the yard.

158

Harp said, "Mr. Jones, we lost too many good men like that. I am sure your son was a good soldier."

Johnson stepped in. "Do want to go back to town, Cal?"

Cal shook his head. "No, tell these young men what your plan is."

Johnson was shaking his head at all the undercurrents that had suddenly infused the situation. He addressed Harp's men. "Cal had a nice little construction company that specialized in home renovations. He sold it and retired a couple of years back and has been kind of odd-jobbing around town. It seemed to me that his kind of experience is exactly what you need here to get this place back together." He looked back and forth. "What do you think, Harp? What do you think, Cal?"

Harp was not one hundred percent sure the man could stand to be around his bunch. "Cal, we would like to have you working with us. We need you. But I got to tell you, we are all kind of getting used to things ourselves. If you can put up with some pretty raw talk about what happened to us, we would like you to help us. We have all agreed that there ain't no peace in running away." Harp looked at each of the men. Each of them nodded. When he saw that, Cal made up his mind. "Let me look around inside just to see the damages."

He came out shaking his head. "I do not believe that our police could do a thing like this. I don't understand, Harry." Johnson was also shaking his head and agreed. Cal said, "I'll be back in the morning with most of the tools we'll need. That okay with you?" All agreed. Everybody shook hands, closing the deal. Somehow, from their eyes, with gazes full of more knowledge than young men should possess, and the grip of strong hands that had saved lives and taken lives, Calvin Jones found a measure of calming which had eluded him since his son's death. Instinctively, he knew this was the right thing to do. He just might find the peace that eluded him by working alongside others who were recovering.

Just as Harry and Cal began the walk to their car, another car pulled up. They all watched as Edie Martin gathered her materials and puffed her way from the car. When the full impact of what she was seeing finally hit, her mouth dropped open. "My Gawd, Harry. What the hell is going on?"

"What do you mean, Edie?" He knew why she was here. He was smiling. "We were just arranging for Calvin to assist Mr. Harper and his men in repairing the damages made to this house by Sheriff Senter's deputies."

While everyone watched, she focused on Johnson. "Men? What do you mean, 'His men'?" She then caught herself and addressed Harp. "Excuse me, Mr. Harper. I kind of had the idea you were about ready to sell the place. What's this about repairing damages? Who are these…these *men?*" She was looking with some puzzlement at the damaged crew standing on the porch. They did not miss the glance or the meaning. "We need to have a talk, Mr. Harper," she said somewhat imperiously, as if she were in charge, and while glaring at everyone present. "And we need to talk privately." She dismissed Bonny, Weeks, and Kip with a sniff.

"Mrs. Martin, anything you want to say to me you can say in front of everyone here." Harp gestured toward his men. "These are my partners." He pointed at Johnson. "He is my banker." Then he pointed at Jones, "And he is my project superintendent." They all grinned at the new title which had just been bestowed upon Jones.

Martin did not think it was funny. "Mr. Harper," she snapped, "I have come to discuss some serious business of great importance, and I think you will want to listen." She stared at Johnson, waiting for him to say something. At this, Johnson knew it was time for him to be professional. "Okay, Edie, we were ready to go anyway." He motioned Jones toward their car and waved at the men on the porch. Jones waved and said he would see them in the morning.

Martin walked away from the house and waited for Harp to join her. When he had gotten closer, she turned her back to the house. "Mr. Harper, I believe that you simply do not appreciate the situation you are in." Harp waited. "To my client, this property is very important and it is very important that we do the sale as quickly as possible. All I can tell you is that it is a piece of a much larger puzzle." Harp just listened, which added to her exasperation. "My client has raised the offer to a flat four million for the property," she said with great satisfaction. She watched Harp for a reaction to that number, but he was careful to reveal nothing. "The only requirement is that the property be vacated within five days and, of course, the mineral rights go to the buyer. You may keep any part of the attached real property you wish. That means the equipment and furnishings." She lowered the paper she was reading from and waited.

"Mrs. Martin, my position hasn't changed. Of course, I am going to sell this place. But I am not in any hurry and I want to spend some time with these guys. You are just going to have to wait." He started to walk away. "Mr. Harper!" she said with surprising vehemence, "You do not have the luxury of taking your time! This deal could fall through!"

Harp stopped and turned back. "What is the real deal here, Mrs. Martin? What the hell is going on? Can you tell me honestly? If we are talking about that gas thing, why not just say so?"

She replied with genuine anguish, "I don't know, damn it. Can't you just give me a date when you will sell? I have to report something to my client!"

"Nope. Can't do that. Talk to you later." Harp walked away in wonder. He could not believe he just turned down four million bucks. If her "client" was willing to offer that much, though, it might not be a bad idea to wait for an even bigger offer. He heard her car door slam loudly and motor race as she tore back down the drive. He was strangely unconcerned. He could not forget how happy he was with nothing. It certainly was less complicated.

"What did she want, Sarge?" Kip asked. Harp was walking through the house picking up broken pieces of glass and wood. He stopped in the office to see what Kip was doing. Kip was trying to make sense out of the mess in there. He had cleared an area and was sitting on the floor looking at his cell phone.

"She brought another offer for this place. I'll give you all the details later. How's it going?"

Kip smiled. "It's better than I thought. They didn't manage to ruin the modem and I've linked up to the internet on my cell phone. So, we are going to have access when we get a computer."

"Good going, Kip." Harp was surprised at the casualness with which he was regarding a windfall of four million bucks. But, he was even more surprised at the feeling that there were things happening here that were more important than money. Must be I'm getting soft-headed, he said to himself.

They spent another night in relative discomfort sacking out

wherever they could find a reasonable spot to throw a quilt or blanket. Something of importance happened during the night. For the first time in a very long time, Weeks slept without the dreams. He slept the night through on a hard mattress foundation and awoke feeling rested. He could not explain what had happened nor could he find words to show the importance of it. There were no zips of passing rounds, no incoming mortars, no red purple splashes of his flesh, their flesh, no screams; finally, just sweet silence. Kip asked him what he was grinning about. Weeks said it was nothing.

They arose early, opened canned fruit, and moaned about the lack of coffee. Their moaning turned to expressions of glee when Calvin Jones arrived pulling a trailer full of equipment behind a pickup. He also carried enough coffee and doughnuts for everyone to totally pig out on sugar and caffeine. Jones drank his coffee and ate one pastry while listening to the jokes and gibes going among Harp's group. He was impressed that men who had been hurt so badly could behave so normally. He was aware of the respect that all felt toward Harp. He was also aware that Harp took that responsibility very seriously.

With breakfast out of the way, Harp got down to business. "Mr. Jones, we are ready to follow your orders. Just tell us what to do and show us how to do it."

Jones responded, "The first thing you got to do is call me Cal. You call me Mr. Jones and I start looking around to see who you're talking to." Heads nodded, smiling.

"The next thing is, I've spend a long time heading up my own crew and I might tend to get a little bossy sometimes. When I do, kind of remind me that I am working for you now." He smiled.

"When it sounds like I am giving an order, act like you heard a polite request."

Weeks, keeping a straight face, said, "Cal, you ain't seen bossy 'till you seen Sergeant Harper give orders!" Kip and Bonny laughed at the comical scowl on Harp's face at this observation. "But, I wouldn't worry, we are all used to complaining about things we don't like — knowing ain't nothing going to change."

Harp resumed after the chuckles ended, "Okay, here's how we're going to start. Bonny is going to head out on his buying trip. He might be gone overnight. I need to do a little transfer operation and will be gone for a couple of hours. Weeks and Kip will stay here and work with Cal. We'll talk about what we are going to do for food later. Questions?" Harp wished he could ask one of the men to come with him to pick up that chest from the storage locker. He would enjoy time together with any one of them on the long drive. But, if he were to get stopped and searched, his ass was grass. So, if he went down, it would be only him charged with the possession of this stuff. He knew he should get rid of it, but that would almost be as difficult as keeping it. Plus, he now had a place for it that was secure. He was tired of hauling it around but would decide later. Bottom line was, he had to go alone.

When Harp stood up, the day began. Cal, Weeks, and Kip went to Cal's trailer to commence setting up equipment. Harp drove off in the Dodge pickup. Bonny took the Ford truck to buy furniture and other supplies. Each of them felt what men need to feel: duty, pride, loyalty, and friendship. For the moment in the lives of these five men, there was the most elusive of all feelings, the feeling of peace.

The first call to Adam was from Edie Martin. She was very

aggravated. "You won't believe what's going on out there. There's four of them now! In addition to Harper, there's a guy with no foot, one with no arm, and one with half his face gone!" She was wiping her face with a handkerchief.

Adam listened in alarm. Who the hell were these new guys? "Did you get any names? Who are they?"

"Harper just said they were his partners. He said Harry was his banker and Cal Jones was his project superintendent. He also said anything I had to say I could say in front of them." Martin was waving her free hand as she talked. "It was like he wanted all of them to know what I was doing. It was like I was wasting his damn time offering four goddamned million dollars! I just don't think this guy Harper has very much business experience. I could just scream!" She collapsed backward into her chair, frantic that her seven percent was getting away.

"Well, what did he say?"

Martin wanted to scream at Adam but took a deep breath and went on. "He said the same thing as he said before. He said, yes, he's going to sell but he says he's not ready yet, whatever the hell that means. The bottom line is that he did not accept the offer. How could a goddamned unemployed retired Army guy turn down four mil?"

Adam did not understand either. But a murmured, "Um, hm," was his sole response.

Martin continued. "I'll tell you something else. Harry Johnson was the one who brought Cal Jones to oversee the repairs. I think Johnson and Harper are real close for some reason. And, dammit all, all the damage those idiot deputies did has only slowed everything down instead of getting us closer to a sale.

To be honest, I don't know what we can do right now." The line clicked and Martin realized Adam had hung up.

Adam didn't know either. He *did* know that it had been mere weeks since he had stumbled across that article in a scientific journal. That information had driven Adam to develop his own study, which had revealed an astounding potential. Only he and one other person knew this so far, but time was running out. In any day, any moment, the same thing could occur to somebody else and then the rush would be on. Even worse, nature could interfere in a big, big way, blowing his plans all to hell and gone. Adam knew that all involved suspected that his acquisitions of property and mineral rights were all about natural gas. That was fine with him. It was the perfect camouflage for his real scheme. Adam realized that it was time to rethink that scheme. So far, his plans had been derailed by the ignorance of the principals involved. He had been certain that Pauline Kuykendahl would sell after her husband died. Then he was certain that her heirs would sell after her death. Adam's people could not find any living relatives and Parsnip was the executor, so buying the property was a given.

Then, somehow, they had come up with a retired Army drunk and again, Adam felt the sale was guaranteed. But, *this* drunk just happened to be a stubborn fool who would rather hang out with some cripples than become an overnight millionaire. Apparently, they just wanted to party for a while and then collect the money when they felt like it. Normally, Adam would have put it on the back burner and waited them out. Now, however, he simply did not have the time for that. It was time to be more aggressive with these fools

There was a number a person could call, with total anonymity of course, and request that things be done. Only the very top of the food chain knew it. He had used it before. It was very simple. You called the number from any untraceable phone, described your need, then mailed twenty thousand dollars in cash to a certain box number. When the money was received, the requisition was met. Adam realized that more fatalities would invite too much speculation. A fire, on the other hand, would be entirely plausible with a house full of handicapped, reckless men. Adam placed the order.

12

HARP HAD PICKED UP THE LOCKER WITH NO TROUBLE.
He did not bother telling the management that the storage unit
was empty. They would know when it was opened at the end of
his contract. He had the assemblage of highly illegal equipment
stored behind the front seats but was still concerned about its
visibility. It could be disastrous if he were stopped and ordered to
open the locker. Then it came to him that he could kill two birds
with one stone. He decided to go grocery shopping again but
with two aims. He wanted lots and lots of those little plastic grocery bags piled up inside the truck cab. Lord knows they needed
everything. When he was done, the entire inside of the truck was
filled with white plastic grocery bags. He made sure that loaves
of bread, cereal boxes, celery stalks and such were evident everywhere. Proud of his camouflage, he resumed the drive home.

As it turned out, he was wise to be prudent. As soon as he
crossed the county line, one of Senter's men began to follow him.
Harp felt that he could very likely be pulled over in Senter's dis-
trict sooner or later. It was sooner. The lights came on and the

siren wailed. Harp immediately drove to the shoulder of the road. He knew the drill, both hands on the steering wheel, license and insurance at the ready. Harp had both.

One of the deputies who had no doubt trashed his house came to the side of the truck. He was a tall round-shouldered local boy whose badge merely said Button. He made it through high school then studied Criminal Justice at the local tech school. He had not been promoted so far. His father was a friend of Sheriff Senter and implored the Sheriff to give him a job. As trained, he stood slightly behind the truck door, hand casually near his weapon. "License and insurance please."

Harp handed them over and asked very politely, "Is there a problem, officer?" But the man had walked off. He was going to go through the whole drill, Harp reasoned, some of the extra attention that Senter had promised. Check the plates to see if it was stolen, or belonged to a wanted person. What Harp did not know was that Deputy Button was reporting Harp's location to the boss and asking for further instructions. Senter asked Button what Harp was driving and carrying. He also asked Button if Harp had done anything he could be charged with. Button reported that Harp had not done anything illegal and his truck was full of groceries. Senter told Button to hassle him a little bit and let him go.

Harp was watching in the rear-view mirror stuck on the side of the door. Button strode toward Harp with a new tension in his walk, as if he were getting prepared for something. Harp knew trouble was coming and prepared himself to remain cool, no matter what. He simply could not allow his truck to be searched. This time Button walked to a stop right outside Harp's window. He was tapping Harp's license and insurance card on this thumbnail.

To Harp, a man familiar with the way men gird for battle, Button was a joke.

"You think you're pretty tough, don't you, Harper." Harp thought, if this kid only knew.

"No sir, I am just an old veteran, trying to get by on my little old farm." Sincerity was dripping from Harp's voice. It was a little too obvious.

"Don't get smart with me, asshole. Just because you got lucky with those jerks at the store doesn't mean you can get away with giving me any shit. Got it?" Button continued, "If I had been there, I would have shoved that pipe up your ass. And that's after I beat your brains out with it."

Meekly, looking at the steering wheel, Harp nodded. If only this idiot knew what he was capable of. Now, Button couldn't stop. "Speaking of that weapon which you so conveniently misplaced, we had a real good time looking for it at your little old farm house." Button leaned down to make sure Harp could see his shit-eating grin. What Button could not have known was that, at that moment, he was probably as close to death as he would ever get. Harp could have snatched him into the cab of the truck and twisted his neck so quickly that Button would be dead without knowing how he died. But, Harp's composure did not break. He said nothing. The white knuckles of the scarred hands gripping the steering wheel might have given him away, had Button had the experience to notice.

"Just as I thought, Harper. All mouth, no action." He straightened up and threw the documents into Harp's lap with a contemptuous flip. "Hit the road, asshole, and watch yourself 'cause we'll be watching you."

Button was standing beside his car, hands on hips, wearing a sneering grin as Harp pulled back onto the road. Watching in the mirror, Harp watched as Button thrust his hips forward and grabbed his crotch as he waved at Harp and pointed down. That gesture was the final straw for Harp. It served to focus his anger and desire for revenge on a name, a person. Button would pay. Harp didn't know how just yet, but he would think of something.

Harp drove into a scene of great activity. Cal's truck, equipment trailer, Bonny's car, the ATV, and the dumpster, were parked helter skelter. As he pulled in, he watched as a large plastic garbage can full of broken sheetrock wafted from the back door to the edge of the dumpster where it was lifted over the edge and the contents spilled. He knew it had to be Weeks because Kip couldn't have carried the thing.

Harp's first duty was to greet a happy dog who had been mostly interested in all that was going on but was still worried that his master was not there. After they were sufficiently reacquainted, Harp gathered up two fistfuls of plastic bag handles and entered the kitchen. He stood there amazed that they had done so much in just a few hours. As far as he could tell, all the broken stuff was gone. The floor was not clean, but it was clear of debris. The runners and rugs were gone, leaving bare hardwood floors. The walls were clear of all paintings and hangings and the overall appearance was stark, with many white patches amid darker wall colors.

Kip and Weeks spied Harp at the same time and yelped greetings from down the hall to the living room. They were covered head to toe in white dust from sanding dry wall patch. Cal was not in sight but Weeks said he was upstairs. Harp motioned for them to come and carry groceries—which included a couple of cases of beer. The fridge and freezer still worked, so they could put the perishables away. They found places to put all the provisions Harp had brought home. Harp asked Weeks to take the strange locker down to the root cellar. They were alone when he made the request. Weeks looked at the markings on the locker and gave Harp a questioning look. Harp just said, "Don't ask." He also told him to be sure Cal was upstairs before he opened the door to the root cellar. Harp was not quite ready to bring Cal into that level of confidence. Weeks understood. Harp went up to the second floor and found Cal cutting a patch for a hole in the sheetrock. Cal stood up slowly from where he had been kneeling on the floor. He too was covered in white dust. He looked somberly at his visitor.

"These are really good boys, Mr. Harper," he said quietly, "How is it that this country can send boys like these off to get maimed and killed? I don't understand politics any more at all." He was shaking his head.

"Cal, I do not think that any country anywhere has ever tried to fight a war with old men. That's what they ought to do. Make the old sonsabitches who start the wars *fight* the wars." They stood for a while in silent agreement before Cal shrugged and went back to work. Both knew that one of the big problems with that approach to war was that young men *wanted* to fight. Old men did not.

"A couple more days and we will be ready to paint," Cal opined. "You got any idea of colors you all would like?" Harp gave it some thought and concluded that it would probably be best to wait and see what the furniture Bonny bought looked like. He conveyed this to Cal who nodded in agreement. The fact was that neither had any idea what color they would like. Harp thought that they would probably paint the old colors back in. That would solve one of the world's most hopeless endeavors: asking a man what color he thought a room should be. Nine times out of ten it would be off white or beige.

It rained during the night. Not especially hard, but enough to bring a new shade of green to all the land around the house. The crew rose early, knowing that Cal would show up any time. It was also easy to get up because they were still sleeping on mattress foundations wrapped in quilts and blankets. But, no matter what, each man rose from his rest looking forward to the day. And, as yet unable to escape a cynicism for which none of them could be blamed, each was secretly cradling this new optimism to his chest, like protecting a newborn from a world he knew with certainty could snatch it away. Harp was getting a sense of this and was frightened at the responsibility it portended. Was he going to be able to protect these guys? Did he deserve their trust and respect?

Weeks made coffee and the smell brought back different memories for each of them. Kip thought of the kitchen in his father's estate. He was not encouraged to mingle with the staff, but he enjoyed having breakfast at the big island in the middle of the room. Everyone was quieter when he was there and that somehow bothered him. He never felt that he had *earned* the privilege that he was accorded by these hard-working people. One could not explain that, however, to a staff that was made separate by the family's wealth. Nevertheless, the kitchen had the wonderful smell of expensive coffee in the morning. Kip was not allowed to drink it when he was a boy, but he would sometimes pour a little in a Coke bottle. He would retreat to his bedroom where he tried to sip it like an adult, smacking his lips and saying, "Man, that's good coffee!"

Weeks thought of his grandfather. His grandfather knew how to enjoy his morning coffee. He would carefully pour the brew into a deep saucer where it would quickly cool, then sip it slowly. The old man had explained once that, during the depression, they made ersatz coffee out of just about any seed they could find and roast. It was always terrible because the memory of good coffee, once you've had it, is indelibly printed on the brain. To a watching young Phillip, it seemed like the revered father of his father was transported as he closed his eyes and slowly sipped the rapidly cooling liquid. Weeks wished he could someday enjoy it the same way. It never worked. All he tasted was coffee. He had no pictures to go with it. His family never had breakfast together. Everybody was working beginning too early in the day. He had the memory of his grandfather, however, and that had to be enough.

Instead of coffee, the young Horace Harper was forever trying to score a stolen soft drink and, better yet, a bottle of beer or wine. He had had no moments when he might have relaxed in a safe warm place while slowly sipping a fine brew. As a matter of fact, in the miserable wet cold of the New Jersey winter, the challenge was often just finding that warm place. Harp was the product of foster homes in the city. His father was a seaman who sailed away when he was three and never sailed back. His mother was drowsily inattentive to anything but her vodka supply which, during a period of overabundance, exceeded the limits of her liver. This was about the time when his nickname became Harp, the short version of his last name. It was what his fellow NCO's called him. Once there were friends from around the world who called him that, but he had no idea where they were now. Most were dead. He secretly liked the name. It gave him an identity separate from the military. Unlike many men with childhood nicknames, he still thought of his with nostalgia.

It was not until he had gone through boot camp and was drawing guard duty that he found the value in strong coffee. Even then he was not drinking for flavor—but for its ability to keep him awake. Finally, during a short stint in Germany, he found that coffee and German pastries were something to which he looked forward. From that time, he made sure that it was there in the morning, hot and black, and sometimes even in the evening. He was one of the lucky ones who slept well after an evening coffee.

Thus, accompanied by large cups of steaming coffee, the limping sergeant, the one-armed man, the one-eyed man, and the mongrel dog, sat quietly on the front porch looking at a refreshed land decorated in wildflowers and many, many shades of green. The ordinary observer would not know it, but this quiet study of Harp's farm included a new level of scrutiny practiced by four individuals whose lives once depended on seeing land as a series of hiding places. They couldn't help it. They sat and slowly rocked and studied the picture and, in time, they relaxed and enjoyed the panorama before them.

This terrain seemed to radiate peace, and these damaged souls felt that peace. The rockers creaked and rhythmically bumped back and forth across joints between boards in the porch floor. Crows cawed in the distance and birds carried out their business with tweets and trills in their usual colorful but harried fashion. It was a memorable moment for each of them.

175

Kip said it first. "I don't want to move, Sarge. I want to sit here and rock and pretend nothing hurts and I can see out of both eyes and I got a future." He rocked some more. "The thing is, right now, I am happy. I didn't think I could ever be happy again."

"You don't have to move if you don't want to," Harp said. "I don't much feel like it either. Also, a man as smart as you has always got a future. Besides, you're rich." They all rocked some more.

As they watched, Cal turned off the road and rolled up the driveway to stop in front of the porch instead of driving around the back as usual. He stepped from his car and took in the scene as the three men and a dog sat and rocked. Cal grinned and said, "Next time I come out here I'm going to bring me a rocker. You all look like you was planted in those chairs and danged if I don't want to just sit up there, too. This is truly some kind of beautiful morning."

"Come on up, Cal." Harp said as he stood up. "You can take my chair while I go feed this ugly beast who calls himself a dog. It won't hurt if we start a little late this morning." Fart and Harp went back in through the front door to the mud room where he was still being fed. The dog was spending more and more time inside as the work progressed and doors stood open. So far, he had been good. Trust was growing that he had been disarmed.

To a man of Cal's age, it was too good an offer to refuse. He joined Weeks and Kip without another word and he too enjoyed the silence of the moment. Weeks asked Cal if he knew how to operate all the equipment on the farm. Cal said that, generally speaking, if it had a motor, he could drive it. Weeks said that he and Bonny wanted to learn how to operate the big tractor with the bush hog attachment. Cal said it would be no problem. They just needed to find the time. Their pleasant interlude was broken by the welcome return of Bonny announced by the very loud horn of his truck. They had not been worried, but each of them was aware of the responsibility they had heaped on Bonny's shoulders. The big Ford cruised up the drive and on around behind the house. They all gathered around him and commenced a ritual of knuckle bumps and back slaps. Bonny was grinning in triumph as he described his buying spree. "Guys, I bought a house full of furniture and I hand-picked every damned piece. You're going to love it! It will all be delivered here tomorrow and, get this, they will even bring it in and put it where we want it!" He was gesturing with both arms. "When they saw how much I was buying, they gave me enough bedding for each of the beds for free!" Having once slept for months in their clothes on cots in hot tents, no one gave the slightest thought to the reality of cheap two hundred count sheets and polyester blankets. It was a non-issue.

Bonny was not done. "Kip, I went to a computer store and got you the best Dell laptop they had. It has all the storage you'll ever need. Something called terabytes." He pulled a large flat box from the front seat of the truck and proudly handed it to Kip, who was eager to get on line. "And," he added with a flourish, "it comes with a free printer and modem." He bowed to a round of applause. With great pride, he handed cash back to Harp. "And I didn't even spend all the money!"

Cal's voice broke into the cheerful banter. "Gentlemen, I hate to be the bearer of bad news, but we are nowhere near ready to bring furniture into this house." He waited out a chorus of exaggerated groans. He continued, "However, if we bust our humps the rest of the day, we can finish patching and sanding the sheetrock and get all the wiring fixed. We can hang lighting fixtures later. After that, we have got to clean everything tonight. We cannot bring new furniture into a house full of plaster dust." He paused while that news was digested. "We can paint around furniture after we bring it in so that is not a problem. You will just have to decide what colors you want." Seeing the looks on their faces, he suggested, "I would go back with the original colors if I were you." This suggestion was received with great relief. Cal turned and strode purposefully toward the house. Harp turned to follow Cal and announced, "You heard the man, let's get started."

Bonny quickly said that he had thought of some more things he needed to buy and would be back in the morning. He was grabbed by several arms and dragged toward the house. After several hours of mudding joints and sanding them smooth, the wall and ceiling repairs were done. Then with brooms, an old vacuum cleaner and lots of rags made from old clothes, they began wiping down the whole house. The dumpster was soon full, the beer was gone, and so was the joyful energy with which they had started. They were ready for the furniture. They were ready for sleep.

But earlier in the evening, while they were working, all the lights were on, a radio was playing, and shouting from room to room was common. A car with lights out silently cruised to a stop on the road at the base of the drive, unnoticed by the busy workers. Deputy Button got out and skulked up the long driveway close enough to see what was going inside the open windows. He saw with surprise a happy crew of workers moving in and out of rooms as they were cleaning the house. Even at a distance he could see that some of the holes that had been patched were ones he had put there himself and grinned with satisfaction. He looked forward to doing it again. All they needed was another excuse to conduct a search, and that was an easy thing to come up with. Button smirked as he unzipped his fly and pissed on the driveway and waved his weenie at the house. Then he sauntered back to his darkened patrol car and quietly drove off.

It was true that none of the men in the house were aware of the deputy's visit. Fart, however, was bothered by all that dust and was hunkered down in the garage. He was aware. He lay in the dark between vehicles. Basically a friendly dog, he was not the kind trained to attack. He was merely inclined to give notice of things that bothered him. This human in the driveway definitely bothered him. He walked over to the open door to the kitchen and, when he saw Harp, emitted a small bark. Harp walked over to the door and watched as his canine friend walked a few steps and looked over his shoulder. It was an instinctual thing for the experienced Army man to follow the dog just to see what the trouble was. He had arrived at a spot in the darkness of the garage just in time to see Button piss on his driveway. It would be a gross understatement to say that this visit pissed him off.

The first thing it did was ignite a hot anger at the contemptuous gesture. But, more rationally, it concerned him that they were obviously not under an intermittent observation like he had assumed. These guys were coming onto his land under cover of darkness, maybe every night. That made it serious. That meant a new level of vigilance would be necessary. He decided not to ruin the mood this evening, but they would have to have a serious

179

meeting in the morning before Cal arrived. After they watched Button return to his darkened car, the dog got a good scruffling and lots of praise for his alertness and Harp went back inside to resume work.

Just after daybreak, after each man had scrounged an early breakfast from the many kinds of food available, the old Sarge called the meeting to order. "We need to talk about some things before Cal gets here. Like I explained before, there is some weird shit going on out here. This place is way too important to someone. I am happy to let them have it, but I want to know what's going on first. You need to know that it is possible that the deaths of Pauline and Lars were maybe not accidents." Harp waited until the shocked murmurs were finished. "I said *maybe*. We don't really know. I do hope to find out some day. Anyway, I bring all this up because we had a visit last night by one of that bunch of deputies who did all this." He waved his arm around the kitchen where they all sat. "This guy, his name is Button, came up the drive and watched us for a while. Fart saw him and let me know. He was here maybe five minutes, and then he pissed on the driveway and wagged his pecker at the house and us." Harp waited until that sunk in. "What could be worse is that these guys could pretty easily find an excuse to come out here and wreck the place again."

"How come these miserable dickwads can do stuff like this and get away with it?" Weeks blurted. "Don't we have any rights at all?"

"We have the right to deny access to our home unless they have a warrant," Harp explained. "But a warrant is an easy thing for a sheriff to get." He waited. "I have said from the beginning that I was going to sell the place. But I mean to sell it in my own good time. And, every time they do something like this, it makes me want to wait even longer before I turn it over to the bastards." Vigorous nodding supported this sentiment. "My feeling right now is that I want to wait a couple of weeks, maybe a month, before I sell it. Is that okay with you?"

The question was answered with a chorus of profane agreement. "I have to tell you that it might get a little hairy out here. We just don't know what's going to happen next, but we need a plan. I got some ideas I want to run by you. But, before we get into planning, I need to know if each of you wants to stay on. Most of the work is done and if any of you want to leave, I'll pay the agreed amount and you can leave with no hard feelings." He quit talking and looked each of them in the eye. "Something I want each of you to completely understand, you are invited to stay as long as you want." Harp had to look down at the floor for a minute. "I *want* you to stay. Okay." They knew that it was a rare time when this hard-assed veteran would get emotional.

Kip said, "I like it here. This is what I need. I am not ready for the world and I know it."

Bonny said, "Sarge, I can go back to what I was doing any time. It's nowhere near as fun as this."

Weeks stood up and said, "You all know that coming out here saved my life. I am not leaving until somebody drags my ass away." He paused, "I can talk about the uh, you know, with you guys and this is the first time I been able to do that."

"Okay, we need to assume that we are under pretty constant surveillance, for what reason I do not know. All I know is that someone is really interested in what we are doing." He told them about the vantage point near the south spring. "I think we need to start keeping a kind of irregular day and night watch going. Maybe we are not in danger but still need to know who is watching and when they are watching. What I would like to propose is that we kind of schedule ourselves to patrol on an irregular basis. Some nights I can't sleep so I'll get up and walk around. If you all did the same, I think we could cover it. What do you say?"

Harp was very pleased when each of the men volunteered for first night watch. "Okay, let's get to work. Cal will be here any minute. And, remember, we don't want to involve Cal in any of this. He will still live here after we're gone. And, Kip, I want you to get busy on the computer. We need information on this natural gas business, particularly in this part of the state." Bonny and Weeks jumped up and left the room.

Kip lagged behind and objected. "Sarge, I need to do my part in the cleanup. It's not fair that you guys have to do all the dirty work while I sit on my ass at a computer."

"Believe me, Kip, what you will be doing is more important than cleaning this place up. We have got to know what we're dealing with here. Why is this place so damned important?" Harp slapped him on the shoulder and gave him a playful shove. Kip smiled and reluctantly returned to the office to finish hooking everything up and start his search. Cal soon drove in with his usual supply of coffee and pastries. He obviously enjoyed bringing these things, so no one mentioned having already eaten or asked about the cost. He was pleased to see that work had already started and he wouldn't have to do any cajoling.

It was a good thing—because a huge van soon powered its way up the drive and stopped near the front steps where its air brakes barked like a startled dog. After talking to Harp and walking around behind the house, the unloading crew decided it would be just as easy going in the front door as the back. They backed the rig close to the front steps and ran a metal bridge to the porch, then wheeled everything in. Bonny beamed with pride as piece after piece of leather furniture in different shades of brown were brought in. Harp's crew told the unloaders where each piece should go and were excitedly dropping into the chairs and sofas as they were set into place. Kip was the only one who thought that having furniture pretty much all the same color might be a little monotonous. But then, he was the only one who had ever lived in a home that had been professionally decorated. He said nothing. Cal watched in amusement, shaking his head at their youthful antics. He too said nothing. He concluded that, if that's what they want to do, then they damned well ought to do it. They surely did earn it.

Mailman Pierce, being naturally nosy and wanting something to report, brought the mail all the way up the drive instead of leaving it in the box on the road. He saw Cal watching and smiling. Pierce eased himself from his old Jeep converted to right-hand drive and walked up to Cal. "What the hell is going on, Cal? It looks like those boys are settling in for a while. Surely they ain't going to try to run this place, are they?"

Cal wondered at the sound of peevishness in Pierce's voice. Why would this postman care? "I'll tell you one thing, Pierce, they are definitely not boys, and they are going to stay for a while."

Pierce immediately changed his tone and said, "Don't get me wrong, Cal. I wish them boys, I mean men, all the luck in the world. But we both know they ain't farmers and this here is a farm. A man's got a right to be curious." Cal said nothing. Feeling slightly rebuffed, Pierce handed Cal a packet of ubiquitous flyers and drove off.

The rest of the day was dedicated to getting everything settled. The beds were made, rugs were laid, the kitchen table and chairs were ready for meals, and the living room was ready for a satisfied review of the day's activities. Comfortably ensconced in the smooth leather of the sofa and recliners, they all put their feet up and enjoyed the first drink of the day. Harp drank bourbon neat and the rest drank beer. All that was left was to paint, and Cal would be back in the morning with shades of paint that would approximate the current colors. They grinned at each other and remained mostly silent, afraid that anything they said would break the mood.

The painting went quickly. Five men with paint rollers and just a passing concern for evenness of application can move pretty damned fast. By noon, every room was done and the furniture was uncovered and pushed back into place. All that was left to work on were the floors. Cal said they would have to be refinished or covered, Harp's option. Harp said that he would decide later. He was so happy to have the house back to a livable condition, he did not want to bother with any more interior work for a long time. But they weren't done. Cal reminded them that outbuildings needed repair, equipment needed maintenance, and lots of junk needed to be gathered and thrown into the dumpster. He added that he did not need to be on hand for that so he guessed he was done. Harp disagreed. "Cal, we don't feel you are done here. You have really helped us and we owe you. I want you to know that you are always welcome out here, and I mean anytime." Harp held out his hand for a shake followed by the others

Bonny said, "Sarge, if it's all right with you, I'm going to have Cal show me how to get the big tractor running and get it hooked up to a mower. I don't even know what a south forty is but I want to go cut the alfalfa on it." They chuckled at the allusion. "Cal, you think you could show me how to do that?" Cal grinned and replied that he would love to. He did not want to go back to the monotonous life he had been living, and operating any kind of big machinery was an old love. "You can also show me what alfalfa is," Bonny said as they walked out the door.

Weeks then asked if he could take the ATV and get to know the place. Harp thought taking the ATV out would be a good idea and suggested that Weeks take the map of the farm with him. Weeks wanted to get the lay of the land and, just for the hell of it, identify places of concealment and ambush. He also wanted some time alone to simply enjoy the ongoing return of sanity. Once unable to stop peering into his own mind and fearing what he might see, Weeks could now look into his head just when he wanted to. He saw that the fog was clearing. He could control his thoughts. He could stop the dance of the demons. Though he knew that many issues remained, some of the rats, spiders, and goblins were gone. Heretofore, he could not imagine ever again feeling contentment. Now, he thought with wry amusement, he was afraid of losing the joy he felt. It would take a good while for his damaged psyche to trust this feeling.

With mild resentment, Kip went back to work on the computer. He had found extensive information on developments in gas drilling and was preparing an informal report in language they all could understand—which meant he had to understand it first. He could not know that the most recent, most staggering development in this part of the state was known to just one man. And that man was desperate to protect this secret as long as he could. It was just a matter of time before everyone knew, but if he could get this farm under his control first, it wouldn't matter who found out. He could not know that there were signs of eminent danger a few hundred yards from the house.

Harp watched as Bonny and Cal drove the tractor from the shed. He watched as Weeks drove off in the ATV with Fart happily sitting in the front seat. He checked on Kip and saw that he was so engrossed in his research, he did not even look up. This was a good moment to get some articles from the root cellar. He still did not want the rest to know what was in the tan locker. Maybe later. For the time being, he removed three things, the night vision goggles, the disabling spray, and a military grade Taser. This Taser was not designed to function like a civilian model. It had the extra power to instantly incapacitate an enemy combatant. The victim did not even twitch but just dropped in his tracks like a stone.

He put the spray, contained in its can which looked like a foot spray, in his shaving kit. The Taser was the only weapon he was going to use for the night patrols. It was quiet, easy to hide, and very effective. He had considered the various firearms and left them there. He was not ready to incriminate the others in the event of another "search" by the Sheriff. That done, this one-time Trenton bar fly who only wanted to be left alone, and who now was somehow responsible for a crew of recovering but damaged soldiers, decided that he needed a nap. He was going to take first watch and he wanted to be ready. As he drifted off, he reviewed the things that needed his attention. He had to get Kip to find

186

an independent water lab to check those samples. He had to re-member to give Kip the jump drive he took from the cabin. And, dammit all, they would have to get out there and see what the hell was so important down in that hole. Then he was sleeping.

He began his watch around nine. It was no problem for him to be wandering around the farmstead in the dark. It was a warm night with a good moon and clear skies and he could see well enough without the goggles. It was, in fact, a peaceful way to reac-quaint himself with the various proximities of the many structures around the house. He smiled as he recalled the events of the day. Plus, for a change he didn't have to talk to anyone. He missed his silent moments at the Battle. Bonny had been so pleased and ex-cited to be operating the tractor and mower. He was now planning to mow anything over a half foot tall. Cal just laughed. Harp didn't care. He had no idea what was growing out there.

Weeks had been gone for a long time in the afternoon and said he had covered just about every square foot of Harp's acreage and found all the boundaries. He had taken Fart with him and both enjoyed the detailed exploration. Harp had even felt a mo-ment's jealousy when Fart quickly climbed aboard with Weeks but realized that their time together was good for both. When they returned, the sorry mutt had anxiously searched for his mas-ter and spent the rest of the day by his side to make up for what might have been perceived as disloyalty. Harp was so pleased to have him back by his side, he was easily forgiven. This mongrel now sat at Harp's feet helping him keep watch.

Weeks had seen each of the springs and saw no problems. The water looked good with no obvious odor. He went to the lookout point and found no indication of recent use. Weeks had even found both old oil wells. They had been capped with a three to four-foot-high system of rusted pipes, bolts, and caps and were now hidden in clumps of bushes. Curiously, he said that they were both hot to the touch and he swore they were vibrating very lightly. He was especially equipped to sense this because he could hold the metal of his prosthetic arm against the metal of the capping apparatus and feel what others might not. None of them had any idea what this development meant but, in any case, it was dismissed as a low priority for now. The small bubbles around the edges of the seals did not even register.

Kip was pleased to report that he had just about finished his research on the fracking business. He said he needed another day and he had to get the printer connected and operable. Bonny reminded everyone that it was a *free* printer. Kip also checked the contents of the jump drive Harp had taken from the hunting camp and said it was just three columns of dates and volume measurement after each date. He also found the address and phone number of a private water lab which offered confidential water quality evaluations. It was, however, close to Pittsburgh and Harp was not ready to commit the time to getting the jars down there. They were safe in the root cellar.

The painting was done and all the other things for which they needed Cal were finished. They all wished they could come up with some more reasons to get him out to the farm but, for the moment, he was not needed. They assured him that he was welcome any time anyway and they looked forward to seeing him soon. He promised he would visit often.

While woolgathering, he heard the back door open quietly. Bonny's voice easily carried in the silence. "Sarge?"

"Over here." He was not ready to go in but knew that Bonny would want to pull his shift. They bumped fists.

"Anything going on?"

"Nah. It's really quiet."

They stood in easy camaraderie and enjoyed the night. "This sure is different than the sandbox, huh, Sarge?"

"No shit."

Even in the dark, Harp could tell that Bonny was ruminating over something.

"Come on, Bonny, you got something on your mind. Spit it out."

"Sarge, I had more fun today than any time in years. I felt like I belonged on that damned tractor. I could feel the thing in my fingers and feet. I could tell how hard it was working through the seat of my pants. Does that make any sense?"

Harp was honest. He laughed and told him no.

Bonny was just slightly miffed. "I'm serious. I got the feeling that this is what I want to do. I want to plant and harvest and mow. I want to be out there, smelling dirt and stuff I just mowed. I want to look at the soil going under my feet and call it mine."

Harp was contrite. "Hey Bonny, I wasn't laughing at you. I just don't feel what you feel. I'll tell you what, though. If you find a way to go after this idea, I'll help you finance it."

"Thanks, Sarge. I'm giving it a lot of thought. Maybe Kip can help me find options." As they stood off to the rear of the house, they had a good vantage point for the road and driveway.

"Look!" Bonny whispered.

They watched as a sheriff's cruiser quietly came to a stop at the base of the drive. Once again, Deputy Button strolled up the drive to a point even closer to the darkened house. Bonny started to move, but Harp grabbed his arm and signaled to be silent. They both held Fart's collar. Harp put his hand over the dog's mouth. Fart remained quiet but quivering. Once again, the lawman unzipped and pissed in the middle of the driveway. They watched as Button again wagged his penis at the house and strolled back down the drive. They did not speak until he had driven off. "That miserable son of a bitch." Bonny exclaimed. "I can't believe he comes all the way out here just to piss on our property!" Harp noted with amusement Bonny's use of "our." He was glad that they were all beginning to feel that way. As far as he was concerned, it *did* belong to all of them. "He's pissing on *us!*"

"Bonny, I agree one hundred percent, but he holds all the cards. Whatever we do, we should be sure it can't come back to us. That's what they all want. Let's all think on it and see if we can come up with a workable plan." Bonny grumbled his agreement. "One thing I think we can be sure of is that the bastard will be back," Harp continued. "Next time we'll be ready." They stood a while longer. Harp said he was turning in and Bonny had the watch.

After breakfast, marked by mounds of bacon and bowls of scrambled eggs cooked by Bonny, Kip announced that he was ready to explain fracking. He knew he would have to stick to the basics because he had learned how complicated the issue could be. "How much do you all know about it?" The answers ranged from zip to nada to no friggin' idea.

"I won't even try to get into the international, social, and political aspects of it. All we need to know is that it has changed the entire world economy already and more changes are coming."

Before going on, Kip looked at his notes to be sure of what he was saying. The audience was aware of the significance of Kip's presentation. They saw a seriously wounded young man with raw and torn face standing and speaking with confidence. In his concentration, he had forgotten his patch. They knew that he could not have done this just a few days ago. They also knew that they were part of this transformation. "The experts, mostly geologists I guess, have known for a long time that there was a layer of rock under us that held huge amounts of natural gas and oil. It's a rock called shale and under us it's called Marcellus Shale. This layer goes from New York, west to Ohio, and all the way down into West Virginia. The trouble is, it is extremely hard layered mineral and the gas and oil are held in those layers in a way that's kind of like a stack of wet windowpanes. You know the water is there but you would have to break the glass to get it out." The speaker began walking back and forth as the three rapt listeners sat with their coffee at the kitchen table.

"Then this guy in Texas figured out in the 1990's on his own that they could drill a hole down to this layer and then go sideways, they knew how to do this already, and then do something called hydraulic fracturing. They go down a mile then go sideways a mile and start fracking."

Weeks interrupted. "I hate to tell you, Mr. Smart ass, that you can't make a drill go sideways when you're a mile underground. You better check that again." He sat back with a smug grin.

Kip was unfazed. Without saying a word, he passed around a picture showing a side-view of an existing well. They all studied the picture while Kip waited. Bonny asked Weeks, "Hey there, Weeks, would you like some ketchup for that crow you're about to eat?" They laughed at Weeks who shrugged and said, "How the fuck would I know." He gave everyone the finger and resumed listening.

Kip continued with a satisfied smirk aimed at Weeks. "What they do after they get that sideways part drilled is to pump sand and water and chemicals into these deep wells at very high pressure. This pressure causes like an explosion that blasts cracks in the shale in thousands of fractures, releasing natural gas and oil which has been bound up in the rock for eons. The sand goes into these cracks and holds them open. All they have to do then is clean out all the loose crap they had put down there and start piping the gas to a collection point."

"When you explain it that way, it sounds pretty damned simple," Harp said. Kip smiled; he was proud of his research. "Actually, the whole process is a maze of problems they have to overcome. The big one is water. It might take millions of gallons of water just to make one well. If they don't have a local source, they have to truck it in. Just doing that influences local traffic patterns and roads, but that's nothing. Then, once they get the gas flowing, they got to ship it or pipe it somewhere where it can be used. This will involve new pipelines across the land around the well." The young researcher shuffled his notes. "There's even talk about the bigger outfits laying pipelines to get water from rivers eighty or a hundred miles away."

He continued. "That stuff they pump down the well has to be just the right combination of water and chemicals to open up and then clean out those fractures so the gas is released. All that fluid, which is full of dangerous chemicals, must be brought up and stored in a way that it can't ever get into local waters. What's worse, it can't be used again. So now you got millions of gallons of toxic liquid junk that you must store, clean, or get rid of."

Bonny asked what kind of shit was in that fluid. "Different drillers use different combinations of chemicals for different sites, but the fracking fluid usually contains hydrochloric acid to dissolve minerals. It might also have other stuff to kill microorganisms and reduce friction. These companies very carefully guard the makeup of their fracking formulas because, if they develop one that works particularly well, they don't want the competition to know about it."

The old sergeant suddenly sensed that something was trying to worm its way out of his subconscious. "Hold up, Kip. So this stuff is nasty and dangerous. Wouldn't you guess that it would have a strong smell and be really bad for animals?"

"Sarge, from what I read, this stuff could kill an animal or person, or at least make them very sick. And yes, it would have a real stink. Almost as bad as Bonny's foot," he couldn't help adding. He dodged the wadded napkin that Bonny threw. "And some of the drillers got off to a bad start when they didn't put the right kind of casing around the pipe down to a level below the local deep water wells. There are a lot of people pissed at the gas companies because they claim that they're getting natural gas in with their house water. They even have pictures of women lighting the methane gas coming out of their kitchen faucets. Of course, the big companies deny it. But, whatever the cause, it happens."

Harp was thinking of the stuff in those jars, the drum that was full of it, and the smell of the one super bad spring. "Guys, I think we have some samples of that stuff." He went on to explain about the springs and the sample taken at the hunting cabin. "If what I think is true, we could have this stuff analyzed and tie it to a particular driller. I'll get it tested."

He apologized for interrupting and motioned for Kip to continue. "People who own the mineral rights to their land are making a bundle off this process. And, it is changing the economy of entire nations. A few years ago, only two percent of U.S. natural gas came from shale. Now it is approaching forty percent. This means we are getting closer to being energy independent as a nation and less reliant on the Arabs for our energy needs. The long-range effect of this might be to bring a lot of manufacturing back into this country. Some of the experts say this is a game-changer."

Kip's audience was silently absorbing all the information. He continued, "We are still in the beginning of this process of change. Development in treating the water coming back from the drilling process is crucial. That fluid is still full of contaminants and is still unusable for any other purpose. You can't even use it again for fracking other wells. But, because so much money is involved, the experts are working hard to come up with a way to clean the stuff or, better yet, not need it at all. They are even talking about waterless fracking with liquefied natural gas instead of water," which got everyone pondering how they could use an explosive gas to produce an explosive gas. "Then, recently, there are some people considering the possibilities that tremors, or small earthquakes, are happening because all the gas, oil, and water being removed has left gaps down there. Then the ground sinks to fill those spaces. Also, the injection of these fluids might be lubricating deep rock faults making it easier to slip."

"Okay, smart ass, what's all that got to do with us?" Harp challenged with a smile to be sure Kip took it the right way. He was very proud of the way Kip stood in front of this rough crew and gave as good as he got.

"It could be a lot of things. They are supposedly drilling on land all around the Sarge's farm. Maybe we have water they want. From what I understand, they cannot send those drills under our land. We own mineral rights all the way to China or Australia, whatever. Maybe they have already drilled under us and don't want us to know. Maybe they are already polluting our water and don't want us to know." Or, Harp thought, maybe they are polluting our water on purpose just to drive us out. He did not share this thought with the others.

"Keep in mind that all the businesses that support this drilling are also expanding. Demand for drillers, tools, pipe, fittings, trucks, housing, and even clothes have skyrocketed. Heck, some companies are even making work clothes especially for gas workers. They need fire-resistant clothes and special shoes to work with this stuff." This last statement jolted Harp. Maybe if Lars had had fire resistant coveralls, he wouldn't have burned to death. Maybe Lars' death was an easy thing to arrange around such an explosive environment. Kip was winding down. "Finally, we are talking big money. I mean *real* big money. This state collected over two hundred million in just the fees they charge the drillers. The overall money generated is in the billions!"

They mulled over the whole enchilada for several minutes. "I keep coming back to the fact that we got those old oil wells but there are no gas wells on this farm," Harp said. "Must be, though, that someone thinks that this is a good place to drill. Why else would they be offering so much money for this place? Even with the possibility of there being gas here, it doesn't make much sense." He continued his musing. "Why don't they just offer me that kind of money for the mineral rights? How do they know what's under this farm?"

"You're right as rain, Sarge. They don't just want the mineral rights. They want us off the place. Why?" Bonny asked.

"If we knew the answer to that, we would know how to react. I also get the feeling that there is something so big that they want to make sure nobody finds out. Right now, we don't know. So, let's just keep on keeping on and take care of our own little pea patch." Harp concluded.

"Kip, thanks for a great report. We'll all hash it out while we do our chores today." Kip grinned like a happy young man and made an elaborate bow at the generous round of applause from his audience.

"Okay, guys, listen up." Harp stood to set the course for the day. "You all realize by now that we have to keep our eyes open all the time. Bonny, you can finish whatever you are cutting out there. Kip, I know you would like to get out some, so I want you and Weeks to kind of patrol the perimeter. Just get out there and ride around and look for anything out of place." Kip pumped his arm in happiness and high-fived Weeks. "I also want you to plan a route from that sharp curve just up the road from the base of the drive to the end of the tunnel in the equipment shed." He paused for effect. "And, I mean across country *in the dark*." He had a malicious smile on his face. "I am planning a little surprise for our visiting deputy." His audience did not know what Harp was planning, but they knew they liked it. Their happy faces showed their support for whatever he did.

"My plans are to go in to the bank and pay Harry Johnson the money I owe him. Fart can come with me. He deserves a good ride." Joking and shoving as they headed out the door, each headed to his assigned duty. Harp stood alone after they had gone, quietly enjoying the memory of the overall feeling of peaceful relaxation which had moments ago pervaded this country kitchen. For the first time, the thought occurred to this committed loner that he might have actually been responsible for making someone happy and, incredibly, he could even keep doing it. This was a revelation to a man whose whole life had been built on a "do your job and I'll do mine and fuck you if you don't like it" philosophy. He shrugged off the thought. Impossible, he concluded.

The meeting with Harry Johnson went well, with the two old soldiers naturally communicating on the same wave length. The loan was repaid with a simple banking maneuver, with Harp very vocal in his appreciation for the trust Johnson had shown. They discussed activities at the farm resulting in a few suggestions about what Harp's crew might do with the land prior to selling. Harp had assured the banker that he still intended to sell but was in no hurry. He told him about the latest offer and Johnson just whistled.

13

AFTER DINNER, AN AMUSED BUT DETERMINED HARP EX-
plained his plan for retribution against the pissing deputy. They
were certain that this guy was dumb enough to keep coming night
after night. And they would be ready for him tonight. Weeks was
the fastest afoot, so it fell to him to play the key role in the plot.
The arrogant deputy did come as expected. Around two in the
morning, in pitch dark, with no lights on at all in the house, he
strolled up the drive and stopped a mere twenty-five feet from
the porch steps and relieved himself. As he was preparing to do
his customary weeny wag, he heard the siren on his car wailing,
saw the lights flashing, and then his police cruiser, with engine
racing and tires squealing, sped off down the road. Button turned
and ran while zipping his fly and cursing. By the time he got to
the road, his car was out of sight. He could hear it but not see it
so he ran toward the sound. A quarter mile down the road and
around a bend in the country road he found it. It was down a
steep bank and into a creek bed. His cruiser was standing on its
nose in the shallow water of the stream. With gun in hand he

began screaming for the driver to come out. He raced in all directions looking for someone to shoot but saw no one and found no sign of the auto thief.

He ran back down the road and up the drive, threatening to kill every one of those crippled sonsabitches in the house. He raced up the steps and began hammering on the front door with his fist, gun at ready. He knew that one of them did it and there was no way he could have gotten back in the house ahead of him. Whichever one wasn't there was the guilty party. The porch light came on and Harp looked out with amused satisfaction. Button's frantic state of mind was evident. The other three inhabitants stood behind him in various types of sleepwear. They all looked mussed and sleepy. Weeks had discarded and hidden the black clothes and gloves and was wearing shorts and sleeveless t-shirt with no prosthesis. Bonny was leaning on a crutch and Kip was not wearing a patch. They looked at each other, grinned and nodded, then Harp turned on the porch lights and opened the door. They all stepped out.

"What's going on, Button?" Harp asked while lazily and pointedly scratching his crotch.

"You know what's going on, you bastard! Don't play dumb with me! Somebody stole my car and wrecked it and I know it was one of you!" He was so angry he was practically dancing. He was also confused because all four were right there in front of him.

"Where was your car?" Bonny asked innocently.

"Right there at the end of your driveway! That's where the goddamned thing was. I turned my back for a minute and it was gone!"

"Well, where were you?" Bonny continued. "Why weren't you in your car?"

"I was right here in front of your..." It hit Button that he would have a difficult time explaining his actions. "It doesn't matter where I was. I was on an investigation when someone drove off in my car."

"Where is your car now?" Weeks asked.

Button screamed, "It's up the goddamned road around the fucking bend and in the fucking creek."

Kip spoke up, "Can I go to the bathroom? I just woke up and I got to go." Without waiting for an answer, he turned and went back inside. He was the least suspicious so Button said nothing.

Harp scratched again and wondered aloud, "I don't know what we can do, deputy. Is there something you want from us?"

Button was about to answer when Kip returned to the porch. He had the cordless phone in his hand. "Hey don't worry, you all. I got it under control. I just called 911 and they said they will send some people right out. They said they would send a wrecker and alert the Sheriff. The dispatcher said he would probably want to be here personally. I don't know why he was laughing." He looked at Harp with sweet innocence, "Did I do good, Sarge?"

Harp picked up on the act immediately and patted him on the shoulder and said, "Good job, Kip. I bet it was just some teenager joyriding and you helped them find that kid."

The crazed deputy was now stomping, spinning, and yelling, "No! No! No! Don't call nobody. I'll take care of it myself!"

It was too late. "Shoot, Deputy Button, we were always taught that it is our duty to report any serious accidents as soon as possible," Kip said. "Isn't that right, Sarge?" Harp nodded and patted his shoulder again.

"Oh, you bastards. You miserable bastards. I know you did this. I don't know how but you did it. We will go over that car until we find evidence to nail the one who did it." He had finally holstered his Glock and was waving one hand back and forth while pointing with the other.

"We had a long day and have a lot to do tomorrow. Do you mind if we go back to bed?" Harp asked in great seriousness. Button was too upset to talk. He sputtered and cursed but just waved them away. Back in the house, with all lights turned off again, they left Deputy Button fuming in the dark. After staring for another half minute and waving a hand as if talking to the house, he walked, slumping and dragging his heels, to wait at his wrecked car for the wrath of the Sheriff. He knew that the talkative wrecker crew would have the story spread far and wide by morning.

In the darkened house, while trying very hard to act like grown-ups, the guilty four watched Button stomp back to the road. Practically giggling with joy, they waited to be sure he was out of earshot before leaping on Weeks and demanding details. He had been picked because he was the fastest runner. Weeks raised his hands for silence. "I got to that shallow ditch on the other side of the road about midnight. I was dressed in all black with gloves and cap just like the Sarge ordered. I was laying on my back looking at the stars and kind of enjoying the quiet. Do you all realize how quiet it is out here in the sticks? You can't hear anything but little bitty sounds of things. There's some quiet things moving and living in the dark. I wonder what they are." He was unaware of his digression as he re-listened to those sounds in his mind. The other three waited impatiently for the narrative to resume. Finally, Kip said, "And?"

"Oh. Yeah. I was laying there out of sight from the road when I saw this car coming up the road and stop. It was just like we planned. I waited until the door opened and closed and then I peeked over the edge of the berm. I watched that asshole walk up the drive. By then I didn't even need the night-scope. Anyway, I waited 'till he was almost at the house, then I eased over to his car, just hoping he left his keys in the ignition. And, he did! That ignorant shit. So, I knew we could go ahead with Plan One. When I got in the car all the interior lights came on so I had to move fast."

Weeks paused in his narrative, recalling the details. He knew that this was a story to be treasured for a lifetime so he wanted to get it right. Harp, Bonny, and Kip waited in eager anticipation. Weeks paced in the middle of the living room. "I didn't know which switches did what so I just turned everything on and hit the gas. These things are fast, by the way. I drove past that curve like we planned and right up to the steep drop off to the creek. I got out, made sure I wasn't leaving anything then I reached in and put it in drive and it started rolling. As soon as I saw for sure it was going over, I put on the goggles and took off running. It's a damned good thing we planned that route or I would have been tied up in one of those barbed wire fences for sure. I think I probably got to the trunk of the Chevy before he got to his car. I was kind of winded but really okay."

He paused for a correction. "Sarge, I could have got to the back door of the house instead of going through the tunnel but

I'm glad we did it this way." Harp waited for an explanation. "I found out that there is one weakness in this arm." He waved his metal appendage. "It is really hard to crawl on your hands and knees. I kind of worked out a way and made it, though. And you guys know the rest." Weeks flopped on the sofa and enjoyed the silence following a story well told.

Their leader was also enjoying the silence. He was a little embarrassed at his joy over what was essentially a childish prank. But, goddamn, it felt good to see Button taken apart. "You guys do what you want, but I am hitting the sack." He checked his watch. "It's a little after two and Senter will probably be here first thing. He will likely want to interview each of us separately, so let's keep our stories straight. We all hit the sack elevenish and nobody got up until Button banged on the door."

Apparently lifting a car from a vertical position was a little complicated. The first wrecker did not have a long enough boom to pick the car straight up, which was necessary to keep from dragging it across the rip rap on the bank of the stream. They had to wait for another, larger wrecker which meant they had to wait while the new crew was wakened and got themselves on the road. Meanwhile, the first wrecker crew smoked and waited—and joked, all at Button's expense. Button, whom they had known all his life, had to pretend not to hear the jokes. He was standing next to Sheriff Senter who calmly leaned against the fender of his car. He was trying to assimilate all the facts. "You say you ran back to the house the minute you saw your car in the creek?"

Button was pathetically obsequious. "Yes sir, I ran as fast as I could and banged on their door. It didn't take no more than two minutes."

"And all four were there?"

"Yup. They all came out looking like they just woke up. That one fella was on crutches, the other one didn't have no arm and the small one didn't have no cover over that face."

"What about the old one?"

"He just came out in shorts and tee shirt. He was limping real bad from the leg that was tore up. To tell you the truth, Sheriff, I don't think any of them could have made it back before I got there. They couldn't have been on the road and the field is open on both sides. I woulda seen 'em."

The Sheriff was not convinced. After the car was finally back on the road and, surprisingly, found in running condition, he paid a visit to the house. He was about ready to place the blame on an unknown local but wanted to satisfy his curiosity. It was right at daylight.

As the lawman pulled up, Harp stepped outside with a cup of coffee in his hand. "Morning Sheriff. Had a little excitement last night?" Senter just sighed and walked up the steps. "You want to come in and grab some coffee?" Harp offered.

Senter thought about it. "You know what, Harper? That sounds real good."

Harp led the way to the kitchen where everyone sat around the table eating different versions of breakfast. Harp pulled out a chair at the end of the table for the visitor. Senter dropped his hat on the table and sat. "Black, if you don't mind." All expressed pleasant good mornings to the Sheriff. Each sat looking comfortably innocent and waited. Weeks slowly finished his toast.

Harp put the mug on the table. "You look a little tired, Sheriff. Bad night?"

"Mr. Harper, you do not know how bad. Last night we had to process three drunk and disorderlies who were putting up a fight, my farm manager called and said a prize boar had eaten some wire and died before we could get it out—and, as you know, one of my cars took a nose dive into Adams Creek." He took a sip, "Good coffee. I thank you." He looked around. "Your house looks real nice, by the way." It sounded sincere.

After smiling at his audience, "My deputy says there is no way that any of you could have driven his car off into the creek and got back here before he did. I guess I have to agree with him. Plus, I know that he is a man who would dearly love to hang something on you guys. So, I guess I gotta believe him." He pushed his hat back and forth with his idle hand. "However, a good lawman, a successful lawman, owes much of his success to trusting his instincts. My instincts tell me that you four are somehow involved in stealing Deputy Button's cruiser. And I would remind you that it is a felony."

He glared at each of the faces around the table one by one. Their open-eyed innocence did not waver a bit. Each had been glared at by much heavier hitters than the Sheriff. Senter sat comfortably looking around the table as he sipped his coffee. Finally, he sighed and smiled. "I can see that I am in the company of innocent men and I have work to do elsewhere. Rest assured, gentlemen, if you keep fucking with me, I will find out and I will catch you. I thank you for the coffee." He put the coffee cup on the table and stood, looking at the four of them for a moment. The Sheriff then shook his head and walked out without another word.

After a long silence, Bonny spoke. "You know, Harp, I think

we have to give that man a little more credit than we have so far. He's got good instincts; you know, like the guys we fought with who could sense when the shit was about to hit the fan."

Harp was thinking the same thing. "I know, Bonny. Let's not underestimate the man."

14

WAITING UNTIL EVERYONE HAD FINISHED EATING, HARP issued the order of the day. "Men, there is something we have to get done." He related the story of the mysterious coordinates and his experience locating the spot. "We don't know what's down there, but it was enough to totally spook Lars and scare Pauline. We need to find out what it is and what it will mean when we go to selling this place." Harp laid out the plan. They would use the winch on the front of the ATV and lower him down the hole. He would get some pictures, then they would study the photos on the computer to figure out what in hell it was all about.

"Questions?"

"Yeah, Sarge, how come you are the one to go down there? It might be a little dicey. Maybe you should let one of us do it."

Harp smiled at the notion that they were protecting him. "Kip has no experience in a climbing harness, Bonny is too big to fit through that opening, and Weeks would not be able to climb the rope back out if it came to that. That leaves me, so I'm doing it."

After they had digested his logic, Harp stood and headed out the back door, "So let's get at it."

They were ready within a half hour. Weeks drove while Bonny, Kip, and Fart rode in the back. With Harp's direction, they came to the spot in front of the overhang and Harp called for him to stop. "Well, where is it?" Weeks asked while looking around.

Harp smiled and stepped down. "This is it."

"*What* is it? There ain't nothing here," Weeks observed.

Their leader started unloading equipment. "Go over there under that little overhang and whistle or something."

With spirited yelping and whistling, the crew heard what Harp had heard: hollow echoes which seemed to come from nowhere. By leaning way over the low bench, they could see the opening which bent back under their feet. As he was assembling his gear, they were estimating the size of the opening from all angles.

"Sarge, are you sure you're going to fit through there?"

"Well, Lars was about my size and he went down there, so I suppose I can." Harp was fitting himself into the rudimentary harness common for rappelling. When he was satisfied that it was well tied, he clipped it onto the hook at the end of the winch cable. He put a high res camera with lots of memory in his shirt pocket, a powerful flashlight in his belt holster, and put on one of Lars' old hard hats with a head lamp attached.

"Okay, the way I see it, I'm going to have to slide down that little overhang on my butt. When I go off the end of it, I'll turn whichever way I need to go on down. Bonny, I want you to operate the winch. Weeks, you'll hang over the edge and relay directions. I don't think we'll need radios." Harp was trying to think of a duty for the sensitive Kip. "Kip, I want you and Fart to keep

208

watch to make sure nobody comes up on us while I'm down there. We don't want any surprises." When all was ready, Harp carefully swung his legs off the low bench and planted his feet on the shelf. With Bonny slowly playing out the cable, Harp pushed away from the bench and slowly sat on the shelf.

"Okay, Bonny, I'm going to slide down this thing until I go off the end. Give me a little at a time." Harp slowly slid out of sight. They heard him say, "Okay, I'm near the edge so I'll turn over on my stomach. Give me a couple of feet. Okay, a couple more. Hold it." They could hear his directions clearly so Weeks would merely look at Bonny who would nod. "Okay, I'm clear of the ledge and hanging freely. Let me down two more feet and I'll get my flashlight out." Harp slowly dropped into the open space. The light from the opening above provided very little illumination for the chamber below. He could tell that he was in a large space. His head was now clear of the ledge, so he could slowly turn in all directions. He saw that there was darkness on all sides. But, before he went any lower, Harp wanted to know what he might be landing on. He directed the powerful beam of his flashlight straight down and found that, contrary to what he had often said, he had not seen everything. Even years in a war zone could not prepare him for what he was seeing. Beneath him was a tangled pile of bones. His first thought was that a hundred years of unlucky animals must have fallen through that crack. But, he knew immediately that this was wrong and that these were human bones. Two things: they were human skulls and damned if some of the skeletons weren't still wearing remnants of clothing.

"Hey, Sarge, what do you see? Find some dinosaur bones?" Weeks yelled, laughing.

"Guys, you are not going to believe this. This is a fucking graveyard down here. There's a pile of bones of must be eighteen, twenty people in it." This announcement was greeted with silence. The silence was broken by Bonny. "You're shittin' us, right Sarge?"

"I wish I was. Somebody dumped a whole bunch of people in this hole and, from the looks of it, they were all killed first." Harp saw a small area where he might place his feet without stepping on any bones. When the bodies slid off the ledge, they landed in all directions so there wasn't a lone pile. "Let me down real slow. I'll tell you when to stop."

Slowly lowered to a spot in the middle of the pile, Harp carefully felt the ground underneath to be sure the footing was solid. "Okay, I'm standing on the floor. I'm going to unhook the harness now so I can walk around. Can you hear me okay?"

"Hell yes, Sarge. It's like you are standing right here in front of us. It's some trick of sound, like you're talking into one of those cheerleader things."

"Good, I'll just be telling you what I see. Like I said, I'm in the middle of eighteen or twenty skeletons that are just kind of tangled together. Some are still wearing pieces of clothing and it looks like they are both men and women. From the looks of their skulls, they were either shot or clubbed to death. They mostly dried out but still have a lot of skin on 'em. There's a few animal skeletons around. It looks like they got in but, I can tell you, there's no way out. So, they just rotted away and dried out along with the poor bastards who were thrown into this hole. From the look of the clothes, these people have been down here a long, long time. Some shoes are real old fashioned with those old timey buckles. Looks like some were wearing moccasins."

Harp carefully stepped free of the bones. "I don't know what caused this cave, but it looks like the top half of a bubble. Maybe it's a volcano thing from a million years ago. It's about thirty feet across and just about perfectly round. The walls all slope up to the hole which is about fourteen feet up and make it impossible to climb out. It's really dry and got a sandy floor. I can see where Lars walked."

He walked away from the sad congregation right under the opening. "What's funny is that there are small footprints in the sand all over the place. There's another small bunch of bones over against the wall straight out from where that ledge points." It hit him then. "Wait a minute! There can't be other bodies away from the main bunch unless they weren't dead when they were put here!" Harp walked toward the separate group of bones feeling mostly curiosity. As he stood there, his flashlight revealed an incredible tragedy. He was thunderstruck. "Those rotten sonsabitches. Those slimy cowardly bastards. Those miserable motherfucking pieces of shit!"

The crew above listened with alarm. "Sarge, what the hell is it!? Sarge?"

"Hold on guys, I need to get my head together." There was a slight catch in his voice. To a group of men who firmly believed that, of all the men in the world, the one who most certainly had his shit together was the Sarge, this statement was literally shocking. After a brief respectful silence, the voice from below returned. "I'm looking at what looks like a young girl. She's got a skirt and necklace of beads. She's lying on her back. Her right ankle is broken. The foot is at right angles to her leg. Lying next to her under her right arm is a really small kid, maybe a baby. I can't see anything wrong with this one. On her left arm is another small kid with a broken femur and broken arm." Harp paused and took a deep breath. He put the flashlight in its holster for a minute and rubbed his face before continuing. "Off to the side, about ten feet away, is another kid, probably a boy. He looks like he wasn't hurt. I think he made the tracks all over the place looking for a way out." Another long pause. "It looks like the girl and those babies died of shock and exposure. The boy probably died of thirst and starvation." Harp studied the clothes. "It looks like they are not wearing heavy clothes so this probably did not happen in cold weather."

Harp concluded, "From what I can see, some group of assholes gathered all these people together and killed the adults with clubs and bullets. They didn't even bother killing the kids. They just threw them down the hole. This shit had to be done while these people were under guard."

"My God, Sarge, what is this? Who could've done this?" Bonny was dumbfounded.

Weeks stood shaking his head. "How can you hate somebody so much that you torture their kids?" He knew the answer to his question because he had seen it. He just didn't want to believe it.

Kip said, "This kind of massacre is a thing that has got to be in the history books. It has to be known to someone somewhere. Sarge, if you were guessing, how long ago do you think it happened?"

"There's no way of telling. The clothes look really old but I don't see a date on anything. Let me look some more." Knowing that this was an explosive discovery and might even be considered a crime scene, Harp was careful to not disturb any of the bones. After studying the main group and finding nothing new, he went back to the children. Leaning over, he could see a flat stone against the girl's spine where it had dropped from the stomach as the body deteriorated. It appeared to have scratches on it, so he felt it would be best to carefully remove it for study. "There's a stone here with some writing on it. I think the girl must have done it." Harp turned the stone until the direction of the writing was correct. "It looks like it says 'malisha done it.'" He carefully placed the stone back where he found it. "She spelled it M-A-L-I-S-H-A-D-O-N-E-I-T. Write that down. Anybody got any ideas?"

He was answered with silence. Of course everyone was trying to guess who Malisha was. "Okay, here's what we have got to do. You guys hook up that emergency light to the ATV power and lower it down. We need to get all this on tape."

"You need one of us to come down?" Bonny asked.

"To tell the truth, guys, if you don't have to see this, then I'd recommend against it. This is as bad as anything I've seen. It's the kids that get you. They might as well have tortured them because that's how they died. Anyway, we're going to have it on tape so we can all look at it back at the house." With good light, Harp took enough time to capture every aspect of the horror for the record. He hated having his tracks all over the area so he was careful to move about as little as necessary. Looking down, however, he saw the distinctive imprint of his boot soles in the sand. He wasn't sure why, but he did not want that on the record. Anyone who saw the film would know that someone had obviously had to have been down there. He just did not want anyone to know that it was *him*. He decided that the boots were worn and it was time to get rid of them anyway. They would be burned as soon as possible.

With the camera in his pocket and harness back on, Harp was slowly lifted from the chamber. As he approached the ledge on his ascent, he called for a stop and slowly swung in a circle studying the scene once more. He wanted to be very sure that he had not missed anything. "Hold up!" Harp saw something that had not been visible from ground level. There was a body at the edge of the pile with an outstretched hand. Something glinted in that hand whenever the flashlight beam passed over it from just this angle. "Let me back down." They carefully lowered Harp back to the floor. Slipping from the harness once again, he went to the body and shown the light on that hand. The hand held a silver cross that was about two inches long and had what looked like a picture of Santa Claus on it. It was the one thing that Harp felt with certainty that he must take back to the world above. Again in the harness, he was lifted to a bright afternoon where three anxious men waited for him to report. They were quiet and patient while Harp made the awkward climb over the bench and eagerly chugged a bottle of water and gathered his thoughts.

"Okay, bottom line: this was a goddamned massacre and it happened a long, *long* time ago. Somebody killed about twenty people and threw the bodies down there. They mostly clubbed them to death but some were shot. There were four kids they didn't even bother killing, they just threw them in the hole. Three of them got broken bones from the fall. One boy, one boy..." Harp stopped and viciously rubbed his face to cover the fact that he, of all people, might have a tear left for anything or anybody in this world. Then he continued, "One boy, maybe five years old, was mostly unhurt and ran and ran all over that hell hole until he laid down and died. All the kids died of shock or thirst or exposure or maybe loss of blood."

Harp sat for a long time looking at the ground. "I am not sure what leads me to think this, but somehow I think these people were Indians." He paused and continued, "Their looks, their clothes, everything points that way. I know they killed Indians back at the beginning of the U.S., but this is different." He held out the cross he had brought up. "For one thing, they were Christians and another is that they were educated." He looked at his silent audience. "It doesn't matter in a way because we don't know enough to deal with this situation. Only the experts would be able to tell what happened here. We have to decide what to do with what we know. Ideas?" He handed over the cross to be passed around and began assembling gear to load back on the ATV.

Bonny was first to speak. "Sarge, it looks like we have to tell somebody about this. This kind of thing is part of history. I don't see how we can keep it to ourselves.

Weeks agreed, but offered a cautionary view. "Bonny is right, Sarge, but this kind of thing would cause a real shitstorm and the whole world would be coming to our farm. Think what would happen if the news people got a hold of it."

Kip was still sitting on the bench. He held the cross in his hand and was studying it closely. "I think we should start with some research, beginning with this cross. It's pretty distinctive and it might tell us who these people are. If we can find out who they were, we might be able to figure out who might have killed them."

Harp agreed. He looked at the others and they nodded. "For

now, we say nothing." He looked at each man sternly and re-peated, "And I mean nothing. We will transfer the pictures on this camera to a jump drive and look at the film tonight on the computer. When you see it, you will see what really pissed me off. Bonny is right; people oughta know who did this." Harp paused, thinking. "Let's remember, this happened a long, long time ago. Keeping it quiet for another few days or couple weeks is not go-ing to hurt anything. And we sure don't want it to hurt us. Let's get back to the house."

Soon the ATV was loaded and with Fart joyously running alongside, everyone was chattering on the way back to the house with minds full of what they had just discovered. That is, every-one but Kip. Harp noticed he was unusually quiet and pensive. Once they had arrived and finished putting equipment away, they gathered in the kitchen. Harp asked Kip what was on his mind. "I'm trying to remember all the facts about something my father ran into when he was building a new office complex in western New York. When they were digging the foundation right in the middle of the whole thing, they uncovered some old bones." Now the other three were listening intently. "Of course my father or-dered everyone to clam up and make no mention of it. There was one guy, though, who told a reporter friend what he had seen. The next thing you know, the state had totally shut down the job. And they kept it shut down for several months until they had totally excavated the whole site. It was an old Indian burial ground. It cost my father millions, which I was happy to see." He added the last with a mean smile.

"Can they do that?" Weeks asked. "Just close everything down on something they don't own?"

Harp Answered. "The government can do anything they want if it's in the law."

"Do you see what I'm saying, though?" Kip asked his friends.

"Naw, I don't get it," Weeks offered.

But Bonny did. "You're saying that, if they knew about this, they would come in here and take over the farm."

Harp nodded. "You can bet your sweet ass they would. If they knew what was down there, it would be headline news everywhere. This farm would be turned into a fucking zoo."

"And," Bonny continued, "they would definitely take over the farm and we wouldn't be able to sell it until they said we could—which could take months, maybe years. We should think about this and try to figure out the timing of it all."

At first nobody got it. Then Bonny grinned maliciously and explained, "We know that some rich son of a bitch is trying to take this place over and it looks like he might do anything to get it." He paused to let that thought sink in. "Suppose the authorities, whoever the hell they are, find out about this *after* we sell it."

Weeks hooted and Kip laughed. "Man, that's cold," Weeks said.

"Sarge, who knows about this?" Bonny asked. He then answered his own question. "Just the four of us. You know there isn't one of us who would ever talk about it. If we sold this place, it would not be a question about the authorities finding out. We stay dumb and mum, and you sell the place, the question would then be *how* to clue in the government people so the sonuvabitch buyer could not prove we knew about it." Bonny glared at Weeks and Kip. They were quick to nod in agreement that they would keep the secret.

His first thought was that there was no way of making this work. Yet, Harp really liked the idea of sticking it to the bastard who was so desperate to buy. He wasn't ready to commit, however. "Okay, let's put this idea on the back burner for now. Let's get some chow and then we'll look at the film on the camera. You all realize that what we have in this camera is pure dynamite. We're going to transfer the images to a jump drive and hide it in the root cellar until our plan gets totally clear." Harp pulled the cross from his pocket and remembered what he had asked Kip to do. "Kip, after we look at these images, which are about as bad as I've seen, do your research on this cross and what happened to those people. This kind of thing has got to be part of the early history of this country." Kip nodded. He was becoming used to being the computer man for the group. He kind of liked the way they all deferred to his knowledge of computers. It made him feel like an equal partner, even though they all were older.

While Kip was at work in the office, the rest were grumbling and going about household chores which had fallen behind. Bathrooms needed cleaning, clothes needed washing, and general dusting was past due. They were finding that, as could be expected, some were messy, some were neat, some didn't mind and some did. They were learning these things about each other and found that, over all, they could laugh about each other's foibles. In other words, they had become a team—in and out of the house.

15

ADAM HAD ASKED FOR FIRE AND FIRE WAS PERRY BECK'S
specialty. Beck had studied the Kuykendahl farm. Using remarkable computer applications, he had looked at it from the air, from
space, and from the road, all while sitting in his neat little condo.
He had studied other properties in the region to compare and
draw certain conclusions. With all information aggregated, he
had focused on a large LPG tank under a small shelter a short
distance from the house. In his experience, he knew that LPG
tanks were built with thick walls to contain the pressure of the
liquefied gas. That called for a special technique using two timed
explosives. It would be easy to loosen fittings and ignite the released gas. But, he needed a violent explosion strong enough to
level the house. That's what the contract called for—very em-
phatically, as a matter of fact. There was no mention of occupants.
Also, he needed to be far away when the explosion occurred. So
he studied the roads, too.

Beck lived to start fires. He had known from childhood that
pyromania was a sickness—but he had secretly embraced it rath-

er than to attempt denial or cure. He had studied the sickness, not to understand it but to learn how to avoid the mistakes others had made. Thus, the difference between Beck and many others with this disorder was that he had never been caught. He had learned to avoid the errors that were products of his condition. As much as he would like to watch his targets burn, for instance, he was never anywhere near the site when the conflagration occurred. As much as he would like to leave a signature at each of his target sites, he had been careful to use random techniques leaving no clues as to his involvement. He had even started practice fires to fine tune different accelerants.

As a result of his occupation, he had been responsible for millions of dollars of damage across the nation and the loss of a great number of human and animal lives. Like a true psychopath, the suffering and loss he left in his path did not concern him. His only concerns were doing good jobs and building his bankroll. Authorities and investigators did not have a clue about his existence. If Beck had any weakness, it was a certainty that he would never be found out.

That's why, as he lay on the ground quivering and suffering violent muscle spasms behind the Kuykendahl house, he was trying to figure out what he had done wrong. His mistake was in making an assumption. He assumed that, because it was 3 a.m. and there was absolute quiet around this house out in the boonies, there would be no one to intrude on his preparations. He did have time to place the two explosive charges and set the timers, which he completed in darkness with a satisfied grin. He was certain that the ensuing explosion would level the house and didn't care. His job was to blow the propane tank. The client wanted a fireball and that was what he would give them. It would probably kill whoever was in the house but, again, who cared.

With his tiny flashlight, he had taken a last look at his hand-iwork and stepped away. He would now proceed back across the nearby pasture to his waiting car. That's when he heard a snap and the strange sound of whipping wires and the painful stick of prongs in his chest and abdomen. He suddenly found that he no longer had any control of his body. Rigid with muscle spasms, then flinging his arms and legs wildly, he was an unhinged puppet at the end of a set of wires steadily delivering massive shocks from a Taser.

Harp and his band had agreed that they should continue keeping a night watch. Too many things had happened. They were soldiers and understood that the price of safety was vigilance. There was some argument over the weapons that the sentry should carry. Harp decided that guarding the farm with lethal weapons might result in an incident that would put them all away. He did not want to take that chance … yet. Bonny had the duty. He was armed with the M-26 military strength Taser and a canister of pepper spray. It was a nice night and he wore the night-vision goggles on his forehead, ready to flip them down if needed. His charge was to alert the house to any threat and to use his weapons as defensive measures only.

Bonny had stood guard many, many times. He understood the importance of alertness. He also understood that you listened for the anomaly. You looked and listened for things that did not belong in the night air. It was nothing but the light scuff of a pant leg against a low bush that alerted him. He was at the back of the house, on the side away from the LPG tanks. Bonny was alive because he trusted his instincts. He pulled the goggles down and hit the "on" button. He made no sound as he stepped around the corner of the house just as Beck stepped back from the tank and bent to pick up a small satchel. The experienced soldier did not pause to study the situation. He saw a man who had just done something to the tanks. That was enough. He fired the Taser at a distance of no more than thirty feet and watched as Beck flopped to the ground and convulsed as the 50,000 volts jolted his body. Beck tried to rise. Bonny jolted him again. He twitched and spasmed as Bonny quickly rolled him over on his stomach and tied his hands behind his back with his own belt. Bonny then used the arsonist's belt to tie his feet. Lastly, he tied his kerchief around the man's eyes and stuffed a rag in his mouth. The last actions were a reflex move coming from experience with terrorist captives. Only when Bonny was certain that Beck was secure did he drag him by the collar of his jacket to the back door where he could watch him while he alerted the house by banging on the door jamb. He stood inside the door and motioned for everyone to remain silent as they gathered in the kitchen. Beck had said nothing. He was still trying to understand what had happened and considering his options. He did know he had been tased.

The lights came on and Harp, Weeks, and Kip followed Bonny from the house. They were all still in various levels of sleepwear. Fart had somehow sensed that Kip suffered most during the night and had been sleeping in his room. When Kip had a nightmare, Fart would lick his hand. His emanations had been controlled lately, so his presence in the house was tolerated.

They stood quietly around the trussed figure on the ground. Beck was now unmoving and listening for any clue to what his captors intended. With all present and still silent, Bonny went through Beck's pockets, shoes, and socks. Beck carried no identification but had a small satchel, a set of keys, and a cheap phone. Everything he needed for the job was attached to the LPG tanks. Only a few minutes had elapsed since he set the timers, so he had about twenty minutes before the explosions. He had planned to be in his car and about 10 miles away when that happened. As Beck considered his fate, Weeks had walked to the tanks with a flashlight. He quickly noted with some horror that there were two charges attached to the LPG tank. He ran back to the group around Beck and motioned for Harp to hurry over and see what he had found. Harp did not hesitate. He motioned for Bonny to come look. Bonny was most familiar with various explosives and was best trained to know what to do. They moved away from the arsonist and the house to talk where they couldn't be heard.

"What was he doing?" he asked Bonny.

"He attached explosives to the LPG tank." Bonny answered grimly as he raised the two bombs for everyone to see. Normally, this would have panicked anyone standing nearby but such was the faith in Bonny that they instead studied the two devices. "They are set to detonate in about twenty minutes, one a split second after the other. Harp raised his eyebrows in the unspoken question all wanted to ask. "Don't worry," Bonny continued with a smile, "I've seen this trigger before and know how to defuse it. They're clear."

"How bad would it have been?" Kip asked.

"There is enough here to blow up the house even without that gas tank touching off. With the tank, I would guess the house would be gone plus a couple of these buildings." Beck had followed instructions on the strength of the blast.

223

Weeks swore. "This guy was going to kill all of us."

Kip was thinking along the same lines as Harp. "Somebody paid this guy to do this."

Harp added, "And it's probably the same asshole who has been trying to get his hands on the farm. Let's think about this."

"If we turned him over to the law, he would go down for sure." Weeks offered. "But, in the meantime we would be stuck again on selling the place. It would take months to clear this up."

"He didn't succeed in blowing us up, so even if he did some time, he would be out in a few years," Bonny added.

"You're both right, which means it's time for a decision." Harp was not sure how far they would go but he was ready. "Do we give him a break or do we treat him like he treated us?"

Kip was the only one who did not get it. "What do you mean, Sarge?" Bonny and Weeks just stared at Kip, who finally got it. "Oh man, can we do this and get away with it?" There was no question he was in. Just about not getting caught.

"I got an idea," Harp said. "Bonny, do you know how to reset the timers on those mothers?"

"No problem."

"Okay. The first thing we're going to do is find out who paid this piece of shit to take us out. That might not be pretty. Kip, maybe you ought to go back in the house."

Kip glared at the trio. "I did not decide to stay here with you assholes just to be a part-time partner. I am in it just as much as any of you. Let's do what we have to do." Each man felt a surge of solidarity at these words coming from the mouth of this very young man. If there had been any doubts about the commitment to one another, they were now gone.

The old Sarge took charge. "The first thing we need to do is find out where his car is and bring it back here. It's got to be close. Weeks, I want you to get the car. No hair, no fiber, no prints, no nothing. Seriously nothing."

Weeks nodded and left.

"Bonny and Kip, we're going to the barn to do some prep."

Weeks entered the barn to find that the others had set up a slanting table and were bringing in buckets of water from the animal trough. "We're going to water-board?" he asked in amazement. "I've heard of it but never seen it!"

Grimly, Harp responded, "I've seen it, and it always worked." He didn't offer where he had seen it.

Kip was confused. "But, it doesn't kill the guy, does it?"

"No, it never killed anyone that I know of," Harp said. "But, they are dead certain that they are going to die by drowning and that's what makes it work."

"You got the car?" Harp asked Weeks, who just came in.

"Yeah, no problem. I put it behind the barn. It's a rental out of Harrisburg. Nothing in it. Rental contract in the glove box." He handed it to Harp.

Beck was brought into the room. He remained blindfolded and gagged with hands still tied. He tried to speak and was ignored. They quickly brought him to the slanted board and tied hands and feet underneath.

Harp had explained how it was done. It was very simple. A soaking wet towel was draped over the victim's face and water was steadily poured on the towel over the mouth. Apart from the inability to breath was the absolute certainty that he was drowning. Even subjects who were exceptionally able to hold their breath eventually gave in to the horror of the sensation and would do anything or say anything to make it stop. So far, nothing had been said to Beck. Without any warning, the gag was pulled from his mouth and the soaking wet towel was quickly put in place. Harp started dribbling water over Beck's nose and mouth and watched as his body went through involuntary paroxysms as it fought for oxygen. Bonny and Kip lost some of their resolve but stayed silent. What they were doing was slowly killing a man by smothering him. It was an ugly, cruel thing to do. After one minute, Harp stopped pouring and pushed the towel clear of Beck's nose and mouth. Beck coughed and gagged, spitting water. When he had caught his breath, and was just capable of speaking, Harp pulled the towel down and began pouring again. He did this for another minute then pushed the towel away. They waited again. Beck unexpectedly started loudly sobbing. He was a broken man. They watched and waited silently. Beck found his voice, "Who are you? What do you want? Please Jesus don't do that again. I'll do anything, say anything. What do you want!" he screamed.

Harp finally spoke. "It's really simple. We want to know who you are and who hired you to blow us up."

"Oh God," Beck pleaded. "I don't know. I do not know.

Harp said, "Hand me the towel."

"No! Let me explain! I'm in the business. Please listen! I get a call from someone somewhere and they give me the job. I never know who orders it."

"What do you do after the job is finished?" Bonny asked.

Beck hesitated, not wanting to answer, until Harp started pressing him down. "Wait! Wait, I make a call on my burner! At the beep, I give a code and say it's done. That's all. I swear it! Then the money comes to my P.O. box through the mail. It's cash in a package."

Weeks was watching. "I don't trust this son of a bitch. He's not telling us something."

Weeks asked, "How much do you get for this job?"

Beck answered, "I get twenty grand." With a touch of desperation, he added, "Let me go and you can have the money. You can have all my money."

Harp conferred with Bonny and Weeks before he came back to Beck. Bonny left. "What's your name?" Harp asked, adopting a friendly manner.

"They just call me Beck."

"The name on the rental contract is Charles Beck," Weeks said.

Kip was curious. "You said that this is what you do. How many of these "jobs" have you done?"

Very reluctant to respond, Beck shrugged. "Answer the man, Beck," Harp said with menace in his voice.

"I guess a hundred or so. I don't count 'em."

Kip continued, "And probably in some of those jobs there were fatalities; men, women, kids?"

Beck explained, "I am not supposed to factor that into the job. If I tried to hit only the places that were empty, I would never get anything done. It's collateral damage. You know how it is." He paused before adding, "Listen, you got to understand. This is a business. People get into financial trouble. I help them get out of trouble. I'm doing them a favor."

Even the most jaded cynic would have cringed at that excuse for the horror he had created. "I'm not the only one doing this.

It happens all the time." Harp shook his head and looked at his band of soldiers with a question in his eyes. They knew what he was asking. Should they proceed as earlier agreed? Each nodded, each aware of the gravity of the decision. The man had tried to kill them. If he lived, he would succeed in other places. This creature might kill many more innocent people.

Harp waited until Weeks untied Beck and helped him to his feet. "Okay, Beck. Here's what we're going to do." The blindfold remained. "We've got your car here. We've got a picture of you and your prints on the explosives. You are now out of the business." Harp handed Beck his phone, "We are going to dial this number and you're going to give the code that the job is done. I'll dial the number, you give the code."

Beck gave him the number and Harp dialed. At the beep, Beck said, "d4779. Done." Harp immediately turned the phone off and removed the battery. Beck was nodding vigorously as Harp spoke, "If you get your ass far away from here and promise to quit this shit, we are going to let you go." Beck was elated. He just wanted to get away as fast as possible. He was going to collect his stash and head south. He would be out of the business for a long, long time. It never occurred to him that this was too easy.

Bonny had been gone for several minutes then came back in and signaled. Harp nodded to Weeks who then brought Beck's car around to the front driveway facing the road. Beck was helped into his car, still blindfolded. Beck sat quietly behind the wheel. "Here's how it's going down, Beck. We've got everything on you. Picture, prints, your explosives, and we've got your car make and license number. We're going to give all this to the sheriff in one hour. What happens to you after that is no concern to us. I would advise getting out of this county as quick as you can. Now, go!" The arsonist did not waste any time. He ripped the blindfold off without looking at them and tore down the drive to the road. They heard his motor whining as Beck raced down the county road, probably heading to the interstate.

It was starting to get light in the east as they turned back toward the house. "How long has he got?" Weeks asked.

Bonny looked at his watch and calculated. "About twelve more minutes. I put his little bag in the trunk with all the explosives and timers in it. It should be clear of any effects.

Kip worried that there would be collateral damage. Bonny explained. "It's a real small charge stuck to the side of the center console. It's shaped toward the driver. It will get him, but I don't think it'll go any farther. There probably won't even be a fire. It's late. I doubt there will be anybody else out there on these roads. When they find his other charge in the trunk, they'll figure out that he's a pro and assume that he got careless with a timer. That's the plan, anyway."

"Weeks, did you wipe it down?" Harp asked.

"Totally. They'll never tie him back to us." They had been extra careful to leave nothing for forensics.

"We okay?" Each man nodded and all fists bumped at the same time. It was, however, more of a commitment than celebration.

***

Before they hit the sack for a little sleep during the remainder of the morning, they removed all signs of the water-boarding and made sure that no tire marks from Beck's car were visible. "Sarge, it just occurred to me that somebody does know about Beck's being here," Kip commented as they entered the kitchen.

"Yeah, I know; the bastard who hired him."

"It's not going to stop, is it Sarge?" Bonny said.

"Nope, I don't think so."

"Listen up, men. You all try to get some sleep. I'm going to stay up and stand watch. I need to think on this some more."

Thirteen miles away, while still in the county, a happy Beck was pointed south and tasting freedom. He could not believe his good luck. He smiled when he saw the sign saying it was just three miles to the interstate. Home free, he said to himself—just before the small charge stuck to the inside of the center console went off. Beck might have had time to wonder at what was happening, but probably not. There wasn't a single blast but a sequence of shocking explosions when all the air bags were actuated at the same time. The effect was to confine the explosive charge to the interior of the car. These incredible safety devices also neatly held Beck in place during the milliseconds his upper body was separated from the lower. There was no fire and only the rear window was blown out by the force of the expanding gases. With Beck's foot off the gas, the car coasted along a shallow ditch and came to a stop against a drainage pipe with its motor still running. The top half of the driver fell to his right after the air bags had deflated. The first people on the scene, well-meaning and intent on helping, did not deserve the hideous vision presented when they looked in the windows.

As planned, the large chunk of explosive concealed in the trunk did not detonate. Further, all the small electronic parts which are used to create a timed explosive were conveniently found in the small black satchel covered with Beck's prints. When these materials were found, it was quickly concluded that this was a case beyond the capabilities of the local police. State explosive experts were called in and an intensive investigation initiated to find out who this guy was and what he was doing with these materials. The obvious assumption was that this was a perpetrator who got careless with his shit. Subsequent investigation did little to change that idea, even though timer pieces remained in the console. Sheriff Senter did not readily accept that conclusion. He was thinking that things like this just did not happen in his county. Until those boys moved into that farm, that is. He sighed. He guessed he would have to drive out there again.

16

A TROUBLED HARP WAS STILL WANDERING AND THINK-
ing as the sun rose in the east. He was accepting the truth that
his stubbornness had placed his crew in danger. Why in hell
didn't he take the damned money and walk away. Beck's action
brought the whole situation into a new light. Of course, the sale
of the farm was a no-brainer. It had never been his intention to
hold on to it. Now, however, the time factor had taken on a new
importance. He would never forgive himself if his stubbornness
brought harm to any of these guys. He had begun to regard them
with a deeper affection; almost like a family. He must be getting
old and soft, he thought.

Making matters worse was the fact that he had developed a
grudging attachment to the house. That morning, as the sun rose
over the low hills to the east and painted the house in morning
colors, Harp stood in the front drive and watched as the house
sat perfectly in its place in the world. When the light had crept
down from the front peak to the windows upstairs, he shrugged
angrily and admonished himself to cut the crap. He took a final

tour around the house before going in and starting breakfast. Yes, he was cooking breakfast. Kip had never cooked a thing in his life, Weeks was too impatient and served everything either burned or raw, and Bonny thought that salt and pepper were the staffs of life and poured them on anything he cooked. Disgusted with himself, Harp found that he secretly enjoyed throwing things together to make a meal. It was especially rewarding when his diners hungrily ate anything put in front of them—even eggs and spam. That made it easy to cook for them.

Once again, just as they had finished eating, the Sheriff pulled into the yard. This time he politely knocked. Gazing down the hall from his chair at the end of the table, Weeks announced that it was the Sheriff. They looked at one another with the big question in their eyes: had they covered their tracks well enough? They smiled and shrugged, "Go let him in, Weeks."

At Weeks' welcome, Senter entered the kitchen and sat at the table with a deep sigh. "Got some coffee?" Harp found a cup and poured. They waited with innocent pleasant expressions. Senter looked around the table, taking time to study each face and sipped his coffee. "You know, a sheriff who's plugged in these days can find out anything about just about anybody. I can learn just about everything I want to know about guys named Harper, Bondurant, Weeks, and Finch-Smithers." He held up his cup for a refill. Harp poured again. They remained silent. "This is good coffee. I thank you." Senter continued, "I found that you were all good soldiers with lots of medals and lots of injuries—which I admire and I thank you for your service. Weeks, you had some trouble but I guess you got it straightened out."

He paused before going on. Weeks shrugged. "What I couldn't

233

find in all that information is why my county has gone to hell since you four got here." Senter leaned back and crossed his legs. He put his Stetson on his knee. "Last night, or early this morning, there was this car in a ditch down by the interstate. There were a few concerned citizens who looked into that car just to be nice and offer help if it was needed. They said that every person who looked into that car puked their guts out."

He took a long sip of coffee and paused to look around the table. "It looked like some damned fool who was into some serious explosives managed to blow himself up. Cut himself in half. Bottom half in the driver's seat, top half in the rider's seat. Very neat. Almost too neat. Like maybe it was planned that way." Senter looked at the ceiling and around the kitchen, taking in all the new paint and repairs. "Then they found this brick of explosives along with timer materials right there in the trunk of this guy's car. Real stupid." The sheriff just shook his head. "Oh, and you know what else? They say he was soaking wet."

Senter widened his eyes comically. "The state guys are pretty sure he was a guy who had been in the business and think they might have a line on him. They even think he was a pro—so they got the fibbies involved. So now, in my quiet and peaceful little county, all of a sudden I got the state crime lab and the F, B, and fucking I trying to figure out for sure who he was and what he was doing here. Then they're asking me if I have any idea what the hell a guy like this is doing in my peaceful little county. I'm just shaking my head and saying I got no fuckin' idea. Do you have any idea what it's like dealing with the FBI? They pat you on the head and kindly ask you to go back to your little office and leave the real investigative work to the pros. Then they cut you out of the loop and act surprised when you express a little dissat-isfaction with their methods."

Senter shook his head in irritation. "And all the time I'm thinking something. I'm thinking about some people they don't even know exist." Senter smiled coldly. "Trouble is, I DO have fucking ideas. I'm saying to myself, suppose this guy was in the area to do a job? What kind of job would it be? It would most likely be burning something down or blowing something up. But who or what would be the target? I know every goddamned square foot of this county. I just about know every mother's son in the county. So I ask myself: what is different around here that would all of a sudden attract that kind of talent?"

Senter leaned forward and pointed at each of them, one by one, and said, "You four are what's different around here. And, no surprise, you four are probably the only characters in the county who know what to do when you catch a piece of shit like the deceased in the act." He sipped his coffee and sighed, "You know, I have been Sheriff all these years and I have never shot anybody. You guys have shot and killed men. You know what it is like to kill people. I don't. Yet, here I am, with the job of making men like you obey the law." He looked around the table. "Make no mistake, irony or not, I will run your asses into that jail downtown in a heartbeat if I find you breaking MY laws."

While the Sheriff sat looking at them, each of Harp's crew solemnly returned his gaze with no expression. Each was think-ing, however, that this guy was no dummy. He had managed to put all the facts together in exactly the right way. They were cool, however, and just sat and waited. Kip, Harp thought, was especially cool because he was so young but very aware of the gravity of what they had done.

After waiting for a couple of minutes, Senter stood and put his hat on. "It has not escaped my attention that anyone who fucks with you guys ends up with his nuts handed back on a platter. I kind of admire that. But let me warn you, don't try it with me. Just get the hell out of my county." He strode toward the door. "I'll let myself out."

He did not hit the siren this time.

They sat for a while, each in his own world. Finally, Harp spoke, using a phrase from long ago. "We all know the price of poker has gone up. Now, some bastard is willing to kill us all just to get his hands on the place. That means that there is somehow a time element in this situation that we do not understand. Whoever wants this place is really desperate."

Bonny leaned back in his chair, thinking out loud. "The thing is, everybody knows you are going to sell and that ain't good enough."

"Maybe we ought to dig in and just wait 'em out," Weeks offered.

"I got to admit that that is most natural for me," Harp said. "The thing is, I don't want to see any of you get hurt just because I got a bug up my ass."

"Don't worry about us, Sarge. Do what you think is optimal for the mission," Bonny suggested, falling into military jargon.

"Yeah, that's what I think," Kip agreed.

Weeks nodded, and said, "There is one thing, though. Are we going to just forget the douchbag who paid this guy to burn us out?"

"No," Harp said. "He's going to pay. I don't know who or how yet, but he'll pay."

"When we sell the place, won't we know who it is? Won't it be the buyer?" Kip asked.

"We'll be closer, but the one son of a bitch who made the call could be buried under layers of corporate bullshit," Bonny said.

"We need to remember that, if people find out what's in that hole up there, the entire damned farm would turn into a zoo. We would never be able to sell it until they had studied the thing to death," Harp said. His mind flashed back to what he had seen and he was angry all over again.

"Wait a minute!" Weeks was excited at a new thought. "Sarge, you said you were going to think about Bonny's idea. You know, what would happen if we sold it and *then* the word got out about it?"

"The buyer would be royally screwed," Harp answered, grinning, happy to be reminded. "Whatever he had planned would have to wait until the whole thing had been studied all to hell and gone." They enjoyed a moment of dreaming of the impact on whoever bought the place.

"I don't know for sure, but if you know something like this and don't reveal it at the time of the sale, you might get charged with fraud," Bonny cautioned. "And say we sell the place. How do we let the history people know about it without letting on that we knew about it beforehand?"

"I hate to say it, Sarge, but I think we need a lawyer," Kip suggested. "We need someone who can handle big, complicated sales like this. But who the hell can we trust around here?"

Harp knew immediately who to call. He wasn't sure, however,

that he established a *business* relationship with this lawyer. He smiled to himself at the thought of trying.

"What are you grinning about, Sarge?" Weeks asked, wondering where the humor was in this situation.

Harp put those thoughts out of his head and answered, "Nothing. Just something about a lawyer I know."

Harp raised a hand to get their attention. "Okay, here's what we're going to do. I'm going to contact this lawyer and try to set up a meeting. Kip, I want you to get busy finding out as much as you can about those poor bastards in that hole up there. Start with that medallion I brought out and see what you can find. Bonny and Weeks, set up a guard schedule. I want an active patrol on all parts of our land all the time. We'll all pull our shifts. I do not feel like we can let our guard down at any time. Remember, we can't attack, but we can retreat to regroup." And, he thought to himself with a strange sense of nervousness and excitement, I have got to call a lawyer named Kowalski.

17

ADAM LEYTON WILLARDE STOOD AT THE WINDOW OF HIS office in Pittsburgh staring at his phone in disbelief. He had just been informed that, not only was the job not done, but the idiot fucker who was supposed to do it was dead, having blown himself up instead. He had also learned that the money he had mailed was not refundable. That was the least of his worries, but it added to his growing anger. What the goddamned hell do I have to do to get those losers off that useless little piece of shit land, he muttered as he gazed down upon the world beneath his building. Willarde was unaccustomed to failure among his staff and was quick to punish anyone who did not deliver exactly what he had ordered. But, even he could not punish a man who rested in two parts on a tray in the morgue. Nor could he punish the contact who hired the two-part man. He was just a number known to very few operators at Willarde's level.

I've got to rethink this mess, he thought. The trouble was, he was running out of time and he was the only one who knew it. Except for that geologist, and he was sworn to secrecy. Willarde wished for a moment that he could consult someone, anyone, on this situation but, if the word got out, it would be a fucking disaster. Even that mealy-mouthed Parsnip did not know the real story.

It started with a convention, Willarde remembered, as he looked down on the rivers of Pittsburgh. It was in Texas and it was a gathering of people interested in, or invested in, the new aspects of drilling for natural gas by fracking. Because the processes were still being developed, there were many key papers presenting recent studies and most were met with genuine interest by the attendees. There was one less attended smaller session, however, *Spontaneous Oil Flow Regeneration in Old Wells Adjacent to Contemporary Hydraulic Fracturing Zones of Certain Dimension and Pattern*, which Willarde attended because he had nothing else to do at the moment.

The main thrust of the paper was that old oil wells were mostly drilled straight down and abandoned too soon when output diminished. Usually the operator was unwilling to invest in deeper drilling when there was no guarantee of new production and the area had already shown signs of depletion. Yet, there were certain geologic formations where new gas fracturing surrounding a once unpromising and weak oil source would also fracture the center of the underlying oil bearing strata, thus freeing the oil from its geologic confinement. Once free, this oil would flow laterally to seek a path of release which would focus on any weakness in the geologic structure. Predictions were that former oil wells of a certain depth in certain areas would become the path for this release. Further, when this happened, it would tend to produce oil in quantities great enough for incredible profits. In other words, some of these abandoned old wells could become gushers, producing incredible riches, and most importantly, with no investment in the costly process of drilling.

Willarde was already a rich man, but the notion of simply uncapping old wells excited him. Through one subterfuge or another, he already owned the mineral rights to thousands of acres of Pennsylvania lands and was gleefully counting the millions that were pouring into his accounts from natural gas production. But, he thought, oil was different. Significant new oil production in the middle of the eastern part of the United States would be a game changer. Using the designs suggested in that paper, Willarde hired an expert geologist to study his fracking empire. Employing those guidelines in his computer records, the expert found a few areas that might qualify. However, the geologist stated, there was one spot where it would be surprising if the reaction *did not* occur. It was a small plot of land in central western Pennsylvania which had old wells that had been prematurely shut down and that was uniformly surrounded by zones of fracking activity at different levels of the strata.

At Willarde's direction, and at a time when Pauline and Lars were not at home, the geologist located the two wells in question. To his horror, the wells seemed almost alive. The old cast iron caps and valves, standing about chest high, were hot to the touch and slightly vibrating. Using his sound probe which magnified internal sounds, he heard the creaking of rock and metal which were the sounds of immense forces at work. He knew this was not gas. This was oil. He considered it amazing that the old metal containing these forces was still holding. His best guess was that it was only a matter of weeks, maybe days, until they blew off.

Basically, it could happen at any time. He was afraid that it might even be possible for the pressure to blow the well casings out of the ground. This would unleash an environmental calamity on anyone nearby, certainly the people at the farmhouse only a few hundred yards away. It would also produce untold wealth to the owner. He could not even guess what would happen if the oil and gas ignited.

The geologist, owner of J.H. Lindsay Geologic Consulting, was an honorable man. He had signed a confidentiality agreement with Willarde and he would abide by it—up to a point. He was seriously concerned about the possible harm that might occur if these old caps failed. He made this clear in his report to Willarde. He stated that he would maintain the secrecy for only a short period during which Willarde had to promise that he would endeavor to alleviate the danger. Willarde agreed and immediately began his efforts to purchase the farm. It never occurred to the geologist that his life might be in danger, not from the wells, but from a man who would stop at nothing to own them.

Willarde hoped that he could secure the farm before it became necessary to take drastic steps to confine the knowledge to himself alone. He was a determined man who placed little value on the lives of individuals who got in his way. After making several very fair offers for the farm—and being turned down by the Kuykendahls—he decided to pay a personal visit to Lars. This was something he avoided, preferring to work through nameless representatives, but this situation had become that important. He just wanted to get the measure of the man. He had driven himself to preserve security. That day, at the remote unmanned well on which Lars was doing maintenance work, Willarde introduced himself to Lars and made another offer for his farm. He was polite and non-confrontational. But, as soon as Lars found out what he wanted, he erupted in anger and, with much profanity, told Willarde again that he would not sell and that he resented the constant pressure from all the frackers.

Willarde, responding in anger, stepped toward Lars who pushed Willarde away. Willarde instinctively pushed back. Lars was off balance and fell backward off the low platform on which they were standing. He landed on a large pointed bolt jutting from a wooden beam on the ground below. Shocked to find that, after a few feeble kicks, Lars was dead, Willarde knew that he could in no way be tied to this accident, even if it really wasn't his fault. In climbing up onto the platform, touching railings, etc., he had no doubt left fingerprints. After scanning the area for witnesses, he opened the valve on a small burn-off gas line at the base of the platform. Then, getting a safe distance away, threw a flaming rag tied to a stick into the cloud of gas now surrounding Lars. The gas ignited with a large thump. The platform and Lars' oil-soaked clothes were soon burning. Willarde was well away when the first responders arrived. The coroner concluded that Lars had opened the valve, created a spark, started a fire and, in a panic, had fallen backward onto the bolt.

Though Willarde had given some consideration to what might happen to Pauline, now that Lars was gone, he had nothing to do with her death. She was carelessly texting on her cell phone and went off the road into a creek and drowned. The coroner correctly cited her death as an accident. To Willarde, it just meant a problem was solved. Consequently, he had been assured by Parsnip that, whether or not an heir was found, and he didn't think there were any, Parsnip, as intermediate executer, would be able to assign the mineral rights—for fracking he would assume—to the land to *protect the interest of the heirs.*

Willarde would be home free. Then, that idiot lawyer had fumbled this simplest task after some New Jersey thug had showed up to claim the farm. Now, he had a farmstead full of crippled veterans who were apparently in no hurry to take his money. Willarde's anger and frustration were beyond description. He was desperate for another plan. Maybe more money would do it, but they had already refused four mill for the fucking place. Who were these guys, anyway?

18

KIP TAPPED THE LAST COMPUTER KEY AND SLUMPED
back in his chair with a sense of sorrow over what he had learned.
He absentmindedly rubbed the scar tissue on his cheek. Oddly
enough, his wound didn't really hurt now, but it was a presence,
a pulling on the surrounding skin that causing a deep, low level
itching. It just pulled on the surrounding normal tissue. It did
not respond to scratching, but a mild, pushing massage—which
he had learned was most effective. He would never have thought
that he could come to accept such horrific damage to his face,
but he was growing cautiously accustomed to it—which was far
beyond where he would have been had he not come to Harp's
farm. Without thinking about it, after he had rubbed his face,
he would then reach down over the side of the chair where Fart
would gently lick his fingers. Then Kip would smile, which was
another thing he was getting used to again.

Apart from the new urge to smile was the feeling of it now
pushing against the scar tissue on his cheek. The dog and the boy
were partners in these changes. The rest of the band recognized

this and were quietly pleased at Kip's improvement. Fart was giving Kip something that no one else could provide, and the rest of the crew were greatly pleased to watch it happen.

A gloomy Kip left the office and went in search of the other three. He had some difficult information to impart. It was late afternoon and they were in the family room downstairs discussing what they might have for dinner. They had gotten tired of Harp's steak and potatoes. Pizza was an option, but they didn't think it could be delivered so far out. Further, they weren't sure if they dared to leave the farm unattended while going into town for some restaurant offerings. It was a lively discussion and Kip's efforts to interrupt were ignored. Finally, he shouted, "Hey!" with some anger in his voice. The others were shocked into silence. This was a voice from the young soldier that they had never heard. Even the old Sarge was silent and respectful. Now, they were listening.

"I think I know what happened up there in that cave." He held up the medal that Harp had brought up from the hole. "This shows what I think is the Moravian Cross. I won't get into what Moravians believed except to say they were Christian. Anybody can look up the details anytime on the web." Kip sat on a bar stool while they listened intently.

"I plugged 'Moravian' into the internet along with words like killing, death, massacre. What I came up with is really unbelievable. Sarge, you said that somehow something in the way the bodies looked made you think they might be Indians. That fits. So I'm going to tell it the way I think it happened."

He looked at his notes. "The Delaware Indians originally lived along the Delaware River in new Jersey." Kip looked at

Sarge. "That means they were Jersey guys like you, Sarge." Harp made a fist and pumped. "But, when the British came here, these Indians were pressured to move westerly in the early 1700's to avoid the colonists. Then they ran into another bunch of Indians, the Iroquois, who drove them further west. They ended up crossing the Ohio River and settling in what is now Ohio. At first, this was French territory, but, when the French left, it became British along with American colonists." Kip was pleased to note that he had a rapt audience.

"When the American Revolution began, these Delaware Indians were torn between support for the British and the new revolutionaries. Many had adopted Christianity and lived in Moravian Church Missions at Schoenbrunn and Gnadenhutten in eastern Ohio. Some tried to remain neutral, but some gave their support to the British. Some were afraid that, if the Americans won against the British, then they would be driven out of their lands again."

Weeks had gone behind the bar and gotten everyone a beer. Kip drank one long pull and continued. "The Americans wanted the Delaware to be their allies in the fight for freedom from British rule, but as the war went on, certain groups did not trust them." Kip took a deep breath before continuing the story. "Now we get into the tragic part of this story. In 1782, some Pennsylvania militiamen, thinking these Indians had carried out several raids, crossed over into Ohio territory and killed about 100 Christian Delawares in what was called the Gnadenhutten Massacre. These righteous bastards killed entire families, including women and children."

He paused and put his notes on the bar and finished his beer.

His audience sat quietly. "Now, I think there was another massacre which nobody knows about. If the bodies in that hole are Indian and if they are Moravian Christian, I think there was another earlier killing of a smaller group that had not gotten far enough west yet. I think there was a small Delaware colony here in these hills that tried to stay neutral and hide out. I think they were discovered during roughly the same time period. I think these bastard militiamen slaughtered them. Maybe to hide what they had done or maybe just to get rid of the bodies, they threw them down in that hole. They didn't even bother killing the kids. They just threw them in."

He held up the stone. "That young girl held the proof in her hand when you found her, Sarge. You said she had written 'Malisha done it.' She was not referring to a person. She was saying the *militia* had done it. She was saying that it was the fucking militia that had killed them." Somehow exhausted from the intensity of this narration, Kip threw his notes on the bar and opened another bottle. "Put it all together: You got the fact that it was obviously a vicious slaughter, you got the Indian look, the Moravian cross and, finally, you got the girl's words." Kip threw himself into one of the recliners, flopped back, and finished. "What you got is an enormous fucking black mark on the history of this state, and a thousand books that will have to be written or re-written."

His audience sat in stunned silence, trying to absorb the enormity of what they had just learned.

"My God," Weeks said.

"Yeah." Bonny said. "It's got mass murder, Indians, tortured kids, national history, a hidden cave, and let's not forget, religion. This whole area would turn into a media nut house."

"A giant cluster-fuck," Harp agreed. "And, don't forget the history and preservation geeks at the state and federal levels. I'm guessing the state would take the whole place over, at least for a while."

Kip reminded Sarge, "Like you said Sarge, if this got out, you would play hell trying to sell the place."

"Okay, you all get started on your watch schedule. We cannot afford to let our guard down now. I'm going to make a phone call." Harp winced as he said the words. He really did not know how to do this. Harp held the phone for a long time before dialing. Finally, he sighed and punched the numbers she had given him. The firm's main receptionist passed him along to Kowalski's secretary.

"Let me talk to Sandra Kowalski, please."

"Your name please."

"Horace B. Harper."

"And what is the nature of your business, Mr. Harper?"

"It's a private matter."

"Hold, please."

Harp held for long enough to get impatient.

"Miss Kowalski is very busy today and …"

Harp interrupted, "Tell her it's real important and I need to talk to her now."

"Please hold."

"She says she does not recall a Horace Harper."

"Tell her that I'm the one who inherited that damned Pennsylvania farm, which means I am a client of hers, dammit."

"Please hold."

"She says she needs some proof of identity before she can make time in her schedule."

"Okay, what does she want?"

"She wants to know the name of the dog at the farm you inherited."

Having gotten used to the name and being preoccupied, he answered simply, "Fart."

"I beg your pardon."

"I said, Fart."

"That is a most insulting suggestion, Mr. Harper, and this conversation is over."

"Wait! You asked for the dog's name! I wasn't telling you to fart!"

"Well, I should hope not. We simply will not put up with such obscene demands."

"It wasn't a demand, dammit all. I would never tell a woman to fart over the phone." Harp realized he had somehow gotten way too deep in an absolutely ridiculous conversation.

There was a long pause during which there were faint screams in the background. The secretary came back. She spoke with a strange choking sound, as if she were trying to swallow while speaking.

But she remained professional and coolly asked, "Miss Kowalski asks if that meant to imply that you might make such demands of another vocation. Like a lawyer perhaps?"

"No, dammit. I wouldn't tell a lawyer to do that either." Harp was sweating and wondering what it would take to get through to Kowalski.

"Hold, please." Now, it really sounded like the secretary was choking on something.

Finally, Kowalski came on the line. She was gasping as if

out of breath. Harp could hear laughing in the background that seemed almost hysterical.

"Hello, Harper. How's the dog?"

"I'm glad I get to give you some laughs, Kowalski. What the hell, you put me on speaker phone so the whole damned office gets a chuckle?"

"Just me and my secretary. She typed up all the papers, so she knew all about your dog. We bring it up once in a while when we need a laugh."

"Wonderful. Let me know when I can call again and brighten your day," Harp started to disconnect.

Sensing that she had taken the joke a little too far, the lawyer quickly recovered. "Hold on, Harper. I know you wouldn't have called unless something is going on. What can I do for you?"

Mollified but still a little miffed, Harp explained, "The situation here at the farm has gotten very strange. We want to sell it and we've got a buyer but there are some things we have to work out first. We need you to advise us."

"Okay. Tell me what you need. And who is 'we'?"

"It's not that simple, Kowalski. You're going to have to come out here."

"Harper, I have a desk full of complicated transactions. I can't simply drop everything and drive out to East Jesus to arrange a land sale."

"Goddammit, somebody has tried to blow us up! They could've killed us all! And, dammit all, listen to me! We have a pile of dead bodies that are part of the deal!"

Stunned, Kowalski was thinking furiously. Now very focused,

she commanded, "Harper, don't say another word! Julie!" muting the phone, she yelled to her secretary, "we need to start recording!"

The phone still muted, she yelled again to her secretary. "Is it done? Good."

Then, mute off, she came back to Harp, "Okay, Horace B. Harper, with your permission, we are recording this conversation. Before we go any further, do you wish to retain me as your legal counsel?"

Harp knew full well what it meant to have a formal agreement with a lawyer. "Yes, and yes, I do."

"Okay, you are now my client and client/attorney agreements are in effect. I agree that my presence will be necessary at your place of residence. Give me a couple of days to give all this other stuff to someone else or get it rescheduled. Okay?"

For a man accustomed to making all the decisions during his lifetime, it was with an odd sense of relief that Harp agreed. "Okay. Good. Call when you get close. We'll be waiting."

"Who is 'we,' Harper?"

"There are four of us. All good men. I'll explain when you get here."

"Four?"

"Yeah"

"See you in a couple of days."

"Roger."

Kowalski was tempted but did not say, "Out."

19

The caps on those old oil wells were not made to contain high pressure. They were placed there to cover an inactive well. Perhaps not really necessary, but required by law and common sense. The good news is that, in those days, all the capping components were made of very heavy, high-quality iron. They had withstood decades of weathering and occasional bumping by farm equipment. They were not designed for the challenge of deep fractures providing new pathways for high pressure petroleum and gas arising from untapped pockets much further underground. Such well caps were a good design in their day, with deep ridge and slot fittings. What was not good in their design were the gaskets, the last defense when a liquid or gas wants to escape.

Contemporary gaskets are made from exotic man-made materials fashioned specifically for the material to be contained and tightly fitted into grooves. The old gaskets were cut from cork, pure and simple. Cork is good in ships and bottles. It makes a wonderful grip on a fishing rod. Generations of people have grown old pinning their notes to sheets of cork. It floats a lure and fishing nets. Cork is everywhere around us. But cork by itself is not meant to hold a very hot liquid under very high pressure for very long. The gaskets on these old well caps were made of cork and installed with no sealing compound.

On the bottom joint of the well to the north of the house, the pressure had squeezed past all mechanical obstructions and confronted the very thin line of cork between the outer flanges. This relentless force had pushed and poked until it found the one microscopic gap between the grains of the cork. Now, it focused on that spot. Instead of pushing at a flat edge, it began to push sideways inside the gap. The gasket was not made to defend itself from this kind of pressure. So the gap grew, micro-millimeter by micro-millimeter.

Over the weeks, the gap grew, unbeknownst to any of the parties now involved with the Kuykendahl farm. The geologist had noticed a sign of very old leakage, but that was attributed to more of a capillary action. This was a real gap which soon developed into tiny channels reaching from the inner edge all the way to the outside of this old oil well stopper. Where the channels met the outside world, the first evidence of the things to come blossomed into small, thick-walled iridescent bubbles. And so, the viscous remnants of plants and animals which flourished in the light of the sun and which died millions of years ago now once again came forth into sunlight. A bubble would form and collapse. Another would form overnight. They now appeared at a rate of one or two a day. Soon, it would be three bubbles a day, then four and, ever more quickly, more and more. Though no one was aware of it, the bubbles were growing even as Kowalski proceeded to Harp's farm.

Harp and his group were now agreed that they needed to sell the farm and they needed to move quickly before knowledge of the massacre got out. But this had nothing to do with the wells. Unaware that the leakage foreshadowed a disaster beyond their wildest imagination, they were simply anxious to get away from the place with the best deal possible. Oddly enough, their goals were now in complete accord with Willarde's. He wanted them gone as soon as possible so he could engineer containment of the source of those bubbles and all that they portended—before the whole damned thing blew up. Unfortunately, he was afraid the time to meet and strike a deal had come and gone. Something had to be done and done now.

20

WHILE WAITING FOR KOWALSKI, HARP FOCUSED ON A
new state of readiness. He wasn't sure what would happen next
and, for a military man responsible for his troops, he decided to
be ready for just about anything. While laughing at the whole
thing, they all practiced the steps that Harp had designed. It
wasn't enough to simply stand watch, as they had been doing.
They needed to be able to act and act quickly, hence the drills. He
wanted to be ready when she arrived. He would now be responsible for her also.

Kowalski called to let them know she had followed her GPS
and was just a couple of miles away after an easy drive. Harp,
Weeks, and Kip came down the steps as she pulled up in front
of the house. Bonny was out happily doing something on the
tractor. They waited until she had stopped and, as women will
always do, fiddled with her purse for a long moment before she
emerged from the car. She stood casually, leaning on the roof of
her Mercedes, looking them over. "I know I have seen a homelier
bunch of misfits somewhere in my life, but I cannot remember

where." Harp grinned and thought, that is Kowalski alright. He thought she looked much better than he remembered. She still had the short curly hair and sunglasses blocked her eyes—but it was easy to see that she was a beautiful woman. She stepped around the front of her car and started toward them with a confident stride. She was wearing stylish boots, tight jeans, and a sheer blouse. They stood and stared.

"When you three idiots are finished gawking, how about getting my stuff out of the trunk? I brought some fresh oysters in that cooler, so don't spill them. There's some crab cakes you need to get in the fridge."

She looked at Weeks, "What do you think, Hook, can you carry a suitcase?"

Then at Kip, "How's about giving him a hand there, Patch. Harper and I have some things to talk over."

Kowalski grabbed Harp's arm, spun him around, and marched him up the steps. "Where's your bedroom, Harper?" Harp pointed. "Well, what are we waiting for?" She pushed him ahead of her and slammed the bedroom door. "I always keep my promises," was all she said.

Weeks and Kip were still standing outside, mouths open, where they had stopped when she walked past them. She had pushed their tough old sergeant into the house like he was a baby.

"Hook?" Weeks said in wonder.

"Patch?" Kip said, not sure yet how to take it.

They looked at each other and started laughing. From that moment, each was a little bit in love with this beautiful, brash lawyer. As they carried the few pieces of luggage, they were shouting back and forth.

"Hey, Hook, can you hook this bag?"

"I don't know, Patch, can you see where you're going?"

"How's about hooking this little thing on your hook, Hook?"

"Can't you see I'm already hooked up, Patch?"

Neither had laughed so hard for a long time. If you asked them, they would say it was more therapeutic than their many sessions with army psychotherapists.

When they had carried all her luggage into the house, they started toward the kitchen to ask where she wanted it. As they passed the master bedroom they heard the unmistakable sounds of enthusiastic lovemaking. Actually, it was the sound of *her* enthusiastic lovemaking. Harp did not make a sound.

In a hushed tone, with not just a little awe, Kip whispered, "So this beautiful woman arrives in a Mercedes, tells us what to do, grabs the Sarge, and pushes him into the bedroom, and then they do it. Just like that. When I grow up, I want to be just like the Sarge."

Weeks whispered, "I would almost give my other arm to fu . ., uh, make love to a woman like that."

When Harp and Kowalski finally emerged, they came to the kitchen where the rest of the bunch sat enjoying a late afternoon beer. Bonny had come in and was trying to describe how powerful the tractor was. The barrister was not the least self-conscious about her recent activity, though everyone else was. So, as was her usual method, she took charge. "Harper, why don't you introduce me."

Harp started with Bonny. "This is Sergeant Marion Bondurant. We call him Bonny." Bonny stood and shook hands with Kowalski.

"This is Corporal Phillip Weeks. We just call him Weeks." Weeks stood up and offered his hand. With a big grin, he said, "You can call me Hook." Kip broke out laughing. Bonny looked on in confusion. He hadn't been there when she arrived. "And this is Private Wellington Kipling Finch-Smithers, the Fourth. We call him Kip." Kip was already standing and said, "You can call me Patch." He and Weeks broke out laughing again.

Bonny, slightly irritated, asked, "What the hell is going on here?" Kowalski smiled, keeping the inside joke inside. She was secretly happy that they had taken it the right way. She was almost weeping inside to see what war had done. She vowed that she would do whatever she could to help this ragtag group sell this place for the max amount.

"Nothing, Bonny. We'll explain later."

"Wait!" Kowalski commanded. They all stopped as if struck. "You forgot someone … or something. Where's the dog. I have got to meet this dog!"

Kip went outside and returned with Fart at his heel. Fart, perhaps the ugliest dog in Pennsylvania and strong as an ox, walked to stand in front of her as if waiting for orders. The cool lawyer dropped to her knees and grabbed his jowls and said in an uncharacteristic soft voice, "Finally we meet." At the sound of this female voice, the dog did just about everything but pee on the floor. He slumped, twisted, whined, wagged his ass, and laid his head on her knee and looked up at her. Kowalski looked into his eyes and said, "I know your story. I'm glad you're okay." She scruffed his head again and stood up. He would follow her anywhere. Harp thought the dog's behavior was disgusting. Some kind of killer guard dog, he mumbled.

"Okay, we have got a lot to talk about and time is wasting. Let's get the oysters steamed and the crab cakes frying. We'll eat, then talk."

They looked at Harp. "Well, you heard the woman. Let's go!" And they jumped to. "Who's got the watch?"

Bonny answered, "Got it, Sarge." He strapped on the belt with the gear and donned the night vision goggles.

Kowalski was amazed. "You have someone out there every night?"

"Every night. We don't dare to let our guard down," Bonny waved and left.

With the table cleared, Harp's attorney laid a legal pad on the table and said, "Let's start at the beginning, but before we do, do each of you agree to engage me as your attorney?" They nodded vigorously. "Good, from now on, anything you say is covered by attorney-client privilege. I know how Harp inherited this farm. Let's take it from the day you arrived here." She was looking at Harp.

Harp started. She laughed when he recounted the manner in which he had retained the mineral rights. She was appalled at the actions of the local police and the thugs at the market. She was surprised at the size of the offer for the land and puzzled at the sense of immediacy in the deal. She could not believe that it was the Sheriff's staff who had wrecked the house.

"Can we tell her about what we did with the police car?" Weeks asked. "And why we did it?"

Kowalski responded, "Why don't you tell me and I'll let you know whether or not you can tell me." She was listening in amazement to what had happened in this strange little town.

When Weeks had finished telling the story with a lot of colorful detail, she giggled and said that it was not germane so it would not be part of the record.

The fate of the arsonist was not mentioned. It was understood that this was a story that each of them would take to the grave. It was certainly key to the narrative, but the agreement was never to tell a soul. To violate that trust would be to betray comrades. That they would not do. To Harp, it was the one unforgivable action that had been taken against him and his men. It was part of the real reason for wanting to sell the property in a certain way and he could not tell her why. Maybe he could someday take care of paybacks by himself. It was late when she asked, "Okay, this is all very interesting. No question that something is going on here that we do not understand. But, you want to sell the property. So let's sell the property. I can draw up the best goddamned sales contract you will ever see and Harp will be a rich man. So what's the problem? Where's this pile of dead bodies you mentioned?"

The Farm crew looked at one another. This was the crux of the whole thing. How would she take it? They had all seen Harp's video. Harp looked at Kip and nodded. Kip got his laptop. The video started with a bouncing, uneven outside shot of the overhang that hid the opening. As the video played, the little microphone picked up the comments of the three on top while Harp descended. She could then hear Harp cursing and exclaiming as he viewed the carnage. The light inside the hole was dim but everything was easily discernible. Kowalski caught her breath when the camera focused on the children. When it finished, the tough attorney who thought she had seen everything was wiping her eyes. Kip then related his theory on who the people were and what had happened to them.

They waited for her to digest it all. "Jesus Christ, Harp. This is on your land?"

"You can almost see the spot from the back yard."

"You know the world has to see this, don't you?"

"Uh huh."

"Does anybody outside this room know about it?"

"Nobody alive. Lars and Pauline knew. They never told because they knew what would happen to their lives if it got out. Pauline just gave me GPS coordinates in a note."

Seeing where this was going, she said, "And if it got out before you sold the farm, it would totally screw the deal because nobody would buy the place with that gigantic stick of dynamite sitting up there on that hill."

"Uh huh."

"And, more than likely, the state would take the land by condemnation until all kinds of study had been done and the total history of the state was re-written to show this incredible atrocity."

Another round of uh huhs.

She looked around the table. They were returning her gaze as if she should continue this line of thought. She got it. "And, you want to sell the place *then* let the world know about it."

They breathed a sigh of relief. Happy to see she got it. "And you want me to set it up."

Kowalski was now shaking her head. "This is fucking unbelievable. You guys want me to write a contract for millions of dollars which will scam the buyer. You want me to take part in an outright fraud. You want me to put my reputation and license on the line so you can screw the buyer and get rich." They nodded. Except for the get rich part, that was pretty much it. She stood and threw her tablet on the table and backed out of the room while pointing her finger at them. They sat in shock. This was not at all the response they expected. She did not, could not, know ALL the things that had been done by this mysterious buyer to drive them from the farm. This person did not deserve a fair deal. He deserved to be screwed. They would have to find another way.

Harp found Sandra Kowalski sitting on the front steps. He sat down beside her. "I'm sorry, Kowalski, we shouldn't have brought you into this. We won't bother you again."

"It's okay. I got to take a nice little trip and meet some great guys. I also kissed a dog named Fart." They both chuckled.

Harp picked his words carefully. "I want you to understand that it is not the money. This place has got to where it's real important to me and those guys in there. When somebody tries to get us off this place using these dirty tactics, it makes us want paybacks. We figured that this was a good way to screw the son of a bitch, whoever he is. We would let him buy it and then watch as the staties or feds took it away from him. It seemed like kind of poetic justice."

The lawyer listened but was shaking her head. "I get it. I even kind of agree with you. But you can't hide such an important asset or liability to the property without negating the sale. The only way you could sell would be to reveal the liability and then hope the buyer wanted the property bad enough to overlook it. But, let me tell you, when pictures of what's inside that cave get out, it will be a national sensation and, I guarantee you, the state will own it."

Harp sighed. She continued. "Those poor people had to come from somewhere. Oh, those poor babies! They were alive when they threw them down there! The historians and preservationists will not rest until they discover everything related to their lives."

Harp said, "Something else to really confuse things, footprints from Lars and me are down there so it will be easy to tell that someone has been there and *didn't* say anything about it." At her look, he explained, "The boots are gone so there is no connection to me. They will probably assume it was Lars."

"Harper, I didn't see how you could have made this anymore impossible, but you just showed me. Way to go, shithead."

They sat for a while enjoying the darkness and quiet. Bonny walked by on his circuit around the house and saw them, waved, and kept walking. "This really is a nice place, isn't it?"

"Yeah, it's funny. I never thought of myself in this kind of place, but it kind of gets inside you after a while."

"You ever think of staying? I mean, if you could?"

"Nah. I'm still a city boy. I like the streets. Maybe I could come out to a place like this once in a while, but I would still want to go back to Trenton. It's what I know."

Determined to take the lead just once in their relationship, Harp said, "Let's go to bed."

Harp stood up and held out his hand. Kowalski smiled and took his hand. Both felt that this could very well be their last time together for a long time so their lovemaking was slower, gentler, and then they fell into deep sleep.

21

THEY WERE AWAKENED BY THE INCREDIBLY LOUD SOUND of an air horn. Three blasts inside the house. Bonny was shouting, "Up everyone! No drill! No lights!" He charged up the stairs and gave three more blasts. "Let's go guys, you know what to do! No lights! No drill!"

Harp jumped from bed and rudely shouted at Kowalski, "Get your stuff together. Get dressed! Don't ask questions, just do it!" He grabbed his kit which was ready and helped a confused Kowalski jam her loose clothes into her suitcase. Harp grabbed her makeup case and threw everything he could see into it. She had not even had time to unpack. When they came from the bedroom, Bonny, Weeks, and Kip were gathered in the kitchen helping each other. Weeks was carrying his arm and his travel kit. Bonny had his small duffel.

"What's up, Bonny?" Harp shouted.

"I counted about six. Dressed like commandos. They are moving in. They're probably outside right now. We don't have long. We need to get downstairs now!"

Kowalski stopped and demanded to know what was going on. Harp said, "We don't have time to explain right now. Just come on." With arms and hands full, they clattered and stumbled down the stairs to the basement.

Within two minutes they were all in the root cellar with the bookcase back in place and the door locked behind them. "Okay, we have a little time now. Let's get dressed. Last check. Have we got everything?" They checked their own gear and each other carefully before responding in the affirmative. Kip helped Weeks with his arm. Kowalski was wearing her jeans and blouse and carrying her boots. Now very angry, she demanded to know what the hell was going on.

Harp explained. "From past experience, we figured that they weren't done with us. We knew we had to have a plan in case they came back. This is part of the plan." Harp pulled the tan footlocker from under the shelves.

"It seems to me that you guys are overreacting. Nobody in this day and age is crazy enough to attack a house full of people and expect to get away with it. I say we should confront these bastards and threaten legal action." She started toward the steel door. At that moment, the first crash sounded over their heads. Following was an incredibly loud cacophony of breakage which was frightening in its volume, even though they were underground. Kowalski cringed away from the door. The sounds then moved downstairs and were right outside the bookcase.

"Okay," Harp ordered, "Into the tunnel. Kip, do you have the computer? The jump drive? Good. You go first. You know the end best. Kowalski, you're next. Follow Kip. Do what Kip says. I'll go next and drag this footlocker. Weeks, you follow me and do the best you can to keep up. Bonny you're last. Pull Kowalski's suitcase. You know what to do. When we're all out, blow it."

Frightened out of her wits, Kowalski nervously inquired as she reluctantly entered the tunnel, "Blow it? What do you mean, blow it?"

"Just move it. I'll explain later." Harp pushed her roughly so that she had to duck and start crawling. The tunnel was dark and long. The city attorney was not used to crawling on hands and knees, so she suddenly stopped for a breather before moving on. Harp was caught unawares and ran nose first into her perfect bottom.

"Harper, goddammit, how can you think of that at a time like this."

Harp laughed at the idea. "The next time you stop, give me a warning and I'll try to keep my face out of your butt."

She laughed. "Likely story. I happen to know you have a filthy mind."

Weeks, who was following closely, observed, "Could you two keep moving? It's hard enough to do this on one arm without having to stop every two minutes."

After about five minutes crawling, they came to the short flight of stairs at the end. Kip had come back down and was waiting. He whispered, "They are in there wrecking the place but they left two guys on watch, one behind the house and I think one in front. We need to be real quiet."

They gathered behind the old car in the equipment shed and watched until Bonny emerged. "Everything set?" Harp asked. Bonny nodded. He looked at Weeks and Kip. "Got everything?"

They gave thumbs up.

"Go ahead, then." Bonny pulled a small remote control from his pocket and pushed a button. There were two quiet thumps underground which probably went unnoticed by the invaders. A hard puff of air and dust whistled out of the tunnel.

"What did you do?" Kowalski asked in a panicked whisper. Harp explained that, if the tunnel was found, they did not want the bad guys to know where it came out. "That would lead them to where we are now." Bonny had set some small charges which would seal it completely. The explosives were compliments of the recently expired Beck.

"We ready?" Harp whispered. "Let's go. Bonny, help me with this footlocker. Everybody be absolutely quiet." They left through a small back door of the shed and headed across the fields toward the point that overlooked the farm. It was just light enough to see each other and follow closely. In a few minutes, they were climbing the path that led to the top of the bluff. Once there, they gathered to look back at the farm. Even from this far away, they could hear the ongoing destruction. They looked back in sorrow at the house that they had grown to regard as a place of peace and healing.

Then the noise stopped. Harp figured the wrecking crew had been in there a total of about twenty minutes. He had no delusions about the state of the house. He knew that this time it would be totally unlivable, even for camping. Harp had left the others and walked to the Ford pickup which was waiting. They had brought it up there as part of their emergency escape plan. They put the footlocker and luggage in the back and loaded up. Harp and Kowalski sat in front and the rest piled into the back seat.

"Sarge, Fart was outside," said a worried Kip.

"I hope he'll go up to the cemetery and hide out there."

"Well, why didn't he see us and come along with us?"

"I don't know, Kip. We'll come back for him after we get set-tled somewhere."

It was a silent group of passengers who rode away from the farm, down the old road past the cabin where Harp had immobi-lized the unfortunate watcher and set him naked next to the road.

"Where are we going?" Kowalski asked.

Harp, a little embarrassed, responded, "I haven't got to that part yet. I guess a motel somewhere. I'm open to ideas."

She thought for a moment then dug her phone out of her purse. "Let me make a call."

She dialed a number. They listened to her side of the conver-sation. "Hey, Tony, sorry to wake you up. It's Sandra Kowalski."

"Yeah, I know. It's five a.m. Sorry about that."

"No, I'm okay, but I want to ask you something."

"Didn't you have a cabin on a lake somewhere?"

"Is anybody there now?"

"Good, I want to borrow it."

"No, I can't tell you where I am now but I am fine. No worries."

"Yeah, you got it. My boyfriend and I want a place to crash."

"Okay. The key's under the red planter."

"There's a Jeep in the garage? Can we use it? Cool."

"No, we won't be there long. Maybe a few days. We won't hurt it."

"No, I won't tell you who the lucky guy is."

"Yeah, I know. I owe you big time."

Laugh. "You should be so lucky."

"Thanks Tony. You know I love you—like a brother." Laugh. "Bye."

She explained to Harp. "That was Anthony Everston, the lawyer who got you out of jail. We were classmates in law school. We dated a few times and ended up at the same firm for a while. He has a cabin on a lake north of Pittsburgh. It should be just a couple of hours from here." Quickly locating the lake on his GPS, Harp pointed the truck in the right direction. He noticed it was just getting light in the East behind them. They rode in silence for a few miles before Kowalski quietly asked, "Harp, what would they have done to us. You know, if we had been in there when they came in?"

"I'm not sure." He had been thinking about that. "I don't think they would have killed us."

"Oh, well, thanks a lot, Mr. Harper, for that encouraging observation."

Harp laughed, "No, what I meant was that this is just another attempt to drive us off the property. I think they would have taken us all outside and made us watch. I'll bet that they were all masked, wearing gloves, carrying no ID or any other way of identifying them. I think they were paid to swoop in, gather us up under gunpoint, ruin the place, and get back out before the law could get there."

Kowalski was no dummy. "This is some serious shit, isn't it?" she said, almost in surprise. The others sat quietly, thinking that she had no idea how serious it was.

"Just to be perfectly clear, you do want to sell the place, right?"

Harp nodded.

"And now, the sooner the better, right?"

Harp nodded again.

"Okay, I got some ideas. Let me think about it some more."

Bonny spoke up in the back. "Sarge, I think we need to call the sheriff. Remember, our cars are all there. Especially hers. They'll be putting out an OPB on her after they see the place."

"Dammit, you are right, Bonny. Kip, did you bring those throw-away phones?"

"Yeah, I've got a couple in my bag."

Harp pulled his phone from his pocket. "Get Senter's number off my phone and dial it after I pull over up here."

Senter answered after the second ring. "Yeah." There was a lot of background noise. Harp had put it on speaker phone.

"Hey Senter, this is Harper. Wanted to you to know that they trashed my house again."

"They, what do you mean, *they*. You bastards stepped over the line this time. I'm going to get you for public endangerment, in-surance fraud, destruction of property, and whatever else I can come up with!" He was shouting loud enough for everyone in the truck to hear. They were astounded to learn that the sheriff was blaming them for destroying the house.

"How did you get there so fast, Senter?'

"Because the fucking place is burning and you can see the flames for fifty goddamned miles!"

Harp was saddened to hear that. "We didn't do it. We're lucky we escaped."

"Escaped what?"

"Due to recent events which you are goddamned well aware of, we had a guard posted. He saw this gang coming in. We only had a few minutes to get out through the tunnel."

"What tunnel?"

"The one Lars built off the root cellar."

"What root cellar?"

"The one behind the shelves in the basement." Harp was enjoying this. "Go look in the trunk of that old Chevy in the equipment shed. That's where we came out."

"Whatever. I am still bringing all you bastards in on a list of charges so fucking long you will never see daylight again! And if I find that you took that lawyer against her will, I will happily add kidnapping to the list. And, yes, we got her ID off the plates of her Mercedes."

Kowalski had had enough. She snatched the phone from Harp's hand. "Listen, Gomer, you ignorant fucking hillbilly, I was *not* taken against my will. If these guys had not been prepared for a fucking all-out attack, I might be charcoal in that fucking fire pit *your constituents* created. We are *lucky* to be alive. Furthermore, you can tell that fucker who is trying so hard to get this place that we were working on the contract to sell it to him."

She paused and took a deep breath. The men sat in appreciative awe. "Furthermore, you miserable excuse for a law man, I am going to do my best at the fucking *state* level to have you investigated for allowing all this shit to happen. Oh, and if you know who the fucker is who is behind this and you don't do something about it, I am going to work extra hard to bring your ass down! I know the Pennsylvania Attorney General and she is going to be *very* interested in all this shit that you have let happen!" In the end, she had been shouting. Her face was red and she was out of breath.

Senter was impressed. His first reaction was anger at the disrespectful language. Then, he realized that he might have been riding the wrong horse politically. Most importantly for his future, he believed everything she said. Unfortunately, that meant that he had to believe everything that Harper had said. He hated that thought. This whole thing had gone too far. And he still had no idea what was so important about this piece of ground. He had long ago figured out by a process of elimination who the buyer most likely was. Maybe it was time to put that knowledge in someone else's hands.

"Let me talk to Harper." They could tell that something had changed. Kowalski passed the phone back to Harp. She was still fuming.

"I want to, ah, have an understanding, Harper."

"I'm listening." There were silent fist pumps around the cab of the truck.

"I'll tell you who I think is behind all this if you give me your word to leave me out of any communications with him. He can't know how you got his name. He's loaded and he's connected and I sure don't need him as a political enemy."

This was easy enough. Harp looked at each of his cohorts. They nodded. Kowalski was last, but she also agreed. "Okay. Deal."

Senter had obviously walked away from the noise of the fire suppression. He spoke very quietly. "I'm pretty sure the man behind all this is a guy named Adam Willarde. That's Willarde with an *e* on the end. I'm pretty sure one of his companies owns land and mineral rights all around this part of the state. If that's true, he owns all the land or rights surrounding your place. It's got to be him." Kowalski wrote the name on a small tablet from her purse. "We never met and as far as I know, nobody has met with him. I think he's over in Pittsburgh. He just calls people and says what he wants done. He says to just call him Adam." Senter paused. "I actually never wanted to know too much because of the political side of things. If it's him, he's a powerful guy with powerful friends, if you know what I mean."

"Bullshit," was all Harp said.

"Let me make something really clear to you, Harper. I don't have the foggiest goddamn idea why he wants your land. It doesn't make any sense, and that's the god's honest truth." Harp looked from person to person in the truck to get some response to Senter's statement. They shrugged and nodded. Nobody was ready to fully trust Senter.

"We all set then?" Senter asked.

Harp turned to Kowalski. She nodded. He said, "Yeah."

"Oh, I forgot to tell you. We found the dog. It looks like they clubbed him. From all the blood around his head, it looks like he tore a chunk out of one of them. He really put up a fight. He's at the vet's and might not make it."

Shock and sorrow momentarily silenced the passengers in the truck. Senter continued, unaware of the bombshell he had just tossed. "I am now going to start an investigation into finding the vandals who trashed your place. I will tell the insurance people that I have been in contact with you and that you were away on vacation and that you have no responsibility for the situation. That suit you?"

Harp, surprised at the depth of his sadness, choked out a "Yes."

"Good. Now all of you do me a favor and get the fuck out of my life." He hung up.

Harp took advantage of the loud expressions of anger and

grief which filled the cab of the truck to quickly wipe away tears. His thoughts were quieter—and more deadly.

"How could they do that? He was just an innocent goddamned dog!" Kip was doing his best not to cry but it wasn't working. Bonny put his arm around his shoulders and said nothing. His sorrow was not quite as personal as the others. "He knew," Kip said. "He knew when I had those nightmares. He knew how to get me through."

"I want to go back and kill those motherfuckers," Weeks said. Then, "Sorry Ma'am."

Kowalski said, "That's okay. I want to go back and kill those motherfuckers too. And don't call me Ma'am. Let's just hope that beautiful old dog makes it." The rest of the trip was made in silence, except for self-conscious sniffing and eye wipes. Each of the riders absorbing the events of the day in his or her own way. Common to each was a promise not to forget and to get even. Harp was the only one who knew *how* he was going to get even. He had all he needed. He had a name, he had the means, and he had the ability. He would take his time and wait until the memory of his association with the farm had grown more distant.

22

EVERSTON'S CABIN WAS A GOOD INDICATION OF HOW well the young lawyer was doing. It was a large log home situated at the end of a small cove. There were no dwellings on either side, so the cove pretty much belonged to him. The lake was like the hundreds that dotted the northeastern part of the country. Elongated and very deep, it was made by the glaciers whose giant ice fingers gouged jagged holes as they retreated north, then filled them with the melting water. The water level on these lakes never changed, so homes could be built right at the shoreline. Everston's *cabin*, if it could be called that, sat just 50 feet from the shore. There was a very nice aluminum dock to the right which was built out into the lake and was headed by a small boat house. The main house had three formal bedrooms, but a bunk room was attached to the back which looked big enough to sleep another ten people. There was a land line which they later found actually had a dial tone. They parked the truck in the empty side of the garage and commenced unloading. Kowalski was shocked to see tears in the eyes of Weeks as he pulled stuff from the truck. He caught her glance and, surprisingly, confided in her. "That farm saved my life. I am really going to miss it." He wiped his eyes and carried more cargo inside. It was all she could do to not start crying with him.

After everything had been moved in and sleeping arrangements had been settled, Harp said, "We've had a long night. Let's crash for a while and then figure out the next step. Kowalski, what are you going to need?"

She had already found the office. No lawyer would ever think of building even a cabin without a computer and printer. "What I need is some sleep … alone," she emphasized. "Then I need to hole up in that office and not be bothered by anybody for a long time. I am going to be writing, printing, and faxing until I come up with a contract that will make you rich and hopefully screw this Willarde with an *e* to the wall." She enjoyed the noisy accolades for a moment, then went to her bedroom.

Kowalski was awakened the next day around noon by the sound of men shouting. Alarmed, she ran to the window of her upstairs room and looked toward the lake. She was soon smiling as she saw Bonny, Weeks, and Kip cavorting in the lake on tubes and floats like a group of kids. As she watched, Harp walked onto the dock and stood next to Kip who had gotten out of the water. They talked for a minute. Harp had turned away as if to return to the house when Kip stepped up beside him and gave him a hip check into the water. Kip quickly jumped back in and joined the others as they whooped and razzed Harp as he surfaced. She could tell that Harp was angry but the joy the others were feeling in watching him get dunked soon had him laughing too. Before long, they were all engaged in noisy horseplay, climbing on and off the dock, splashing, and throwing balls back and forth.

My God, she thought, look at them. Stumps and scars, dreadfully hurt by who knows what and look at them: now they are playing like children swimming on the first day of summer. She realized that she *owed* them the best she could do in selling that goddamned farm. The well-known New Jersey real estate lawyer went to the office, turned on the computer, and began writing.

She wrote and printed for almost two days. Her laptop contained almost all the forms she would need. She was also in constant contact with her office, obtaining additional materials and legal information. She would appear for food but quickly return to finish the project. At the middle of the second day, she emerged with a thick sheaf of paper and called a meeting. "Guys, are you going to trust me with this? It's either all the way or not at all."

She received enthusiastic nods all around. "What do you want to get for the farm?"

"They've offered me four mill. I guess that would be plenty," Harp shrugged. The numbers were unreal to him.

"Wrong. If they offer that, you can get more. I'm going to ask for eight. By the time you pay all your fees and taxes, you might end up with five and a half. Is that okay?" Nods again. No one believed that this might actually happen and it was all Harp's money, so they were agreeable. All business, Kowalski started laying documents on the table in front of Harp. Sign here. Sign here. Initial here. Sign here. And so on.

When they were done, she explained, "You have given me power of attorney to represent you in the sale of this property to the son of a bitch who wants it. I will meet with this so-called attorney Andrew Parsnip and conduct the sale. I will make sure the money goes into Harry Johnson's bank. I will not sign the papers until Mr. Johnson has the money which will be immediately wired to my escrow account." She paused, "I think I have found a way to let the authorities know about that dreadful cave up there in such a way that your foreknowledge will not be an issue. We will be covering the possibility but, hopefully, neither Parsnip nor the buyer will consider it important enough to stop the deal." She pulled out one more document. "Harper, do you have a will?"

"Hell no. Don't have anything and don't have anyone to leave it to."

"That's changed. You are now a millionaire and you got people."

Harp looked around, "You know, that's right. Okay, if anything happens to me, I want everything to go to these guys."

"Aw, shit, Sarge, you don't have to do that." They were suddenly very uncomfortable with the size of this development.

"Yeah, come on. We don't deserve all this stuff."

"Like I told you, Sarge, I already got big bucks coming. I don't need this."

Harp just looked at his lawyer lover and said, "Do it."

She smiled, "I already have. I figured that's what you would do."

"Smart ass."

"You are absolutely right." She continued, "Okay. I am going to set up a meeting in Johnson's office with the buyer on the line in a conference call." After carefully replacing all the documents back in her briefcase, she abruptly switched moods and asked, "What's a lady got to do to get a drink around here?"

23

THE DOOR OPENED TO THE CONFERENCE ROOM OF HAR-
ry Johnson's bank and the woman who strode into the room was
the woman Phoebe Loftus always wished herself to be. Tall, el-
egant, with beautiful long neck and fabulous legs, Sandra Kowalski casually threw her $5000 coat over a chair and approached
the table where Johnson and Andrew Parsnip were seated. Both
leaped to their feet and introduced themselves. Parsnip then introduced Loftus as his secretary. Loftus finally gathered herself
and hurried around the table to indicate where Kowalski would
sit. Kowalski ignored Loftus and walked around the table to sit
between Johnson and Parsnip.

She smiled at Loftus and sweetly said, "Thank you, Feedy."

Loftus corrected her, somewhat frostily, "It's Phoebe, not
Feedy."

"Ah, yes, the Phoebe. A gray nondescript bird that eats bugs
and sits on a limb bouncing its little ass up and down," Kowalski said nonchalantly as she removed a pile of documents from
her incredibly expensive briefcase. Johnson, who had dealt with

Loftus often over the years was struck with a fit of coughing as a diplomatic alternative to the guffaw he was trying to stifle.

As Loftus crumpled into a chair, Kowalski, who now commanded the room asked, "Are we all set…the conference call set up?" She removed a small very expensive voice recorder, turned it on, checked it, and set it in the middle of the table.

"All set," Johnson said.

Parsnip, trying to recover some poise, said, "I have arranged everything according to our agreement. The buyer will join us via phone conference when you are ready. I am authorized to act in his stead on all matters relating to this contract."

"And I am authorized to represent the seller." She proffered the Power of Attorney signed by Harp and witnessed by Bonny. Parsnip's power of attorney was signed by the secretary of a corporation. Each agreed that everything was in order.

"Okay, let's get this show on the road."

Johnson directed a staffer to dial the number that Parsnip had provided. When Willarde answered, Parsnip said to the room, "We are speaking to Adam, who wishes to remain anonymous. Adam, we are here in the bank conference room. Present are Harry Johnson, Phoebe Loftus, Sandra Kowalski, and me. Are you ready to proceed?"

"Thank you, Andrew. Hello, Mr. Johnson and Ms. Kowalski. You may call me Adam. Let us proceed." The underlying smugness and sense of superiority in his voice was unmistakable.

"If you don't mind, Mr. Adam Willarde, I would not presume to address such an imminent individual by his first name. And, I am *Miss* Kowalski." She paused, "And I am recording these proceedings." Johnson, Parsnip, and Loftus sat in stunned silence.

Johnson thought: so the bastard who is behind all the crap at the farm is Adam Willarde. He had heard of his dealings on mineral rights in the area. Parsnip thought: Oh, Jesus, I hope he doesn't think that I'm the one who let his name out.

Willarde thought: so this bitch found out. So what? He would just have to be a little more careful now that his name could be associated with events at the farm. "Of course, Miss Kowalski. I understand the need to remain professional. I'm sure you are not accustomed to deals of this magnitude and you want your behavior to be unquestioned." The condescension in his voice was blatant.

You smarmy son of a bitch, she thought. "Mr. Willarde, I assure you that this is one of the *smallest* deals I have managed this year." She picked up a copy of an official offer during the silence that followed that statement. Continuing, she asked, "I know you have received the selling price put on the table by my client, Horace B. Harper. Do you find it acceptable?"

Parsnip spoke up, "That is an impossible figure. There is no way that we can in good conscience pay that much for this small farm."

Kowalski did not even look at Parsnip. "What do *you* think, Mr. Willarde? Is $7,454,677 too much for this land—along with its mineral rights, of course?"

"Of course it's too much. There's no way I could justify paying that much for such a small plot of land. It's simply not feasible."

"You wouldn't know, I'm sure, that the owner has already had an offer of four million." She paused and checked her notes. "Then, because of some extreme difficulty in trying to develop a domicile and live on this property, the seller has determined that, in his words, 'He will be damned if he will be driven off.'"

"It still far exceeds the value of the land."

She continued, "As a result, the seller has begun to pursue sale of the mineral rights with an outfit located in, let's see, ah, yes, Lubbock, Texas." She could not have imagined the panic this caused on the other end of this conversation. Oh, my God, Willarde thought. How far have they gone with this? If another oil man looked at those wells, the whole area would go nuts.

"Now, Miss Kowalski, let's not be too hasty." Parsnip could not help it. He was staring at the speaker with eyes opened wide and mouth agape.

"Would you mind sharing with me how you arrived at that figure?" Willarde was very calm.

"My client was offered four. Now he wants five. But he wants five *clear*. I calculate that the number I gave you will take care of taxes and fees, leaving him five clear. Any less and he is ready to look elsewhere."

"And you will be helping him look." It was not a question.

"That is correct. Contacts have been made." Johnson and Parsnip were looking back and forth from the speaker to Kowalski. Johnson was in a state of awe. Parsnip was close to a nervous breakdown. He was very concerned that Willarde was losing it. Kowalski was staring at the speaker and praying that Willarde would fall for it.

"If I agree to this number, how soon can I take ownership?"

"You can have it today. We have the deed ready to execute. When you wire the money to Mr. Johnson's bank, and Mr. Johnson affirms the transfer is complete and irrevocable, the farm is yours." She smiled. "Of course, you wouldn't know that the house is destroyed and the owner no longer has any interest in the remaining assets."

Parsnip could not contain it any longer, "Adam, ah, Mr. Willarde, there is a clause in the contract which is unusual and I really think we should discuss it."

You saw it, Kowalski thought, you sneaky little bastard.

"Okay, Andy. What is it?" Now, he was impatient.

Parsnip continued, "It says, and I quote, that you will agree to maintain and allow access to the small family cemetery and maintain, preserve, and protect other historical sites located within the boundaries of the farm and, given the historical nature of this part of the state and country, you will not hold the seller responsible for discovery of any future sites of said interest."

"That sounds pretty harmless to me, Andy. Of course the family can visit the cemetery. Are you aware of any other historical sites out there?" Willarde knew that the cemetery was toast. He had moved graves before and he could do it again.

"No, but…"

Willarde cut him off. "Then go ahead and sign it, Andy."

"But, sir…"

"Sign it!" What they didn't know was that Willarde had at one time or another had the whole farm thoroughly studied and mapped. He was already acquainted with just about every square foot of the property. He *knew* there was nothing there other than the little cemetery. Parsnip signed and initialed the clause. With this item out of the way, the remainder of the sales documents were initialed and signed and the sale was complete. After receiving assurance of same from Parsnip, Willarde said, "Now, if you will wait a moment, I will order the transfer by wire from my bank in Pittsburgh to Mr. Johnson's bank."

Johnson got up and left the room. Once outside the door, he

made an exuberant fist pump. Kowalski found it difficult to keep a straight face, but she was pro all the way. She sat idly spinning her Mont Blanc, not looking at any of the others. She stifled an obvious yawn. Parsnip and Loftus were still wondering what had just happened. They had seen millions change hands but felt as though they were mere observers rather than key participants. Within five minutes, Johnson re-entered the room trying to contain his joy. It was with good reason that he had come to despise the person who had caused Harper and the Kuykendahls so much grief. He was enjoying this payback. With a professional smile, he announced, "The transfer is complete. The amount of $7,454,677.00 has been deposited in the account of Mr. Harper. Access to the account is available only to Mr. Harper and Miss Kowalski."

Johnson smiled as he watched Parsnip and Kowalski complete the documents necessary to transfer the deed. He noted that Loftus was staring at Kowalski with an odd mixture of hate and envy. He didn't blame her. If he were a woman, he would feel the same way.

"Are you still there, Mr. Willarde?"

"Yes."

"We are done. The farm is now yours, free and clear."

"Andy, do you have everything you need? Are the mineral rights in order?"

"Yes, sir. We've got it all. The land and all rights pertaining thereunto are yours."

"Good. Send me the papers as soon as possible." They heard the loud click as he hung up. Willarde breathed a great sigh of relief as he put the phone down. "Got the bastards!" he said to himself. We'll be pumping oil within months. All we have to do is run pipes to those wellheads to prevent a blowout. Parsnip and Loftus silently gathered the documents. He shook hands with Johnson and Kowalski and they left without another word. Parsnip's instincts told him that something was wrong with the deal but could not put his finger on it.

After they had gone, Kowalski and Johnson regarded each other with mutual respect and admiration. He was first to speak, "Miss Kowalski, I want to thank you for what you have done for those guys. They deserve every break we can get for them."

She responded thoughtfully, "You know, I haven't paid much attention to what guys like this are doing. But you're right. They do deserve whatever we can give them. This was a pleasure. Plus, the chance to stick it to a real dicksnot like Willarde made it fun."

"I agree with you on every point. But, back to business. You have put roughly seven and a half million in my little bank. What do you want me to do with it?"

"First, I want you to take one percent as a fee. Then, I want you to transfer every bit of this money to my escrow account." She gave him the bank and account number.

"That's very generous. May I ask why you want to move the funds so quickly?" He was still fully aware of his responsibility to his depositor.

"I do not trust this guy. I want this money where Willarde cannot touch it through attachment, legal maneuvers, or whatever. If I have it, I know it's safe. Keep whatever Harper had in his account before. I know he will want to continue to bank with you." She saw the question in Johnson's eyes and smiled. "Don't worry. Harper knows about it and likes the idea. You can call him to check if you like."

"No need, Sandra. If he trusts you, I trust you."

Again, Johnson left the room. Kowalski was standing at the window with her coat on, briefcase in hand, when he returned. "Attorney Sandra Kowalski, you now have another $7,380,130 in your escrow account. I have retained the 1% fee. I thank you. The bank thanks you."

Still staring out the window, Kowalski said, "This has been a trip, Harry. Getting the money for those guys is one of the best things I have done in some time."

Johnson, sensing her mood, gently asked, "Why aren't we happier, then?"

"I guess it's because this has been one of the most exciting few days in my life and it's over. My life has been threatened, I've escaped by crawling through a tunnel, I've hidden out in a cabin with a bunch of heroes, and I've beaten the snot out of a true son of a bitch." She turned to face him. "Now, I go back to my firm and quietly put together more killer deals and make a lot more money." She laughed, "And all of you will be back here and I will probably never see you again."

"Well, young lady, you are always welcome in my bank." She smiled, they warmly shook hands, and she left. She knew better than to go see the guys again. If she did, it would just make it harder to go back to her real life. She would see Harper again, she knew. But, she was damned if she could picture any way that they had a future. He was a fierce, beat-up forty-some-year-old drunken mute who drove her crazy, and she was an otherwise in-control attorney who couldn't afford to go crazy.

24

AS KOWALSKI DROVE TOWARD TRENTON, TWO JUBILANT meetings were being arranged. One was called by Adam Willarde and the other was called by Harp Harper. The meeting called by Willarde was to assemble his key staff and announce, much to their surprise, that they were back in the Pennsylvania oil business. They began immediately to call in the teams and equipment needed to develop these wells. It would be a tremendously complicated operation—complicated mostly by the need to transport the oil to market. Fortunately, there were still oil and gas lines crisscrossing the area and they could be adapted to this new cargo. They would have to be found and connections arranged. The main thrust at the beginning was to install new wellheads that would hold the pressure. If those old heads cracked, the mess would bring every EPA regulator in the state. Within two days, the Kuykendahl farm was a beehive of equipment and men. The remains of the house were bulldozed and crushed into the basement, along with some of the lesser outbuildings that were in the way. Bonny's car was taken to a tow company yard and the rest of the vehicles were assumed to belong to the company and put to use by workers.

The other meeting was at the cabin where Harp, Bonny, Weeks, and Kip remained. They were a stunned bunch of men. Harp had just announced that the deal was done and he was now a multi-millionaire. He could not think of it as *his* money alone. In Harp's mind, it belonged to all of them. "So, what are we going to do with it?" he asked. "I don't need it. I wouldn't know what to do with this much money. Ideas?"

Bonny and Weeks looked at each other and nodded in agreement. "Sarge, we've been talking about that. You know, the time we spent back there on that farm was really good for all of us." Kip was nodding in agreement. He had been part of the conversation. Taking a deep breath, Bonny continued. "Maybe we could do it again. Maybe we could find a place where we could just relax and do the work of running a farm. I don't know what it is, but I just want to get out there and grow something. I want to breathe that air."

Weeks chimed in, "And I want to work with him. I want to stay on a place where the world can't get to me. I ain't ready yet."

Harp was thinking. "What about you, Kip?"

"Well, I guess I can live in the world now. I'm going to inherit a bundle in a few years, so I should probably go to college and learn how to manage it. I guess I can go out there." He paused, almost unprepared for the attachment he felt at the moment. "But, it doesn't matter what I do, you guys are family and I hope I can always meet up with you wherever you are. I might need to crash once in a while with the real people."

His wish was met by loud agreement that he was one of them

forever, no matter what happened. Each loudly expressed regret at the realization that this meant that Kip was leaving. "Hey, I'm not leaving tomorrow. I want to be part of finding the new place. Don't kick me out yet!" Relieved to know that Kip would be around for a little longer, they pummeled and hugged him with rough pleasure. Harp was impressed at the notion that Bonny had presented. Though he couldn't express it, he felt the same as Kip. He knew, however, that he was simply not cut out for life out in the country. It was quiet, sure, but to him it was a little *too* quiet. There just wasn't much about it that appealed to him. He wanted to get back to the city. The decision he was about to announce was easy.

"Here's what I want you to do. No, as a matter of fact, I *order* you to do. Kowalski says we are going to clear about five mill when everything is settled. I want you guys to take three million and buy the kind of place you want. I'll leave it up to you. Me? I'm going back to the city."

"No way!" was shouted by his audience. "We can't just take that kind of money," Bonny said. "It's your money, Sarge!"

"Guys, how much money do you think I can spend? He pointed at each of them. "And, if you hadn't been there to back me up, I might not be here. You take that money and I'm still going to have too much to ever spend. Just shut up and take it. That's an order!" Bonny, Weeks, and Kip looked at each other, accepting the fact, marveling at the opportunity, and wondering how to start. Kip offered that they should probably form a corporation to start and then arrange for the money to be transferred. As Harp looked on with a smile, they talked about corporate names and where they might start looking for land they could love like they loved Harp's first farm. He was pleased to see that they wanted Kowalski to handle everything. He knew she would do it. She probably had the connections to find just the right kind of property.

"Sarge, there's still something we need to talk about." It was Bonny, the quiet one. "This guy tried to kill us and damned near killed Fart." Weeks and Kip were nodding. "We don't see how we can just walk away from that. It just ain't right that he can get away with it." Fart was still hanging on and would join them wherever they went if he survived.

Harp was way ahead of them. "We are not walking away from it. But here's what I want you to do: Forget about it. Anything can happen down the road." He was being purposely vague. "Whatever happens, I want all of you to be totally unaware and uninvolved." He met the eyes of each of them and held the gaze until he knew that they understood. Something *was* going to happen to Willarde and Sarge was going to take care of it. They understood and they accepted.

25

THE CALL DID NOT GO INTO SHERIFF SENTER'S OFFICE. It went to the State Police Post near Bardberg. It was a frantic, almost screaming message from a hunter who had found a cave full of bodies. The operator, who dealt with fairly routine calls normally, was immediately struck by the sound of panic in the caller's voice. It also sounded like the caller had a minor speech impediment.

"I want to report a cave full of bodies! They must be twenty, thirty of 'em! Kids too!"

"Hold on, sir. Calm down. Can you repeat that?"

"I tell you I saw a pile of bodies. They was skeletons! Down in this hole!"

"Can you give me your name please? Where is your location?"

"I ain't gonna get involved in this, lady! I just wanna tell you where they're at!"

"Okay, sir. What is the location of the bodies?'

"I was huntin' on this place and sat down on this neat little rock bench and my rifle fell down behind me and it went down in this hole! I went down there to get it and they was all these bodies there and they was ...!"

"Where, sir!" she interrupted. Now she was desperate to get the location while she had him on line.

"It was up there where all that dang oil equipment is, dang it! It's like this little outcrop with a low rock wall in front of it!"

"Can you please calm down and be more specific on the location."

"Calm down? You want me to calm down after I seen that!?" Now there were several troopers standing near the operator listening. One of them was the charge officer. While listening to the conversation, he called area headquarters and told them something big was coming in.

"Okay, sir. Can you help us get to this place, GPS or something?"

"Yeah, I can do that. Hold on." The excited caller gave the coordinates. "Just so's you know, I am a long way from that god awful place and I ain't never going back there. This here is a pay phone so you ain't going to find me. I don't want nothin' to do with this whole dang thing." There was a bang and a click as he hung up.

Bonny took the wadded up piece of paper towel out of his mouth. He carefully wiped the telephone free of his fingerprints and returned to his car. He had a long day's drive ahead of him to get back with the guys. It was worth it in taking this final step in sticking it to Willarde. It had been kind of fun impersonating a panicked hunter. He thought he had sounded pretty authentic. He was curious about how the investigators would tackle this project, but wouldn't stick around to watch.

Still wary of this being a crank call, the first trooper to reach the farm was skeptical. He drove up the driveway which was now lined on both sides by equipment. He talked to the site manager who assured him that there was nothing to worry about. But, he said that the police could look around as much as they wanted but should watch out for the heavy equipment. This trooper tried to drive to the coordinates but soon learned his low-slung car could not cross some of the field terraces. He related same to his post and said they would need to bring up an SUV. Within the hour, the taller vehicle had driven up to the place indicated by the coordinates. Like everyone else when they approached the site, the troopers saw nothing exceptional or suspicious. This time was different, however, because, with the caller's description, they could more easily identify the exact spot. Leaning way over the rock bench and looking down, they saw the opening. They saw the rope marks where someone had gone down there. Now it was serious. This could really be something big.

The tension and excitement mounted as these men relayed the situation back to their post. The commander decided that the crime scene guys needed to be present before proceeding. The crime scene guys, not having any idea of the depth, called a unit outfitted for entering caves and holes. They now knew that investigators would have to be lowered into the hole. Soon there were several police vehicles gathered in the area. The oil men below were getting very curious, so crime scene tape was put out to close off the area.

The first man carried strong lights and a camera. As he was being lowered and as soon as the scene became clear, he called for them to stop. He knew this was a massive crime scene. They were looking at the pictures from his camera on a monitor on top as the suspended trooper slowly panned the carnage. The lieutenant in charge said suddenly, "Stop! Bring him up! Now!" He realized that he was dealing with a *historical* crime scene and any further intrusion at this point would be a serious blunder. He conferred by radio with the post commander. The post commander patched him through to regional headquarters. Regional headquarters decided right off that the state historical commission needed to know. State headquarters was then notified and directed a delegation from its office to be present.

Within two days, there were 17 state vehicles at the site and a temporary field headquarters had been set up with several tents and trailers. Everyone who had seen the video agreed that this had to be handled *exactly* right. The project supervisor who had quickly granted access to the property was now wishing he had asked more questions. Now it was too late. He called his supervisor who called Willarde's office. Willarde, believing everything had been taken care of, was traveling out of the country.

Sheriff Senter, believing everything had been settled, took a long overdue trout fishing trip to the Poconos. He had given orders not to be bothered unless it was a dire emergency. Not knowing what constituted "dire," his staff, while aware of considerable activity at the farm, decided that they had better not bother the boss. The FBI, learning that there were bodies of people who had obviously been slain, sent a delegation to determine the need for its involvement. Upon learning the facts surrounding the situation, it agreed to let the state take the lead, but they would remain on site just in case.

After the first investigators had entered and exited the cavern in shock, it was decided that, to protect the geologic integrity of the location, meaning they didn't want to see that dome collapse, all activity around the nearby well-heads had to cease. When asked how long, the state people said that it could very well take weeks to do a complete examination of the site of the massacre. They realized that it had become a key historical site along with being a fascinating crime scene. The experts were drooling over the potential. Some were already outlining their books. Willarde's crew said that there was no way they could stop their work. They were still bound by Willarde not to reveal what they were doing. They had only managed to safely cap one of the wells and had started work on the other. They knew the other well was ready to blow at any moment. It was actively bubbling now. The state people were adamant. Willarde's people were ordered to stop all activity immediately. The armed state troopers enforced the order. If Willarde had been available, he might have been able to quickly secure an injunction stopping the state instead of being the one who was stopped. He was lazing on his yacht with a paid companion whose measurements were arranged precisely as ordered. If he had been available, they might have gotten the new iron on the second well. Just one more day of work would have done it.

It would be some time before Harp found out how well his plan had worked. The second wellhead suddenly blew off and sent rich black oil a hundred feet into the air. The state people watched in wonder after they heard the explosion as the metal gave way. A deep black plume then shot upward and was caught by the wind. It was blowing away from them, fortunately. Deep pools of oil quickly formed underneath. Oil droplets were drifting in the breeze across the fields, coating hay and brush. There weren't many gushers in this part of the country, so capping them off was kind of a specialized capability. The experts who could do it were hours away and the local boss did not have the authority to engage them.

As is common around construction sites, there are always burn piles where construction residue is burned, then buried. The oil workers had left behind a burned pile of broken hardwood pallets. They forgot about it because they thought it had gone out. It still contained some glowing embers, however. The state historical officials saw a small flicker of light down low near a puddle of oil. They watched as it grew and crept across the grass toward the well. They watched as it ignited the spray from the well and then caught the methane mixed in with the oil. They watched as the well became a giant blowtorch that sounded like a jet engine. It was spewing droplets of burning oil which ignited everything they touched, including trucks, cars, and materials. The state people at the cavern were safe more than a quarter mile away. They had all the radios the government could provide. They began calling fire departments, the Forestry Department, the U.S. Forest Service, the Ag Department, anybody who had fire suppression capability. The column of smoke reached more than a thousand feet in minutes, alerting everyone within a hundred miles that some calamity was under way.

It didn't take long before the area around the well was contained and crews were on hand to quench any blaze that popped up on surrounding areas. But the well went on roaring and burning and polluting as crowds of hundreds of people watched from roads and hills and choked up all traffic in the area. Everyone was waiting for the crew that could douse the flames and stop the gusher. Senter had finally been called and was on his way back. He was beyond anger upon finding out all the enforcement agencies now on *his* patch and he had not been made aware. He was cursing Harper and Willarde all the way, somehow certain that all of this had been avoidable—but he didn't know how. What the fuck was this cave about? Hundreds of bodies? What bodies? What cave?

Willarde was not found until well after the fire was out and the well capped. He listened in open-mouthed wonder as his associates described all that had transpired. His anger turned to red-faced apoplexy when he learned the cost of containing the well—along with the eventual EPA fines. And this did not include the cost of returning the land around the well to its former state. All of the hundreds of truckloads of polluted soil would have to be dug up and taken to an approved disposal site. The costs for the whole mess would run into the millions. The EPA said they would have to give a hard look at his plans for piping oil from these wells. The permit process could take months. To make matters worse, the State Police said that he could not do anything to prepare for pumping oil and developing that source of income without their permission. The whole area was being treated as a crime scene.

The state historical commission said he couldn't do a thing until they had fully examined the cavern and everybody in it in great detail. They had an Executive Order from the Governor, for God's sake. There were weeks of investigation pending, they said, in that hole full of bodies. He knew this had to be bullshit because he knew everything there was to know about that goddamned farm. In casting about wildly for any solution, it occurred to Willarde that he might sue to get some of his money back if he could claim and prove that that bastard Harper had sold him the land under false pretenses. He called Parsnip to file an injunction locally, only to find that his lawyer on the scene had suddenly taken his family on an extended trip to Disneyland and was out of touch. Willarde raged that the little son of a bitch was fired and he conveyed this message to Miss Loftus who was almost catatonic from the series of events transpiring of late.

Next, he had his high-priced Pittsburgh lawyers call Harry Johnson in an attempt to freeze the money until he could figure something out. Johnson laughed and said that the money was gone within ten minutes of arriving at his bank. And, no, he was not at liberty to divulge where the money was sent. Harry Johnson quickly called Kowalski and told her of the query. She assured Johnson that the money was safe and untouchable.

Willarde personally called Kowalski to demand the return of the money on the basis that they had sold him the land under false pretenses. She knew what was happening on the farm and reminded Willarde that the seller had admitted the presence of sites of historical significance and Willarde had agreed to maintain, preserve, and protect same. As for the money, she was pleased to tell Willarde that a big chunk of it was already gone. This was the money transferred to a new account held by the Bondurant and Weeks Corporation just established to invest in promising farmland. The Corporation was funded by a three-million-dollar donation from an anonymous contributor. And, no, she was not at liberty to divulge the owners of the new account.

26

THE PRINCIPALS IN THIS NEW CORPORATION, INCLUDING Bonny as President, Weeks as Vice President, and Kip Finch-Smithers as Chief Financial Officer, had agreed that their new property would be somewhere south where winter ice and snow would not shut them down. They eventually settled on North Carolina as having the perfect balance of seasons. They soon realized that they simply did not have the knowledge and experience to find and buy what they wanted. Through Kowalski, they hired a broker whom she vetted. Actually, Kowalski told this broker that if he so much as took one penny more than the agreed fee and if he did not find exactly the right property, she was going to make sure that his ass was hung from the tallest tree in North Carolina. The broker, like everyone else, immediately fell under her spell and was determined to do exactly as he had promised.

They were, within days, looking at many promising properties. They were having difficulty maintaining straight faces as brokers and sellers casually discussed multi-million dollar numbers in their presence as if they were accustomed to such discussions. They resisted the constant wish to grin and slap high fives as they considered and re-considered their good fortune. They were determined, however, to give it their all, no matter what, because of a deep sense of debt to the Sarge.

Willarde again contacted Kowalski and upped the pressure to reveal where "his" money was. At first she laughed it off. No one, she thought, would actually threaten a respected attorney in a big firm known statewide and demand return of lawfully gained assets. But, as she found, this was not necessarily true. Walking back to work from lunch in mid-week, she was suddenly and expertly whisked into a black limousine by two very large men in dark suits. She found herself alone in the back seat with Adam Willarde. He smoothly introduced himself. She was very frightened, but she was still pure Kowalski. "I don't know who you are, asshole, but what I do know is that there are probably twenty cameras that just recorded this abduction. Your license plate and the faces of those two goons who dragged me off the street are a matter of record."

Willarde calmly waited. "Miss Kowalski, this is not abduction. I merely wished to have a private conversation regarding the Bardberg property." Kowalski studied his face as he spoke. She had come in contact with many bad guys through her years of practice. She was aware that a handsome, smiling face could have ice-cold, merciless eyes. This is what she saw in Willarde. "We are talking about millions of dollars of *my* money. I did not want to bother you in your condo on Twelfth Street, or your parent's house up in Princeton, or even at your brother's home in Washington. He has lovely children, by the way. Two little girls and one boy. So full of life." The smile remained as Kowalski took all this in. She was suddenly very afraid for her family.

"I am positive that you all knew about that fucking cave and you knew what would happen once that kind of discovery was made public. In other words, you fucked me. I would like to impress upon you that Adam Willarde does not like to be fucked unless he chooses the fuckee. In my mind, you made a fool of me. You embarrassed me. One way or another, you will have to pay for that."

Kowalski tried to keep her wits about her but she was scared and she knew her voice was shaky. "Everything in that contract was legal and evident. So, what makes you think we should do anything just because you're not happy with it?"

"'Should' is not the operative word here, Miss Kowalski. 'Will' is more appropriate."

"Okay, what 'will' we have to do to get you off our backs?"

Willarde said, "Simple. If you will pay for the cleanup and cover all the additional costs associated with the discovery of that cave, I will take no legal action to secure the return of my money."

"I don't see how you can blame my client for the mess caused by that blown oil well which *you* chose not to reveal at the time of purchase." She added, "Further, I really don't see what legal action is available to you."

"There are times when it becomes necessary to augment legal action with additional incentives. Get what I mean? The bottom line is, if that cave hadn't been found, the blow-out would never have happened." Willarde studied his fingernails. "Here's what I propose. I will give you two weeks to put together a fund sufficient for my needs."

All she wanted was to get out of this fucking car. But she said, "It's not my money. Suppose Harper refuses?"

Willarde laughed grimly. "That's not an option. I know he will do what you suggest. I'm sure he will understand your love and devotion towards your sweet family." He made a gun with his fist, pointed it at Kowalski, and winked. This courageous, outspoken lawyer understood and was deeply worried. She did not think that Willarde was bluffing.

Kowalski heard the doors unlock. Willarde flipped his hand toward the door. She opened her door and turned to step out. "How will I contact you?"

"Don't worry. My representative will be in touch, quite regularly, as a matter of fact. Oh, one other thing. Contact with any of the various branches of law enforcement will do no good and might instead cause me to rethink my peaceful approach to this little problem." She knew who he was talking about. He just smiled as if he could see her thoughts.

The limo quietly pulled into traffic as Kowalski stood on the curb trying to keep from shaking. She noted the license number and almost ran to her office. Once there, she ordered her secretary to find out everything she could about Adam Willarde. Even though he had a penchant for anonymity, he was too active in the business world to fly totally under the radar. Her secretary soon found an article in a business weekly about Willarde and his early foray into the fracking business. The article included enough background to lead her on to other sources for pictures and details about his family and business. Before the day was over, Sandra Kowalski had put together a file with all these details and that file was now on her desk in front of her. And now, she didn't know what to do next. So…she called Harp. At least she *tried* to call him—only to find that this primitive bastard *still* did not have a goddamned cell phone. It was getting late in the afternoon so she knew where to find him. It would be just like him, she thought, a freaking millionaire, to be back in that same smelly joint where she first found him. She was right. Soon she was walking through that damned door again. This time a car was waiting. This time she would not be drinking.

As she entered the place, she flashed back on her last visit, as much as she remembered, that is. It was clear the bartender remembered her because he grinned widely as she walked toward Harper. He, on the other hand, groaned as his head sunk to his arms crossed on the bar edge. The bartender strolled down the bar with eyebrows raised in question. Kowalski raised a hand and said, "Don't even think about it." He strolled back to the other end of the bar still grinning. It looked like Harper was wearing the same clothes as when she first saw him. Cheap short-sleeved shirt, khakis, boat shoes, nothing new. She sat on the stool next to him and just looked at him for a moment. She was still somewhat surprised at her feelings from just being near him. She supposed, with a sigh, that this would never be explained.

"Harper, we need to talk." She put the file on the bar.

He groaned again.

"I turn you into a business dynamo and millionaire and you're still not glad to see me."

Harp looked up. "Oh, I'm glad to see you, Kowalski. But somehow I just know you bring trouble. I thought I was done with trouble. I don't want trouble. I want to drink and read and sleep. No trouble."

"Sorry, Harper. I wouldn't be here if I could go anywhere else."

Harp quickly saw that this was a different Kowalski. There was a tension there that his threat radar felt immediately. He *did* care about her. He just had found nowhere to fit that feeling into his life. So, he listened.

"Okay, what's up?" She was surprised at the sudden concern in his voice. The effect was that she found herself wiping tears away. Seeing this, Harp knew that, whatever was bothering her, it was serious.

As he listened intently, she related the contact by Willarde and expressed the fear she felt for her family. Though still determined that Willarde would pay for events of the recent past, Harp had decided that the man had paid through the nose because of all the things that had happened on the farm after he had bought it. Also, Harp knew, they *had* tricked Willarde, whether or not it was a legal thing. All things considered, Harp was about ready to just let it go. He liked the peace he was enjoying again. He would not try to punish the man any further. But now the guy was threatening Kowalski and her family—even the little children. He knew immediately that he would have to do something. He should have done something already. Innocent people could pay for his inaction. He understood what he had to do, but he also knew that Kowalski must not have the slightest inkling of what it was. He had to totally deflect her thoughts away from that possibility. He had quickly run through the various options available and concluded that a man like Willarde would not settle until he had gotten his revenge. She could not know that he had gone into operational mode. His *old* operational mode.

"Okay, let's pay the guy. I don't want any trouble for you or the guys."

She reacted in shock. This was the last thing she expected from this tough guy. "What!? We're just going to roll over after all we went through to stick it to this bastard?"

"Sure," Harp said casually, as if it were no big deal. "Figure out how much I can pay him from what is left and we'll send him a check. Tell him that's all there is. It should be a couple million, shouldn't it?" He loudly sipped his bourbon.

Kowalski found it difficult to conceal her scorn. She had hoped that Harper would join her in somehow fighting Willarde and protecting her. At least come up with ideas. Suddenly Harper looked like a shallow, weak excuse for a man, ready to give in when confronted with a serious challenge like this. All he wanted was booze and books. She was disgusted with him—and with herself for caring about him. Sure, they could pay Willarde, but that man still knew all about her and her family. How could she ever stop worrying about that?

27

COLDLY, SHE STOOD AND REACHED FOR THE FILE. HARP
pulled it toward him. "Just leave it. Let me look it over at least. He
said we've got two weeks. We can at least wait that long before
we pay him." Harp took a long drink of bourbon and waved for
another. Kowalski glared at him for a moment, and then quickly
strode from the bar. Those hard hitting heels walked out of the
bar and, he assumed, out of his life. After she had gone, Harp was
all business. He knew that a man like Willarde wasn't going to
walk away. Not only had he lost a ton of money, but he had been
humiliated and outfoxed in a business deal. Now this unscru-
pulous bastard had put together that intel on Kowalski and her
family. No matter what concessions they made, Willarde could
still get to her any time he wished. He had shown that already
with the possibly fatal attacks at the farm. He could always find
someone to do his dirty work.

Though Harp had known immediately what the options were,
he didn't know where. He began a study of this file in a manner
unlike anyone but a person with his training. The file had just

become the background data package for a *mission*. After he was sure that Kowalski was in a cab and gone, Harp paid his tab and hurried home. He had some serious homework to do. Deadly serious. He knew from experience that there were many long-range opportunities a target offered in the course of everyday activities. For what Harp wanted to do, however, it required a distant hide with a guarantee of anonymity matched with a very particular background beyond the target.

It was a surprisingly good file, with information going back to when Willarde was a student at Penn and preparing to join his father's brokerage. He was a good student, graduating Summa Cum Laude in finance, and was a natural in the business world. He came out of school ready to play rough and dirty if that's what it took. He was also a very good golfer, playing on the team which took many awards during his years in college. Willarde continued to play the game as he advanced up the ladder in his father's business. Both were members of the super elite Green Regal Hills Country Club. The packet included an article about father and son having the same start time on Saturday morning for more than ten years — which ended after the death of Adam Willarde's father years ago. After considering other locales and the odds of success, Harp settled on the golf course and the assumption that Willarde still played there. He also started with the assumption that 18 holes on a long-standing golf course on rolling hills would offer target opportunities from multiple directions. Now, he only had to find the tee times.

"Hello, this is Regal Hills. How can I help you?"

"Pro shop, please. Who's got the duty this morning?"

"Paul is working it today. I'll connect you." Harp waited.

"Hello, Pro Shop, how can I help you?"

"Hey, Paul?"

"Yeah."

"Hey Paul, this is Don. I was supposed to meet Adam Willarde after his round and misplaced my book. Does he tee off at 10 a.m. Saturday as usual?"

"Let me check. No, his group is teeing off at 9:30." Harp was grimly pleased. Willarde had taken great pains to remain the reclusive millionaire operating behind the scenes. So the file had offered little information on his current activities. After trying to find different venues, including ski vacations, yachting, mountain lodges, etc., Harp had concluded that the inherent open design of golf courses with many long open vistas provided his best chance, and it worked.

"Okay, thanks." Now Harp knew where he would be Saturday morning and, from the files, he knew what the guy looked like. He hoped that the son of a bitch hadn't changed much.

Aerial views available via the internet soon revealed the most ideal view. The sixth hole was a straight shot of 400 yards and then a dogleg to the left to the cup. Where the dogleg bent to the left, there was a clear view of the end of the long leg of the sixth hole, leaving a clear shot from the nearest group of buildings in a large sprawling group of condos about 600 to 700 yards away—which was very doable. Now, Harp had three days to find where he would shoot from. He settled on a vacant semi-furnished third floor unit about a half mile away. It was retained the next day by a company for a temporary project in the city. A six-month lease was taken by a Mr. Truet Kent via a cash payment delivered by courier. The manager was happy to let the property for cash, no questions asked, because it was in a troubled area. The view of the sixth hole was barely visible but could be seen clearly with good binoculars.

In the tan foot locker were two special 50 caliber cartridges. Rather than the usual lead, steel, or exploding projectiles, these cartridges fired a very small flechette. It was a tiny arrow or dart with an arrowhead and three fins. It was encased in a unique jacket which fell away after it left the barrel of the rifle. It was made of super hard alloy of tungsten carbide and had the unique ability to travel *through* things at very high speed with little loss in velocity. It was said that, in instances of actual use, it would easily go through the cab of a military truck and the three people sitting there, then exit through the steel door on the other side of the cab. Harp had heard about them but had never actually seen one used. He wanted to use it on Willarde because he planned for it to disappear after the hit, leaving no trace. He hoped it would go through the target without the usual explosive force of the regular fifty.

The lessee of the condo arrived early in the morning. His crushable canvas hat was pulled down over his eyes and ears and he was wearing sunglasses. He was carrying a golf bag and suit-case. With lights off, a quick check showed the sliding glass doors were functioning. The curtains were closed and the setup began. Harp moved the kitchen table into a spot well back from the sliding glass doors. Harp removed screws from the bottom of the golf bag and set it aside. Using chairs and other small items from around the unit, everything was positioned just right. The golf bag was laid across the backs of two chairs and tied in place with towels. It was Harp's silencer. He knew there would be a very loud concussive noise from the fifty but hoped that it would be reduced to more of a thump than a sharp bang. Still, he wore large lens shooting glasses, a handkerchief tied across his nose and mouth, and earplugs. Any doubt he might have had at this point was eliminated by the memory of the target's efforts to kill him and his men. The mission was a go.

It worked. When Harp pulled the trigger, it sounded more like a door being slammed extra hard than a gunshot. No one in neighboring apartments even paused to listen for more. For Harp, the blow-back from the golf bag was shocking and stung his face but he had expected it and shrugged it off.

The flechette zipped through Adam Willarde; rib, lung, heart, lung, rib—from side to side as he was leaning over practicing his swing for a short iron shot to the green. It had made a snapping sound as it traveled at supersonic speed through the air, but Willarde's golfing partners were drinking and laughing many feet away and paid no attention. The projectile went on to easily pass through a smaller tree before burying itself about fifty feet off the ground in a large pine far down a long slope away from the course. It would remain there until noisily passed through a wood chipper years later as part of a load of mulch.

Adam Willarde had a moment of puzzlement at the tremendous pain in his chest. He had time enough to think he was having a heart attack—then he was dead. After he fell forward, one of the other golfers began CPR while the others called for an ambulance. Because his heart had been stopped immediately, there was no bleeding. Due to the size of the round, there were just two tiny holes in his body. They virtually disappeared under Willarde's arms in the fabric of the wind breaker pullover. During these frantic activities, no one thought to relate the sound they had heard to Willarde's collapse. Then there was some delay as the EMT's could not find their way to this spot on the sixth hole. Once there, they attempted to get a pulse where he lay. Failing that, they quickly loaded him into the ambulance where they employed all their skills to no avail as the vehicle raced to the hospital. His golfing partners, shocked at this turn of events, gathered all their equipment and, contrary to common humor, returned to the clubhouse rather than finish the round.

An internist at the hospital where they were employing the best techniques available to revive the man was the first to notice the small oddly shaped holes, entering and exiting. He thought he had seen everything, but this was truly odd. Getting no response to the paddles, he quickly ordered an open heart massage. When they opened they found blood in the chest cavity and then, on further examination, the heart pierced side to side, obviously by the thing that had penetrated his body. With this discovery, Willarde was officially declared dead. Because of the wounds, an immediate autopsy was ordered and the police were contacted. Consequently, there was no law enforcement until Willarde lay naked on a stainless steel table at the morgue. Then, even more hours later, the forensic pathologist at the morgue was mystified when he read the physician's report. After a long examination of the body, out of curiosity, Dr. Bob Grier gently pushed a thin metal rod into the entry wound and found that it easily went straight through to the exit wound. He straightened and said, "I'll be double damned."

Detective Joe Stephens, who had drawn the case, was quickly called and watched as it was done again. He whistled in amazement. "Jesus Christ, Doc, this guy has been shot! What the hell was he shot with?"

"I don't know," Grier said, as he wiped his hands on his apron. "I have never seen a wound like this. Let me explain something. This thing that went through him was so small and so fast it did not even develop the typical shock wave. The exit hole is shaped outwardly but not much bigger than the entry hole. It was like he was killed with that rod you see there." He shook his head. "But, the entry wound has exceedingly small radial cuts around the center, almost as if the projectile had fins. The thing was maybe three eights inch total at its widest point. Strange. Really Strange."

"You mean it could be an arrow?" Stephens had handled many homicides, but none where the victim was killed with an arrow.

"No, I don't think it was an arrow—shaped like a very small arrow, maybe. All I can say for sure at this point is that the deceased was killed by a projectile that penetrated his upper torso from right to left, piercing the heart and lungs, causing death instantaneously. It went through so fast it had the effect of an arrow, or a solid rod." He smiled grimly. "We will know what that projectile was when you find it."

Finding that projectile had, because of the sequence of events, become impossible. All the golfing partners had gone home and had become very difficult to contact. When contacted, about the only thing they could accurately describe was that it had happened on the sixth hole. None related the snapping sound. None could accurately place Willarde at the moment he was shot. They only knew *about* where he was standing when he fell but the angle of his body was pretty subjective. The only thing that could be concluded was that the shot came from the right of Willarde. The result was that the direction from which the projectile was fired was in an arc of almost 130 degrees. Standing on the sixth hole and studying that arc, Detective Stephens sighed. It was slightly elevated and presented a view of literally hundreds of doors, windows, parking lots, rooftops, and thousands of trees. That also meant that, if you took a range of, say, a thousand yards, the location of the shooter could be just about anywhere out there. Making matters worse was that, to the *left* of Willarde, there was 180 degrees of buildings, trees, soil and structures in general which could have absorbed this tiny projectile. Nobody had called in any impacts or wounds by bullets or other objects, so it could have landed anywhere.

In one of those sets of sliding doors, the curtains were drawn and the occupant had arranged everything precisely as found. That occupant had left while Willarde was still lying on the ground. He was wearing his hat and golfing gloves and carrying a golf bag and a suitcase which he placed in the trunk of a rental car and slowly drove away. He drove only to a rental return lot where he transferred those items to an old Dodge truck. This was the part that Harp didn't like. He had to hurry back to Trenton with the murder weapon in his possession. It was a chance he was willing to take. Oddly enough, he felt that, if he got caught, it would be kind of okay. What he had done needed doing for Kowalski and the guys. He was at peace with that. As it turned out, it was a long, hard drive, but the trip went without a hitch. He was back in the Battle at 5 p.m.

28

GIVEN THE CIRCUMSTANCES AND THE PROMINENCE OF
the deceased, a task force was formed to investigate possible locations. Part of that investigation focused on the weapon. Soon,
casting about for any new ideas, a military advisor, Marine MSgt.
Bob Ames, was brought in to help identify the type of round. A
weapons specialist, he suspected what it was but could not, however, tell much without seeing it. Therefore, he could not identify
the rifle from which it came. What he *could* say for certain was
that this was very unlikely a civilian weapon. And, he added, this
was not a type of round available to the public. Further, it might
be one that was discontinued a long time ago. And, he concluded,
if this was a military weapon and the ammo he suspected, then
the shooter sure as hell knew what he was doing.

Back in Trenton, Harp was back into his old routine. The
quick drive home had given him more than enough time to return, store the foot locker, and show up at the Battle around his
normal time. The authorities kept the media in the dark because
they did not have a clue as to the culprit. It was two days before

the story of Willarde's death reached the papers. Then, all of a sudden, it was everywhere. Harp saw it, of course, but ignored it. He was entering into information hibernation so that when and if he was confronted, his declaration of innocence would be believable. The first person to bring it to him personally was Kowalski. She found him in the same seat in the Battle. She strode into the bar again and stood behind Harp. She had a newspaper under her arm. She looked at him in the mirror. He looked back. She appeared more puzzled than anything else.

"Talk to me, Harper!"

Harp swung around on his stool and smiled. "Hey, Kowalski. What's up?'

"You know about Willarde, don't you?"

"What? He decided to take the deal?" Harp shrugged. "Let him have the money. We've got enough left." He turned and picked up his whiskey and took a sip.

Kowalski opened the paper and slapped it on the bar. "*This* is what I'm talking about, Harper. Somebody killed the son of a bitch. Don't sit there sucking on a glass of booze and tell me you are so out of touch you haven't heard about this."

Harp shrugged, "I had a couple of days where maybe I was a little under the weather. What happened?"

"He was fucking *assassinated, that's what!*"

"Holy shit! Somebody took him out?" Harp picked up the paper and started to read.

Kowalski sat on the next stool and leaned forward. She stared at Harp with great intensity. "Okay, Harper. Play dumb. I just wanted you to know that the FBI is in this and they are looking at everything this guy has done for the past few years. They are looking at anyone who might have a grudge. They have been to see me and I told them everything I knew about that god damned farm and what happened out there. I told them about Willarde pulling me into his car. I told them absolutely everything. I do not think I am a suspect because I have got a perfect alibi. Harper…" She paused and glared as he returned her look with bland preoccupation. "… but, they were interested in you. Again, I told them everything. I'm surprised they haven't got to you yet."

"Well, fuck 'em. Let them come. Didn't you tell them I said go ahead and pay the man?"

"Yes, and I told them I was disgusted with you for rolling over on the deal."

"I thought it would just be less trouble for everybody. Plus, I just want to get back to my old life."

Kowalski looked around the Battle, shook her head, and responded with scorn. "Which I see you've managed to do."

Harp shrugged, "It's what I know."

She paused, thinking, and studied his face. "I wonder what you actually *do* know, Harper."

"Not much. I just know what I like and it took a long time to know that." He was too casual.

"All right, Harper. I came here to learn something and, as usual, I got nothing. You know they're coming and, as your lawyer, I advise you not to bullshit them. If you need me, call me." She put her card in his shirt pocket and turned to leave. After few steps, she stopped and turned around. She walked back and studied his eyes for a few seconds. Entertaining a totally new line of thought, she suddenly asked, "What did you do in the Army, Harper?"

Damn! Harp thought. "I was just an ordinary grunt, Kow-

317

alski. Nothing special." Again, he gave her the bland look. She slowly shook her head as she looked at him. She reached out and gently pushed his hair away from the ear with the missing top. "Sure, Harper."

Harper watched as this long-legged beautiful woman quickly pushed through the door and left. He did not show the ache he felt. He wondered if he would ever be able to touch her again.

29

THE FIBBIES DID FINALLY COME FOR HIM. HE STUCK TO
his story. He never wanted the damned farm and he never wanted the damned money. He was even ready to give the fucking
money back to that bastard Willarde and had instructed same
to his lawyer. No, he did not have an alibi. He lived alone and
nobody visited his apartment. The people in the bar could at-
test that he was there pretty much at his normal times every day,
including the day the man was shot. They noticed him mostly
because they didn't like him. The agents did not like it, but could
not come up with anything solid. Even his service record showed
nothing except a long list of medals for courage and valor. He had
looked very good as a suspect at first but, after a day of intense
questioning turned up nothing, he was moved down the list. But,
he would remain under consideration for the time being because
they had nothing else.

The FBI had a victim with a hole through his chest and that
was all. They had a motive but did not have the shooter, the gun,
the bullet, or the place from which the shot was fired. To com-

plicate things, they eventually found a raft of people who, to put it kindly, did not mourn Willarde's death. Harp remained a person of interest but, with absolutely nothing to go on, they soon discontinued active consideration. Willarde's death remained a frustration at several levels of law enforcement. In meeting after meeting, it was concluded that they had nothing to move forward on. In response to continuing public pressure, however, they continued to maintain that they had several promising leads they were pursuing. With Willarde dead, the charges for the cleanup work at the farm were assessed against his estate. His estate was so large that the heirs considered those expenses to be inconsequential and signed off with no objections even before probate. It was either that or a lifetime of litigation. The executor assigned one of the company's field men to oversee the project and the heirs promptly forgot about it.

As weeks went by, Harp was happy to resume his former lifestyle. He had decided to spend some of his new wealth and bought a downtown two-bedroom, two-bath condo. He considered himself a pussy for enjoying large rooms, good heat and air, and an elevator. Harp even decided that he would hook up to the internet so he could stay in touch with the guys. His new home even came with a parking spot. He had sold the old truck and bought a new Ford SUV. He had no idea how to operate half its features and would sit for at least a minute each time he got in it just staring at its shiny complicated dash. He would shake his head and sigh before pushing the start button while the key remained in his pocket. He promised himself that he would someday figure out how to operate the radio.

30

BONNY, WEEKS, AND KIP HAD FOUND THE PERFECT FARM
in North Carolina near Goldsboro. It was larger than Harp's
farm but was currently operating successfully growing soy beans
and corn with a small row crop operation providing vegetables
to local businesses. It also had a small herd of Angus beef cattle
on a good-sized pasture. The guys fell in love with it from the
moment they first laid eyes on it. Another key factor was a nearby
VA Center for their ongoing medical needs. As for managing the
operation, however, they were smart enough to know they were
in way over their heads. Wisely, they were going to pay the seller,
who wanted to relax in his old age, to remain as farm manager for
a year. Bonny was determined that he could learn to manage the
operation. Weeks was being trained by Kip to oversee the financ-
es using computer programs. They agreed that Weeks needed formal training beyond what Kip could provide. Weeks determined
that he would, come hell or high water, take some courses at a
nearby community college. His mind was now his own and he
was ready for the world.

Kip was going home in a few weeks. He had several operations coming up and decided that his parents' home would be the best place to recuperate. His parents were delighted. They said it would be different now. Even his father unbent enough to ask Kip if he would please come home. Though they understood the logic, Bonny and Weeks were unhappy at this development. They were losing a brother. Kip said he would be back but they knew that was unlikely. When soldiers go home, like it or not, that's often their permanent base.

They had brought Fart with them, first to another interim country home while they looked, and then to their new home in North Carolina. Fart had survived the beating and was found by one of the troopers who called Harry Johnson. Johnson knew about Fart from his visits during the work on the house. He directed that he be taken to the local veterinarian and that every effort be made to treat and rehabilitate the dog. The vet said he should be put down, but Harry was adamant. Harp's crew were elated to find that Fart was recovering. As soon as he was able to travel, they went back to get him. He rode from Pennsylvania to North Carolina on a large soft cushion in the back of an SUV with his head in Kip's lap. Kip became the dog's keeper. He provided the almost round-the-clock care Fart needed, including constant medication and massage. Fart was never the same, however. He was fairly old in dog years to begin with. Where the bones had been broken, arthritis had set in and he was seriously hobbled in his movements. He died after less than a year at his new home. They believed he had died happy. Bonny had called Harp with the sad news and Harp had outwardly shrugged it off. He was accustomed to walking away from loss and this was no different.

The guys finally convinced Harp to drive down for a visit. He knew they wanted his approval, but he would have approved anything they selected. Once there, they excitedly led him through a large well-kept farm house to what would be the Sergeant H. B. Harper Memorial Bedroom. It was upstairs front with a beautiful view across the fields. Harp was deeply satisfied at their happiness while brusquely evading all the affection they showed as they drove around the fields of their new domain. They begged him to move in to their new home. Once again, while agreeing that it was a beautiful place and that he would certainly visit often, Harp knew that the city was his home. But, before he left, they wanted to show him one more thing.

They took him to a small granite stone on a rise overlooking the farm. It was in the shade of an old maple tree. It was destined to become a puzzle for generations to come. All it said was "FART — He Was a Good Soldier." Harp had successfully pushed away any melancholy thoughts about this animal that had given him his trust. But seeing this grave and marker for some strange reason almost brought him to his knees with a sudden rush of intense overwhelming sorrow. He hadn't cried when buddies died and he wasn't going to cry over a goddamn dog. But it took every iota of his will to stand there without breaking down. As before, he managed it. All he said was, "Thanks, guys. This is perfect."

He found himself looking forward to going back to Trenton after just three days. In their excitement, they had talked and talked about what they were going to do with the land. After listening for hours about crops, fences, livestock, and tractors, he found himself craving the resigned gloom of the Battle.

31

AND THAT WAS WHERE HE FOUND HIMSELF LATE ON A quiet Wednesday afternoon, starting his third drink. Harp was glad to be back in the dim shadowed silence of the Battle. He had finally slipped into what was almost a post-action slowdown. With the knowledge that the action was over and he had so much money and life was short, Harp had switched to a much more expensive bourbon. He was now deeply interested in analyzing its fine qualities. The new libation had required that he speak to the bartender—but only that one time, he hoped. It was served with a raised eyebrow but nothing else. The world around him had finally settled down and left him right where he wanted to be. He was content for the first time in a long time. He sat chin on knuckles, staring into his bourbon and trying to get back to the fine balance he had achieved before it all began.

Harp, lost in thought, was not aware that two men had entered the Battle and approached until they had mounted stools on his right and left. Irritated at this intrusion, he looked up at the back bar mirror. He thought there was something familiar about these guys. The connection didn't come until they spoke. They smiled cheerfully as he studied them in the mirror. He then realized that they were the two spooks who had left him on his own in that house in Pakistan.

Uh, oh. He knew this could not be good.

The two men ordered drinks from a surprised bartender. One got a draft beer and the other scotch rocks. It was evident that these guys were supremely confident no matter where they sat. Neither was dressed in a way that would be memorable. They were clean-shaven, short-haired, average-sized and had sunglasses pushed up on top of their heads. They wore loose jackets over shirts, jeans, and black sneakers. They had those eyes, though, which were very comfortable meeting other eyes. Not quite insolent or mocking, but somehow superior. "You remember us, Sergeant Harper?" The one on the left asked with a smile. They both watched Harp in the mirror.

Harp remembered.

Harp was not happy. "Yeah, I remember you. Spooks. You left me on my own in that shithole. Pat and Tim. Thanks a lot, by the way."

"Hey, that's good, Harper. I'm Pat, he's Tim."

The other one said, "Nope, you're Mike and I'm Bill."

"I know, dickwad, but that's who we were during that op. Gimme a break."

"God, it's hard to keep these things straight. I have to check my wallet to see who I am. Whatever. I'm Mike today." They did not offer to shake hands.

"We didn't mean to leave you alone in that shitpit," Mike continued, "but Tim slash Bill here got shot in the ass and we had to lay up 'cause he was bleeding all over everything."

"Yeah, we had to lay up so that fucking raghead doc could dig pieces of tee shirt out of the new hole in my ass."

Mike shrugged. "That's all I could find to stop the bleeding. You should be thankful that I was so inventive in a time of great need."

"True," Bill admitted, "but you didn't have to stick your dirty damned thumb two inches into my heretofore well-shaped gluteus maximus."

Mike looked around the Battle and sipped his beer. "Well, it worked. You owe me a tee shirt, by the way. White, extra-large." Then, looking at Harp, "Speaking of shitholes, how come with all your money you still hang out in a shithole like this?"

Slightly offended, Harp answered. "Fuck you, I like it. It's quiet. Or," he added pointedly, "it used to be quiet." Then Harp was thinking fast; how did these guys find out about the money? What else did they know? "I'm a civilian, and what I do with my money is my business. Why don't you two go back into the bushes and spy on somebody else?"

The other one spoke as if Harp had not uttered a word. "In a roundabout way, your name came up relating to a recent homicide. As a matter of fact, the way it happened was almost comical."

Mike interjected, with a laugh, "Yeah, it turns out this military advisor over in Pittsburgh filled out a report on a local murder case where he had been called to identify a kind of bullet. Actually, all they had was a weird hole made by an unidentified projectile. The Medical Examiner was pretty sure that this guy Willarde had been offed by a small finned object, a really special little killer. The military guy said there was only one thing that would grease right through a body like that. He also said there was only one caliber in these things that could shoot one of those little fuckers over a long, long range. It's a fifty."

Bill laughed, "This guy's report says that it was damned near impossible to tell because that kind of ammo ain't in no way available to you members of the general public and they do not have a shell casing." He took a sip and added. "Not to mention the fact that that little projectile could be anywhere. It wouldn't even slow down going through that fucker's chest." To illustrate, he poked one side of his chest with a finger and made a throwing motion away from the other side making a "poosh" sound.

"Anyway, because of this ammo, this story gets bounced up the Fed ladder and around certain circles and it comes to us just as a kind of gossip, you know what I mean?" Mike asked. "Big shot in Pittsburgh gets offed by a weird old maybe military round from what has to be a really long, long distance shot. We all laughed."

Bill continued. "Of course, we wouldn't have thought nothing about it until something even funnier came up. Your name came up as a person of interest." He laughed coldly. "Ain't that something? They got a guy who's been knocked off by a practically antique round from a distance like from Rico to Rosco and *your* name is somehow attached. Who-ee! What are the odds?"

"What the fuck is Rico to Rosco?" Mike asked in wonder.

"Its places near where I grew up, thank you very much," Bill replied, as they both leaned forward and were talking in front of Harp's face. "And I would appreciate it if you did not interrupt me whilst I am explaining my logic to Sergeant Harper."

"Is this in these United States? Cause, if you're a fucking foreigner, I got to turn you in. They hand out rewards and medals for shit like this," Mike argued. They spoke as if Harp was not sitting there listening. "I'm gonna have to have your badge and sidearm."

"Yes, shit heel, it's in the U.S. and I would appreciate it if I could now continue my astute observation and the only way you'll get my sidearm is when I shove it up your ass. Also, as you know, I do not carry a badge. Now, where was I?"

"Somewhere between Rico and Rosco, I believe," Bill offered.

Harp looked at the ceiling and shook his head in wonder. This supposedly humorous badinage was plainly a way these guys got through many tense and lonely missions. "Fuckin' clowns."

Mike, ignoring Harp, continued. "Bill and me then got to thinking about that round and the kind of weapon you'd have to have to shoot it. Then we asked ourselves, "Selves, what do you suppose ever happened to that old foot locker full of toys that we left with Sergeant Harper? Anyway, we know there was a couple of those old specialty rounds and a Barrett in there, amongst a few other things, which happens to shoot a fifty." Mike grinned. "Then we says, 'you don't suppose that old boy somehow got our old toys back to the States and has been using some of those doodads in a personal kind of way.'"

Bill continued, "Then we says, 'fuck, he was a career NCO, been all over the world, done everything, been shot at and shit on, got a bunch of medals, plus he knows ins and outs of military supply tricks.' Then we remember we gave him that *temporary* set of fake credentials so we says, of course he knows how to get that shit back to the States." He held up his hands and interlocked two fingers from each. "So we put two and two together and find it equals you."

Mike's turn. "Then, we did a little inside investigating, at which we are quite good, thank you, and learned the whole story about what happened out there in Hicksville. We found out that this guy was a supreme scuzbucket and he was about to put the screws to you and your little four-man squad—which operation, by the way, we find very inspirational."

Harp was just watching in the mirror as they bounced the story back and forth and felt a growing sense of dread. He was beginning to get a bad idea on the point of all their horseshit. The thought was chilling. Each had ordered another drink and stopped long enough to appreciate their libations. Harp knew that they were here for a reason. He also knew it would not be a good one. The curious bartender had wandered over to eavesdrop. Mike waved him away with a cold look and a pointed gesture.

"So, we says to ourselfs, 'selfs, the facts don't lie. That guy has been done by our good ol' Sergeant Harper.' We looks at each other and says, yup, he was shot by Harp. Can we call you Harp?"

Mike added, "Course we don't blame you. The guy needed killing. Also, if we calculate right, it was a helluva shot. We truly admire such expertise. It makes me envious. Experience has shown that I have to be practically standing right next to somebody to kill 'im. It is disadvantageous." He was proud of that word and said it again to the mirror. "And, let me add, that shot in 'stan was one of the prettiest things we have seen in a long while."

Bill summarized. "Now, if we was to put all of this together for the 'authorities' and then we found that ol' desert tan lock-er—which you don't know we can do—in storage somewhere close by, you would be in shit all the way up to over your head. They don't have nothing without our help and that old locker."

He took another sip of his drink and asked Mike, "Did you know that ol' government issue thing has an RFID tag?"

"It does seem like I do recall absolutely nothin' about that." Mike observed. "What the fuck is an RFID tag?"

Harp was cursing himself because he hadn't taken the time to dump that damned locker.

Bill said, "I wasn't talking to you. I was asking a reasonable question for our old friend Harp. An RFID tag is one of those things they put on stuff so you can't walk out the door without setting off alarms, radio frequency ID tag, or something like that. Which, by the way, I happen to know you have done." He nodded his head sagely. "I have seen your record."

"So that's how the fuckers got me. Amazin'." Mike shook his head. "Doesn't matter. I was a child just doing childish things."

"You were eighteen and already had a record, asshole," Bill said and continued, "Anyway, all we got to do is get one of our detectors anywhere near that old thing and it will beep us right into its little cache of secrets." As an afterthought, he added, "I believe those military grade things will light up a receiver even from say a helicopter. Fuckin' amazing, if you ask me."

Mike added, "And once we get that box, we kind of suspect we got us a suspect." Bill did the thumb up finger point and raised eyebrows at Mike in recognition of the word play. "Course you wouldn't have been dumb enough to put that empty fifty back in there with the rifle. Those kind of rounds have a special marking. Tells exactly what they are."

Harp cringed inwardly. That was precisely what he had done. His face showed nothing but their finely tuned interrogation antenna sensed it. They grinned.

"And we could do our civic duty and inform the authorities who are most anxious to know who this culprit is," Bill said. He was watching Harp in the mirror. Much more sharply now. "The upgrade from suspect to culprit is a humongous jump, don't you think, Sergeant Harper?"

Mike quickly said, "Of course we would never do that. You're one of us, you know."

Son of a bitch, Harp thought. One of them? It had never occurred to him that he would join such a deadly fraternity just by following orders. It was the fucking Army, for Christ's sake! He was *ordered* to help them.

He had to ask, "Who the fuck do you guys work for, anyway? Pentagon? CIA? Or is it some little building in backwater Virginia where an old man sits in a dusty library and pushes buttons."

"Well, hell," Bill moaned, "now we're going to hafta kill our ol' friend Harp. He found us out."

"Yeah," Mike agreed, "I was going to say the old line about if we told 'im, we're gonna have to kill 'im. Now we got no choice."

"Yeah, like that little fuck in Thailand, who you wrongfully concluded had found it out and we had to terminate his membership among us living."

Bill observed, "Actually you terminated him maybe a little too impetuously. I thought he might have just been guessing."

"I consider his demise one of the vagaries of our profession," Mike said loftily. "We are responsible to a higher calling."

"Well, you put a knife right in his vagaries and he sure won't be doin' any more calling."

"Doesn't matter," Mike said. "It seemed like the right thing at

331

the time. And, I would appreciate you not revealing my impulsiveness to our friend here. He will think I am not levelheaded."

Bill offered a solution. "I just had a thought, which as you know happens quite often. Maybe we won't have to kill ol' Harp after all."

32

HARP SAT UP STRAIGHT AND PLANTED HIS FISTS ON THE
bar, getting ready for the bad news. He looked at Mike. He
looked at Bill. He looked at both in the mirror. The bullshit was
over, he knew. "Okay, I know you guys didn't go to all this trouble
just to be my pals. What do you miserable bastards want?"

Mike looked at Bill, who nodded, smiled again, this time icily,
and said, "We got another job for you."

Bill added, "Here." He pointed his hand up and moved it in a
circle. Mike watched Harp.

Harp turned to Bill with an incredulous look. "Here? You
mean here inside the U.S.?

Bill just met his eyes with a cold, steady gaze. He said nothing.
It was clear the answer was yes. Harp asked, "How do I know
you're just bluffing. There's no way you could find that foot locker.
Fuckin RFID tag is bullshit."

Mike reached into the inner pocket of his jacket. He removed
a plastic wrapped 50 caliber brass shell and stood it on the bar.
"It's got your prints all over it." Harp was slowly shaking his head.

"We've got the rifle too. More prints." He added, "If you want, we can give you the address of the storage unit where we found it." Harp just closed his eyes and looked down.

"Your country needs you," Bill added. "These are perilous times for all intelligence agencies. We need to survive."

His future from this moment on hit Harp like an arctic blast. He realized he was now a dead man. He simply would not do this, no matter what the cost. And, if he didn't do it, he could die in prison — or would have to be capped simply for knowing about this shit. If he did the job, probably at some serious personal danger, he would again know too much and would eventually have to be eliminated. Not to mention the fact that he had serious moral and ethical objections to this kind of operation within the States. He had sworn allegiance to the United States and it was a point of honor to keep that promise. He knew that, whatever they said or did, he would not be part of it.

Realizing that he was truly fucked, he began considering ways to stay alive. The first step would be to get away from these killers. But, they were consummate pros who had seen everything. Pure bullshit or bluff weren't going to work. They calmly sat watching his face as if they were reading his thoughts. They were used to being right and, right now, they were. He definitely was trying to come up with a way out of this hole he had dug for himself. They sat and waited.

"And I suppose you've got a car outside waiting," Harp guessed.

"Brown Ford," Mike said with a shrug. "Backup if we need it." It seemed to Harp that Mike showed a touch of regret at what he was doing. This only added to Harp's instinctual sense that he was not meant to survive this mission. However, the Old

Sarge knew something they didn't know. Putting it to work was a different matter. There was something they did not know about Harp's activities over recent weeks.

The way he saw it, he now had three choices: say yes, die,... or say bye.

33

HARP WAS OF GREATER THAN AVERAGE INTELLIGENCE to begin with. Then, he had learned through a lifetime of violence that a big part of staying alive in any situation is to know how you're going to get out before you go in. Events in his recent past showed him that he was walking a kind of tightrope. Two men had died, and way too much Federal and state attention had been, and still was, focused on him and that damned farm that had been his inheritance. He was, or had been until this moment, free through good luck and careful planning. But he knew that he had done too much and gotten away with too much to ever completely assume that it was over and he had gotten a walk. One thing was certain even before these guys showed up: Harp could not go to jail. To him, life in a cell was the same as death. If he ever was doomed to prison, he knew there were only two things he could do: die or disappear. The first was something he could do himself and of which he was fully capable and ready; the second was the one he had prepared for. As it turned out, his preparations were on the mark. He was ready to disappear. He just had to somehow get away from two incredibly capable Feds who knew everything about him. He had to assume his condo was being watched. Shit, he had to assume his life was being watched. They probably knew where he bought his groceries and where he bought his liquor. They would know about the new farm and Kowalski. His new truck was probably already bugged.

His only remaining hope was that they would not know about his new identity. This was done in a way described in great detail on the internet for people who wanted or needed to have a new identity. He located the grave of a stillborn male child buried in a distant cemetery about the time he was born. He requested a copy of the birth certificate for that child via the internet. With the birth certificate, citing a house fire where all documentation was lost, he requested a new Social Security card. With both, he secured a new driver's license. The picture on the license showed a middle-aged, clean shaven man with a receding hairline and glasses—head turned slightly to the left to hide the ear. These documents were all he had. He hoped it was enough. There was no background like jobs, service, health, etc. He would have to cover these things as situations arose. All this had taken several weeks after his return to Trenton. It was time well spent.

There was one more thing, however. His money from the sale of the farm still resided in Kowalski's account minus a withdrawal for the condo and car. He did not want to involve her in any future activities, so he left the rest alone. But, he still had the money in Harry Johnson's bank. He had asked Harry to send $200,000 of it to him at his condo address in cash, shipping it in a USPS Priority Mail Medium Flat Rate box. Johnson had questioned the shipping method, but Harp had been adamant and the banker reluctantly complied. Involving no other bank or their questions, the money arrived safely and was put to good use. How good was soon to be shown.

34

THERE WERE REALLY ONLY TWO PLACES FOR WHICH
Harp needed escape plans. The condo was easy. The Battle was
a lot more tricky. It was an old bar in an old building that was
nothing but a long, narrow rectangle. All the rooms were on one
side with the kitchen and storage behind the bar and a long hall
with restrooms on the same side as the kitchen. The other side
was just the few booths, tables, and chairs, then the pool table at
the end. On past the pool table was an emergency exit with a dim
sign over the door. This exit was the obvious escape path—but
Harp wondered if it was *too* obvious.

Harp had noticed that when beer bottles were taken behind
the bar, they somehow quietly disappeared. He heard a faint
clinking as the bottles rolled somewhere, then stopped. Much as
he hated to, he asked about it. It was a series of very slightly sloped
ramps running in opposite directions that gently eased a glass
bottle all the way down to a collection point in the basement. By
itself, that information was only mildly interesting. Yet, it caused
Harp to file away the information that there was indeed a working

basement under the Battle. But, how to get there. This was important because the only ways out at street level were the front door
and the exit door at the back—which were both in plain sight.

Harp listened one afternoon as a man in a beer company
uniform came striding through saying only that he was picking
up empties. The bartender just nodded and said nothing. Harp,
curious about how this worked, casually followed the man as he
walked to the rear of the building. Stepping around a short partition that blocked the hall to the restrooms, he saw the man going
down stairs under a large hatch. The hatch was the same size as
its attached mat in front of a chewed up dart board. The man left
the hatch up as he worked in the basement. In about a half hour,
the man passed behind Harp and said to the bartender, "Sixteen
cases," and kept walking. He was picked up by a large beer truck
in front of the Battle. The bartender made a note and stuck it
on the spike next to the cash register. Harp was surprised at the
amount of beer being sold here.

Harp thought it safe to assume that the empties had been
taken outside from the basement and loaded behind the building.
As it happened, he would soon find out.

"I gotta take a piss," Harp announced and started to stand up.
He left his drink, his wallet, a cell phone, and keys where they
had been on the bar. He wouldn't have any use for these things
where he was going.

Mike laid a hand on his arm and said, "Wait a sec." He looked
at Bill and motioned his head toward the restrooms. Bill strolled
beyond the partition and came back after a thorough study and,
nodding his head, said, "It's tight. No doors, hatches, windows.
He can pee without me."

Mike turned to look squarely at Harp and spoke. There was no more bullshit. The message could not be clearer. "We have no room for fucking around, Sergeant. Your ass is ours. Do... you... read...me?" Experienced as he was, Harp felt a small chill at the true meaning of those words. They only reinforced his determination to get away—far, far, away. He could still be, however, just as cold blooded as they were. He did not show the slightest fear.

"Yeah, I got you, asshole. I won't fuck around. Now, could I please go to the shitter?"

He knew when he stood up he was committed. He would either get away through that hatch or be trapped in whatever this place had as a basement. All things considered, it was a gamble he was willing to take.

He walked slowly, maybe emphasizing the limp for effect. He knew they were watching. They were so confident that they had him, however, they did not feel the need to follow him to the bathroom. As soon as he was out of sight, he moved quickly to the trap door. He lifted the edge of the mat and saw the large iron handle recessed in the hardwood door. Slowly lifting the door to minimize noise, he opened it just wide enough to step down under it and quickly but quietly lowered it back in place. He found he was correct in his assumption that there would be a light switch close by the bottom of the stairs. He could see it when he lifted the hatch. In pitch darkness, now with some emergency, he felt for the switch and flipped it up. Quickly noting the location of the door to the alley, he ran around old tables, stacks of chairs, and discarded bar junk to the rear of the basement and studied the manner in which it was secured. It was just a large sliding bolt with a security clip on a chain. No lock.

D.E. HOPPER

Now he knew he could get out. But he had four miles to go and hadn't really planned out this part of the escape from the Battle. He sure couldn't call a cab. He couldn't hitch a ride. The best he could come up with was to get there on foot. There were always any number of idiots who ran for fun on the streets at any time of day. How to look like one of them? He pulled off his khakis and cut the legs off just below the pockets. He removed the Hawaiian shirt and tucked the sleeves of his t-shirt in. As a final touch, he tied his large, red handkerchief around his head, pulling it down close to his eyebrows.

Harp was hurrying because he understood how high the stakes were in this game. But it still took about two minutes. He knew that was too long for a typical visit to the john and they would be looking for him. Leaving his wallet, keys, and phone on the bar bought him that time. Smart as they were, they assumed no one who was escaping would leave such things behind. In this case, everything he left was part of a life, part of an identity Harp was leaving behind. Mike and Bill immediately began careful inspection of the wallet and keys. The wallet showed nothing unexpected. It held a driver's license, his VA ID card, a credit card, cash, and vehicle registration. They checked the phone for recent calls and messages. There were none of either. These actions, however, took just long enough for Harp's needs. He had a precious few extra seconds to get out of the basement and then get out of whatever alley access he would find behind the Battle.

Harp went up a short flight of stairs and slid the bolt. There was no one else in the alley. He ran quickly past dumpsters and other trash receptacles, one in which he threw his shirt and pant legs, to the mouth of the long alley and, without pausing, set out

342

on a leisurely pace on city sidewalks away from the Battle to a place of safety four miles away. He knew he could run four miles with little trouble — as long as his leg did not cramp up. He was now just another late afternoon running dude in a strange outfit, wearing white socks and boat shoes and cutoff khakis instead of the usual high dollar gear. No one took a second look.

In the Battle, without the ready cooperation of the angry bartender who could not figure out what the hell happened and what it had to do with him, Mike and Bill finally found Harp's means of escape. By then, Harp was several blocks away, running on narrow streets away from major thoroughfares becoming less and less visible as dusk turned into darkness. He carried nothing but a few twenties, his knife, and a coded magnetic card.

35

IT WAS A COLD BUT PLEASANT MORNING IN THE WEST-
ern area of Trenton, an industrial area, when the gates slowly
opened and a medium-sized fairly modern but nothing special
motor home slowly drove from a vast storage complex. It had
Pennsylvania plates and had been stored for several weeks. It
started easily. It had two full gas tanks, up-to-date maintenance,
and was ready for a long, long ride. As it slowly drove away from
the gate, a small motorcycle and woman's bicycle could be seen
clipped into a rack on the back. Painted in large flamboyant let-
tering above the bikes and under the large rear window were the
words, "Ken and Sadie. Just Dreamin' and Drivin'."

The motor home drove steadily west on Highway 1 out of
Trenton, keeping off interstates for now, through Lancaster, York,
Gettysburg, and points south, one small city after another. The
driver had no destination other than away. Cold weather was
coming, so he was heading south. First south, then west. Arizona
seemed as good a destination as any. After a couple of days of
poking along on surface roads, he got on I-40 at Greensboro,

NC, and drove all the way to Winslow, AZ, and the Homolovi State Park. He slept well at rest stops along the way, marveling at their existence. They had parking, food, some security, bathrooms, snacks, and maps. He was getting into the ease of it—always moving, taking his time, looking at the often beautiful country-side he had never seen before. He was learning that driving a large rig like this took some extra care when it came to passing, turning, going under things, and especially backing up. Fortu-nately, his new abode had all the new electronic features that pretty much told him when he was about to do something stupid. It also had another feature about which he would say nothing to anybody. It had a little over two hundred thousand dollars in cash scattered throughout the camper in compartments, behind pan-els, and even in a magnetic box attached to the frame underneath as a last resort.

With the camper was a how-to book and it was a damned good thing it was there. When he backed into his spot in the park, he had a good idea about the rules and how to handle all the hookups. Once settled with water and power on line, he final-ly relaxed. Only now did he take one bottle from the entire case of Pappy thoughtfully stowed away in a closet and crack the seal. He stretched out on the sofa, sipped the Pappy and went through the checklist again. He felt he was safe but knew he could nev-er take it for granted. His name was Kenneth Nelson, age 49, from Elm, Pennsylvania. His wife Sadie had died recently and he didn't want to talk about it. This was a memorial trip taken in her memory. She so loved to travel.

Thus, Horace B. Harper, aka Harp, aka Ken, five days after leaving Trenton, NJ, finally fell into a deep peaceful sleep on a big double bed in a motor home on a sandy pad off a dirt road in the quiet empty stillness of the Homolovi State Park near Winslow, Arizona.

36

THE OPEN SPACES AND FAIRLY EMPTY ROADS PROVIDED A
great place to re-learn riding the bicycle and motorcycle. He had
ridden both before so it wasn't too difficult. When he felt he was
ready to ride without hurting himself or a hapless pedestrian, he
rode the motorcycle into Winslow. He needed basic provisions.
A two-wheel vehicle and helmet, he found, provided what was
probably the best disguise anybody could imagine.

Harp spent two weeks at Homolovi Park. He was polite but
distant with other campers. This became much easier after he had
explained to the first inquiring neighbor that Sadie had recently
died and he wasn't ready to talk about it. Once the word had gotten around, people just smiled sadly and left him alone. He felt
shitty about lying to these well-intentioned people.

Harp finally got around to mounting his dish antenna. He
found that his apprehension about the real intent of Mike and
Bill was well placed. The news world was agog about an attempted assassination of the President just three days before. The at-

tempt failed because the assassin was quickly located and killed by the Secret Service right at the spot from which he was planning the shot. It was almost as if the attempt was known of beforehand, said one report. Somehow, a Secret Service squad got there before the gun was fired.

"Yeah, they knew," Harp said to himself as he watched reports. It confirmed his suspicion that *he* was supposed to be that person and that he was not supposed to survive. It also became crystal clear at this moment that Harp was presently in danger and would be from now on. He was the only person outside the agency who knew what those slick fuckers had pulled off.

Harp was trying to wrap his mind around the method and ultimate results. Then it hit him. This was a sham assassination. It was done only to show that it could be done. According to the news reports, the shooter had a clear shot where it was not supposed to be possible. As a result of the quick elimination of the purported assassin, the Secret Service gained three things: It regained control of the activities of a reckless President, put the trust of the President and Congress in the hands of the Secret Service, and it would do wonders for the needy Secret Service budget. Not to mention the fact that it scared the shit out of the President. It was a brilliant political maneuver and it worked perfectly. And, all it cost was one poor fool who thought he could trust Mike and Bill when they promised no one would get hurt. It was just an exercise, they told Harp's replacement. For the sake of authenticity, they needed a pissed-off experienced sniper who was expendable. Apparently, they found someone just like Harp. Harp wondered who it was.

Now there was just one big remaining problem for the agency.

Harp was out there and Harp could figure out what had happened. Which meant he had to keep moving. He had to stay invisible. He had to stay clean. But for how long? They had all the tools at their disposal. If he left one tiny clue on his travels, his ass was cooked. He figured the best thing he could do for the time being was to keep moving.

Starvation State Park in Utah, near Duchesne, was the next stop. An easy day's drive from Winslow, it was an active camping area on Starvation Lake but, now that it was getting colder, there were many empty spots on the big oval loop next to the lake. It was easy to avoid interaction with other campers. A camping pro by now, he had backed into a slot and hooked up in half an hour. Stocked up on provisions before leaving Homolovi, he was ready to stay for as many days as he felt like. Instead of running to keep the leg loose, he got into hiking and exploring. A new sort of thinking was developing. He found himself starting to get curious about things. His life so far had somehow required little curiosity. There had always been an objective, a solution, an action, a post op examination of tactics, and finally, recuperation. It was all either written or experience-based. In that environment, curiosity might get you killed.

From time to time, he would think of the world he left behind. Harp assumed the condo was being watched but concluded it should be okay otherwise. It was paid for and all services were auto-deducted from his checking. His disability checks were deposited electronically. The new SUV had probably been towed by now. As far as he knew, all farm sale money was still in Kowalski's escrow account and that was fine with him. She still had his power of attorney. Though he felt he had no choice but to take off like he had, he still felt guilty when it came to Kowalski. He wished he could have explained what really happened.

For now, Harp felt he had no choice but to be careful and keep moving. He found that state and national parks and interstate rest stops were best. The parks worried him because he had to sign in. This put a signature and license on the record, but he had to take that chance if he wanted power and water. Besides, he had to remind himself, who could possibly know or give a shit about Kenneth Nelson. With his maps and guide books, Harp found that he could easily drive just a few miles and set up at a new site. He thus wandered to where it was warm for the winter and cool for spring and summer. He enjoyed the guessing game involved in chasing the frost line as it crept northward.

37

THEY FOUND HIM AROUND FIVE IN THE AFTERNOON AT slot No. 12 at the Pinon Flats Campground on the edge of the Great Sand Dunes National Park and Preserve near Aspen, Colorado. Harp was washing dishes. Through the window over the sink, he could see the lone car coming from a long way off. It was a four-door sedan which was very out of place in this isolated world of campers and SUV's. He figured it was about time. Because it was off season, his was the only vehicle in the campground. Maybe it was nothing, but Harp prepared for the worst. He had just enough time to get ready.

When the car pulled up, Harp was sitting on a camp stool at a small camp table near the steps of his camper. He was wearing t-shirt and shorts. On the table was a bottle of beer, a paper plate with a sandwich, a pack of cold cuts, a bottle of mustard, and a loaf of bread. It was them. They sat in the car watching. The grinning and joking was gone. Harp sipped the beer, took a bite from the sandwich, and sat waiting with the beer in one hand

and the sandwich in the other. Then another sip and another bite, chewing and waiting.

The car was slightly lower than Harp's camping spot and about twenty yards away. In the car, they studied Harp. They could see everything. Under the table, under the chair, everything was clear. No weapons of any kind in sight. The rider said to the driver, "What do you think?"

The driver said, "I don't know. He looks okay. We approach smart and be ready. I think we got him. Let's not underestimate this guy, though. We do *not* want this fucker to get away again."

The rider said, "Okay, you get out first, stay behind the car. I'll approach." The driver got out and with Glock in hand, held down on Harp.

The rider then slid from the front seat and stood behind the door for a moment. With his Sig drawn and ready, he stepped into the open.

Harp sipped the beer and ate more sandwich. He smiled and asked, "What took you so long?"

"You're a tricky son of a bitch, Harper." the rider answered. He slowly moved forward, still looking everywhere for anything out of place. Any threat at all. He saw nothing to worry about. His Sig was up and cupped. There was no more banter.

"Yeah, it was good while it lasted, wasn't it. I thought you would figure it out before now, though." He laughed and added, "You guys want a beer? A sandwich?" He held them both up, both hands full. Harp's relaxed casual attitude and visible hands brought the driver from behind the car. He began approaching but was still thirty feet away. Then he was just twenty feet away, weapon up and ready. The rider was just ten feet away.

Harp had only one shot at making this work. While still smiling, he toasted the rider with the bottle of beer, casually laid the food on the plate and, in the same motion, picked up the old police 38 caliber revolver. It was behind the loaf of bread. The first bullet entered the head of the rider just below his right eye. As he fell, Harp was also falling. He fell to the left where, after landing, he fired four aimed shots at the driver, who was in the process of emptying his pistol, mostly into the ground in front of Harp.

These guys were not trained for a fire fight in the open. It was not their style. They were trick and trap operators—not the move and shoot kind. The driver reacted in shock and surprise instead of cool analysis of the situation. Harp was hit but the driver was hit worse. He was wearing a ballistic vest but Harp hit him in the neck, groin, and middle of the vest. One shot had missed. The shot to the vest had probably spoiled his aim. He lay on his back with blood pumping out from both wounds. He had dropped his Sig and was weakly reaching for it in the sand. Harp kicked it away. This one was Mike, he thought. Mike was looking at Harp with a strange intensity. He shook his head slowly in what seemed to be wonder. He weakly smiled and rasped, "Shot by Harp. God…damn." and died. Harp did not have to use his last bullet.

Moving quickly, Harp ignored the bleeding from the wound in his bad leg and circled the camper looking for any witnesses. He was alone. The wound on his leg was straight through on the side, so he duct-taped a clean dish towel covering entry and exit and went to work. He first hauled the bodies into the camper and put them on a plastic tarp in his bedroom. He cleared the area of any sign of what had just happened, pushing deep sand over the area where Mike had bled out.

353

Dressed in his ridiculous bicycle riding outfit, he locked the camper door and left a note saying he was going for a ride. He put his bike in the trunk of their car and drove to a point on the highway several miles where there was no sign of human activity in either direction. The note on the dash said, *Motor quit. Gone for help.* He rode the ten miles back to the camper in agony, swearing all the way. The biker pants hid the wound which now put a new vicious sting over the ongoing ache from his old wounds. He knew if he slowed down, he would go down.

It was dark when the camper left Pinon Flats heading south, the only way out, then east. He was pleased to see the rental car was still there as he drove past. He thought he might make it to dawn before the bodies began to smell. He was almost right. At about five A.M., his nose told him he absolutely had to find a road off the beaten path to dig a very deep hole. This was the West and it was full of sand, long straight roads, and lonely spots where things could be buried. Now in even more pain, even though he had popped a bunch of his more powerful pain meds, Harp found a turnoff which apparently went nowhere. He was on a small rise and there was just light enough to see that he was truly alone as far as the eye could see. A small patch of dunes which had crept over some vegetation near the road was perfect.

The base of those dunes soon hid the single grave of two operatives of some government agency, most likely American, who had set out to illegally eliminate another American and had failed. In the grave were two clothed bodies along with the bloody tarp. Their wallets and the rental papers from the car were soaked in gasoline and had quickly burned with the ashes scattered while Harp dug. The contents of their wallets had been as expected;

354

just two innocuous ID's that said nothing. They certainly weren't Mike and Bill or Pat and Tim. Harp recognized the irony of one false identity burying two other false identities. He wondered at what point somebody somewhere would recognize that they were missing. Had they been heroes in the service of their country? He didn't know. All he did know was that they were killers and he was their target. The dunes would soon creep over this grave, assuring that the final question would never be answered. The old revolver, sold to Kenneth Nelson at a shady pawnshop that asked nothing of the buyer now had a scarred inner barrel and filed off firing pin. It was dipped in bleach, wrapped in wet rags and buried deep in a separate grave further down the road. It was already badly worn and would soon rust away.

After taking great pains to wipe out any signs that Harp and his camper had been there, Harp hit the road once again. This time, however, he was doing it with a different kind of desperation. He really needed to thoroughly treat the leg and he was very, very tired. He took a chance and got on I-70 East, praying for a rest stop and no cops. The rest stop near Edson, Kansas, was an answer to his prayers. He cleaned the wounds again, this time with soap and water followed by hydrogen peroxide — noting that the wounds were normally pink but not infected. The exit wound was a nasty looking hole, but he knew it too would heal. He had been shot before. He knew what a wound was supposed to look like. He slept the dreamless, motionless sleep of a man who was physically exhausted, mentally stressed, in pain, and suffering from a recent loss of blood. One thing he did not feel was regret. He was happy to be alive.

38

SERGEANT HORACE B. "HARP" HARPER WOKE UP IN A FLAT, featureless part of Kansas alongside a busy interstate highway, wondering if it was worth it to keep running. Whenever an honest man asks himself a question like that, he already knows what he is going to do. Harp set course for a beautiful piece of land near Goldsboro, NC, the new home of Bonny, Weeks, and Kip. He had not contacted his squad since he left Trenton weeks ago for fear of getting them involved. He had no idea of developments over the past several months. For Harp, the journey was coming to an end. This visit to these guys was, in his mind, kind of a goodbye. He was going home to Trenton without knowing what would happen when he got there. He just wanted to see them one more time. This time was it. He was done running.

It took three days. Harp left the camper at the nearby Busco Beach and ATV Park and rode the motorcycle to the farm, arriving right at dusk when he figured they would all be at the house. Motorcycles were not the usual visitor so Bonny and Weeks had come out on the porch to check out who it was. Harp sat for a moment, still wearing the helmet and goggles, and tried to compose himself. He swung off the bike stiffly because the leg was still very sore. He removed the headgear. Their suspicion quickly turned to amazement. Any notion that he might not have been missed was dispelled in a crazy moment of yelping, cussing, slapping, and hugging as they tried to fit many months of worry and affection into a few seconds of physical expression.

Bonny and Weeks dragged Harp into the kitchen where they quickly opened bottles of beer. Before drinking, they smiled and quietly touched the bottles in a toast to each other. Harp's first question was, "Where's Kip?" Weeks explained with obvious sadness that Kip had had some recurring problems with bone chips still under the skin of his cheek. He had gone home earlier than planned to see a specialist. His parents were deeply involved in his recovery now and paying for everything. Bonny added that Kip probably wouldn't be back for quite a while.

In response to Harp's questions about the farm, they described a difficult first year but said that they made a little money. Weeks was doing well in school and had taken over the financial management of the farm. Bonny reported kiddingly that Weeks had a girlfriend and teased that it might be getting serious.

"I hope so," Weeks said, then smiled and shrugged.

Still in the kitchen, standing around the kitchen island, Bonny held up his hand as if to halt everything. "Okay, Sarge, would you please tell us what the hell is going on? Where have you been? What have you been doing? No bullshit, please." He continued, "A few months ago, these two weird dudes came by trying to act real casual, but we could tell they were way too interested in knowing where you were. These dudes had a very strange vibe.

All of us picked up on it. We couldn't tell them a thing because we didn't know a damned thing. We didn't know where you were or why you left."

Harp was staggered by the implications and now doubly glad that that pair was permanently inoperative. But, he still didn't know where their orders came from. All he knew was that he could not drag these guys into the shit with him.

"Listen, guys. You remember back when we were active, sometimes it was better to not know *why* you did what you did. This is one of those situations. I really think it is much better, much safer, if you don't know."

Bonny and Weeks looked at each other. Almost in unison, they said, "bullshit."

Harp shrugged and said firmly, "Well, that's the way it is." They weren't about to argue with the Sarge. They nodded glumly. "I can tell you this much, I've been on the move — seeing the country in a camper which is up in Busco Beach. I've got the motorcycle and a ten-speed and it's been a pretty good trip."

"But now," Harp explained, "I'm going back to Trenton." What he was thinking and what he didn't add was: he was going back to face the music, one way or another.

"That reminds me," Bonny said, "Your lawyer Kowalski has been in touch a couple of times to ask if we knew where you were. She said you need to call her. Something about the estate." They both grinned, remembering Harp and Kowalski.

Oh, hell, thought Harp, I've got to do it. "Yeah, I'll be talking to her when I get back home."

Harp was still concerned about the possibility of hurting these guys with his continued presence so he announced, "I've got to go. I need to hit the road tonight. I'm sorry I can't explain. Just trust me." They were shocked and disappointed but, again, they accepted the Sarge's decision without question. After an emotional farewell, Harp quickly rode back to the camper and was soon on the road north. He figured that he would have the camper back in storage and get back to his condo about daylight. He would ask the maintenance guy for a key to his door.

39

HE MADE IT JUST BEFORE SUNRISE. WITH THE CAMPER stowed and locked, Harp walked through the streets of Trenton and enjoyed it. He felt he was back where he was supposed to be. The sounds and smells of an awakening city made him smile, in spite of all that was portended in this return. Somehow the combined aromas of baking bread, breakfast cooking, and diesel fumes were a welcome reminder that this was his home. The pleasure ended when he approached the front of his building. Somehow, impossibly, his arrival was expected. The same technology that allowed the recently deceased agents to find him while out in the middle of nowhere allowed another kind of agent to be sitting on his doorstep when he came home. A tall man carrying a black valise stood up from a low wall where he had been sitting. He was dressed in a three-piece gray suit with a perfectly knotted tie. He was totally out of place in this neighborhood but seemed completely at ease.

Harp sighed. He considered options but concluded, to hell with it. He was tired of considering options. He walked up to the man and stopped almost within reach and waited. The man smiled and appeared to be comfortable and unafraid. "Sergeant Harper?"

"That's me." The man waited. "I'd ask you up but I don't have a key."

The man opened the valise and Harp thought, I guess this is it. Instead of a weapon, the man produced a small ring of keys. "No problem. I have your keys right here." He handed them to Harp, who was mystified. "I'm sure you remember which one." He gestured at Harp to go ahead. They took the elevator and rode in silence. The man calmly stood with his back to Harp, who was slowly shaking his head in puzzlement.

When they were inside, the man closed the door behind them as Harp stared at his keys, desperately trying to comprehend the impossible. The lights worked. The place looked normal but smelled empty. The man again reached into the valise as Harp again waited for the worst. The man smiled, shook his head, then brought out the wallet and phone Harp had left on the bar many, many months ago. With them was a folder. He opened the folder to show Harp pictures of two men. It was Mike and Bill.

"We have just one question: Are you aware of the location of these two individuals?" Harp noted that it was a very specific question. Just the location? He then realized that there was only one way that Harp could be alive and know their "location."

Upon posing this question, the man's friendly demeanor was gone and replaced by a steely gaze. Harp knew his answer was critical but could not ignore the implications of that gaze. It seemed to be asking a question and making a statement at the same time. To say yes was an irreversible admission with unknown consequences. Having made up his mind, Harp stepped closer and steadily met the man's eyes for a long moment and, with the slightest nod and a long, slow blink followed by an equally intense gaze, said, "No."

For several seconds, the man studied Harp with an equally direct look, then smiled and said, "Good." He added, "We lost contact with them several days ago. Maybe we will never know what happened to them." He picked up his bag and almost as an afterthought, said, "It was a rogue operation and the D.C. end has been cleaned up." He snapped the bag closed and headed for the door. "We are happy to know that this operation has been successfully, um…terminated."

Harp, in disbelief that this nightmare may be over, followed him and asked, "What about me?"

"You? Why, Sergeant Harper, you are in the clear with the thanks of a grateful Nation." The man opened the door and paused. "As long as you never say one fucking word about anything you have seen, or heard." He smiled, pointed his hand like a gun and added, "Or done." Then he was gone.

40

THE NEXT DAY, A LITTLE EARLIER THAN USUAL, HARP entered the Battle and walked directly to his favorite stool. Despite the many months which had passed, the bartender did not hesitate and went right to Harp's brand. He poured the bourbon neat with the small chaser. He paused in front of Harp with his hands still on the glasses and raised his eyebrows in question. He remembered the escape through the cellar and the ensuing bedlam.

"Don't ask," Harp said in a not unfriendly way. The bartender left the drinks, smiled, and walked away.

Harp savored the Battle ambiance as a big part of coming home: the look, the smell, the sound, all of it ... the Battle and his city. With one more wound and raft of new memories to ponder, he was truly home. He went so far as to shift around on the stool, roll his shoulders, give a thankful sigh, and then lean on the bar. Only the bartender, the man who had been waiting for him at his condo, and one other person knew he was home. Just after his second bourbon was delivered, he heard something else that was familiar. He heard the sound of hard heels striding across the old wood floor. They stopped behind his left shoulder. He continued staring at his drink.

She waited, then sighed, hitched a long perfect leg up on the next stool, slid her shapely butt the rest of the way, and slapped an expensive leather briefcase on the bar. It landed way too close to his second bourbon of the day.

"You're a hard man to find," Kowalski said. This time he turned toward her and smiled.

End

ABOUT THE AUTHOR

D.E. HOPPER IS A FAMILY MAN AND VETERAN WHO EN-
joys the extreme good fortune of having a loving wife and two
smart, healthy sons. Using the wonderful G.I. Bill, he worked his
way through three college degrees. He remains especially proud
of having served his country at many locations around the world
during a four-year stint in the Air Force Strategic Air Command,
mainly in a Reconnaissance Wing. He is reasonably literate with
experience in technical writing, editing, and writing for personal
pleasure. *Shot by Harp* is his first novel.

CPSIA information can be obtained
at www.ICGtesting.com
Printed in the USA
FFHW021640030419
51491428-56936FF